PRAISE FOR

Life and Other Love Songs

"*Life and Other Love Songs* is a precisely observed, often beautiful book about family, love, loss, and the hidden history that shapes lives. . . . The prose is beautiful and poignant."

—*The New York Times*

"This novel wields themes of generational trauma, class, and race as pickaxes, excavating a Black family's history and making room for the future to bloom."
—*Essence*

"Riveting, rhythmic, transcendent . . . a stellar family saga."

—Jacqueline Woodson, *New York Times* bestselling author of *Red at the Bone*

"*Life and Other Love Songs* builds beautifully—we care about these characters while coming to understand that the ground beneath their feet is constructed of secrets. Anissa Gray's novel feels musical in structure—the octaves rise when the music calls for it; truths are revealed by the invisible beats of this gorgeous, rich story."

—Ann Napolitano, *New York Times* bestselling author of *Dear Edward* and Oprah Book Club selection *Hello Beautiful*

"Anissa Gray's *Life and Other Love Songs* is one of those rare novels that pulled me out of my life for a few days. The characters are real, vivid, complex—as in life. It's a story that explores the depths of darkness and fear, yet offers a window into hope."

—Mary Beth Keane, *New York Times* bestselling author of *Ask Again, Yes*

"Anissa Gray is a genius . . . magnificent!"

—Caroline Kepnes, *New York Times* bestselling author of *You*

"Cleverly structured and emotionally precise . . . *Life and Other Love Songs* is a powerhouse ballad about a family whose histories—shared and individual—will pierce straight to the heart. With empathy and insight, Anissa Gray writes an expertly crafted family drama perfect for fans of Celeste Ng."

—Tara Conklin, *New York Times* bestselling author of *The Last Romantics*

"*Life and Other Love Songs* is a harsh, sometimes haunting, astonishingly moving, exceptionally complex novel about family and music and hurt and fear and pride and love and loss. Anissa Gray tells this story with such grace, insight, and precision that readers will think of these characters long after they close the book. This is what writing should be."

—LaToya Watkins, author of *Perish*

"Gray does not disappoint."

—*Publishers Weekly*

"The trajectory of Gray's flawed but relatable characters offers hope that even deep, long-festering wounds can heal."

—*Kirkus Reviews*

"Gray shows the complex natures of these broken characters and how abuse, deceit, and life's struggles are all made worse by racism, poverty, and homophobia. A great pick for book clubs and an essential purchase."

—*Library Journal*

"Humming with heart and just enough suspense to keep the pages turning, this is arresting."

—*Booklist*

"Anissa Gray delivers in a clear and lyrical voice that with honesty and love, there is hope for a better tomorrow."

—*The Atlanta Journal-Constitution*

"A powerful narrative that explores the realities of race, class, and generational history in the twentieth century."   —The Root

Other Titles by Anissa Gray

THE CARE AND FEEDING OF RAVENOUSLY HUNGRY GIRLS

Life

AND OTHER

Love Songs

———

ANISSA GRAY

BERKLEY

New York

BERKLEY
An imprint of Penguin Random House LLC
penguinrandomhouse.com

ISBN: 9781984802477

The Library of Congress has cataloged the Berkley hardcover edition of this book as follows:

Names: Gray, Anissa, author
Title: Life and other love songs / Anissa Gray
Description: New York: Berkley, [2023]
Identifiers: LCCN 2022032817 (print) | LCCN 2022032818 (ebook) |
ISBN 9781984802460 (hardcover) | ISBN 9781984802484 (ebook)
Subjects: LCGFT: Novels.
Classification: LCC PS3607.R3876 L54 2023 (print) |
LCC PS3607.R3876 (ebook) | DDC 813/.6—dc23/eng/20220711
LC record available at https://lccn.loc.gov/2022032817
LC ebook record available at https://lccn.loc.gov/202203281

Berkley hardcover edition / April 2023
Berkley trade paperback edition / March 2024

Printed in the United States of America
1st Printing

Book design by George Towne

For Katherine

When I die, Hallelujah, by and by,
I'll fly away

"I'LL FLY AWAY," ALBERT E. BRUMLEY

Life

AND OTHER

Love Songs

Prologue

Trinity

It wasn't like any funeral or burial or postburial I'd ever imagined. Not that I'd ever really imagined those things. But as I watched the cars line up along the curb, freshly arrived from the cemetery, all I could think about was the incredible strangeness of the funeral, burial and now, postburial we were all enduring. Everyone was piling out of their cars. They formed a kind of procession that moved over neatly mowed grass to the sidewalk. They made their way up the sloped driveway to the stone walkway and approached the tan brick house and the unlocked screen door that belonged to what was left of my family.

I hung back, leaving the hosting duties to my mother, a more than capable committee of one. She was standing next to the white maple coffee table where she'd stacked coasters and yellow, square cocktail napkins. She'd cooked, too, because the days of people bringing over casseroles and platters of food to fortify our bereaved family had ended years ago. Mrs. Neilson, though, from next door had come by with a vanilla pound cake earlier. The same pale, bland, aggressively bumpy cake she'd brought us when we moved to Bloomfield Hills fifteen years ago. And then again, years later, after my dad vanished.

My grandmother made a spot for the cake on the dining table where we'd set up a crowded buffet of roasted chicken, sliced and splayed artfully on two big platters with sprigs of parsley. There were also boiled potatoes, green beans and assorted sweets. I hefted the cake up next to a platter of brownies and chocolate chip cookies that my mother had bought at the A&P. She was a master of most of the homemaking arts. She crocheted scarves and sewed complete outfits with personalized labels embroidered with *Created by Deborah Armstead*. She could pack a good lunch and cook an even better dinner, but she'd never been much of a baker.

"Cut her some slack," my father used to say in a kind of backhanded defense of her various sagging cakes and soggy pies. "When I met her, she was just as likely to burn water as not."

My mother was standing perfect-posture tall in the living room, a pale-yellow room made brighter by the scent of hyacinths carried in on the breeze. She was smoothing her navy blue skirt and matching jacket, smiling as the first of the visitors came through the door. Her long, blue-black hair that people had admired for as long as I could remember was pulled into a neat bun. She was graying at her temples.

I'd noticed the graying earlier that morning as I sat on the bathroom counter, watching her get ready and listening to her lay out the plans for the day. Only partly listening, actually. I'd mostly been enjoying the steam facial from the mug of coffee I had cradled in my hands, until she asked: "You think they'll come? You know, with how long it's been?"

"Yes." I wanted to add: They'll come *precisely because* it's been so long. And because this is strange. But I didn't say that. I didn't want to risk an argument.

"It's time to try and go on."

"You definitely seem ready to do that," I murmured into my coffee mug, at risk of starting that argument I thought I wanted to avoid.

We regarded each other's reflections in the bathroom mirror. Her honey-colored skin was clear and smooth and not made up yet. She looked younger than her forty-five years. I, on the other hand, looked like an aging hooker who'd had a particularly bad night. My puffy-eyed face was a giant smear of blush and mascara from the day before because I'd been too wiped out to wash after my ten-hour drive home. My mother in the mirror was working her jaw, like she was biting back a particularly bitter critique.

"What do you think I should be doing, Trinity?" she asked finally.

"Not burying an empty casket. For starters."

"Goddamn it—" She stopped for a moment, closing her eyes and gripping the counter, like she might collapse. "He's gone."

"I know that."

"Do you?"

Did I?

He wasn't just gone. He was presumed dead. It suddenly felt claustrophobic in that bathroom.

My mother let out a heavy breath, and when I looked at her reflection again, she was every year of her age. And more. There were the crow's feet feathering out from the corners of her eyes. The deep furrow between her eyebrows, as if she'd endured a lifetime of worry. I noticed my mother's hand trembling as she slid a bobby pin in her hair to fix the bun at the back of her head. I wondered if she was drinking again.

Careful with her . . . It wasn't so much that my mother was delicate. It was more that she was already broken and shoddily held together in places.

When she made for the bathroom door, brushing past my shoulder, she'd said, "Please fix your face. And put on something decent. Let's agree on at least that much for today. Okay?"

Peeking around the doorway to the crowded living room now, I adjusted a rogue shoulder pad under my decent burgundy blouse and secured it under a bra strap as I tried to work up the—well, I didn't quite know what to call it. Nerve? Gumption? Moxie? Whatever it would take for me to go out there and be a normal human. I took a deep breath and dove into the front room, landing in the arms of neighbors and my father's former colleagues, many of whom I knew only vaguely.

I turned when I felt a tap on the shoulder and heard my name: "Trinity!"

Mr. Adler, my father's cheek-pinching, quarter-behind-the-ear-discovering boss, was there with his wife. He was my mother's boss now. In the days after my father's disappearance, the Adlers were the main deliverers of casseroles, cakes and a few dishes my mother and I couldn't identify—even after copious amounts of poking and debate. The Adlers were also the bearers of reassurances: "The police are on it. They'll find him."

"So, a journalist?" Mr. Adler was saying. "We got ourselves another Barbara Walters here?"

I smiled awkwardly. "Working on it, I guess."

"A reporter." Mrs. Adler nodded approvingly. "That's what your mom tells us."

My eyes darted over to my mother, who was standing in a clutch of neighbors—quite possibly, at that very moment, embellishing my resume to them, too. "Well," I said, "I'm actually more of a . . . radio newsreader."

"Don't sell yourself short, young lady."

"Your dad never would have," Mr. Adler said. "He was a real go-getter."

"And so funny," Mrs. Adler added. "Just a hoot, when he wanted to be. He—"

Mr. Adler cut in with a return to go-getting, recalling the many Saturdays and late nights my dad could be found "burning the midnight oil" at work. I recalled that time, too, but not nearly as fondly.

"We still miss him," Mr. Adler said. "He was one of our rising stars."

Mrs. Adler nodded, looking grim. "I can't believe that just, poof . . ." She threw her hands up and simulated emptiness in the air.

Mr. Adler shot her a look that said, *You'll upset the girl!*

And boy was he right. Mrs. Adler's words and hand gesture had conjured up a terrible image. Poof. A puff of smoke. The wave of a magician's wand. My father in one moment there on a sidewalk waving goodbye after a birthday lunch. Then, poof, nowhere. I felt tears rise.

Mrs. Adler squeezed my arm. "Oh! I didn't mean—"

"No, no. It's okay. Seriously." I wiped at my eyes, embarrassed. I hadn't cried, not even once today. Not once since the day he disappeared. I'd spent that time in a state of disbelief, waiting for the next wave of the magician's wand and my father's reappearance, maybe in the front yard cutting the grass or out back tending the garden. Or even popping up on the cracked, black-gum-dotted sidewalk where he was last seen. Like an amnesia patient who couldn't say where he'd been or who he was but had somehow known to return to that spot.

Mrs. Adler was rubbing my arm, still apologizing. "I'm fine," I said, gently removing her hand. "It's okay."

There was an awkward transition to a conversation about Mr. Adler's upcoming retirement. But I was recalling the police officers coming to the house, standing near where I now stood with the Adlers. I was remembering my mother's distressing trip to the morgue. I saw again my father's dark blue suit jacket and black leather briefcase. Two of the things he'd left behind at the office, as if he'd be back for them in no time.

I suddenly felt like I was breathing through a pinhole. Trapped in a tight space. I came back to Mr. and Mrs. Adler talking about the multitiered crystal chandelier they'd ordered for the foyer of their retirement home in Naples. Just as Mrs. Adler was moving on to the master bedroom, I excused myself. I wanted to leave the house altogether, but go where? I stepped gingerly through a thicket of people, careful of toes. I went through the dining room, passing the buffet table. The chicken was about halfway gone, with vultures circling. I went on to the kitchen for a glass of water and stood at the sink, feeling marginally better with each swallow.

I returned to the fringes of the room. Standing on the outside of things, I could see that the mood was much lighter than it had been before. The breezy conversations sometimes whipped up into great gusts of laughter. A few of the mourners were making their way around the room, balancing plates and wineglasses, spilling off into the dining room and the kitchen.

And then it hit me: *This is a party.* My mother had thrown a *party*.

I searched for her in the crowded living room. She was nowhere to be found.

Whatever there was of grief in that room, it collected itself and followed me out the front door and onto the porch. The warmth of the day had dipped with the sun, but it was still a nice night. I hugged myself against the chill and looked up at the sky and a crescent moon. I'd long ago put heaven in the same category as Santa's North Pole, but I sometimes found myself wondering whether my father was up there. I wondered about him all the time because absence was not the same as death. It was worse, given all of the not knowing. A person can't just disappear from a Detroit sidewalk—*poof*—into thin air. Dead or alive, the missing are somewhere here on earth. But how do you find them?

I jumped, startled by the sound of the door opening and closing behind me. It was just my grandmother. My father's mother.

"Didn't mean to scare you." She swirled the ice in her glass. A vodka tonic. "You doing okay out here, little girl?"

"Oh, you know . . ." I slid my arm around her waist and rested my head on her shoulder. "Do you think Dad would have liked this? All of it . . . It feels like a bad play, you know?" Complete with a chorus of mourners costumed in black. A generic monologue-cum-eulogy from a clergyman who, because he didn't know my father, described him vaguely as a "loving husband," a "dearly beloved father" and a "faithful friend," which, to me, anyone would have said about a husband/father/friend who was marginally better than terrible. He didn't even get his name right. He kept calling him Daniel. It was Daniel Ozro Armstead Junior. But everyone who knew my father called him Oz.

My grandmother shrugged and shook her head. "I cain't tell you what your daddy would or wouldn't've liked. You know how it was with us."

The strains of an old song drifted out the door behind us: *You won't regret it, no, no, young girls they don't forget it . . .*

"I don't understand. Mom wouldn't even consider declaring him dead, then suddenly, it was all she wanted to do. And now we have this. A *party*. With *music*. I don't get it."

My grandmother cradled her glass to her chest, her eyes shining. "We all trying to live through our moments, Trinity. That might mean crying a bucket of tears . . . or playing some good old Otis Redding." She waved her drink toward the house. "Got to live through it, little girl. Heartbreaks today, joys from yesterday . . . and God knows what all tomorrow."

Before

He imagined it must be love.

Deborah

1962–1963

I was getting ready for another one of our rent parties. Despite the fact that me and my roommates, all four of us, worked, we were barely getting by. We lived as close as sailors in a submarine in our little one-bedroom above a beauty shop on Twelfth Street. Out the windows of our apartment, down on the street, red and green lights were blinking and giving our place a festive glow, never mind the cracked plaster and worn-out radiator.

I was crawling around on my hands and knees, running a line of beige tape along the checkerboard floor to mark off where we were going to put a stage for the party. I stood up and rubbed the soreness out of my knees, then put the roll of tape around my wrist like a bracelet. I stepped back to get a good look at things.

"What do you think?" I asked my roommate Mary, who was at my shoulder breathing hot judgment.

"I don't know, Deborah. I—"

"The band can squeeze in in the corner right behind us," I said, waving the roll of tape toward the tight space where our singing group and the band would soon be. "It's just a three-piece. And us girls, we can be kind of close in together up in front of them, don't you think?"

"We're gonna have to get awful close . . ."

"Look, we needed a stage, so I made one. If you can do better, be my guest." I tossed the roll of tape on the coffee table. "I'm going to change." I stalked off toward the bedroom me and Mary shared with our two other roommates, who, right then, were trying to make more dancing space by pushing our Christmas tree into a corner. The lights were still on it and the ornaments were dangling and swinging, so it was a delicate business.

In the bedroom, where Mary had followed me, we stood in the narrow space between the two sets of bunk beds and shimmied into matching black cocktail dresses. The third dress for our third member was spread out on one of the bottom bunks, waiting for its wearer. The dresses were on the fancy side for a rent party, but we always wanted to do things at the highest level. Mary zipped me up and I turned around to return the favor. I'd made the dresses myself, so I was surprised to find a thread sprouting up from the seam on her shoulder. I was usually more careful than that with my creations. I didn't want to go pulling on the thing and making a bigger problem for myself, and I didn't have scissors handy, so I smoothed the thread down.

As we got ourselves made up, our third member, Celeste, came falling through the door, saying something about missing the bus and apologizing like she'd killed somebody with her lateness.

"You got time," I told her. "We've been waiting for it to fill up some more so we can make a real entrance." We'd heard a steady stream of arrivals on the other side of the door, and it was getting loud out there. Probably full up by now. Butterflies swarmed in my belly. We were eighteen now and graduated, but we'd been performing together at talent shows and anyplace that would have us since eleventh grade, and my nerves still weren't used to it. As Celeste wiggled into her dress, I peeked out at the living room. It was as crowded as it

sounded, busting with people pressed in together, twisting and bopping. The overflow was in the galley kitchen, with no space to spare.
The windows were fogged up from warm breath and bodies. So much
so that the lights down on Twelfth Street looked like twinkling red
and green stars now. I signaled one of our roommates out in the living
room and flashed ten fingers as I mouthed, *Ten minutes.*

She nodded.

I pointed to the kitchen, trying to get her to see there were a
bunch of people sitting on the pull-down table. We couldn't afford
to fix that thing if they broke it down.

She looked at me like, *What?*

I gave up and closed the door.

Mary was at the dresser filling three shot glasses with bourbon.
It was a pre-performance ritual. A taste of Kentucky, where she was
from. I was a Detroit girl. I'd never seen another city or town, except in pictures.

Mary passed the two of us our shot glasses and we all three toasted.

"Sing strong, sisters," she said.

I tipped my glass back and let the bourbon slide down. I closed
my eyes as the warmth of it melted at least some of the butterflies
away. Just then, we heard our name—the Belle Tones! We did a
three-way hug and hurried out the door, shoulders square, chin up,
boobs out. I took my place in the center of our trio. We barely fit
behind the tape. The pointy toes of my pumps were hanging over
the edge.

Being lead singer, I was automatically lead talker, which didn't
suit me. Still, I thanked everybody for coming out and pointed to
the tip jar on the floor: "It's coming on Christmas," I reminded
them, "so give generously. Paper money, if you please!" Everybody
laughed, and a couple people tossed a few coins into the jar to get
us started.

I thanked them, and we went into a set of covers from the Mar-velettes. I always had a good bit of stage fright, with shaking legs and a dry mouth. I kept a glass of water close and took a sip before getting into that first song. But the water didn't help the shaking. One time in high school, I'd had the shakes so bad that I just up and ran off-stage in the middle of the song. I'd since learned that closing my eyes through the first few notes helped me relax. It helped me concentrate on the words, because singing, to me, was telling a story and the story I was laying out with that first song was about being desperate to hear from the one you love. How bad would that feel to be waiting like that for something as simple as a letter? I didn't know, but I let my imagination and the melody carry me till I was relaxed enough to open my eyes all the way. That eye-opening was always like showing up at a surprise party where everybody was waiting for me.

When we finished, people came up in a rush. Out the corner of my eye, I could see rising coins and even a few bills in the tip jar. As I pushed through the crowd, sweaty and still smiling, I noticed one person who hadn't rushed at us. It was a boy in a gray sweater vest and starched white shirt, standing in the far corner of the room. His shirt was buttoned all the way to the neck. He was by himself, holding on to a paper plate. On that plate sat a potato that he kept trying to keep from rolling off whenever somebody bumped up against him. He hadn't joined the crowd, but he'd glanced at me a couple times before looking away when he saw me noticing. That was way different from the boys in my neighborhood who had no shame in their game. The apartment was full of boys like that, and, quiet as it's kept, I could've had just about any one of them. That wasn't bragging. It was a simple truth.

Mary was all of a sudden at my shoulder. "Look like you got an admirer," she said, handing me a cup of tea with honey. We always had that to soothe the voice after a performance.

"Not my type," I said.

"Just as well," Mary said. "Them short fellas are more trouble than they're worth. Always got something to prove."

I kept feeling that boy looking at me. When I swayed by him close, I could see his eyes trying not to meet mine. Those eyes, behind professor-style round glasses, were heavy with thick lashes. Finally, he looked. He smiled, and I saw he was a little bit bucktoothed. But what I noticed most was that the smile on his lips wasn't echoing back in those soft, serious brown eyes. I think it was that mismatch that made me curious and had me edging my way between gyrating bodies to get to him.

"You enjoying yourself?" I asked.

"Yeah." He nodded in the direction of the "stage," looking shy. "That was a nice performance."

I thanked him and found myself going on a ramble about how we didn't have our own songs yet, but we practiced faithfully, and we'd perfected our sound in one of the stairwells of the towers where Celeste lived in the projects I'd not long ago moved out of. I trailed off to a stop, wondering what the hell had gotten hold of me. I wasn't a rambler.

He smiled, and that time it was everywhere on his face. It was in his eyes, on his mouth, in the dimple in his right cheek. "Guess I'll be able to say I knew you when," he said, glancing around the apartment like he'd just arrived and was trying to get the lay of things. "This your place?"

"It is. In all its glory. I share it with some girlfriends." I put out a hand to shake. "I'm Deborah."

"Oz," he said, shaking back with a firm, all-business grip.

"Like the Wizard of?"

"I don't know," he laughed. "Maybe. Can't say I've seen it."

I raised my teacup and pointed toward the kitchen. "There's

rum punch in there, if you can get to it." I glanced at his plate. "To wash down that potato."

He looked like I'd accused him of stealing the potato. "No, no. I'm . . . I'm full." He rubbed his stomach and slid the plate onto a side table. "But some punch, that'd be good."

I could hear a southern accent. "Where you from?" I hadn't seen him around.

"Uh, just a couple blocks away. Came with some family." He rose up on his tiptoes and looked around the room. "Looks like it's just me now."

"You don't sound like you're originally from around here," I said, more to the point.

"Oh." He gave an embarrassed half laugh, half throat clearing. "Alabama."

I ticked off the names of a couple people at the party who were from Alabama. He didn't know them. I wasn't sure what to say next. It seemed right to say it was nice meeting you and good night and for him to go on to the kitchen for his punch and for me to go back to dancing. But what I did was lead Oz through a tight knot of sweaty bodies to the kitchen and ladle punch into a cup for him. We wedged ourselves between the wall and the pull-down table, which, miracle of miracles, still stood, and we started a whole new conversation, standing so close I could smell the sweet, boozy punch on his breath as I sipped my tea. He was nervous as anything and nowhere near flirty. *A real southern gentleman*, I thought. He said he hadn't long moved up from Alabama. It was just him, his mama and his brother now, living with a bunch of family. They'd lost his daddy and their house to a fire.

I told him I was sorry for his loss, but all I could think about was how much I loved the rich timbre of his voice and the soft, rounded vowels that made *fire* sound like *far*.

I kept talking, more than was normal. I'd never talked to anybody—any boy—who leaned in only to hear me better and looked at me the way Oz looked at me. Like I was more than pretty. Like I was smart and interesting and had good conversation.

"You're going to be a real star," he said, that smile coming back to his eyes. "I can't wait to see you shine."

It was a corny line, but with the way he was looking at me, it seemed like something true.

Oz stayed there talking to me till he caught sight of his brother stumbling toward the door. His brother, Tommy, was a sweet-faced boy who'd had too much to drink and had fallen asleep on a pile of coats on the bunk beds. Tommy was with a boy I knew.

Oz said he had to see his brother home—even though Tommy told him he most definitely didn't have to.

I told Oz the boy Tommy was with, Lloyd, was Mary's big brother. "He'll get him home safe," I said. "You're not going to find anybody better than Lloyd."

But Oz wouldn't hear it. Said he couldn't leave his brother to some boy like that.

That winter turned to spring and I saw no sign of Oz. He wasn't at a single club or party. And I know this because I looked for him. It was like he'd just popped up at my apartment from out of nowhere, then disappeared right back to wherever he'd come from. When I asked around about him, nobody even knew who he was.

But I was lucky to work with his cousin in the hospital kitchen, which, turned out, was how he'd ended up at the party in the first place. She was the only one I could talk to about him, but I had to be careful about that. Willa Mae was the type who, unlike me, liked working when she was at work. She ping-ponged through that kitchen carrying heavy trays stacked with dishes and glasses like it was nothing, even though she was malnutrition skinny. Where I couldn't wait for my shift to be done, Willa Mae would be over there signing up for as many doubles as they'd give her, and the girl was barely sixteen. She wasn't really the type to tolerate being interrupted with silly, girlish questions about a boy.

Still, I'd sometimes ask: How does Oz spend his time?

She'd come back with: Doing his stuff.

I'd once risked: So, is he seeing anybody?

She'd said: Not that I know, but then I don't know all his business.

Willa Mae was at the sink beside me humming off-tune to the radio we kept on the shelf over the station. She was frowning. It made her face, which was blasted with acne, not that nice to look at. She hunched over the sink, scrubbing hard at something, the tops of her rubber gloves coming up to her bony elbows.

"Willa Mae," I called.

She grunted to let me know she'd heard me, but she didn't look up from her work.

I didn't want to make her mad, but I wanted to get her talking, so I blurted out: "I think a person's got to have high hopes."

She stopped scrubbing, but her hands were still in the sink. "What're you going on about?" She fixed her eyes on me. They were like Oz's, heavy-lashed and soft brown. The two of them were cousins on his daddy's side, she'd told me, which made me think Oz's dead daddy had had those eyes, too.

I wasn't sure what I was going on about, but I patched it together. "Just, I don't know. I was thinking about that thing you told me one time about how you, Oz and Tommy were doers and not daydreamers. Is that true? I mean . . . is Oz really like that?"

"When you come up like we did, ain't no imaginings, like you be going on and on about," she said. "It's just doing and taking things as they come."

I didn't know anything about how Oz had come up. One time, I'd heard Willa Mae mention an "old aunt" who'd raised her. But she wasn't too chatty about all that, otherwise. "And how did y'all come up," I asked. "How was that?"

"Hard," she said, all of a sudden easing back from me and looking on guard.

"I'm sorry. I didn't mean to—"

"That's fine," she said, and went back to scrubbing in her dirty water.

All I knew of Alabama was what I'd seen on the news or heard about from other people. The Freedom Riders getting attacked by a white mob. Folks down there doing sit-ins and marches were getting spit at, beaten, having dogs and fire hoses set loose on them. They were even getting killed. I knew that.

"Yeah," I said. "I've been hearing about how bad it is down there with the marches and stuff."

She glanced over at me, her acne-pocked face scrunched up like she smelled something bad. "And you think it's better up this way?" She laughed. "Might not be no 'colored' signs keeping us where they want us, but go on out there to Dearborn and tell old Mayor Hubbard you wanna move in. See what he say."

My face burned. My sister would tell me sometimes: "You don't care about important things, Deborah. Just whatever boy you're running up behind and whatever you can sing into a microphone." I hadn't thought that much about anybody keeping me where they wanted me. But truth be told, I couldn't just go anyplace or live wherever I wanted to. No Negro could. Not with neighborhood covenants and such that kept us out. Or just knowing we weren't welcome. You don't need a sign for that.

I apologized to Willa Mae for causing offense. She kept staring at me, like she was trying to figure me out, which made me feel that much more embarrassed. "What?"

"All that . . . that kinda thing down South that you heard of? That ain't what I was talking about, necessarily." She took off her gloves and leaned on the counter. "White folk wasn't all we had to worry about," she said. "Sometimes hurt can be put on you by the ones that's closest to you and supposed to love you best. That's what I meant by hard."

I stayed quiet because I didn't want to say something stupid again.

"I know you like Oz," she said, fiddling with the fingers of one of her rubber gloves. "And he like you, too, but . . . well, I think he might be scared. He seen a lotta bad. So . . ."

"He's different," I said, more interested in him now than before. "I could see it. Just that first night." That *only* night. I took off my rubber gloves and tried to flex the shrunken raisin feeling out of my fingers because both of the gloves had holes that let in water. "I'd like to see him again," I said. "What should I do?"

She shrugged. "Dunno." She put her gloves back on and started scrubbing again, then said: "But I believe it'll happen. I dreamed it. Saw y'all together clear as day." People paid attention when Willa Mae talked about a dream. There were signs and omens in her dreams. She'd said back when she was a girl, the "old aunt" had taught her how to touch the supernatural, which, on top of dreams, meant Willa Mae could conjure up curses and cures, too. I'd never seen her curse or cure anybody, but the two times she came to work and announced she'd been dreaming about fish, two dishwashers turned up pregnant. And she'd helped people hit the numbers off her dreams, too. A lot. I knew it was probably some kind of witchcraft, which was wrong, but quiet as it's kept, I wanted to believe in this dream she'd had of me and Oz. While I watched her scrub and thought about all that, she stopped for a second and cut her eyes at me. "Be good to him," she said. "When he do come around, don't hurt him. Oz ain't been with a lotta girls. He's, um . . ."

"A virgin?" I leaned in and whispered. "I am, too."

She rolled her eyes and said something in a voice even quieter than mine. I could hardly hear what she said over the sound of water spraying and dishes clanking. I reached up and turned down the radio and leaned in closer. "He's what, now?"

"Fragile," she said, louder. "Kinda sensitive, I think I might wanna say."

I'd never heard anybody talk about a boy that way. "Can you—" I didn't know what to ask her to do. She'd told me before that she'd passed on messages from me, but she'd never brought a message back. "Can you, I don't know . . ."

Willa Mae sighed. "You're a good kid, so I suppose."

I laughed. "*Kid*? I'm older than you, Miss Woman!"

"Years-wise, maybe. But life-wise?" She shook her head. "You ain't seen enough of life yet. Anyways, I'll deal with Oz. Now let me get back to my work." She sounded tough and mean, but Willa was smiling, which was something I wasn't used to seeing.

"Thank you!" I threw my arms around her as she tried to rack the long baking sheet she'd been working on.

"All right now, that's plenty," she said as she twisted loose. She went over to the other side of the room to unload the latest batch of dirty dishes, mumbling that she hadn't even done anything yet. But she'd already seen it in a dream, which was enough for me. I let my mind go off to my own dreamland, and for the rest of my shift, I thought about what it might mean to be a fragile boy. I did know what it meant to be sensitive. To have a heart that could be pricked by words. Especially words set to music.

Oz

1963

Oz shrugged out of his heavy work jacket and kicked off his boots at the back door. The chill from the linoleum floor radiated up through his sweat socks as he crossed into the kitchen. There was the faintest suggestion of light coming through the window over the kitchen sink. With every breath, he could almost taste the leftovers from last night's dinner—cabbage, onions and neck bones. He sniffed under his arms and realized that the onion smell was coming from him. He could use a shower. But he'd wait until later, even though it meant he'd be left with cold water. Just getting home from work as the sun was coming up and everyone in the house was still asleep—that was his precious time alone.

When he, his mother, brother and cousin had arrived in Detroit last year, they'd moved in with his mother's sister, who already had a houseful, with her three children and her boyfriend. Every morning when Oz got home, he cherished the quiet. In the stillness of that hour, what Oz enjoyed most was standing at the kitchen counter in the dim light with nothing but the sound of the percolator gurgling and the smell of a perfect cup of coffee brewing.

He unpacked his lunchbox on the counter, carefully folding the wax paper he'd wrapped his peanut butter sandwich in so that the paper could be used again. He screwed off the top of his Thermos and dumped out the old coffee. He washed everything and put it beside the sink to dry. He grabbed his blue mug down from the cabinet to have it at the ready. He looked out the window over the sink, waiting for his coffee to finish and watching the sky split off into fantastic gradations of pink and blue and white. A miracle of light unfolding over a city that in so many ways felt like a foreign country to him. It was his second December in Detroit.

As Oz poured his coffee, a tiny shiver ran through him. He couldn't stand the winters here. Hated huddling miserably on the bus or hunching over as he walked along ice-slick sidewalks. It took forever for his feet to warm up after coming in from that. He wiggled his toes to further encourage the warm-up, which would be slow, given the cool floor under his feet. He couldn't get used to the cold and, even after more than a year, he still wasn't comfortable with the pace of the city and the packed-in feeling he had from living so close to so many people. Sometimes he wished he were back home in Alabama. He was wishing that now as he stood looking out at the square, snow-covered backyard and the garage and back gate that led to the alley. Then he caught himself. How easy it was to slip into wishful thinking and willful forgetting. There was no home left in Alabama.

"Let it be," he said quietly, before taking a sip from his hand-warming cup of coffee.

From the day Oz had arrived up North, he'd pictured himself like a squirrel on the side of the road, twitchy and jumpy, trying to get across a busy street. He felt always in danger of being run over. Especially at parties. He'd gone to three in his first three months of arriving in Detroit, more than he'd been to in all of his seventeen years in Alabama.

He smiled and lifted his cup for another sip as he remembered

Deborah's party last December. He'd found himself alone after Tommy had drifted off and Willa Mae had, earlier in the evening, told him she was leaving to get some sleep for her early shift. Standing there at the party without his brother and his cousin, Oz had been keenly aware of himself in that crowd: a short, sweater-vest-wearing wallflower surrounded by some of the coolest people he'd ever seen. And there was Deborah on the other side of the room, her dark hair teased into a halo around her head and flipped up at the ends. She was sipping from a white porcelain teacup when everyone else had paper cups. She was in the black, breast-hugging dress she'd performed in so beautifully. She looked like one of those fast girls who paid Oz no attention. He'd been sneaking glances at her all night. Then suddenly, she was looking back at him. She was weaving her way through a couple dozen people on the "dance floor," coming right over to him, of all people, as he stood holding a paper plate with a baked potato on it that he was *this close* to picking up and eating with his hands because it would be his only dinner and he'd dropped his fork. Oz was amazed that he'd captured her attention and heart-thumping nervous because he didn't know what to do with it. He didn't have a lot to say, which was typical for him. His usual conversational limitations were made worse by her very presence. As she talked, he could not stop looking at her face. He could not stop wanting to trace a line between the light freckles on her cheeks to make a constellation. Maybe Virgo. He kept asking himself, *What does this girl want with me?*

In the days that followed, every time Oz talked about asking Deborah for a date, Tommy would suggest that Deborah was out of Oz's league while at the same time saying Oz should give it a shot. Tommy was never quite sure in the ways of love.

Oz finally made his decision after a serious sit-down with Willa Mae. He didn't believe in any of her dreams or the signs she claimed to see, but he did pay attention when she gave him a stern talking-to: "She like you," Willa Mae had told him. "Trust me. I cain't get my work done for hearing about it."

He'd chased down Deborah over the summer. He'd waited for her one day outside of work and followed her across the street to Hitsville, where she went almost every day. The two-story white house, trimmed in blue, was home to Motown and everything she cared about.

"I've seen Smokey Robinson, Martha Reeves, you name it," she said, motioning for him to sit on the grass next to her. "It's only a matter of time before somebody discovers me and I'll be in there making my own records. Watch and see."

As Oz sat across from Deborah on the damp grass, he had to concentrate hard on what she was saying, because he kept getting distracted by what he was seeing. He was mesmerized—almost hypnotized—by a lock of hair that kept dipping in her eyes whenever she excitedly jerked her head while talking about some singer or song. And when she finally tucked those unruly strands behind her ear, it was the movement of her hands that caught Oz's eye. He kept imagining those fingers touching him. He glanced at his own hands, wondering what it would be like to touch her.

When Oz asked her out on a date, he was unprepared when she said yes. Had he expected her to say no? He cast about for some ideas: Dinner? A picnic? She loved music—a concert? Deborah said she wanted to go to the movies. When Oz told her he'd never been to a movie before, she stared at him with her mouth agape, like she was looking upon a specimen at a freak show.

"Now, how is it you've never been to a movie?" she wanted to know.

"It was a sin," he said. "My mama and daddy, well, mostly my daddy, he didn't believe in it." Oz wasn't sure what he believed, but he'd always feared judgment for doing wrong. He reminded him-self, though, that he wasn't that same Alabama boy. Or at least, he was working hard not to be.

"Well," Deborah said, "the movies are exactly where we're going."

She made it feel like an event. When he picked her up in the Ford he'd borrowed from his aunt, she had on what looked like a party dress, with its wide, swinging skirt. At the concession stand, Deborah made sure Oz had popcorn with just the right amount of butter and salt.

"It's for the whole experience," she said. "Everything you see, hear and taste is part of the *experience*."

Then, she told him to wait in the aisle as she squeezed by maybe a dozen people so she could try out three different spots in the the-ater to be certain the two of them had the best seats in the house. He was half-embarrassed, half-enchanted as he stood holding his bag of popcorn, watching until Deborah motioned him over to sit beside her in the "most perfect seat."

Perfect seat or not, Oz wasn't sure how much of the movie he actually watched. As a blonde cozied up to Sean Connery on a train, Oz leaned in closer to Deborah. She smelled of, what? Fading flowers. And butter. She was eating most of the popcorn. Some-times, when she reached into the bag and took out a handful, she would graze his hand or his leg, sending shock waves through him. And even if he could have focused on the film through all of that, Deborah kept up near-constant commentary, her breath tickling his ear as she whispered: "This movie doesn't make sense" or "I don't see what the big deal is about James Bond." And so on. Lis-tening to her, he thought about how palm-sweating anxious he'd been at her party and on the lawn outside of Hitsville and when he'd picked her up for their date, but as he breathed her in, he sud-denly felt calm and relaxed, as if drugged. He sank deeper into the cushion of his seat. When Deborah finished eating his popcorn, he got up the courage and reached over to string his fingers through hers, thinking, *I could never be 007, because Deborah would be the death of me.*

That summer unfurled into a fall and a winter full of firsts. There was, of course, that first movie. Then, his first nice restaurant. Followed by his first full night with Deborah, and his very first time.

Oz would think about her all day if he could, but he had work to do now. He turned on the faucet and splashed cold water on his face with both hands and shook his head briskly like a dog, as if to clear his mind. Then, a light went on. He swung around and looked. It was his mother. Pearl.

"What are you doing up now?" he asked, catching himself too late to tamp down the annoyance in his voice.

"Well, good morning to you, too," she said.

"Sorry." He reached for a dish towel to dry his face.

She pulled the belt of her terry cloth robe tight around her as she hovered in the doorway. Oz could tell she was weighing whether to disturb him or not. But she already had.

"Just having a cup of coffee," he said, motioning toward the coffee maker. He made himself say it: "You want a cup?"

She slid into a chair at the table. "I'd appreciate that." She rubbed her eyes with rough hands. Pearl was not a yielding, soft, feminine beauty. She had worked the fields down South since she was a child. Her hands were calloused. Her mahogany skin was creased from too much time frowning into the sun.

Oz shuffled over to the cabinet and grabbed down a mug for her. Got the sugar and milk, too, because that's how she took it.

"That'll be some good fuel for the day," Pearl said. "I couldn't sleep last night. But what else is new?" She patted the scarf on her head, as if to check that it was still there, then rested her head against the wall and closed her eyes. Growing up, Oz knew his mother slept, but he'd never seen her looking well rested. Especially in those last years before they headed north. Fled north. Pearl's eyes were always bloodshot and puffy back then. Oz remembered that she used to move slowly sometimes, too, like she was pushing a boulder out in front of her. Back in those days, which were not so long ago, Pearl was the one who could be found in the kitchen before sunup. Oz would hear her sometimes, tipping around on the rotting floorboards, the smell of bacon and coffee flavoring the air. She was making sure his father's breakfast was ready whenever he was—which could have been at any time of the morning. By the haggard look of her, no one ever would have guessed that Pearl was as young as she was. She had married and had Oz by the time she was fourteen. She had Tommy at sixteen. For Oz, she was some-where between mother and sister—but distant on either count.

Thinking about how young she'd been and how young she *still* was—Pearl was thirty-three now—Oz felt something tug at his heart as he set her coffee in front of her with the box of sugar cubes and the milk. She looked up at him, and he could see the hope in her eyes. The desire for him to sit across from her and talk, like he used to do when he was a boy. But those days were long past. There'd been too much time and tragedy between then and now.

Oz went over to the counter and grabbed his mug. He usually liked to study at this hour. He'd just started college in September. School had been a real struggle because, growing up, so much of his time had been spent working their peanut farm and playing catch-up on his schoolwork. Still, he'd managed to graduate after many late nights with his head in a book. Now, his college work was waiting for him on the kitchen table across from Pearl. He liked to do as much as he could before his aunt and her boyfriend made him clear out so they could take over the kitchen table, which may as well have been the whole downstairs. They'd sit on the phone for the better part of the day, loudly reeling off digits—"Two-seven-six? And how much on that number?"—as they took bets. Or they'd obsess about what was in the "bank" from the previous day's bets.

"I'm going to go on up and get a shower," Oz told his mother, crossing back over to the kitchen table and scooping up his schoolbooks. "I'll get a shot at some hot water for a change."

"Enjoy it. You deserve it."

He could see Pearl working to hold that smile steady. Her face appeared tight with the effort of it. He turned and hurried out the doorway, taking the stairs two at a time, the coffee dribbling over the side of his mug. Unsteady in his socks on the slick hardwood floor, he went carefully and quietly to the room he shared with Tommy and his aunt's two boys. He put his books and mug on the dresser and undressed. He tiptoed out the door in his underwear and went across the hall to the bathroom. It was nice to beat the crowd. There were no wet, soggy towels hanging off the sink or draped over the toilet. No white globs of toothpaste clinging to the sink or speckling the mirror. No empty toilet paper roll that he'd have to refill.

First, he stood in front of the mirror as he did every day and practiced saying *A, E, I, O, U,* exaggerating his mouth movements around every letter. He reeled off a number of words and phrases, slowly enunciating every syllable: *I can't. Good afternoon. How are you all? Aren't you? Store, for*—making sure to get the vowel and consonant sounds just right. Over the past few months, he'd been working on losing his southern accent and speaking with perfect diction. He still had some distance to go, but he had at least excised words like *ain't* and *cain't* and *y'all* from his vocabulary.

When he was done, he waited for the water to warm up, then stepped into the heat of the shower and let it rain down on top of his head. He could hear the housemates moving around now. The opening and closing of doors. The creak of the stairs. He imagined a line slowly forming at the door, with everyone arguing over who needed to use the bathroom most urgently. He thought about Pearl downstairs at the kitchen table. He couldn't stick around and let her say whatever it was her mouth was twitching to say. He needed time and distance from what used to be. He was creating a new self. One he could live with. After all, it was Pearl herself who'd said that was what they all had to do. If they were to survive.

It was time for a Christmas present for Deborah. Oz had given it a lot of thought and even written down a few options in his spiral-bound notebook, where he listed all of his goals and priorities. There was a list about college and how much it cost and what classes he would take. He kept a record of his pay, along with how much he could save for "the future"—which had its own page decorated with rocket ships in the four corners—and how much he'd have to give to his aunt and his mother to help pay the bills. He also wrote down goals for his next job. He'd jotted down *OFFICE*, but nothing specific because Oz had never been beyond the peanut fields in Alabama or the factory floor here, so he couldn't say specifically what went on in an office. But he did know that he wanted to go to work in a suit and tie and have some say in how things were done.

His focus was on Deborah now, and he flipped through to the page with Christmas gift options. He kept coming back to one: *RING*. He'd written that word in bold capital letters in the right-hand corner of the page and circled it. The very thought of *wanting* to marry Deborah had surprised him. They'd only been together for six months. But more than that, Oz had seen only one marriage up close, and so much heartache had come from it. He had been sure he wanted no part of any marriage. But there was something about Deborah. Whenever Oz was with her, he didn't worry so much about Pearl and the things she might say and the memories she might call forth. In fact, just like that night in the theater, something in him went still and settled down, like a soothed child. He'd never felt anything like it, so he imagined it must be love.

Deborah

1963–1964

Oz picked me up from my parents' place on Christmas night. Snuggled up beside him in the front seat of the car, it was like me and him were in the middle of one of those snow globes, with snowflakes swirling all around. As he hunched over the steering wheel to see through to where we were going, which was to my apartment, I told him about the new dress I'd gotten for Christmas from my parents. Then I described the skirt I'd made for my sister.

"Just a simple A-line," I said. "But I did it in black velvet. She loved it."

He glanced at me. "If this singing thing doesn't work out, you can always go with being a seamstress."

"Don't say stuff like that!" As much as I liked sewing, and as good as I was at it—if I did say so myself—that wasn't what I was after. "Are you trying to jinx me?"

He chuckled. "I don't think anybody could stop you doing what you want to do, Deborah—jinx or not."

When we got to my apartment, we had the place all to ourselves. It was freezing in there, so I went over and turned up the heat first thing, at the risk of upsetting the radiator.

"Just a second!" I said, running from the living room back to my bedroom to get his present. I was worried because he had two boxes for me—one big rectangular one and a medium-sized square one, both wrapped in red paper with silver stick-on bows. I just had the one present for him, though my wrapping was much better than his. I didn't go in for stick-ons. I tied my own bows.

When I came back to the living room with my small box, Oz was on the couch with his two boxes balanced on his knees. He was also rubbing his hands together to warm up.

"You want me maybe to go a little higher with the heat?" I asked.

We both glanced over at the radiator, which was giving off a wheezing, coughing death rattle.

"Best not to," he said. He patted the sofa. "Come on and sit down next to me."

"Oh! Wait!" I dropped my gift beside him and scrambled over to the record player to put on Nat King Cole's Christmas album. I plugged in the Christmas tree. At the sight of its red, white and green glow, I opened my arms to make sure he was taking it all in: "We've got to have the right mood."

"Of course," he said.

I sat down close to him and asked if he wanted me to open the gifts he'd gotten for me first, because, well, that's what I wanted to do.

He gripped the boxes, like I might snatch them out of his hands. "No. I'll open yours first."

"Okay . . ." I handed over what I had for him, wondering why he was holding on to those boxes so tight.

After he opened my present, his face scrunched up in confusion as he fiddled with one of the clasps.

"Cuff links," I said. "For when you get that office job."

The cuff links were silver, with his initials engraved on them.

I'd taken in *a lot* of sewing to make some extra money to pay for them. He touched them and nodded, then looked at me like he'd never seen anything so nice. "Thank you," he whispered as he leaned in to kiss me. Then, all of a sudden, he started moving his hands around, like he didn't know what to do with them. Like he was nervous. "Okay," he said. "You ready for yours?"

"I think so," I said. "Are you?"

He didn't answer. He shoved the big box my way. I opened it to find a red sweater. His lips twitched into a smile when I told him I liked it. Then he gave me the smaller box. It had candy cane socks in it. I didn't like that gift as much, but I don't think he noticed because he was sweating and patting his pockets and putting his cuff links box on the side table. Then he got down on one knee. He pulled a gold band with a small glittery diamond out of his pocket.

"Will you . . . ?" he asked, looking like he was scared I'd tell him no.

But my yes came easy. I'd already dreamed of a life with Oz.

When my sister, Asaline, got married, she had the wedding at Second Baptist. The same church where my mama was a proud, nononsense, white-gloved usher, pointing people to open pews and keeping an eye out for trouble. Me and Asaline were raised in that church, and everybody would expect me to get married there. Especially my mama.

But Oz said he couldn't do it. Couldn't get married in *any* church. How was I going to tell my family this? I thought it'd be best to tell everybody in one go at our Friday family dinner. I brought it up real casual, like it was a whole lot of nothing. Mama stood at the stove frying chicken, taking it all in. She was in her black slip-on house shoes, still wearing her navy blue maid's uniform. My sister, Asaline, was there, too. Just like me, she came every Friday for dinner. The three of us were together in the little U-shaped kitchen, with me and Asaline behind Mama's back at the kitchen table.

"And if not at a church, where?" Mama asked.

"Well——" I hemmed and hawed a little because this was probably worse than the "no church" news. Even I was still trying to be all right with it. "We're thinking about doing it at his house," I said.

I waited for Mama to turn around and say something, but she kept her back to me.

Asaline looked across the table at me and made a face like, *Are you crazy?*

Oz lived with more than half a dozen relatives but had promised we could make things special. He said he just couldn't go in a church. He told me he hadn't even gone in one for his own daddy's funeral. I didn't know what to make of that and he wouldn't talk about it, except to say, "The last time I was in a church was because of Pearl. And it was . . ." He paused. "It was a dark time."

With the quiet thickening between us, Mama finally spoke up: "If ya'll're gon' get married, Deborah"—she took a long pause as she turned around real slow—"you don't get married in somebody's house like that. Especially over there with all them worldly folk and their foolishness."

"What foolishness, Mama?" I leaned back in my chair and crossed my arms. Asaline turned and looked out the window to the road that ran in front of the apartment, which meant she had, for all intents and purposes, left the room.

"You think I'm brand-new or something?" Mama asked.

I don't think my mama was even new when she was born. She was an old soul with her own way of seeing the world and talking about it. *Foolishness* was her word for anything she thought immoral, illegal or otherwise ill-advised. I imagined in this case, she'd heard

Oz's aunt and her boyfriend ran numbers out of their house. But they were nice people who, to my mind, were just getting by the best they could, like anybody else. Like Skeet, who lived down the block and had a "boutique" where he sold boosted women's clothes out of a back room in his apartment. Or Mrs. Walker, who lived in one of the towers and ran a whole beauty salon out of her apartment, which was where Mama got her hair done every other Saturday, knowing good and well Mrs. Walker didn't have anything close to a beautician's license.

"Mama, if you're talking about their numbers—"

"You was raised better than that, Deborah." She turned back toward the stove and stabbed at a couple drumsticks in the pan with her fork. They hissed and spit back oil.

Daddy had been listening from his easy chair in the other room where he was watching *Rawhide* with Asaline's husband and their little boy, a fat crier who, for one time in his short life, was quiet. Daddy took the opportunity to repeat what he'd said when he first met Oz, after Oz had maybe talked too much about his college classes and how nobody could pay him enough to keep working the graveyard shift—or any shift for GM—breaking his back for the rest of his life. Daddy, who worked dayside at a Chrysler plant, had pulled me aside to whisper, "That little uppity country nigga's too slick for his own good. You sure you wanna get mixed up with that?"

Daddy said those words again now from his easy chair in the other room, adding, "Your mama's right."

I looked out the kitchen window, trying to escape like Asaline. Out there on the sidewalk, I spotted a boy I'd grown up with. He was swaying from side to side like he was balancing in a boat on choppy waters. His coat was flapping open in the winter wind. He was bone-showing skinny enough to be blown right off his feet. But I didn't think he'd even feel the pain of falling because this boy was the biggest gutter drunk I'd ever seen.

It hadn't always been that way. Back when we were kids, me and him and all of our friends used to have so much fun chasing each other around these projects. Whenever we tried to hide in the stairwells during hide-and-seek, he almost always gave us away because he talked so much, going on and on about this thing or another and then giving his two cents on it all. Which was why we called him just that. Two Cents. I'd constantly have to tell him to zip it before clamping my hand over my own mouth to keep quiet as a mouse because of the way sound carried.

When I got older, around twelve or so, me and my little singing group at the time, we'd practice in those stairwells, our voices bouncing off the walls and swelling into something bigger than we could imagine. Two Cents would sometimes show up and drum out a beat for us on the handrails, constantly interrupting us to talk about a bad note somebody had hit or a song we might want to try. We let him stay because he was the sweetest chatterbox of a boy anybody could imagine. But look at him now.

Two Cents caught sight of me in the window staring at him. He raised a hand and smiled, then started talking. All I could make out from reading his lips was, *Hey, sis.* I noticed he was missing a block of teeth across the front. I blew him a kiss. He pretended to catch it, moving in slow, drunk motion.

I heard Asaline say: "Oz is nice."

I turned away from the window and Two Cents. I mouthed *Thank you* to my sister as she got up and went over to the stove to peek in one of the pots. Asaline was lovely, with her dark hair pulled into a roll at the back of her head. Her working hairstyle. She had on a maid's uniform, just like Mama's, but hers was black. She was Mama's mirror image, just from a different angle and another stage in life.

"I'm sure Oz'll come around," Asaline said. "Just give him a little time."

Mama limped over to the refrigerator on her bad knees and took out some buttermilk. She limped back to the counter to finish making her hot water corn bread, glancing over at me like a warning: *Heed what I say.*

I turned and looked out the window again. Two Cents was weaving his way up the sidewalk. A woman quick-stepped her way around him, like he was something to be scared of. The woman was carrying a grocery bag and pulling a little girl by the hand. By the look of her white, comfortable work shoes, I imagined she had a job and a life like Mama's and Asaline's: cleaning somebody's house, ironing somebody's clothes, washing somebody's dishes. I didn't want that life. I didn't want the kind of men they'd married either. Men who couldn't see much beyond the assembly line and the end of their shift. Me and Oz, we were after more. I blew on the window and drew a heart with an arrow through it.

While I waited for Oz to come around to understanding he'd have to go in a church, I kept busy with my music. I walked over to Hitsville every day after work at the hospital, rain or shine. The white two-story house with *Hitsville U.S.A.* written across it in blue was like my second home, even though I'd never been inside. I was standing outside under an umbrella in a spring rain when good fortune finally shined on me. A boy who looked like he was built for basketball was on his way into the building, but he stopped halfway up the sidewalk and came back to talk to me.

"What're you doing out here in the rain?" He ducked under my umbrella and held it up higher over his head. "I've seen you out here before."

I'd seen him a time or two before, too. "Trying to get discovered," I said. "So, did I?"

He smiled and told me his name was Robert. "You aren't gonna get far standing out here." He nodded toward the house. "Come on in."

Robert was an engineer and a songwriter with an easy way about him. From the day I met him, he'd let me come in and watch him work. He was as patient as a schoolteacher whenever I slid up next to him on the piano bench. "We're making music, not just sounds," he'd say as he tinkled the keys, trying to put together the right notes. "That takes something special. Some people got it. Some people don't."

He'd give me lyrics to try out. I'd sing. He'd play. One time he put together a song with me sitting right there next to him. It felt like a magic trick. The song was about a girl playing hard to get— but the boy got her in the end. He winked at me a lot while he sang it. After that, he started looking at me with moony eyes. Sometimes he'd joke about taking me out. But I could tell he wasn't joking.

When I told him I had a boyfriend, a *fiancé*—a word I loved saying—he said, "Yeah, that's what y'all girls always say. There's always somebody else." Then he told me how much trouble he had finding the right things to say or the right ways to be with girls. How none of them ever seemed to like him in the way he liked them.

I felt sorry for him. I told him the right girl was out there. "She's just waiting for you to find her."

He hung his head and his long fingers danced over the keys. It was a pretty sound. But sad, too. "I don't think I'll find a girl out there as nice and sweet as you, Deborah," he said.

He started saying that to me a lot, mostly when I was next to him on the piano bench. He looked at me in that moony way of his all the time, too. One time, he slid his big basketball-palming hand up my thigh while he was playing a high note he wanted me to hit.

I stopped sitting around with him at the piano.

But I appreciated Robert introducing me to other songwriters, producers and singers. And the fact that he never pretended he could make me a star. "I can parade you around," he'd say. "But I'm not big-time enough to get you signed. You're going to have to show them what you got."

Soon enough, producers and everybody else had me running out to pick up snacks or whatever they needed. When I wasn't being an errand girl or being introduced to somebody else or avoiding Robert and his hands and eyes at the piano, I'd sit in the little reception room on the long, hard bench they had out there and people-watch, which was where I'd spotted all the Miracles and Marvin Gaye. Nobody complained about my hanging around. Not even when I crept down the stairs that led to the studio. I'd sit to one side on a step and scrunch myself into a corner to watch the singers and musicians record through a dreamy haze of cigarette smoke that filled the studio. When they needed an extra pair of hands for clapping, I'd jump up to show them that mine were right there. They started letting me do some *ooh*s and *aah*s sometimes, too. The first time I stood in that studio under the microphone, I knew I was exactly where I was meant to be, which made it that much harder for me to go to work at the hospital.

Every day at work, I'd stand at my sink daydreaming myself back to that studio. I worried sometimes that I was going to be trapped in that hospital kitchen forever. I saw every second I spent there as a warning. All I had to do to give that warning weight was look around. There were women who'd raised families, had grandbabies and were still there on their feet and swollen ankles all day, scraping plates and slaving over metal sinks.

I was standing at my own sink thinking about all that on the day I heard what I'd been waiting my whole life to hear. I screamed at the sound of it.

Everybody looked at me like I'd lost my mind.

"What is it?" Willa Mae abandoned a tray of glasses she was working on and scrambled over to me. "What's wrong?"

"Listen!" I peeled off my gloves and turned up the radio.

"What?" a girl at the sink behind me said. "That's just 'My Guy.' It's good but it ain't worth all a' what'choo doin'."

"That's me, though!" I said.

"Girl, please," somebody said. "Mary Wells don't need no help from you!"

"The handclaps! I'm doing *handclaps*."

When I told the girls all about being an errand girl and sometimes going in the studio, they got quiet like they were trying to figure out whether to be impressed or not. Some of them leaned in toward the radio to listen closer. I clapped my hands at the point where I came in. "See?"

Just then, Willa Mae clapped *her* hands and said, "Well, congratulations! Next time, it'll be you singing on a record and all us clapping for you! Uh . . . like fans. Not on the record."

She grabbed me and the two of us danced around the kitchen together. The other girls must've decided my handclaps were something to celebrate, too, because they started dancing and whooping right along with us.

I was still dancing inside when me and Mary went out that night. Her big brother, Lloyd, was behind the wheel and Tommy was in the passenger seat next to him. After meeting at my rent party a couple years back, the two of them had become close as anything. I hardly ever saw one without the other. And at times, like now when they probably thought nobody was paying attention, they had a playfulness with each other that, if I didn't know better, I'd say was flirty. From the backseat next to Mary, I watched them argue over the radio dial. Lloyd wanted something that'd make him dance. Tommy wanted to keep it mellow. But it wasn't real arguing. They were laughing and trading soft glances. And when their hands met at the radio dial, there was some finger wrestling that lingered and looked like something tender.

"Would y'all two settle on something already?" Mary complained. "You sound like an old, bickering married couple up there."

Tommy snatched his hand from the dial, like it was all of a sudden hot to the touch, which made me think about Tommy's hands in general. It was hard not to notice his messed-up palms that looked all melty. But it was one of those things you had a feeling you shouldn't ask about.

Lloyd's hand was perfect, just like the rest of him, and he drew it back slower. Tommy leaned forward again and clicked off the radio in one quick motion, then turned and looked out the window, giving off a deep silence that was different from his everyday silences. Tommy was quiet most all the time because of a bad stutter. Oz would always say: "Don't let the silence fool you. There's a lot there with my little brother."

Mary turned to me. "So, Potato Boy ain't changed his mind about getting married at church?"

"Don't call him that." Mary had called Oz Potato Boy ever since meeting him at our rent party. "And to answer your question, no. His mind's made up. Bad memories of church and his mama and daddy or something."

Tommy glanced over the backseat at me.

I all of a sudden felt like I was talking out of turn. Still, I low-ered my voice and finished what I was saying: "He got so, I don't know, touchy about all of it, I just gave up."

"Well, what matters is y'all getting married and being together forever, right? Don't matter where you do it."

"Tell that to my mama," I mumbled, staring straight ahead. We were coming up on the house where the party was. People were hanging out on the porch, taking in the summer air.

"Looks like a full house," Lloyd said.

Lloyd loved a good party. He was wearing a black suit and shiny black leather shoes. With his wavy hair slicked back and his thin mustache, he was always the best-looking boy in any room. Tommy couldn't even compete. He was a lot like Oz. Good-looking enough, but not a head turner. It took getting to know him to see him. But then, Tommy was a hard one to get to know.

Tommy and Lloyd opened our doors. Lloyd offered his sister his elbow and Tommy gave me his. It was definitely a full house. And the place was rocking to the beat of the Miracles coming off the hi-fi. Lloyd and Tommy took off to go talk to somebody they knew across the room. Me and Mary went looking for the punch bowl. Along the way, I hugged and kissed a bunch of friends—Celeste and a good many people we knew from the gigs we played. As we bopped our way to the kitchen, we spotted Joe, owner of Joe's Rec-ord Shop, which was right down on Twelfth Street, close to where we lived. Joe was one of my biggest fans. I scooped myself some punch and told Mary I was going over to talk to him.

"Have fun getting bored to death," Mary said, then went off on her own.

Me and Joe fell into a conversation about the Belle Tones and when we were going to get our break and how, when we did, he'd give our record pride of place in the window. Then, sure enough, Joe started telling me a John Lee Hooker story. He was deep into God knew how many drinks, so there was no stopping him when he got on to reminiscing about the "old neighborhood," Black Bottom, and his old record store on Hastings Street and what it was like when they "kicked us out to build that damn highway," and so on and so forth. Unlike Mary, I liked Joe's stories, but I'd heard about enough. When he took a break from talking to sip his drink, I excused myself to go to the bathroom.

I worked my way up through the line, and when it was finally my turn, there came Robert out of nowhere, sliding into the bathroom behind me and closing the door.

"Can I talk to you?" he asked.

"Sure," I said. "When I'm finished, we can talk as long as you want to, okay?" I motioned for him to leave.

He put his hand on the doorknob and started to go. Then he turned and said, "You know, I really mean it when I say there's nobody as nice and sweet as you, Deborah. Not to me. Nobody in the world."

"Thanks, Robert. That's sweet." It wasn't sweet. It was sweet the first few times, but I'd stopped liking that after he got all touchy on the piano bench. And I didn't like how he was looking at me. It wasn't his usual moony way. It was something . . . different. Wolfish. I motioned toward the door behind him again. He was almost as tall as the frame. "Why don't we both go, okay?" I said. "And we can talk out there."

He shook his head. "You really don't like me, do you?"

"Of course I like you. What's this?"

"I saw you come in with somebody."

"That's Tommy. My fiancé's brother."

His mouth twitched. He looked over his shoulder at the closed door behind him. Then he turned his eyes back to me. His face was a blot of sadness and confusion. He stepped closer, and I could smell the booze coming off him like cologne. He leaned in and tried to kiss me. I pushed him away. He closed his eyes and shook his head. He mumbled, "*Fiancé*," then stumbled forward and tried to kiss me again. Once again I shoved him back. The door all of a sudden felt a mile away. Then, it was like the music dropped out on the other side of it, and all I could hear was my heart thumping. And a whisper in my head: *Get to that door, Deborah.*

"You're my good friend," I said, inching closer to the door, trying to figure out a way around him.

He looked at the door in a fidgety way. "Why do y'all always say that? I don't want to be your *friend*."

"You've been drinking, Robert," I said. "Come on. Let's go out there and talk." I stepped around him, but his hand darted out. Strong as anything, he held me around the waist. He pulled me toward him and clamped a hand over my mouth. I tried to scream, but my voice was so muffled and the music was so loud . . . He pulled me down to the cold floor tiles, the whole time saying, "*Shhh, it's all right if we like each other.*" He was bigger than me. He was heavier than me. He was stronger than me. I was buried alive beneath him. The air left my lungs as he shoved my skirt up.

Why's he doing this to me?

When it was over, he got to his feet and apologized as he zipped up. He was looking at the floor and then the door, like he couldn't wait to be gone. Then he apologized again and promised that this didn't change anything. He'd still help me.

I heard myself say, "Okay."

He left. As I stood there on shaky legs, I could hear him on the other side of the door telling somebody, "Just give her a minute. You know how girls are."

I threw up. I held the rim of the toilet and the counter and pulled myself up with trembling arms. Standing in the middle of the floor, I felt lost. Like there was no door. No window. No way out. I couldn't get enough air. I squeezed my eyes shut, trying to catch my breath. After struggling for I don't know how long, I could finally breathe well enough. And everything went still.

I used the bathroom and washed myself at the sink, moving on automatic, like I was following some kind of terrible choreography I didn't even know I knew.

When I came out of the bathroom, I looked around the room real careful, not wanting my eyes to fall on Robert. I spotted Tommy in a far corner. He looked so much like Oz, which was who I wanted to see most right then. Tears came to my eyes. A cry rose in my throat. I put my hand over my mouth and swallowed it all down. I went over to Tommy. He was talking to Lloyd and a boy I didn't know. I interrupted and asked Tommy and Lloyd to take me home.

Tommy raised an eyebrow and studied my face. "Y-y-y-you okay?"

I told him I was fine.

He looked at me closer.

I could feel the sting of tears again.

Tommy nodded slowly, like maybe he didn't know exactly, but he knew something of a hurt so deep, you can't speak its name. He told Lloyd to go find Mary so we could leave.

Lloyd hesitated for a second, and Tommy put his hand on Lloyd's shoulder. Lloyd nodded and went off. When he got back with Mary, he asked me what was wrong.

I was about to say *Nothing*, but Tommy told him to leave me be. As we headed for the door, I felt like the ground was shifting. Like I might sink right through the floor. Tommy reached his melty, scarred hand down and grabbed mine. He held on real tight.

I married Oz on the last Saturday of August in 1964. His aunt's duplex smelled of fried fish and air freshener. The dingy floral couch and chair had been shoved up against a back wall to make way for a handful of folding chairs that somebody had gotten from some church basement somewhere. But every light was on in the apartment and the sun was shining through open windows. It didn't burn off all the dankness, but it was okay because there was Oz waiting for me at the other end of the room in his black suit and tie, looking as handsome and happy as I'd ever seen him.

Later, when me and Oz were in bed on the one night we took for a honeymoon at a motel we couldn't afford, he laid his head on my belly. I'd told him a week before that I was pregnant. Was it his? Was it Robert's? I thought that, somehow, by telling Oz, it would make me believe the baby was his. I thought it would make me not want to claw my insides out so much. I thought it would make me feel like I could live with it.

Oz was making plans. We were standing outside the apartment building where we now lived in a one-bedroom with my sister, brother-in-law and their little boy. It had only been a couple weeks, but there were nonstop arguments over the bathroom or who was making too much noise or who'd eaten too much of something. I leaned back against the wrought iron gate and looked up at the moon. It occurred to me that it was a Saturday night, a night when most couples were probably out at parties or someplace where they could have a good time. I hadn't been to a party since that night.

Under the streetlight, Oz was lit like a star in a black-and-white movie, which made what he was saying seem more dramatic. "It's time to get serious about things," he said. "We're about to have a family."

My stomach lurched at that, and I felt like I might be sick.

"We need our own place, don't you think?"

I stared off at an old man making his way down the sidewalk. I wondered where he was getting off to at that hour. It was after ten o'clock and depending on where he was going, it might not be safe. I felt a flutter of worry in my stomach. I worried all the time now.

"Do you hear me, Deborah?"

I looked back at Oz and blinked.

"It's time to go," he said. "I know you feel it, too. I can see how you've been acting. So down and everything." He paced back and forth along the sidewalk in front of me, with his hands clasped together behind his back.

Oz had been working as much overtime as he could and going to school between all of that. He kept all of his paychecks written down in a black notebook and was always checking to see how he was coming along. He was working on himself, too. When he could get more than a second alone in the bathroom, he'd be in there telling jokes and acting like he was having a conversation with somebody. It was his way of trying to get over his shyness. He practiced the right ways of speaking, too. Every time I heard him in there saying "A, E, I, O, U," holding each letter for a long time, my heart broke a little. I loved the softness of his southern accent, but he wanted it gone. Said he couldn't lose it fast enough.

As he paced, Oz started talking about how much apartments

cost. He was looking straight ahead, his forehead knotted up in concentration. "But don't worry," he said, turning to me.

There was something about the way he looked, earnest and innocent, that made me feel like a liar. I started to cry.

He looked panicked. "Why are you crying? I said not to worry. We'll find our own place. I promise."

I opened my mouth and closed it like a fish.

He searched my eyes. "What is it?"

I heard myself telling him everything that had happened at the party. I told him that I didn't know if we were having a family because how did I know if the baby was his?

As I spoke, he put his hands to his stomach, like he was the one carrying something that had been forced on him. His eyes glistened under the streetlights.

"Why didn't you tell me?" he said. "Before?"

I shook my head. "I didn't know how." But there was also this: *Because you'd leave me.*

I told my sister. I needed her to tell me what to do. Not knowing, she told Mama. Mama was the last person I ever wanted to tell something like that to, but she was also the one person I most wanted to know. Everybody felt that way about her. From all over the projects, women came to her to talk about their problems, and she always knew the right thing to say or the best thing to do. In this case, she went in her bedroom and slammed the door on me and Asaline. I could hear her crying.

A few days later, Mama pulled me aside after a Friday dinner and told me she knew a woman who knew of a woman, a midwife, who could "deal with this kind of foolishness."

Oz insisted on driving us. He held my hand across the front seat for most of the ride. We pulled up on a quiet street lit by dim streetlamps. It felt safe enough. But I could hear the wail of a siren in the distance. A dog barking, not far away. Mama took a piece of paper out of her bra, which was where she kept small items of importance. She checked the numbers on the paper against what was on the building. We were at the right place. We got out of the car and went up to an ordinary-looking apartment building. A converted row house. When we got inside and moved to go up the stairs, Mama stopped and put a hand on Oz's arm.

"This here's women's work," she said.

Part of me wanted him to come. But most of me wanted him not to see me this way. Besides, Oz and Tommy had already done their "men's work" by tracking Robert down. Oz had come home with bloody knuckles and a bloodstained sweater vest. I told him not to tell me what they'd done, but I liked knowing they'd done something that had drawn blood.

"Mama's right," I said to Oz. "Just wait for us."

He looked from my mother to my sister, then back to me and nodded. "Whatever you want."

He stood at the bottom of the stairs with one hand in his pocket, while holding his black fedora against his thigh with the other. He'd dressed like he was going to a funeral. He had on a black suit and tie. His shoes were shiny and brand-new. He stared up at us as we climbed the stairs in the dim light and found apartment 2B. We were met by a round, wrinkly-skinned woman who reminded me of a plump raisin. She was wearing one of those aprons that put me in the mind of a sleeveless pullover dress. It had red flowers on the body and gingham at the shoulders. She looked clean, and her apartment did, too. She led us to a small room decorated with a brown paisley wallpaper that made the room darker than I imagined it was naturally. There was a young woman. A girl, on closer look. Maybe fifteen or so. She was sitting on the edge of one of the two wingback chairs in the room. She was prim and almost still, except for her right leg agitating up and down, fast as a jackhammer. She was light-skinned and her cheeks were flushed and damp.

"Don't mind her," the midwife said, noticing me noticing the girl. "She ain't quite ready for her turn yet."

I nodded to the girl, who nodded back politely, then put a Kleenex to her nose and stared at the wall. There were two little boys sitting on the floor in front of a snowy TV screen giving directions to a third boy who was standing up, trying to get the rabbit-ear antennas pointed in a useful direction. Mama smiled at them, but they never looked away from the TV and the antennas. I knew it was killing her not to say something about disrespectful children along with something biblical. But then, she'd backed off the Bible lately, given what was going on with me.

I all of a sudden felt warm and sweaty under my arms. I leaned on Asaline. My stomach rolled from the smell of the apartment. It revived the nausea I'd been feeling off and on for weeks.

"Smell like you got something good going for dinner," Mama said, like we'd just stopped by for a visit.

"Liver and onions," the midwife said.

My stomach lurched at the thought of it, and I swallowed the spit pooling in my mouth. Asaline slid her arm around my waist as she smiled politely.

"Could never get these two to eat liver and onions," Mama said, pointing to me and Asaline.

I swallowed again, trying not to be sick.

The midwife nodded then asked about the money.

Mama blinked, obviously shocked by the reminder of why we were all there. She reached into her bra and pulled out the payment we'd scraped together between the three of us and Oz and his

mother, aunt and cousins. The midwife put the wad in her apron
pocket and asked Mama and Asaline to have a seat on the couch.
She led me back to the kitchen, where she told me to leave my
blouse on, but take off the rest of my clothes. She went over to close
the kitchen door, then came back and held out a towel to me.

"Use it to wrap up," she said.

I hesitated, looking at the towel like I'd never seen such a thing.
My eyes moved to the sink, which was clear of any dishes. They
landed on the stove where the pot of thick brown gravy, covering
the liver and onions, bubbled like a brew in a witch's cauldron. My
stomach heaved. She'd somehow anticipated the moment, moving
with quicksilver speed for a woman of her size and age, snatching
up a garbage can and shoving it in my face. I went down on my
knees, retching for the longest to the sounds of gunshots and
neighing horses coming from the TV in the other room. Seemed
they'd gotten the signal right.

When I finally stood, sweaty and still dry heaving, the midwife
said, "You all right?"

She pushed the towel toward me again.

I nodded and accepted the towel to wipe my mouth and sweaty
face.

"All right, then. Let's go on 'head and get them clothes off."

I hesitated again as I watched her pull on a pair of yellow rubber
gloves. Dishwashing gloves. *What the hell am I doing here?* I looked
around the kitchen, thinking about the girl who wasn't ready for
her turn yet. *How do you get ready for something like this?* I wondered if
Mama had been fooled. Did this woman even know what she was
doing? I'd heard stories about "messed-up" girls or girls who just
out and out died from this. Maybe I should've just tried throwing
myself down some stairs or drinking some bleach. My mind whip-
sawed from one "remedy" I'd heard about to another.

As I stood there shaking and sweating, with the towel up to my mouth, the midwife said, "You ain't got nothing I ain't seen aplenty of before, dear." She laughed. "Go on now."

I shimmied out of my skirt and folded it up real neat. I hesitated as I got ready to take off my panties. I glanced at her. She gave me a tired smile, then nodded encouragement. I pulled my underwear down as quick as I could and wrapped the towel around my waist, just like she'd told me to do. She motioned toward the tiled kitchen table, and I moved to take out a chair.

"No, girl," she laughed. "Get on up there."

"What?"

"The table. Spread your towel out and lay on it."

I gripped the terry cloth tight, twisting it into a knot as I looked at the table, wondering if it could hold my weight. Wondering if they'd have their liver and onions there after. I dry heaved again.

"Maybe we should—"

"No. No. It's fine. I'm fine." I knew all those other "remedies" wouldn't work just from the stories of two girls in the kitchen at the hospital. "I'm fine." I put my hand over my mouth and pushed back the convulsions. I just wanted it over with.

"Good," she said. "Now, please, get on up there and relax."

Relax? I spread my towel on the cold table and climbed up on top of it. She threw another towel over me and spread my trembling legs, apologizing for not having anything for the pain. "But maybe you'll remember," she said, "and not end up back here." She nodded toward the front room. "It's twice for that high-yellow hussy out there."

Hussy? She was just a girl.

She pushed my legs up in the air where she wanted them and promised to work quick. Then I felt something sharp at my core. I jerked away, but she tightened her hold on my leg. Waves of pain shot through me.

"Quiet, quiet," she said. "You don't want them out there to hear, do you?"

She held my legs firm. She was so much stronger than she looked. I don't know how much time passed. I closed my eyes and bit down on another towel she'd given me to keep me from crying out. Tears slid down the sides of my face.

When I opened my eyes again, there was blood in the kitchen sink, just across from me. The dishwashing gloves were draped there like dangling, mangled hands. I was pulled off the table and made to stand on wobbly legs. I glanced back at the table with its blood-soaked towel. And there was darkness. Then there was light. Then I was leaning on Mama and Asaline and the midwife was saying, "I packed her with some gauze. She can expect some cramping, but she'll be fine. Maybe give her some aspirin when you get home. And menstrual pads."

Oz ran up the stairs two at a time the second he saw us come out the door. He carried me down and laid me on the backseat, where he stayed with me.

Oz

Oz tried never to miss a performance. He got comfortable in a booth next to Willa Mae, waiting for Deborah's group to come onstage. Willa Mae looked down at her watch and, as if on cue, the band started playing. And there was Deborah, snapping her fingers as she glided up to the microphone.

Oz smiled and leaned forward to watch her go. She and her group were far from the amateurs they'd been during that apartment performance some years back. They were poised now. More professional. And Deborah was as polished as any star out there, in Oz's view. She never put a foot wrong or missed a note with her soaring soprano.

Willa Mae leaned over and whispered loudly over the music, "You and Deborah all settled in? Y'all liking the new place?"

Oz shrugged. "It'll do." He and Deborah had just moved out of Deborah's sister and brother-in-law's place. They now lived with Pearl in a nice house on Edison. Willa Mae had come over with candles and a plastic bag full of something or other she planned to burn to bring "good energy" to their new home, but Oz had vetoed her "Voodoo witchcraft." He and Deborah would bring their own good energy, he told her.

The house belonged to Pearl's boyfriend, Mr. Burton, a tall, square man with round features who looked every part the stable husband. But Pearl always made clear she had no intention of marrying him: "I been there before," she'd say. "I don't mean to pass that way again."

"We're saving up for our own place," Oz said to Willa Mae. "Hopefully it won't be long. We drive around sometimes 'house shopping.' That's what Deborah calls it. Trying to see ourselves in different places."

"And where you see yourself?"

Oz shrugged. "I don't know yet."

"Well," Willa Mae said, "when me and Deborah was out *clothes* shopping the other day—"

"Which she knows we can't afford."

"Hey, I did my best to keep her outta trouble," Willa Mae said. "Anyways, when we was out, she told me she'd like a place with a lotta windows. I don't know if that'll help you whittle things down."

Oz smiled. "Yes, I know. She wants a lot of light."

A couple of months ago, with Deborah packed with gauze and resting at her parents' house, Oz couldn't have imagined them anyplace other than the darkness of that moment. He'd talked to Willa Mae about everything. The rape. The abortion. The merciless, bloody beat-down he and Tommy had given Robert. Everything. Willa Mae had said only, "Ain't nobody never like they was. Not after." Then she'd fixed Oz with a hard stare. "But you better not leave her. If you do, you ain't no better than the one that did her bad."

Leaving Deborah had never occurred to Oz. "I could never do that," he'd said.

Deborah was smiling as she leaned into the microphone and hummed her part of the harmony. Oz watched her closely all the time to see if what Willa Mae had said was true. To see the differences in her. She'd been distant and quiet, right after. But she seemed okay now, as far as he could see. She smiled and laughed a little less. But she was back to shopping with Willa Mae and hanging around with her mother and her sister like she liked to do. She was making their little attic apartment a home, sewing curtains and getting better at cooking. And, of course, she was back onstage. She told Oz all the time that she was fine.

Just then, Lloyd slid into the booth next to him and leaned in to say his hellos. Lloyd was managing Deborah and the group now. He slouched down and bopped his head to the music. He tapped the ash from his cigarette. He waved and winked at whoever caught his eye. When the club owner stopped by the table, Lloyd sat up straighter and left his cigarette to burn in the ashtray. Oz heard him tell the owner that the girls would be glad to come back and perform anytime. That they'd iron out details on payment later. How was next weekend?

Oz leaned forward, ready to cut in and tell him that he and Deborah had plans for next weekend, but Lloyd and the club owner were locked in conversation. Oz cleared his throat. They couldn't hear him. Then the club owner left and Lloyd turned to Oz and said, "I got us some dates in Chicago and Milwaukee. It'll be more exposure. What do you think, man?"

Lloyd was chewing on his cocktail straw. He was always fidgety when Oz saw him—chewing on something, picking at something, flicking nonexistent ash off his cigarette. Oz had a low tolerance for people who let so much of themselves show.

He glanced around reflexively looking for Tommy. But for once, Tommy wasn't with Lloyd. Every time Oz turned around, those two were together—and Oz didn't like what he was seeing between his brother and Lloyd. It recalled a different time. A different Oz.

"I said, what do you think?" Lloyd said, breaking into Oz's thoughts.

"I don't know," Oz said. "Deborah . . . we have some new things happening now."

Lloyd nodded and grinned. "Yeah, man. Y'all just moved and you're trying to get settled and everything. I know, I know."

"Right."

Lloyd went on: "Thing is, I think we need to strike while the iron's hot. That old man they had managing them before, he wasn't aggressive enough." Lloyd sat back and put his hands up, like he was pausing Oz before Oz could speak. "And I understand about everything y'all have going on. I do. We'll go out a few times and get back, then she's all yours." He smiled. "Until the next time."

"She's already all mine."

Lloyd laughed and put his hands up again. "Hey, man, you don't have to worry about me."

Oz sat back and watched his wife onstage. That first time he'd seen her perform he'd told her she would be a star. He had no doubt about it. Just look at her. But he'd never thought of what it would take for her to *become* a star. He'd never considered what it would mean to have her out on the road, with him back at home. And now that he was considering it, he felt a little bit, he didn't know . . . just *bothered* by the whole thing. He was reminded of what Robert had done to her and feared that might happen again out there. He felt this tiny seed of worry taking root in him. He was worried about all the dangers. Worried about himself and the life he and Deborah were making here at home. What would their new place be like—how would he feel—with her not here?

"It's just a few dates," Deborah told him as she finished packing up. She was always rushing around, doing things last-minute.

Oz slid back the curtains Deborah had made and looked out the window. A white van was idling on the street next to a mound of snow on the curb. Fresh snowflakes were falling. Near as Oz could tell, that was Lloyd behind the wheel, and he was honking the horn for the fifth time.

"That's going to be an uncomfortable trip," Oz said. "Riding around with everybody crammed in that van like that. You sure you really want to do this?"

Deborah snapped the suitcase closures shut and lifted the suitcase off the bed. "I do, Oz," she said as she came over and wrapped her arms around him. She looked him in the eye and held his gaze for a second. "It's all going to be fine. Safe, too." They never talked about what had happened, but it was always there. An unwelcome, silent specter.

Oz held on to her and looked around their little place. They were standing next to their bed and a chest of drawers—the only pieces of furniture they had so far. At the other end of the apartment, there were piles of clothes that still needed to be hung up or put in drawers. There were crates of albums and a few boxes of books and dishes that still needed unpacking. His eye caught on the cigar box. It was made of blond, unfinished wood. It was wedged between two crates. He felt a ripple of panic pass through him. He'd meant to hide that box away in the chest of drawers, but there it was, its brass closure winking in the lamplight. Oz had not opened it since the day he'd closed it in Alabama. But it called to him sometimes. He turned away, unnerved, sweat pooling on his brow. As he wiped at it, Deborah asked if he was okay.

"Yes," he said. But the sight of that cigar box, the thought of her leaving . . . Everything was so unsettled and not at all what Oz had planned. He felt that sense of bother again. A quickening of that worry seed.

He gave Deborah a half-hearted squeeze, then reached down

and hefted her suitcase up and waited while she ran into the bathroom to make sure she had all of her makeup and perfumes. He followed her downstairs and out to the van. He kissed her, helped her in and loaded the suitcase in the back. He pounded on the side of the van a couple of times as a signal that they could go.

Deborah toured most weekends—and some weekdays—for the next few months. She only stopped when she got pregnant and too uncomfortable to be bumping around in that van. *This is it*, Oz thought. *I let her have her shot. But she's back now. Everything will settle into place.*

They started driving around house shopping again, even though they couldn't afford to buy anything just yet. Deborah would talk about all of the things she wanted: the windows, a lot more room than they had now, a nice kitchen.

"We'll see what we can afford," Oz said. He'd been keeping a close eye on the slowly rising number in their bank book and measuring it against the budget he kept in his notebook, including all the costs associated with a new baby.

Their daughter, Trinity Marie Armstead, arrived in early October 1965—a month early, but without trouble. It took Oz several weeks before he would hold her.

"I've never held anybody so small," he whispered as Deborah positioned their sleeping daughter in his arms. Oz was sitting in a rocking chair, but afraid to move.

"Watch her head," Deborah said quietly.

Oz tensed.

Deborah laughed. "You won't break her." She bent and kissed Oz on his ear. "You're going to be a good father, Oz. Just relax."

Oz rocked Trinity a little but kept the arm that held her rigid. He did not want to risk dropping her.

The words *good father* echoed in his mind as he looked down at his daughter's abundant curls and tiny fingers. He thought of his own father. He hadn't allowed himself to think of him in a long while because of all that it recalled. A different time. A different Oz. That blond cigar box. Suddenly, tears came to his eyes. He gazed at the bundle in his arms through blurred vision. He touched his index finger to his daughter's. Her sleepy eyes fluttered open just a crack.

"Here I am, Trinity," he whispered. "I'll do my best to be good for you," he promised. "And your mother, too."

Trinity closed her eyes again, as if satisfied with what he'd had to say. He rocked her, feeling marginally more confident, given her contentment.

"See," Deborah said, "look at you go. You're a natural."

He didn't feel like a natural. But he felt like he might be able to keep his promise. He felt like he was getting a chance to redeem all that he tried not to recall. He felt like he, Deborah and Trinity could be a family in a home of their own somewhere, just like he and Deborah talked about. A place with a lot of windows. And so much light.

After

Everything that had ever

meant anything to me.

Deborah

Oz's birthday coffee mug was waiting for him on the counter. It said *World's Best Dad*. On the buffet table in the dining room, we had Oz's birthday cake from the bakery with its thirty-seven candles waiting to be lit. There was Neapolitan ice cream in the freezer. I had tea sandwiches and those little quiches and potato chips and French onion dip laid out on the table, too. The dip had gone bad, having sat out warm all night. The tiki torches on the patio had burned out, but we didn't need their light. The sun was up and bright, blazing through the big picture window. It was late morning now and Oz hadn't come home.

I couldn't take my eyes off the bunch of blue and white balloons floating over the bar cart in the corner. They were just to the right of the police officer, who stood framed in the entry to the living room. I was having a problem focusing on that officer. Same went for the one who was sitting across from me in one of two leather chairs. Pearl sat in the other chair, twin to his. She was on the edge of it, wringing a napkin in her hands. I was in a corner of the couch with my party dress and heels still on. Those balloons floating high in the room seemed to ground me.

"He talking to you," Pearl said to me.

I looked at the officer across from me. He was holding a pen and a little notebook. He wanted to know:

Are you his wife? *Yes, I'm Oz's wife. For seventeen years. I'm Deborah Armstead.*

When did you last see him? *Yesterday morning. In the kitchen. On his way to work.*

How did he seem? *Fine. He forgot his coffee mug, though.* I pointed toward the kitchen. *It was a birthday present from our daughter.*

And he drove to work, right? *Yes.*

There was hope hanging on every word I said. If I just gave them the right answer, a lightbulb might go off and they'd say, "Ah, yes. Okay. We know exactly where to find your husband, Mrs. Armstead."

But instead, they came at me with more questions. They wanted to know who'd seen him last and where. The one who'd seen him last wasn't there, so Pearl offered the *where*: "He was at a barbecue restaurant."

"It was for his birthday," I added. "He went on his lunch break." I'd talked to him just before he left the office.

"The place was down off Woodward, I think," Pearl added. "He was with—"

But Pearl cut herself off when the officer stopped writing in his notebook. The tips of his ears got red and he leaned in. "Anywhere around, um, Cass Corridor?"

Pearl turned her head a little in the direction of the officer, squinting like she could see where this was going and she didn't like it one bit. He was trying to take us down drug- and crime-infested blocks where every bad thing you could imagine getting into or getting after you could be found.

"Restaurant's called the Lion's Den," I said, trying not to think about all the bad. It was a stretch to call it a restaurant. It wasn't much more than a spare room with plastic tables and chairs.

The officer nodded. "Now look, I'm sure I don't have to tell you what kind of stuff goes on around there."

Pearl stood. "Ozro ain't no druggie, if that's what you working yourself up to." She paused. "Or out looking for no prostitute either, thank you very much."

The officer's partner, still standing in the entryway to the living room, said, "Ma'am, that's not what he's saying. He's just saying it's a bad part of town, is all. Just maybe . . . maybe a bad thing happened. That's all."

"That's all?" I said.

He looked at the floor.

"We're going to have to give it some time," said his partner across from me in the chair. The partner was older and seemed like he'd been at this kind of thing longer. "Sometimes you just . . . you just don't know what you don't know about people, ma'am. Even, begging your pardon, husbands." He stood up, shifting his weight from one foot to the other. He gazed around the room like he was hunting for the exit.

I got to my feet. "Oz should've been home last night. After work. For his birthday party."

The officer snapped his notebook shut. "Give it some time, then file a formal police report if you need to, okay?" He nodded toward me. "But I think he'll show."

"And how would you know?" Pearl asked.

They left without saying.

I kept calling Oz's office. No answer. Me and Pearl called around to hospitals. Nobody by the name of Daniel Ozro Armstead Junior had been admitted anywhere.

They found Oz's car later that morning parked in its usual space at work. And there was his dark blue suit jacket, still hanging over the back of his chair. His black briefcase was sitting next to his desk, where he always kept it.

It was too quiet. I filled the house with *Songs in the Key of Life* while I sat by the phone waiting for a call from the police or anybody who could say where Oz might be. Music was still my best company, even though I'd given up singing years ago—or more like, it had given up on me. As song after song played in the background, I roamed the house, checking through old boxes in closets, the pockets of Oz's clothes and everything in his basement office. I didn't know just what I was looking for, but I was thinking about what that policeman had said: *Sometimes you just . . . you just don't know what you don't know about people, ma'am. Even, begging your pardon, husbands.*

Down in Oz's office, everything was in its place, just the way Oz liked it. I found his notebooks stacked on the shelf of his bookcase, next to the full set of *Encyclopaedia Britannica*s. The writing in the notebooks was neat and tidy, in Oz's straight-lined block letters. He'd written page after page of the things he meant to do, which included saving, spending and potential job promotions. I was going through the last notebook when the phone rang. It was a call to go down to the morgue.

After hanging up, I sat there shaking and staring at the phone, till it came to me to call Pearl. She met me there. We leaned on each other as we walked arm in arm down a long, freezing hallway with buzzing lights over our heads, in the company of a police officer. He took us into a windowed room where we looked out at a steel table with a body on it.

"Is this him?" the officer asked.

I turned away.

"Come on now, Deborah," Pearl said.

I held her a little tighter as I looked at the face. *A dead body*, I thought. *A corpse*. He was about Oz's complexion, though the brown of his skin had a gray tinge to it. His head was scraped up on the side, right where Oz had these small, fine scars on his face. Oz had told me his scars came from "being on the wrong side of breaking glass" when he was a teenager. I put my hand to my mouth and swallowed the rising bile.

"It ain't him," Pearl said. "That ain't Oz."

I nodded. I knew it. Still, my mind, my ears, my eyes had confused me and carried me off. I couldn't stop worrying: *What if Oz is rotting away in some morgue somewhere? What if he was in the wrong place at the wrong time, like the police thought? What if he's a John Doe in some hospital?*

All that wondering followed me home, and there wasn't a single song that could drown it out, so I didn't turn the music on this time. I sat with my thoughts and a glass of wine, waiting for the drink to do its soothing work as I went through the last pages of that last notebook I'd been looking at earlier. On one page, from just a couple months ago, there was a note that said: *Just tell her*. It was squished in among doodles of cars and these creepy faces that didn't have eyes, a nose or a mouth. I went through all of Oz's notebooks again, wondering if I was the *her* he'd meant to tell. And then I got mad at him and threw one of the notebooks across the room. Why couldn't the pages read like a diary? Why didn't he write down a record of himself or what he had going on? That was just like him. He couldn't, he *wouldn't*, talk through anything. That had been the problem in the months before he vanished.

I got up, finished my glass of wine and went to bed. I couldn't sleep. I slid over to Oz's cold, empty side and stared into the darkness.

Days later, the police brought Oz's suit jacket and briefcase home from the office. I sat on my bedroom floor trying to make sense out of the spreadsheets he'd been carrying around. My heart skipped when I found mini tapes and a tape recorder in a pocket of the briefcase. I couldn't get the little tapes in the player fast enough. My hands shook every time. I listened with the recorder right up at my ear, trying not to miss a word. But nothing he said meant anything to me. Oz was just reminding himself to do this or that at work. I went through the pockets of Oz's jacket and didn't find anything either.

I was coming to see that Oz didn't leave stray pieces of himself lying around or forgotten. There weren't any old receipts or balled-up, scribbled notes to himself. No real thoughts caught on tape. None of life's little breadcrumbs that might lead somewhere.

Trinity came in and found me there on the floor with a spreadsheet I didn't understand and the open briefcase. My baby was sixteen now and smart as anything. She was short, like Oz, but in the face she looked more like me with her narrow nose and almond eyes. She sat down and leaned in toward me for a second. She was trying to sniff out alcohol on my breath, in a way she probably thought I didn't notice. I'd had too much to drink last night. And the night before. And more nights than either one of us could count, for most of her life. But I hadn't had anything to drink today. Not yet.

She relaxed and settled in next to me, hugging her knees to her chest. She said, "I don't understand. Where is he?"

Me and Trinity talked about all kinds of things. The boys she liked, the bullies at school and what she'd do when she grew up, but this? How do you look into the confused eyes of your child and tell her, *I don't have any answers*? But that was what I told her.

She didn't say anything back. She just leaned forward, grabbed the tape recorder and pressed Play. She closed the empty briefcase, then curled into my side, like she used to do when she was little and scared. We listened to Oz's voice fill the room: *Call John about the problem with Al* . . .

I whispered in her ear, "It's going to be all right, Trin." But I didn't know if I believed that.

After weeks and weeks of nothing, we hired a private investigator. He was an ex–Detroit detective who claimed to know every corner of the city and most of the people in the worst parts of it. He worked for months before finally telling us that he couldn't find any signs of foul play. Not a single John Doe—dead or alive—who fit Oz's description. The detective didn't dig up any big secrets either. None of the things that might make a man up and walk off from his wife and child.

Trinity

1982

The Pretenders were playing in the background as I settled in. I hated the Pretenders. Still do, but in my high school, back in 1982, that was a highly controversial position to take. You'd be interrogated: What about "Message of Love"? What about "Back on the Chain Gang"? What about Chrissie Hynde? How can you explain that you respect Chrissie Hynde as a person and even a musician, but still don't like the music? You can't.

Anyway, I was in the newsroom trying to edit an article about the school mascot, and the Pretenders were loud. I took my fingers out of my ears and asked Matt the Graphics Guy if he wanted me to finish the layout for him. "I don't mind," I said.

Matt was known to be devoted to the newspaper, in lieu of having any live, human friends. I expected him to say no, but I held my breath and hoped as he looked up at me from the light table. He scratched at his wispy, white-blond mustache. "You know . . . um, well, sure." He went over to the boom box, popped his cassette out and slid it in its case. "See you tomorrow, Trinity," he said, shouldering his way out through the heavy classroom door with something of a pep in his step. I wondered where he was headed.

Matt and I had made out once earlier in the year right there in the newsroom. It was completely spontaneous and unsatisfying. I couldn't say why it had happened, beyond the fact that I was a magnet for lonely, wayward weirdos. Which was probably the exact thing he would have said, if asked about me.

After Matt was gone, I took in a big, refreshing breath of that silence and looked out the wall of windows to the back lawn of the school. The "newsroom" was housed in a multipurpose room that had mostly been set aside for the purposes of the newspaper staff. A couple of the windows were cranked open. The air coming in smelled of autumn leaves. I could hear the guys practicing out on the football field. I had attended only one football game in high school, and that was as a fill-in for our sports reporter when he was out with mono.

I turned back to the Wite-Out-blotted page in front of me. It was a terrible article. It was about a girl taking over the Spartan mascot uniform for the first time in school history. It was written as more of a screed on how Spartans were, in fact, male warriors. I hunched over the typewriter and did the best I could to make it better. When I was finished, I yanked the page out—loving that *zzzzzzzzip* sound of the typewriter roller. It always had a celebratory *The End* ring to it for me. I got up and went over to the light table where Matt had the front page laid out.

The door to the multipurpose room opened. My math teacher popped his bushy, gray head in. "Burning the midnight oil again, I see."

I looked up at the clock. "It's barely five o'clock, Mr. Steadman."

"Midnight in school hours," he said. "Anyway, all work and no play, young lady." He wagged a finger. "Go home, Ms. Armstead. Find something fun to do."

"In a little while," I said.

He saluted and moved to close the door, but my best friend

edged up beside him. "Same goes for you, Virginia," he said as he stepped aside so she could scoot past him. "Go home and have some fun."

When he closed the door, Virginia dropped her book bag on the table. "You know, I don't think I've ever said anything like this before, but what the hell: I agree with Mr. Steadman. Let's go do something fun!"

I pointed to the light table. "Can't you see I have work to do?"

"You and your work." She plopped down in a chair, her unruly red hair on the verge of liberating itself from the ponytail holder at the back of her head. "How long is this going to take? I've been hanging around for, like, forever, waiting for you."

I looked through the pages and the ads Matt was working with. Layout wasn't my area, but I'd done it a few times and was okay at it. "I don't know. Maybe an hour? A *quiet* hour?"

She pulled out a novel—*Chances*—and made a zipping motion at her lips.

Virginia and I had known each other since we were nine. She lived in the house across the street and on the day my family had moved in, she'd stopped over to give me a hamster as a housewarming gift. My mother was not pleased, but she'd let me keep it. I hadn't been without a hamster since that day, with the latest being Sniffy V, successor to Sniffys I to IV. I also hadn't been without Virginia. She was my best and only friend. And she'd been all but omnipresent all day, keeping a worried eye on me because it was the first anniversary of my father's disappearance.

I shook that out of my mind as I grabbed a razor blade and got down to business measuring, cutting and fitting. Virginia put her book down and went over to the boom box. She gave me a look that said *Please?* as her hand hovered over the radio dial.

"Fine," I mumbled.

It was Top 40 favorites. Kool and the Gang. John Cougar.
Nothing too edgy or too moody. The work went fast with that kind
of soundtrack. When I was finished, I turned off the light table and
Virginia helped me tidy up the newsroom. It was after six now
and time to go before they kicked us out. As we headed out the
door, I slung my backpack over my shoulder. Not even I was nerd
enough to put both arms through the straps. Usually.

We waved to the janitor.

He waved back and pointed off to a freshly mopped portion of
the floor ahead of us. "Watch yourself, now," he said.

We gave him a thumbs-up and snugged up close to the lockers
and each other to avoid it. But my sneakers still got wet. They
squeaked with every step as we kept moving down the hall. I pre-
ferred school when it was empty. Just the janitor and the odd
teacher. No jackasses ricocheting through the halls. None of their
eyes on me. I was still known as the Girl Whose Father Vanished.

"A boy asked me yesterday if my father ran away," I said. "If he
was a deadbeat dad."

"Who asked you that?"

"Just this kid." Giving a name would make that kid ripe for
retaliation, which was Virginia's thing. She often threw herself between me and those types of questions like a human shield. A
sharp-tongued shield.

"Just ignore them," she said. "They don't know you. They don't
know your dad. They're just looking for a diversion from their own
miserable lives." She pointed up to the huge banner over our heads
that said *Good Luck, Class of 1983!* "Soon enough we'll be in college
with real people and this whole high school experience will be like
a bad dream."

"Hope so," I said.

I was one of the best students in school. I didn't worry about getting into a good college and meeting real people. The question for me was: *How far away should I go?* Virginia would go as far as her average grades would take her. That much I was sure of—she had a need for adventure. But change was harder for me.

"Well, look who it is!" Pearl pulled me through the door and bear-hugged me in her all-encompassing way. Then she held me out at arm's length, like she hadn't seen me in years. "Wait, what're you doing here?" She waved the question away and looped her arm through mine. "Don't matter. It's good to see you. And look like you got here right on time to be of some use."

I raised an eyebrow.

"You'll see." I let her guide me down the hall. She stopped at the entrance to the living room.

"Samuel!" she called out to her boyfriend. Mr. Burton was sitting in his leather easy chair, the only piece of modern furniture in the room. The rest of the space was filled with fussy pieces from a more formal era, preserved under plastic. I was always tempted to tell her what an old-lady thing that was to do, but I knew better. Pearl saw herself as a modern woman. And she acted like one, too. She was the furthest thing from grandmotherly one could imagine. I didn't even call her Grandma, Gran or any derivative of *grandmother*. She'd always insisted on being called by her first name, Pearl.

"Look who's here!" Pearl said to Mr. Burton.

He looked up from his transistor radio, which he was always either listening to or tinkering with.

"Hi, Mr. Burton," I said, waving from the doorway.

"It's good to see you, dear." He smiled, and his eyes crinkled behind his horn-rimmed glasses. He was the exact opposite of

Pearl: old, slow, stoic. He pointed to the single white earphone in his ear. "Trying to catch a game. You wanna listen?"

"Next time," I said, going over to kiss his cheek.

"All right, then." Mr. Burton patted my hand. "Have fun with my Pearl."

I followed Pearl down the hall. "You want some dinner? Made pork chops and we got a couple left over in there." She pointed off vaguely in the direction of the kitchen.

I declined. Still, I knew I'd be leaving with a pork chop sandwich, whether I wanted it or not.

"How's your mama?" Pearl asked, glancing at me over her shoulder. "What's she up to?"

"I don't know."

Pearl threw me a look over her shoulder. At the end of the hall, she opened the door to the office and waved me in. "She know where you at tonight?"

I shrugged. "I'm sure she'll guess." I'd dropped Virginia off at her house, declining all of her fun ideas: the mall, watching TV, prank phone calls. Even though her house was right across the street from *my* house, I didn't go home. I made the half-hour drive into Detroit to Pearl's house instead. Home wasn't where I wanted to be right now. Not on the anniversary. My mother would be there. Probably acting upbeat, as if nothing at all was wrong. Or maybe she'd be like she was most often these days, sitting at the kitchen table or on the couch staring at the phone, with a glass of wine or a cocktail close at hand. Probably her second or third glass. Maybe fourth.

"You might wanna call her while you here," Pearl said. "Let her know."

"I won't stay too late," I said, collapsing onto the love seat that lined one wall of her tiny office. The rectangular room was full with the love seat and floor-to-ceiling bookcases brimming with encyclo-pedias, romance novels and old issues of *Jet* and *Ebony* magazines. It was a lot. Her desk faced a wall with a window that looked out on the side yard to the small garden I'd planted with my father when I was a kid and we lived upstairs. Pearl had kept it going after we'd moved. She would revive it, come spring, like a memorial.

Pearl settled into her desk chair and pulled a sheet of paper from her typewriter, a turquoise Smith Corona that I'd taught my-self to type on when I was little. I'd sit at Pearl's desk, a pen tucked behind my ear, pounding out articles from old news magazines, word for word, pretending I'd written them myself. It was how I became an overly articulate student who rarely spoke in class. Typ-ing out all of those articles, I would imagine myself writing about things I cared about, rather than what I was actually doing, which was copying down someone's analysis of U.S.-Soviet relations or political commentary.

Pearl handed over the piece of paper she'd pulled from the type-writer. "I been working on this letter," she said.

I scanned the paper. It was a letter to Mayor Young. Pearl had once loved him, but now . . .

"There are a lot of exclamation marks in here," I mumbled, finishing the letter and chewing on the red editing pen she'd given me. "And some strong language, Pearl."

"Nothing he ain't heard—or said—before." She raised her chin in defiance.

"Right . . ." I said, smiling to myself about the strong language and extreme Pearlness of it all.

She was devoted to the city of Detroit and had made it her mis-sion to help save it. In addition to sending frequent letters to the mayor, she also engaged in a kind of letter-to-the-editor activism, writing to the *Detroit Free Press* about stories and events she saw as racist or sexist or just plain ridiculous. She was printed twice. Both letters included blistering attacks on Coleman Young. The clippings were framed right there on a wall near her desk, along with family pictures, including various ones of me, a kind of life progression, from infancy onward. There was also a picture of my father and Tommy when they were boys. The only one that had survived their house going up in flames, she'd told me.

"So, you gon' wordsmith it for me?" Pearl asked.

I sighed and handed the letter and the pen back to her. "Maybe later. I'm pretty wiped."

She took off her glasses and let them dangle around her neck on their lanyard. Another old-lady thing I turned a blind eye to. She crossed her arms and said quietly, "I know. It's October. I miss your daddy, too."

"He'll come back," I said. "Or we'll find him." I paused for a second, considering whether to say what I couldn't stop thinking about. "Can I tell you something?" I asked.

"Of course."

I took a moment, then said, "I kind of feel like I need to be around, you know? Close by, for when he's back."

Pearl side-eyed me. "And what's that mean?"

"Just . . . I've been thinking about school. College. Where to go."

She nodded slowly, still looking at me that way.

"I mean, I was thinking about applying to schools out East or on the West Coast, like Berkeley. Wouldn't someplace like Berkeley be cool?"

"That's a little too flower-child hippie for my tastes, but if that's what you want . . ."

"I don't know what I want. I feel like I should be close. For Dad."

Pearl got up and came over to sit next to me on the couch. She tapped me on the forehead. "Look here. God gave you this brain and that good schooling so you'd have choices. Somebody like me? I didn't have many choices. I spent most of my life making do with what came at me. You understand?"

"No," I said. "What were your choices? What came at you?"

She blinked, then shook her head. "That don't matter. It's *your* choices that matter. If you wanna go to the moon to go to school, you do that. If you just wanna go up here to Wayne State, then do that. But choose to do what you wanna do, okay?"

She held my gaze until I nodded.

"Good. Me and your mama, we'll worry about your daddy. And you know if we get him back, he'll find you wherever you are. Because he loves you."

I nodded again, but I was still unsure.

She hugged me. Grandmotherly or not, Pearl was the most comfort in the world.

She pointed across the room to that picture of my father and Tommy. They were standing in a dirt field with a shack that appeared near collapse off behind them. My father had on short pants. Tommy had on long ones. "You know this here's back in Alabama," she said, rocking me from side to side. I knew the story, but I let her tell it again. "Oh, I guess your daddy must've been around eleven here, so Thomas was about nine. They were good boys." She rocked me a little slower now and her hand tightened around my shoulder. "They were good." Her voice broke.

"It's okay," I said. "We're both just missing him right now. That's all."

She smiled and kissed my forehead. "That's just so, Ms. Trinity. That's just so." She looked over at the picture again. "But I don't want you missing him so much you miss your chance at life." She gave my shoulder a squeeze. "Okay. Enough of that." She stood and walked toward the door. "Come on."

"Where?"

"Downstairs."

"Oh, God. No. Not that," I said, wiping at tears.

"Come on. It'll be good for both of us. Get this sadness worked out a little. And your competitive juices flowing for them college applications."

"I either get in or I don't, Pearl. It's not a blood sport."

I followed her down the dark, narrow stairs to her basement. She went over and pulled the string on the naked lightbulb. There waiting for us was a torture device. Her Ping-Pong table. She threw me a paddle. "All right, little girl, best two out of three."

It was no contest. She was always merciless and given to trash-talking as she destroyed me. But when it was over, she was good about not rubbing it in. With Pearl, when a thing was done, it was done.

"You gotta know how to keep keeping on," she'd say. "Always eyes forward."

At home, I stood over the sink in the kitchen looking out the window while I ate the pork chop sandwich that Pearl, as expected, had forced on me. It was a good one, as she was an aggressive seasoner. Out in the backyard, it was dark, but there was light enough from the neighbors' homes. My eyes drifted to the edge of the backyard and the place where the bird was buried. I'd found that bird splayed and broken on the porch when I was about ten. About a year after we'd moved into our house—our suburban *dream* house, as my father called it—with its many windows and a sliding glass door. The bird had crashed into the big picture window at the front of the house. A robin. We'd talked about "robin redbreasts" in school and had a painting of one up on the wall in my classroom, as it was the state bird. The bird on the porch was still warm. Its head was turned at an odd angle and there was a small puddle of blood. I backed away from it and ran all the way down the porch steps. I stood in the front yard, my chest heaving, watching it from that safe distance. Then I wondered, *What are you running from?* I inched forward, noting with every step that the bird had not risen up to attack me. Back on the porch, I looked down at its still chest. I felt a rush of grief. It was as if I'd known that bird, given how much I'd been taught about robin redbreasts in school.

My father found me. Told me it wasn't as bad as all of that. "We just need to lay him to rest," he said. "Give him some dignity in death." He went to the garage and got his shovel to scoop up the bird. I followed him as he walked over trimmed grass to the backyard. He laid the shovel down in the shade carefully. It looked like the bird could lift its brown wings at any moment and take flight. I held my breath, willing it to. We went in the house and found a shoebox from my mother's side of the closet to use as a casket.

Outside again, my father knelt and dug a rectangular hole with his garden trowel, as I hugged the bird's shoebox casket to my chest.

"Where do birds go when they die?" I asked him.

"Heaven."

"Just like people?"

He'd stopped with his trowel still stuck in the ground and squinted up at the afternoon sky, like he was taking a thorough inventory of heaven's current occupants. "Not all people can go there. You have to be good to make it in. To *do* good." He was quiet for a second, then motioned for me to put the box in the hole. After I did, he stepped back and prayed in a halting, unsure way. He told me it was the only prayer he could remember because he hadn't been to church in so long. I wouldn't have known the difference. I couldn't remember ever going to church at all. He didn't allow it.

From my place in the kitchen, years away from that moment, I whispered, "Where are you?"

"Trin . . ."

The sound of my name startled me. It was my mother. I turned, knowing full well what I would find, given the thick sound of her voice. She was listing to the side, as if caught in a light breeze. I threw what was left of my pork chop sandwich away and asked her what she wanted.

"Why didn't you call?" Her words were slurred.

"I was at Pearl's. Where else would I be? Either there or Virginia's. That's it."

"I was worried."

"Ma, there's nothing to worry about."

My mother was an alcoholic. It had started long before my father's disappearance. But, back then, I rarely ever saw her drunk. And when I did, she wasn't a staggering, scene-causing lush like, say, Mr. Harrison down the street. The whole neighborhood at one time or another had witnessed him swerving into the family driveway or chasing Mrs. Harrison or the Harrison kids out into their front yard. Back in those days, my mother had been a quiet drinker, mostly in the evenings and at night. The morning after, there she would be, as sure as sunrise, getting me up for school, shuffling from my bedroom to the bathroom with her eyes half-closed, brutally hungover. I always knew to keep my voice down as she combed my hair with hands that vibrated like they were electrified. When she was done, I knew not to complain about the part that usually lurched and meandered down, roughly, the center of my scalp like a drunk person. I didn't say anything about the ponytails either.

They usually sat asymmetrically on either side of my head—one up and a little bit forward and the other one down closer to my ear, making me that much more conspicuous at school. Already, I had the uncomfortable distinction of being the only black girl, which—depending on the day and whether any bigoted statements were made during it—usually left me feeling like anything from a basic outsider to a complete outcast.

Seeing me out the door, my mother would hand me my lunch—which always had a Twinkie or, better yet, a Hostess HoHo for dessert—kiss my forehead and hold my face between her vibrating hands and whisper, "I love you."

That wasn't anything to be nostalgic for, but compared to how she was now? My father's disappearance had made her drinking worse.

"It scares me when you don't come home," she said, propping herself up against the doorframe.

"It scares me when you drink like this," I said.

She lowered her eyes.

"Look, Mom, I'm home. Okay?" I held my arms out, as if to prove my existence. "Now you can go to bed."

She stared back at me with glassy eyes.

She wouldn't go to bed. Or, at least, she wouldn't go to sleep. She had problems sleeping. Getting up from bed and going to the bathroom often meant passing her in the hallway, where she moved zombie-like up and down the hall, sometimes carrying the phone with its long white cord trailing behind her like a threadbare wedding dress train. She was taking "nerve pills" now, which she said helped her relax and focus. They were no help at all, as far as I could see. She wasn't focused. She was scattered, like she'd been blown apart and couldn't quite put herself back in order properly. And all the while, in that scattered state, she talked about whether to hire another private detective to look for my father. She worried about all of the bills that needed paying and how she was going to go about doing that. She had a job now, but that wasn't going well . . .

Sometimes I hated her for the way she was. Sometimes I loved her so much it broke my heart.

I grabbed her around the waist and led her back to her room, then went on to mine and closed the door.

Deborah

The hum of the photocopier had a rhythm to it. Like a lullaby. Part of me wished I could crawl right up inside it, snugged up warm against all those rollers. I'd probably sleep in there for days, given how tired and hungover I was.

"Deborah?"

I jumped.

It was another secretary. What was her name? Sarah? Sandy? Susan?

"Sorry to startle you," she said. She waved a sheet of paper at me. She was polite enough about it, but I got her: *You're done. I'm up next.*

I apologized and scooped up my copies, then headed for the door.

"Deborah?" It was Sarah/Sandy/Susan again. She was at the copier holding up the sheet I'd left on the tray.

Stupid. "So forgetful," I said. "Thank you." I hurried over and grabbed the original from her. I forgot the originals all the time. I had no idea what I was doing. This was my first job since I was a teenager, slaving over that sink at the hospital. A few months after Oz disappeared, his boss, Mr. Adler, offered me a job, telling me with pity in his eyes: "You're going to need money, Deborah. To take care of your daughter. Oz would want this."

I was working in the same building and on the same floor that Oz had worked on. With somebody new in Oz's office, I couldn't go near it. Every day, I took the emergency stairs so I wouldn't have to pass it as I made my way to my desk outside Mr. Adler's office.

Typing was part of my job, but I had to hunt and peck my way to getting anything done. It took me forever to put together a decent memo. I was hit or miss on dictation. Half the time, people just gave up on getting any meeting minutes out of me. That first month, Mr. Adler used to call me into his office to talk about what I could be doing better, which was everything except for his coffee—I made a good cup—but we'd always end up talking about Oz. I'd start crying or go quiet on him. He'd try and make me feel better by telling me what a rising star Oz had been and how much they'd loved him.

After a while, Mr. Adler just let me be about all that. He would overcompliment me the few times I got something right. He was a nice man. Everybody was nice. They'd sent me flowers and condolences and sympathy cards, like I was a widow.

But Oz wasn't dead to me.

I was at my desk one afternoon pecking out a memo when I felt a shadow over me. I looked up and it was Mr. Adler's belly hovering over my desk.

"Deborah, would you mind stepping into my office?"

Oh, Lord, I thought. *They've finally come to their senses. They're going to fire me.*

I followed Mr. Adler into his office and sat on the edge of the chair across from him. I listened to him go on about selling cars and trucks and how important it was to get the message right. I waited for him to wind up to giving me my pink slip. My heart fluttered and I wondered if he could see my blouse trembling over my chest. What would I do for money now? I never wanted to be a pity case, but this job was all I had. I'd fight for it. *That's what I'll do*, I said to myself. I wasn't *that* bad, was I? I was working on things with the copier. I wasn't fast with my memos, but they were in good shape when I finally finished. I opened my mouth to start selling myself before he could say, *We're letting you go.*

But then he cut me off.

"I'd like you to go over and have a talk with our advertising folks. I've told them all about you." He started scribbling on a piece of paper. "They're out in Warren. They'll be expecting you."

"Why would you be telling somebody all about me?"

He laughed. "About your singing and that. You know."

He slid the piece of paper across the desk to me. He'd written down the address and a name. "I don't understand," I said. "What is this? You sending me off to get a new job?"

"Yes. I mean, well, no. See, that's our ad agency that does all of our stuff for Chevy. I told them I had somebody who might be able to put a little spice in some of our jingles. I think they'll love you." He paused. "Now, I can't make any promises. They make their own decisions. But I think you'll do well." He winked at me.

I looked down at the paper, not knowing whether to be offended or interested. Jingles? That wasn't real singing. Besides . . . "I don't sing anymore, Mr. Adler," I said.

He waved my words away. "You should. You're just terrific, Deborah. Remember that time Linda and I joined Oz at one of your shows? Where was that . . . ?" He looked up to the sky, like the answer was up there. "Can't recall, but I do remember that you were outstanding."

I nodded and thanked him. But I didn't want to hear that. I didn't want to remember. All the hope and the highs, then the depths of the lows of my career. Those days were long over, and they'd ended in the worst way. Mr. Adler rearranged a ragged stack of papers on his desk, which was usually his signal for you to leave. "Anyway, I thought it could be a good thing for you in addition to what you do for us now, of course," he said. "And I hear the money's not bad."

I looked at the paper again. "I'll think about it, Mr. Adler . . ."

"Well, look, just give it a go, huh? See what you think. If you hate it, no harm, no foul, right?"

I told him okay, then went back out to my desk.

At home after work, I was staring into my almost empty refrigerator, wondering what to make for dinner. I had some eggs. There was relish, mayonnaise, ketchup and half a carton of milk, too. Even with the job and Pearl's and Tommy's help, it was hard keeping me and Trinity fed, along with hanging on to the house and keeping the lights and gas on.

"What about eggs?" I said. I looked over to the breadbox, like it had thoughts on things. "And maybe some cinnamon toast. I don't think Trinity'll complain much about that." I took four eggs out of the fridge. There were two left that I'd save for Trinity for later in the week. I rationed now. Kept a count of every ounce of food and every cent.

At the sound of the doorbell, I fumbled and almost dropped my four precious eggs on my way to the counter. I got them arranged safe and sound in the bowl to wait for me to do my scramble, then hurried out to the foyer and opened the door. There stood Tommy, with his heavy coat hanging open. He was wearing paint-spattered jeans and an old T-shirt dotted with holes like he'd been shot up on his way to the house.

"You're dressed like you're about to do some serious work around here, Tommy," I said, hugging him tight around the neck.

Tommy stepped in and closed the door. "Just the usual," he said, shrugging out of his coat and hanging it up. Tommy had assigned himself caretaker of the house in Oz's stead. He came around to change furnace filters, climb up to the attic to do whatever he did up there and roam the basement with a flashlight, looking for moisture and signs of rodents, especially around wintertime, which it was now. When I'd explained to him that Oz never did any of that stuff, he said he knew, but he felt responsible.

He kicked off his boots and went down the hall. "Trin home?" he called out, reaching up and pulling the string to open the attic door.

"At school late again," I said as I watched him disappear into the ceiling. "That newspaper, as usual. But she shouldn't be long getting home." I worried about her all the time. It was like I couldn't function if I didn't know where she was. She'd called earlier in the evening to let me know her schedule. She'd been doing better with that since the last time she came home and found me "in a state." I didn't like her seeing me that way. I kept saying I'd stop drinking and maybe cut back on my nerve pills, but the expectation of getting home and having a glass of something was what got me through the days at work. Glass after glass at home got me through the nights. Quiet as it's kept, I almost couldn't wait for Tommy to leave so I could start my evening.

I went to the kitchen and rummaged around in the fridge, looking for something to offer Tommy for dinner. The two eggs I had left weren't enough. And I needed those. I closed the refrigerator and checked the cabinets. Maybe some beans?

Tommy came out of the attic, wiping his hands on his jeans. He asked how I was doing.

I sat down at the kitchen table. "I've been better," I said. I looked over at the phone and told him we'd been getting hang-ups for a little while now. Not a lot, but enough to be noticeable. I was never far from the phone, and when it rang, I jumped on it. Whoever was on the other end of the line never hung up right off. They lingered there for a second, breathing. I'd hold the phone to my ear, waiting, before the sound of the click cut off the call. "Do you think it could be him?" I asked Tommy. "I mean, maybe he's hurt and in trouble. I don't know."

Tommy took a seat across from me and stared out at the mounds of snow covering the patio. Shoveling was Oz's job. To let somebody else do it in his absence felt like allowing for the fact that maybe he wouldn't be back. I didn't do anything about the snow on the patio last winter. I'd just let it melt on its own. I imagined I'd do the same this year.

"Oz was m-m-m-more likely to hurt himself than be hurt," Tommy said finally. "He wouldn't want no help."

"What?" He didn't need to say it again. I'd heard him, but I didn't believe him and told him as much. "Why would you say something like that?"

Tommy had been the last person to see Oz. He'd met him for that birthday lunch at the barbecue place. And Tommy had been swimming in guilt ever since. Whenever he talked about that day, he spoke like he should've seen his brother safely back to work after their lunch, despite the fact that they were both grown men. Despite the fact that, from the time they were boys, the way I'd heard it, nobody ever expected much from Tommy, given his bad stutter and his quiet way.

Tommy swallowed. His eyes were shining. "Y-y-y-you weren't there, Deborah," he said.

"Tommy, what happened?" He'd never said much about that day. Never explained his guilt, no matter how hard we pressed him. He'd say only: "I shhh-should've kept a closer eye." And now, he said it again.

"A closer eye out for *what*? You always say that. But when Oz left the house that morning, he was fine. Fine when I talked to him before he met you for lunch. He was going to bring home some ice. If there was something, I would've seen."

"Really?"

Tommy knew better. And I did, too. There'd been a lot for me to see through in the months before Oz vanished. I had my own guilt about the way all of that had gone down, and me and Oz had never gotten a chance to make it right. "What am I missing, Tommy?" I asked, trying to keep him from clamming up, like he usually did.

He said he didn't know. He went back to the hang-ups I'd brought up earlier. He said they were strange. Said he'd gotten a few, too, with somebody sitting there breathing on the other end of the line. But he said he felt silly thinking maybe it was Oz. Then he mumbled something about Oz always being the strong one, of the two of them.

All of a sudden, I thought about Willa Mae calling Oz fragile. I hadn't thought about that in a long time. I'd been so young and head over heels that it had just slipped to the back of my mind. "Willa Mae said one time that Oz was fragile," I said. "What did she mean by that?"

Tears came to Tommy's eyes again. He was quiet for a second. "M-m-m-me and Oz, we saw a lot, coming up. It left a mark." His eyes dropped to his scarred hands. He pulled them back from the table and slid them in his pockets.

"How?"

"That's for him to say, not me."

"Well, he's not here, is he, Tommy?"

Tommy's mouth started working, like the words were jammed up behind his teeth and he was trying to spit them out. I waited, like everybody did with him when he was struggling. But I couldn't keep my usual patience. "Damn it, Tommy, say what you mean for once!"

He struggled for a second more, then got up and left the room. He showed up again within minutes. He was out in the backyard, without his coat, shoveling the snow off the patio, looking like Oz.

Trinity

1983

I was ready to take myself to college. I'd given it a lot of thought, just like I'd done with picking a school. I wasn't sure if I was making the right choices, but they were *my* choices, like Pearl had said.

I stood in the middle of my bedroom, a pink shrine to my younger self, doing a last bit of inventory. There was the princess phone on the white wicker bedside table and the yellowing white ruffled bed skirt. Above the bed, there was a framed reprint of a little black girl in pink with bare feet, braiding an old woman's hair. I'd always loved that picture, but looking at it now, I suddenly felt trapped in my childhood and thought I would die if I stayed. I went over to the dresser and grabbed the last garbage bag of my stuff. That one held some clothes and a few Prince and Michael Jackson cassettes that were bulging through the plastic, as if trying to escape.

"Not so fast, you guys," I said, heaving the bag over my shoulder. "You're coming with me." I carried the bag out to my car and stuffed it in the hatchback. My last major load. I wiped the sweat from my forehead and gave my underarms a sniff. "Yep," I said, "pretty ripe." I went back in the house and poured myself a glass of water and tossed it back. I stood there for a second, dreading what came next.

How do I say goodbye to my mother?

I didn't want my mother along to take me to school because I couldn't deal with her sadness or the possibility that she might stop somewhere and get drunk and not be able to make it home. I had this recurring nightmare about her passing out and having to share my twin bed in my dorm room and then me trying to explain all of this to my new roommate. I found her sitting in one of the low leather chairs in the front room with her purse in her lap. I got close to her so I could see her eyes. Smell her. Her eyes were clear. There was nothing but the smell of cigarettes, Jean Naté and breath mints. It was still a little early in the day for her to drink. I tried not to think about what she might be like when I left.

"What are you doing?" I asked her.

"Nothing. I was just being quiet for a minute. That's all." Her eyes moved to the picture window. "It's getting late."

I looked at my watch. "It's just a little after noon," I said. "I'll get there well before dark." I'd decided on Ohio State—far enough away, but close enough to drive home in a hurry, if she needed me.

My mother nodded, but was otherwise still, with her hands on either side of her purse. There was a look of mild surprise on her face when her eyes met mine again. She said, "I thought we might get rain, but we did okay, didn't we?"

I glanced out the window. It was a beautiful summer day, with a few fluffs of clouds in the sky. "Yeah," I said. "I guess we did."

She went quiet in a way that filled the room. There was only the sound of my hamster, Sniffy V, scurrying around in his cage, as if impatient to get on the road. My mother's brow was furrowed, and she was fiddling with the zipper on her purse. She wouldn't make eye contact with me. I looked away, too. I went over and turned on the lamp. Then all of the lights, as if to banish the awkwardness to the corners of the room. I looked over at the upright piano where

I'd struggled for years. I remembered my last piano recital. I was fourteen, squinting out into a crowd of polite applause after a calamitous rendition of "Ode to Joy." My father wasn't there, which was usually the case. He worked so much. Or at least, that's what he told us. Kids see more than they're told, and I could discern through my parents' smiles and reassurances that neither one of them was always honest. Especially in those months before the vanishing.

But at my recitals, there was always my mother, second row center, sitting by herself, wearing movie star sunglasses that were as big as soup cans. She'd be smiling through a hangover, as if I'd played like a kid who didn't have a weak left hand and stubby fingers that made the piano a bad fit. She'd be clapping ecstatically like I was the most talented kid in the room.

I went over and opened up the piano bench to see if my old music was still in there. I found "Ode to Joy" and held it up so she could see it. "Remember this? My farewell performance?"

"You weren't as bad as you thought," she said, laughing.

"Go ahead. You can tell me the truth. I can handle it."

She laughed again. "I think you should've stuck with it. That's all I'll say. I always wanted to play, but . . ." She shrugged. "Never happened."

I remembered her in her sparkly dresses, back when we lived with Pearl, getting ready to go out to a club, smelling of cigarettes and wine. Then, as I grew up, she stopped going out at night and my father never wanted to discuss her booking new gigs. She never talked about any of that unless she'd been drinking. She'd said to me once: "You know what Oz said to me one time? He said, 'You're going to be a real star. I can't wait to see you shine.' And I came so close, Trin. *So* close. You have no idea."

I put the sheet music back in the piano bench.

She got up and smoothed her pants.

"I have something for you," she said. "Can I get it? Before you go?"

"Definitely."

She left and returned with a black leather briefcase and a dark blue suit jacket slung over her arm, as if on her way out the door on a business trip.

"Dad's things," I said.

She nodded.

I had not thought of them since the day the police brought them to the house. She and I had sat on her bedroom floor going through printouts and listening to my father's tapes. We played them on the little tape recorder that he also had in the briefcase. It was all notes to himself. Reminders to pull a file or talk to his boss about some issue. All work related. The police had said there was nothing of importance in either the jacket or the briefcase. But those tapes and the sound of his voice, reminding himself of meetings and deadlines, were a comfort to both me and my mother that day, as I sat curled up in her arms, listening to her say, "It's okay, Trin. It's going to be all right."

Now, here stood my mother in the middle of the living room, holding both the jacket and the briefcase out to me. "I want you to have them," she said. "It's not much . . ." Her voice caught. "But they're his."

"Are you sure?"

She nodded but seemed unable to speak.

I got up from the piano bench and took what she had for me.

She sat in the chair again and hugged her purse to her chest. "I'm proud of you, Trin." She smiled. "From the piano to school to just being the best kid I know. I'm so proud. And your daddy, I know he would be just . . . just so happy to see who you're becoming."

Those words, the briefcase, the suit jacket—I heard myself say, "I'm sorry to leave you. I don't know what to do . . ."

"I don't either." Thick tears slipped down her cheeks, and she hugged her purse tighter. "And I don't know what I can say to you to make myself or any of this better. But—" She looked off to the side and shook her head, like something had come to her mind but she was having second thoughts about saying it.

"What?" I said.

She turned her eyes to me again. "Do the next right thing. It's something we drunks tell ourselves. In those meetings and what have you." She looked down and seemed embarrassed. My mother had gone to AA a couple of times, but it had never stuck.

I glanced down at the briefcase in my hand and the jacket over my arm. "It feels so strange," I said, "that he's gone. Like this. Doesn't it?"

She leaned forward, maintaining the same straight-backed posture I had—or, rather, that she had given me—and said, "I'll always need to find him." She rummaged through her purse for Kleenex. She held one out to me and pressed a sheet to her eyes. "But . . . I don't—" She looked up at me, her eyes red and brimming with tears. "What I mean to say is, I need to figure out life from here." She stood up and held me by the shoulders, looking me in the eyes. "The one thing I do know is that it's time for you to go, Trin. So you can figure out life from here, too. Okay?" She bent and opened her purse again to pull out another Kleenex. Watching her stoop down, fractured and fully herself, for the first time I think I saw her, and I wondered what it was like to be Deborah. Not my mother, but the woman who'd lost her husband in the same way I'd lost my dad. I wanted to tell her I didn't know how to be happy or how to live, and I could see that she didn't either and that maybe I shouldn't leave at all. But, at the same time, I knew that to stay would be to remain an outsider. Sometimes an outcast. The lone black girl in the neighborhood who'd managed to make only one true friend in her whole life. I stood frozen, not knowing what to do or say.

But then my mother was guiding me toward the front door by the arm with my hamster cage in her hand. Virginia—my one true friend—was running across the street from her house, a blur of electric energy, a duffel bag and snacks for the road. She'd soon be off to USC, but for now, she was joining me for the ride and everything that came with arriving fresh on campus. Virginia threw her arms around my mother and promised that we'd be safe, then hopped in the passenger seat and propped her bare feet up on the dash.

My mother hugged me tight for a long time and whispered, "This is the next right thing, Trin. For you and me both. I truly believe it." She tucked me into the driver's seat of my car and stood in the driveway waving goodbye with a balled-up Kleenex in her hand as I backed out.

"So," Virginia said, "looks like we're on our way. College! Real people! Real life!"

"Yeah," I said, both happy and sad. As I paused at the stop sign at the end of the road, I said to myself, *Choose happy, Trin.*

Deborah

1985–1987

I cracked the window and lit a cigarette. It was starting to cloud over. Snowflakes were drifting down, light as feathers. I blew a stream of smoke up toward the crack in the window and sat back, trying to get myself together enough to go in that church, walk around to the fellowship room, sit in one of the folding chairs and blend in as best I could. The anonymous part of Alcoholics Anonymous fit me just about right.

I'd started dealing with myself not long after Trinity left for college. I had just over two years of sobriety now. No more booze. No more nerve pills. The fact that my own child didn't want me with her on a big day like her first day of college? That was the bottom I needed to hit. At least that time. I always worried that I had room yet to fall.

I looked at my watch. I needed to get on in the meeting. I got out of the car and walked up the hill to the double doors that had crosses for handles. I followed the hallway to the fellowship room, which was about half-full. At the back of the room there was coffee as usual, so I poured some for myself in one of the foam cups they always had there. I dumped in lots of artificial creamer and my usual four sugars. I hunted around for a seat in the middle of the pack. Waved to a woman I knew. She lived on my street. Another housewife.

You're not a housewife anymore, I reminded myself. Sometimes it was easy to forget that, given that I lived in the same house and saw all the same faces every day. I was something else, but I still wasn't sure just what that was. I was a secretary, I guess. I could say at least that much about myself, even if I wasn't the best one you'd ever find. But I'd settled in there at work. They didn't look at me like the pitiful widow anymore. People forget over time, never mind if you're still keeping company with your loss.

The chair got up to do the welcome and then somebody else read through the twelve steps. I wondered what I might do when the meeting was over. For some reason, I always wanted a drink after a meeting. I wasn't strong. But I didn't want to do anything to mess up the little bit of good I had going. I listened real close to everybody's share and tried to take it all in as a warning to myself: That could be you with the DUIs or the lost job or the kids who won't talk to you anymore.

At the end of the meeting, as I headed for the door, I heard my name. I turned around and damned if it wasn't a familiar face—grown older, and with a full set of teeth. But not much else had changed about him. He was as skinny as he used to be back in the day. He did have a kind of laid-back cool to him now, though, standing there with his fedora angled to the side and his long, Shaft-looking leather coat.

"Two Cents," I said, still surprised.

He took off his hat and gave me a big hug. "Funny meeting you here, sis."

"Me? What're you doing out here in the suburbs? It's a long way from the projects."

He laughed and shrugged. "I like to meeting-hop. See how everybody else is doing it."

"Well, you look good," I said. Honestly, I was surprised he was still alive. Last time I came across Two Cents, I thought his days were numbered. That was back in the early seventies. I'd gone to the projects to visit my parents. Two Cents hadn't long been back from Vietnam. I got off the bus and found him nodding out on the bus stop bench, dirty as anything, with a rope barely holding up his pants. He smelled like he'd peed himself. I helped him home. His mama met me at the door and thanked me. She told me, "All this time I was worried 'bout the war killin' him. But now I believe this heroin's gon' be the thing that take him."

Yet here he was, very much alive and not letting me get a word in as he told me about what he had going on. He had a good job at a parts factory and was running an after-hours club at night. The club was his baby, he said. "You should come by and check us out," he added.

"Clubs aren't as fun for me as they used to be," I told him. I hadn't been to one in years.

"Well, you ain't been to mine." He smiled with that mouthful of teeth that I imagined must've been dentures, given the past state of his mouth. "But if it's too much temptation, with, you know, keeping it sober and everything, I understand that, too, sis."

I told him I'd think about it.

For months, every time I saw him at a meeting after that, he worried me half to death about dropping by. "When're you going to hop off to another meeting someplace else and leave me alone?" I asked him.

He laughed and kept showing up and bothering me till I gave up and went to his little club one night. It was a lounge with a couple dozen round tables fitted tight in the room. It was packed. The ceiling was low, which gave it an intimate feel. Being on my own, I took a seat at the bar, even though I knew it wasn't the best idea. As soon as I could get the bartender's attention, I ordered a club soda just to have something in my hand, which I hoped would fool my mind. But my eyes kept going back to the bottles lined up behind the bar. Drinking had been my companion, my most dependable comfort, and I missed it. I made myself get up and go to the other side of the room. I stood there against the wall, hoping the low light made me less noticeable. I was able to focus a little better on what was happening on the stage, which looked like it had been built into the space as an afterthought and didn't really belong. The young woman who'd been singing was just wrapping up, which was fine with me. She had some pitch problems. Next came an older man with a rich, sweet voice, but he didn't sing a single original note. It was like listening to a Luther Vandross impersonator. Just as I was getting ready to leave, there came Two Cents, loping over with his hands in the pockets of his baggy pants.

"What're you doing over here holding up the wall, sis?"

"Just enjoying the music."

He nodded. "You like it?"

"It's not bad."

"But not good?"

I shrugged. "Good enough."

"Well, you were always better than good enough. I heard you and your group one time. At the Twenty Grand, I think it was. Years back. Y'all was something."

We'd only performed at the Twenty Grand one time, and he was right. We were something. That was our big break. It was the biggest show we'd ever done. But it turned out to be one of our last. It wasn't something I wanted to talk about. But, as was his way, Two Cents kept going: "Yeah, seeing y'all, it took me back to when you used to practice with your little friends." He smiled big. "Remember that? With me on 'drums'?"

I nodded again at another memory that was sweet, but bitter, too. A lot of good any of it had done me.

"The fact that y'all didn't hit it big," Two Cents said, "I'll never understand."

"I don't understand it either," I said, glancing down at my watch, past ready to be gone. "It's after my bedtime. I should probably be getting home. It was good—"

"Wait." He jerked his head toward the stage. "How'd you like to do something for us? I'm not gon' lie. I can't pay you much, but I can slide a few bills your way."

The most singing I'd done recently was jingles. I'd done what Mr. Adler had asked and gone out to Warren to see their advertising people. It wasn't something I ever thought I'd do, singing little nothing songs. Still, that's what I did now, from time to time. Sing the praises of the Chevy Nova for extra money. But there wasn't enough money in the world to get me back up on a stage. Not after what I'd been through with all that.

"I don't think so," I said. "That kind of performing—it's not my thing anymore."

"Aw, come on now," he said. "I think it's time for a comeback."

"You've got to make it someplace before coming back. And I never made it."

"Maybe we can help you get there this time around." He looked around the club. "Sometimes we get some cats in here who can make that happen."

I laughed. "I've heard that before."

He eyed me close for a second. "You got a minute?"

I glanced at my watch again. "I don't know . . ."

"Just give me a second, sis. I wanna show you something. Come on."

He led me down a narrow hall to a dark, wood-paneled office that could barely fit the desk and two chairs it had in it. Lining the walls behind the desk, he had pictures of himself with a handful of stars. And some of the pictures looked like they were taken right there in the club. There was Two Cents with Berry Gordy at one of the tables in the main room. Stevie Wonder was in one of the office chairs. Anita Baker was posing with her arm around a woman out in the lobby.

"You can see, this might not be a bad place to blow the cobwebs off them vocals and take another shot," he said.

There was an excited, hopeful tingle in my chest—but I did my best to ignore it. I walked back out to the main room with Two Cents, who was still trying to talk me into a "comeback." I looked around at the full tables and at the man up onstage sounding like Luther Vandross. He had his eyes closed, lost in that song. I would do that, too. I remembered what it was like to be up there, nervous as anything, but so sure of who I was and what I was doing that I couldn't *not* get out there. And the thrill of it all . . . the audience clapping with me, dancing with me and hanging on every note, every word. I told stories with songs. I lived through music. And yet here I was now, singing little nothing lyrics about Chevys when I could be up there. Like him, soaking it all in.

That excited, hopeful tingle in my chest spread to every part of me. I didn't want to want it like I did. That had always been my problem. All that wanting. And for what?

"I'll think about it," I said.

I was surprised to see Tommy. He'd been MIA over the past month or so, and suddenly there he was at my door.

"How y-y-y-you doing, there?" he asked.

"Doing good. I could ask you the same thing. Where've you been keeping yourself?"

He came in and closed the door. "Here and there," he said as he followed me through the foyer.

"I'mma have myself a Pepsi," I said over my shoulder. "You want anything?" I added real quick: "I've got plenty." That wasn't always the case, and Tommy knew it. Living for one was cheaper than having Trinity with me, but money was still always tight.

"Some Pepsi would be good," Tommy said. "Thanks."

I poured two glasses—not full because, well, plenty wasn't really what I had.

"Talked to Trinity yesterday," Tommy said. "S-s-s-sounds good."

"She's talking about traveling around Europe on some big grad-uation trip with Virginia. How she's going to finance all that along with student loans, I don't know. I just hope they stay out of trouble."

"Well, she's getting s-s-s-some help from me."

"I should've known."

Tommy tilted his head to the side and looked at me, asking one of his silent questions.

"What?"

"Y-y-y-you look good. Happy."

"I'm doing okay." I paused. I hadn't told anybody—I wasn't sure why not. But now, like a confession I said, "I've, uh, I've been singing at this club. Friday and Saturday nights." Of course I'd said yes to performing. I knew I would when I told Two Cents I'd think about it. I'd reasoned that it would be some good outside money, like my little jingle gig. But it was more than that. I felt it the first night I stepped out into the light on that stage. Even with my nerves, I had an allover sense of peace when I sang those first notes into the microphone. And when I finished my set, everything just felt right, and I wondered how I'd been able to live without it for so long.

Tommy reached over and squeezed my hand. "W-w-w-well, keep at it. Looks good on you."

"I feel like I'm coming along, Tommy. Like I finally got something good going, you know?" I didn't want to keep going on and on about how good it all was, though I could've. So I asked, "What about you?"

He shifted in his chair and wiped the condensation off his glass in long strips. He shrugged but had a guilty look about him. I was reminded that Tommy had turned up out of the blue, and it wasn't for home maintenance. He was here for a reason. "What's going on, Tommy?"

"If I tell you something, can y-y-y-you keep it?"

"Who am I going to tell?"

"You might tell M-M-M-Mama?"

"I won't. I promise."

"Lloyd's home," he said. "Came back last m-m-m-month."

I hadn't seen Lloyd since back when he used to manage us. Before he up and left town and took my one opportunity—*my career*—with him. I had to bite my tongue to keep from blurting out what I truly felt. Instead, I said, "I just saw his mama, what, last week? She didn't say word one about him being home."

"Yeah," Tommy said, real quiet. "They don't want him."

"Don't *want* him?" That was the craziest thing I'd ever heard. There was no child more loved and indulged than Lloyd, an only son.

"He's sick," Tommy said.

"But if he's sick—"

"H-h-h-he . . . he's got . . . you know . . . that thing. What they get—what w-w-w-we . . ." He sat up tall and cleared his throat. "But he'll be okay."

"Okay . . ." I didn't want to get in his business, but I wanted to know what "that thing" was. "Is it cancer? What is it?"

"N-n-n-no, not cancer. He's just . . . he's . . . pneumonia." Tommy glanced at his watch and stood. "I'd better get on back and see about him."

For the first time, I noticed how tired Tommy looked. His shoulders were stooped. He had dark circles under his eyes. "You sure this is just . . . not that bad?"

He nodded. "Look," he said. "Lloyd told me to ask you to come see him, so . . . It's important to him."

There'd been a lot of water under the bridge with Lloyd. He was a big part of the reason I'd stopped singing. I would've been fine to never see him again, but I looked at Tommy, who was staring down at the table. I remembered the silent boy he used to be. How he'd held my hand real tight and guided me out of that party on one of the worst nights of my life. Me and him, we'd had a bond ever since. There wasn't much I wouldn't do for Tommy.

I felt at home in the club. I ate my meals there most Friday and Saturday nights after performing, because I never liked eating before going onstage. I was backstage in the cramped office with Two Cents after the show, balancing a half-full salad bowl on my knees, when he asked me if I could do a Sunday. It wasn't like I had plans, so I told him yes.

"Good. This high-powered cat I know gon' be in the house. I want him to see you."

"What 'cat'?"

"Nobody you know or need to worry about, sis. I don't want you getting all nervous."

I stopped eating, with a forkful of salad hovering between the bowl and my mouth. "Well, now I'm nervous."

"Don't worry about it," he said. "Just do your thing, like you do."

I thought about it all week. Was this just Two Cents big-talking? Or could this be somebody important? That Sunday morning, it was all I could think about as I went to the closet to pick out something to wear for the night. I usually cycled through a couple nice gowns that had held up pretty good from my old singing days. But I'd bought a new one not long ago, and I'd been saving it. For what, I didn't know. I pulled it out of the closet and held it up. It was black silk with lace across the front. I had it pinned for where I needed to shorten it.

"I think tonight's your night," I said to the dress.

I held it to me and danced around the bedroom, then down the stairs to the kitchen, all the while humming my set list.

In the kitchen, I opened my sewing cabinet and said to my old Singer, "It's been a long time, old girl, hasn't it?" The cabinet was stocked with that sewing machine, my scissors, all colors of thread and more. At the back of the cabinet were the labels I used to sew in that said *Created by Deborah Armstead*. I'd retired it all after Trinity declared she wanted "real clothes"—Gloria Vanderbilt instead of Deborah Armstead creations. I didn't do much more than mending after that.

In no time, I had my dress hemmed, ironed and under plastic. I decided I'd stop by and see Lloyd on my way to the club. That way, if things went bad between us, I could tell him I had someplace to be, and I wouldn't be lying. As I hung my plastic-covered dress on the hook in the backseat and set my makeup case on the floorboard, I thought to myself, *He should be glad I'm giving him any time at all.*

Tommy was at work, so I let myself in and found Lloyd alone in the apartment. He was as handsome as ever, with his hair slicked back in waves. But he was skinnier than I remembered. His cheeks were sunken in. Tommy had told me the pneumonia was all but cleared up. But Lloyd didn't look good, which made me feel bad for him and a little less mad at him. "Well, look at you," I said as I bent to kiss him on the forehead.

He pulled away but smiled. "It's good to see you, Deborah. Thank you for coming."

"Of course," I said.

He was quiet and all of a sudden it felt strange and heavy in the room. I really wanted a cigarette, but thought that wouldn't be the best idea, what with the pneumonia.

"You mind if I open those?" I asked, pointing to the curtains. I went over and started pulling them back even before he said he didn't mind. It was a blue-sky fall day, with the sun just starting to slide down the edge of the sky. "There we go. We'll just lighten it up in here a little." The room was clean and in good order. On the bedside table, there was a glass of water with a straw in it, along with a couple pill bottles and a half glass of white liquid.

"That's a special milkshake that Tommy makes me drink," Lloyd said, rolling his eyes, but sounding like a man who knew he was cared for. Loved even, by the sweet smile on his face. This put me off for a second. I was thinking back to how Tommy and Lloyd used to be. Always together. Flirty and tender with one another. And Lloyd—I'd learned he was a homosexual way back when we used to go out on the road. Were Tommy and Lloyd *together* together? How had I not known that till now? "It's Tommy's way of fattening me up," Lloyd was saying, still going on about the milk-shake. "Never thought I'd get tired of milkshakes, but I am."

I sat down on the edge of the bed, trying to act like I wasn't hip to anything. "You'll pick your weight back up once you kick this."

He went quiet.

I tried to think of something to say. I didn't want to ask him about his family, given that they didn't want him. I damn sure wasn't going to ask about him and Tommy. I filled the void by talking about my own work. He nodded along, no doubt already having been told by Tommy that I was a secretary. I told Lloyd about singing at the club and how I had what could be a big performance coming up tonight.

He wished me luck.

I mentioned the jingles, too. I was embarrassed telling him about that because he'd think it wasn't real singing, just like I thought. But he wanted to know more.

"The studios are nice. Modern and clean. It's not what I was expecting. Honestly, I don't know what I was expecting. Anyway, the little songs are way shorter than anything we're used to. Thirty seconds or what have you. Everybody seems to like what I bring to things, though."

Lloyd smiled his wide, white-toothed smile. "I'm sure they do. You were always so good, Deborah. Better than you even knew."

We both went quiet, no doubt feeling the churn of the water under the bridge.

He shifted in bed, sitting up a little bit more. He turned and looked out the window. I could see the line of his cheekbone press-ing against his skin. I wondered if he was sicker than he was letting on, and if maybe that was why he wanted me here.

"Look, Deborah," Lloyd said. "The reason I wanted you to

come was, I wanted to talk about why I left the way I did and everything that went down with the Belle Tones."

It had all happened so fast. That show at the Twenty Grand. A big break. A world of promises.

Lloyd shifted again in bed. I got up to help him with the pillow. He thanked me, even as he nudged me away.

"I'm guessing Oz never told you before he . . . you know . . . ?"

"Before we lost him?" I was confused by the mention of Oz. "What would he have to tell about any of that? What would he know?"

Lloyd looked down at his hands. "First off, I'm sorry about what you're going through." He shook his head. "Oz should be the one telling this. But then, he's not here to do that."

So, Lloyd told it. The whole time he spoke, it was like bees were in my ears. I had to strain to hear him. I had to strain to *believe* him. Because he was talking about Oz and everything that had ever meant anything to me.

It took a lot, walking up the stairs to get to the stage. The lights were too bright, even though they were low. The piano tinkling in the background was too loud, even though the pianist was playing real soft. I wasn't even sure how I'd gotten myself to the club after leaving Lloyd. How I'd slipped into my freshly hemmed gown and the patent leather heels. How I'd put on the face that everybody was looking at now.

Just get through it, I told myself. *You can deal with what Lloyd said later.* But how?

I gripped the microphone and swallowed. My mouth was dry. My legs were wobbly. My stomach seized up. *You shouldn't've come here tonight*, I told myself. But I didn't even know how to miss a show once I'd booked it. So, here I was, in front of a full house. My eyes fixed on the sparkling bottles that lined the bar at the back of the room. I thought, *Wouldn't it be nice to have a shot of bourbon? For old times' sake?* As I adjusted my mic stand, I signaled a waiter and had him bring me a drink. I introduced myself to the audience and asked them how they liked my new dress. The applause that came back was like a shot of something warm and soothing. When my bourbon got to me, I drank it down like a chaser. I sang those first few lyrics, "Strange love . . . I'm experiencing . . ." I sipped through the first few songs of my set. I felt steadier, but not better. I kept hearing Lloyd's words over the sound of my voice. I tried singing louder. I raised a hand for a refill, and the bartender obliged, sending somebody over to trade out the glass I had on the stool next to me for another that had fresh ice cubes floating and glimmering in amber. By the time I got to the next-to-last song in my set, "My Funny Valentine," I'd had at least two more refills and the bartender wouldn't send over another.

Two Cents was there next to the stage. I hadn't seen him in the room earlier, but there he was all of a sudden, swimming in my vision. I could see the look he was giving me. I'd seen it before in the eyes of other people, namely Trinity. It was pity. Worry. He had his hands out, like he might catch me. But I didn't feel like I was about to fall. My body was heavy and, yes, my tongue was a little thick, but I had a set to finish. I turned my attention back to the audience, but out the corner of my eye, I could see Two Cents waving me off the stage. I wasn't done, was I? I took a bow and stumbled. I grabbed on to the mic stand and stool to steady myself. The crowd said, *Whoa!* as my ankle turned, but I caught myself. I looked out at them. They weren't with me anymore, cheering me, embracing me. They were embarrassed for me. Laughing at me. I staggered back. I stepped down off the stage. I felt myself floating. Then falling. I'd missed a step. I tried to keep my feet, but there was nothing I could do. I went down hard, my head smacking the ground. I heard shocked gasps. Somebody yelled out for help.

Two Cents rushed over to pull me up, and I kicked him back. I didn't want anybody's help. Lloyd had said he was helping me. Oz had said he was helping me. It was all a lie . . . *You're going to be a star. I can't wait to see you shine.* Something warm dribbled into my eyes. I was half-blind. I touched my face. It was blood. I crawled away on my hands and knees like a dog on the sticky floor. I groped for a chair or table to pull myself up. I scrambled to my feet and found my purse. Somebody asked, "You okay?"

Two Cents came up from behind. "Nope," he said as he pried my car keys from my hand.

I twisted around and pushed against his bony ribs. I dug my nails into his closed fist that held my keys. I told him I needed to go home. I told him I needed to think. I told him I didn't know what to think.

He blocked my swinging, clawing hands and got me out the door to my car.

I gave up the fight. My head felt like it was about to bust open from my fall. Blood and tears were making it hard to see. Two Cents settled me in the passenger seat and pressed his handkerchief to my eyes. Then he held it to the cut on my forehead. "I'm so sorry, sis," he said. "This is my fault."

As we sped away from the club, the lights out the car window blurred into glowing threads that stretched from here to nowhere. I closed my eyes and saw myself staggering off that stage. Staggering out of Lloyd's apartment, with his words still buzzing in my head.

Before

A kind of Pandora's box of memories.

Oz

1967–1968

All hell broke loose while Deborah was out on a short tour, but Oz was safe at home. He was getting Trinity down to sleep, which, as was typical, took considerable effort. She was closing in on two years old now and had opinions. Oz waltzed her across the narrow room, talking to her about how much she'd have to look forward to when she got bigger.

"There are bikes that you can ride really fast," he said. She blinked back at him with her big, curious eyes, as if to say, *Tell me more.* "But maybe a tricycle to start." He tried to think of other fun things she might like. "And lots of candy on Halloween. Now, that's going to blow your mind." He slowed his waltz to a gentle sway until her eyelids drooped and her head dropped to his shoulder. He stood there swaying a little longer, to make sure she was good and gone. He kissed her on her forehead and whispered, "You just can't stand to go to sleep. You're scared of missing something, aren't you?" He put her down in her crib. "You're like your mama that way."

Oz stood over her crib holding his breath, hoping she was really out, because she was masterful at waiting just until he thought he had some time for himself and then, *bam.* Crying. Pearl would tell him to let her cry. She'd wear herself out. But, when Oz was a boy, he'd spent so many nights crying himself to sleep or, worse, watching Tommy *not* cry when he had every reason to, that he could not bear it for his little girl. He stood watching her last little twitch and the slowing of her breath.

Just as he tiptoed into the kitchenette, he heard Tommy thundering up the stairs, yelling his name. Oz froze. His eyes darted over to the crib. Trinity was stirring and whimpering. He couldn't spend another hour getting her back to sleep. He had to study. He ran as quickly and quietly as he could to the door to head off his brother. Oz shoved Tommy out the door before he could get over the threshold. He whispered, "She's sleeping!" Then Oz noticed Tommy's face was glistening with sweat. His brother was struggling to catch his breath.

"Take it easy," Oz whispered, closing the door behind them. He put both hands on Tommy's shoulders and looked in his eyes, trying to calm him. Agitation, distress—it only made Tommy's stuttering worse.

They stood together on the landing until Tommy's breath came slower and his shoulders relaxed. Oz let him go. Tommy wiped his face with his T-shirt and pointed off in the direction of the window. "It's getting w-w-w-worse," he said.

Oz looked out the window, even though he couldn't see anything. He'd heard that rioting and looting had erupted down on Twelfth Street after some partiers were hauled off by police in the middle of the night. He could hear the faint sound of sirens in the distance. Oz looked over his shoulder at the closed door to the apartment, then back at Tommy. "Stay here and watch Trin. I'm going to see what's going on."

Tommy shook his head and stood to his full height, which was a couple of inches taller than Oz. Tommy was bigger, too. Broader. But he was more cautious than Oz. While Oz may have been good at making and writing down his plans, Tommy was the type to question every one of them.

"All right," Oz said. "Mama can watch her."

The two of them went downstairs and found Pearl in the front room watching a rerun of *The FBI* with Mr. Burton. They told her where they were going. She looked from one of them to the other. "Don't y'all go over there," she said finally. "That ain't got nothing to do with y'all."

Mr. Burton said nothing. He was a quiet, contained man. A World War II veteran who was a good decade older than Pearl. He liked an orderly home, an orderly schedule at the plant where he worked and orderly behavior. Oz and Tommy got along well with him, because he did not pretend to be their father. He never inserted himself in their conversations with Pearl when it sounded like those conversations were anything close to contentious, as this one was.

"Look," Oz said to Pearl, "we won't be long."

She sighed and rose from the couch. She pushed past both Oz and Tommy and went to the doorway, headed for the attic apartment. She paused and looked over her shoulder at them. "Y'all stick together," she said.

Those were the words she'd spoken countless times when Oz and Tommy were younger and things were bad: *Y'all stick together.* Oz's mind suddenly hurtled back to a time when he was a teenager in Alabama, sweating and trembling as he stood in a church, begging Pearl to help him. To help *them all* stick together. But that help never came. And now, to hear his mother say those words—*Y'all stick together*—so casually, in the face of that memory, that tragedy, Oz ignited in rage.

"We always stick together," he snapped. "We had to, didn't we? Because where were you?"

Pearl went statue-still. She gripped the stair railing like she might topple over.

Oz turned and left. He could feel Tommy hesitating behind him as he went out the front door. Outside, the heat of the evening pressed in on him. Oz could hear the sirens much louder now, but up and down the block it was calm. It was a middle-class neighborhood filled with autoworkers, teachers, one preacher and a small business owner who had a shop over on Twelfth Street.

"Y-y-y-you ain't gotta be that way with her," Tommy said, stalking up to Oz's side. There wasn't much that seemed to make Tommy angry or get him talking, but Oz's feelings about Pearl and conjuring up old memories qualified.

"I'm sorry," Oz mumbled. "I just get—"

"W-w-w-well, just stop it," Tommy snapped.

Oz sped up to a jog. Tommy ran with him. They followed the sounds of sirens and breaking glass. As they got closer and chaos came into view, everything around them seemed to stop in the heat and tension of the moment. It was as if all sound was silenced in the mouths of the protesters. Flying bottles were suspended in the air and the air itself stood still. Police cars clogged the streets. The cops stood behind masks and shields. But they were outnumbered. Crowds were bunched up on corners and packed in along the street. There were men and women of all ages. Kids were straddling their bicycles, as if pausing to watch a parade. A boy on his bike turned and looked at Oz and, just like that, everyone and everything was reanimated. There was the sound of the seething crowd meeting unheeded orders from police. He searched the faces around him. He knew a few of them. Worked with one of them. A man with a little boy around Trinity's age. What surprised Oz was that the crowd was not in retreat. Just about everyone was advancing. It was as if they were connected through centuries of collective memory. Shared fury.

Oz looked down the street toward Euclid, where Deborah used to live in an apartment above a beauty shop on the corner of Twelfth. He craned his neck but couldn't see much. Something in him was desperate to know that the place where she'd once lived—the place where they'd met—was okay. She was on her way home from her tour. Would they drive through here? How many streets in Detroit looked like this? His heart hammered his rib cage. As he imagined every kind of danger she might meet on her way home, there was an explosion. He ducked and whipped his head around. He saw flashes of orange light in the distance. Was that the dry cleaner's up the street? Flames were jumping and Oz stumbled back, even though he was a safe distance away. The crowd lurched forward to get a better look. Tommy held Oz's arm, probably thinking he was going with them. But Oz couldn't move. His eyes were locked on the flames as they licked the outside of the building. *Y'all stick together.* For a moment he was no longer on this block but in Alabama on an evening much darker than this one. An evening where he was standing in front of a serpentine line of fire, their house fully engulfed and illuminating everything around.

The crash of breaking glass pulled him back to the present. Oz reached up to touch his face. Touch scars from cuts that were long healed. Fine lines that dotted his forehead and right cheek. He looked at Tommy and saw the flames dancing in his brother's eyes. Tommy was breathing hard as if he'd just stopped dead from a run.

"It's all right, Tommy," Oz said. "We're here. Not there."

The two returned to the house in silence, Oz's mind still hundreds of miles away and several years back. At home, he eyed the chest of drawers where he kept that cigar box made of blond, unfinished wood. Its brass closure was shut tight, but still it called out to him sometimes. The call was louder than ever. But he ignored it, like always, because it was a kind of Pandora's box of memories.

The following day, about ten or so men in the neighborhood all drifted down the street and came together on Pearl's porch in the hours before curfew. They all watched tanks roll down the main drag. Mr. Burton sat in his lawn chair shaking his head, saying quietly, "I never thought I'd see the like. It's like Vietnam come here to America."

"What did you expect?" asked the teacher who lived down the street. "They're burning it all down. Even businesses owned by Negroes."

Eyes darted toward the drugstore owner. His business was a burned-out shell now. He, like some of the other black business owners, had tried painting *We Are Soul Brothers* on the window of his shop. The hope was that it would be like a biblical act of painting blood on the doorpost, a sign for the angels of destruction to stay their hands. But there was no Passover. No saving anything.

The preacher who lived next door reached up to touch his white clerical collar. "People lashing out," he said. "They calling this a riot? This ain't no riot. It's a uprising. A *rebellion*. If only it was something—"

"Ain't nothing," said Pearl. She and Willa Mae were the only women on the porch. "You beat somebody down enough, they liable to do anything. Even to their own."

Willa Mae nodded, with a far-off look. Oz got up and went down the steps. He stood in the yard, his sweat-saturated T-shirt clinging to his back in the heat. The conversation on the porch seesawed between understanding and anger over what had been lost to the flames: the pharmacy, the butcher shop, the cleaner's, Joe's Record Shop. Could they rebuild?

Oz felt a hand on his shoulder. It was Willa Mae. He sat on the curb, and she eased herself down next to him.

"It's scary," she said.

Oz nodded, thinking about snipers and stray bullets. Deborah had made it home safely that morning. Tonight, she and Pearl planned to sleep on the floor with Trinity between them in a dresser drawer they'd pulled out and lined with blankets, while Oz, Mr. Burton and Tommy would trade off keeping watch, at the ready with Mr. Burton's shotgun.

Willa Mae stared off at the red brick house across the street. Her face, pockmarked with acne scars, was serious and set. "Look here," she said. "I'm going back."

"Back where?" But it hit Oz as soon as the words were out of his mouth. She was going home. "Why would you do that?"

"I been having this dream. The same one, over and over and—"

"Stop it with that. You know I don't—"

"I don't care what you don't believe in. I'm telling you anyways." There was something about the shattered look in her eye that made Oz pipe down and listen. "In my dream, it was me and Aunt Bee on that old couch out in the front room of Grandmama's house. Remember that old nasty couch? Where Pearl slept that time?"

"Yes," Oz mumbled, not wanting any more reminders of that place or that time.

"In my dream, Aunt Bee's apologizing. She was dying, I think. And she wanted to make it right with me."

Back when Pearl, Oz, Tommy and Willa Mae left Alabama, they were all running away from something. For Willa Mae, it was Aunt Bee, Oz's father's sister. She'd raised Willa Mae from the time Willa was in diapers. That was after Willa's mother, another sister, had drowned, either by accident or intention—one was just as likely as the other. As for Willa's father, he was nothing more than a whispered best-guess, and Grandmama was mostly confined to a bed in a back room. The aunt was all Willa had. And the aunt had a kind of darkness that could eclipse all light in her.

"You never know what you're going to get with that woman," Oz said. "I don't know why you want to risk opening old wounds with her because of some Voodoo dream of yours."

"It was a sign. I know it. I need to go and see her. See if I got a chance at . . . at something . . ." She paused, kneading her hands in her lap. "And as for my wounds, Oz, they never closed. Me and you, we got different hurts. You heal yours the way you see fit and leave me to mine." She hugged her knees to her bony chest and looked up and down the street, her eyes flooded with tears. "With folk setting the world on fire all around me, I think now's about the time to get outta here and go see what's true."

Oz nodded reluctantly, knowing there was no talking Willa out of anything once she got locked on to it. "I'll miss you, Old Willa," he said, reviving the name he'd called her when they were kids.

She turned away. Oz imagined she didn't want him to see her crying. They sat in silence until there was movement from the porch. Everyone was migrating down the steps. Oz expected them all to drift back to their homes, lock up and keep curfew. But then he heard someone say, "We should do something."

Oz and Willa Mae watched the men from the porch head down to the end of the street. Someone brought out two tall garbage cans and flipped them bottom side up. Two men laid a wooden rod across the cans while two others disappeared into a garage. When the two emerged from the garage, they were carrying a sign that read *Keep Out*. They hung it over the rod. They had to know some flimsy sign wouldn't save them if the anger of the crowd turned down their street or if police or the National Guard somehow took their quiet neighborhood for a sniper's nest. Police had just shot up an apartment, claiming they'd seen a sniper. A four-year-old girl was dead now, with no sniper to be found and scarcely a word of apology.

Willa Mae stood and brushed off her pants. She looked down at Oz. "I'll be around for a couple days before I go, so . . ."

Oz told her that they'd go out for a drink or something. He watched her walk down the street. "Hey!" he called out. "You're coming back, right?"

She turned but kept walking backward. "Depend how things go. My dreams ain't always what I think." She waved goodbye and turned off toward the bus stop.

It would be curfew soon. Oz sat out on the porch swing with the shotgun resting across his lap like a sleeping child. He'd fired a shotgun for the first time, outside of target practice, when he was a boy. He was with his father that day. The two of them, walking through the lush peanut field after a summer rain. Oz had the gun and was responsible for keeping an eye out for snakes. Every so often, his father would look back at him and smile encouragement.

His father was a short, soft-spoken man. He wore round, rimless glasses that made him look professorial, though he could barely read. Still, he was a teacher to Oz. He taught Oz everything he knew about the land and animals, and Oz took to it like those things were already programmed in his genes. It was as if the same rich Alabama soil that collected itself under his father's fingernails grew up naturally under Oz's. That soil squished under Oz's boots as he followed behind his father a few paces back. Oz was walking with long strides, trying to land each step in the imprint his father's boots left behind. Up ahead, he spotted movement. A copperhead, right there at his father's foot. Oz aimed and fired. His father jumped and whipped his head around to look at Oz. Oz pointed to the now dead snake.

His father let out a long, low whistle. "You might've saved my life," he said. "That's my boy."

Whenever his father would say *That's my boy* to him—and he said it plenty—Oz would feel a mix of pride and guilt. They were words his father never would have said to Tommy. They were for Oz alone.

As Oz came back to himself, he said aloud, "You're not Willa Mae. Don't go back to that place."

"Who're you talking to?" Oz looked up and saw Deborah coming out the front door.

"Nobody," he said.

She sat on the porch swing beside him. She took out a cigarette and lit it—a habit she'd picked up out "on the road." That and making after-dinner drinks. Although, he'd noticed she'd lately been having a drink before dinner, as well.

She'd made rum and Cokes for both herself and him and they sipped in silence, under a sky that glowed red in the distance.

"Willa Mae's leaving," Oz said. "Going back home."

"Yeah?" Deborah took a drag from her cigarette and stared off straight ahead. "She's been talking about going back to mend fences and—"

"Not every fence can be mended," Oz cut in.

"That woman raised her, Oz. She's got to try." Deborah blew out a stream of smoke to the side. "But I'mma miss that one. If not for her, there might not be an us." She leaned into him and rubbed his earlobe.

"I miss you," Oz said quietly.

"I miss you, too."

He glanced at her. "Well, why don't you stay home? With all of this going on, what if something had happened to you out there on the road?" Oz worried about her all the time. But there was something else, too. Deborah had always calmed his mind. Marshaled his thoughts in the right direction, knowingly or not. She was the center of his well-planned life, which still consisted of saving for their dream house and the hope of a good office job when he graduated from college, which would be next year, if he kept at it. Whenever Deborah was away and his mind roamed too often to the worst parts of the past, he felt the throb of his old hurts because, in truth, they were no more healed than Willa Mae's.

"What I do, Oz, it's important to me," Deborah said. She stubbed out her cigarette and grabbed his hand. "I know what you're scared of, but it'll be okay."

He nodded, even though Deborah couldn't begin to know his deepest fears. He put his arm around her and the two of them watched as smoke floated like acrid clouds across the sky.

Almost a year after the riots had passed, they were living in ruins. It wasn't obvious from the view out the window at Pearl's. Their street was the same. But a few blocks away, it was as if the end of the world had come. So much of the West Side—and beyond—was a burned-out collage of empty lots and hollow buildings. It was all far enough away for Oz to feel at a remove, but still too close for him to ignore it.

He led Trinity out of the house and over to the side yard, where he was planning to put in a garden. It was April and the weather had been nice. "You stay close to Daddy," he told her. "I'm going to see if we can get something in the ground."

Trinity watched Oz with almost adultlike concentration as he turned over the soil. He crouched down and grabbed a handful of dirt and showed it to her. "Why don't we try our peas and spinach. And maybe some onions?"

She poked a finger in the dirt, as if testing his suggestion.

"You know your daddy's a country boy. Me and your uncle Tommy. This is what we grew up doing." But Trinity wasn't listening. She'd abandoned him and was digging deep in the soil with her hands.

Oz heard footsteps approaching and low talk. It was his brother and Lloyd. The two of them were walking shoulder to shoulder; their faces were almost touching as they whispered and laughed together. When their eyes met, there was something there. Oz couldn't stand the look of it. He pulled Trinity away from the dirt and wiped off her hands, meeting only minimal resistance.

He went over and sat on the porch steps as Lloyd and Tommy squatted down to ask Trinity about her day and what she had planned for later. Both Lloyd and Tommy listened intently and exchanged smiles as Trinity said something about her doll, Candy, and waxed on for a few seconds about peas and onions. Oz squinted and shaded his eyes from the sun as the two men strode up to him. Lloyd said his hellos then told Tommy, "I'm gonna go in and say hi to your mama."

Tommy nodded and watched him go.

"Don't you get enough of hanging around with him?" Oz asked, not caring if Lloyd heard him through the screen door. Oz knew things about Lloyd. Deborah had told him Lloyd was a homosexual and had been arrested at one of those clubs while they were down playing a gig in Chicago. Oz had shared this with Tommy a few months back. He'd warned him: "I don't like it, Tommy. You know what kind of bad can come from this. Do I need to remind you of all that?"

Tommy had looked unwell. He was unable to meet Oz's eyes. "H-h-h-he ain't like that. I ain't either." Tommy had avoided Oz for days after that.

Now, instead of answering Oz's question about hanging around with Lloyd, Tommy pulled a white envelope from his back pocket. He held it out to Oz.

"What's this?" Oz asked, taking it. The envelope had already been ripped open. Oz pulled the letter out and unfolded it. ORDER TO REPORT FOR INDUCTION was printed across the top of the page.

He looked up at Tommy in disbelief then at the letter again. He saw the date Tommy was expected to report: May 23, 1968. "That's next month!"

Tommy nodded.

Oz stuffed the letter back in the envelope, tearing it in the process. "They're going to send you over there, and for what? So you can end up—" He pointed down the street. "You knew Michael, right? That boy is dead and gone. It's not enough for them to kill us here at home, they want us to go overseas and die, too." He shook his head. "I don't want you going."

"Ain't n-n-n-nothing I can do about it."

Oz inclined his head vaguely in the direction of the river. "You can go to Canada. That's what these white boys are doing."

Tommy glanced over his shoulder at Trinity, who had hopped on her scooter and was bumping along the walkway. He said in a low voice, "I ain't n-n-n-no pussy, Oz."

Oz knew what Tommy meant by that. Oz recalled his brother as he once was: string-bean skinny and scared, looking on as Oz and his father sparred in the backyard. Tommy always dreaded his turn. But Oz had nothing to fear. Oz had quick hands and fast feet. When he swung at his father, he'd swing hard, just as he'd been told to do. He missed most times, but not always. As his father shook off the punches Oz landed, he'd smile and say, "So, you Sonny Liston now?"

Then it was Tommy's turn. Tommy was the kind of boy who needed "toughening up," his father would say. He would taunt Tommy every time he put Tommy down in the dirt: "You gon' stay down there like a stuttering little pussy?"

Tommy would get up, bouncing on spindly legs that were skin-stripped and scarred from an earlier time when Tommy was mistaken for a pussy. Tommy would fix his eyes on their father's left hand, trying to anticipate the next jab so he could step back and circle out of the way. Oz had taught him to do that, saying, "You have to learn to protect yourself. Make him chase you. Tire him out. Block him."

But Tommy could never block what was coming for him. It was usually a jab to the face that would send his head snapping back. Tommy would go down and get up again and again, even though Oz pleaded with him to stay down and let him count him out. Tommy never listened. With no ropes to fall back on to steady himself, Tommy would stumble around in a cloud of dust, knee-walking punch-drunk. Swaying. Swallowing blood. Lips swelling. Oz would stand there watching it all, torn between his father and his brother. Helpless to do anything, one way or the other. And Pearl was nowhere to be found. Not there to tell his father to stop. To leave Tommy alone. She was hardly ever there when they needed her.

As Oz stood with his brother all these years later, he said what he never had in front of their father: "I know you're your own man, Tommy, but I wish—" Oz couldn't say the rest. He didn't know what he would do if something happened to Tommy. He told himself that after all he and Tommy had endured together, his brother knew how he felt. He handed the draft notice back.

As Tommy climbed the stairs to the porch, Oz asked him: "What are you going to tell them? About your legs? Your hands? At your physical. You know you have to get one."

Tommy reached down, as if to cover his legs, which were almost always hidden under long pants to conceal the scars that crisscrossed their way up from ankle to thigh. Tommy's hands were just as bad. The palms looked like they were made of melted wax. "N-n-n-nothing to tell," he said, disappearing through the screen door.

But there was a lot to tell. In some ways, those scars—and the ones that dotted Oz's forehead and right cheek—revealed everything about wounds that might never heal.

Deborah

I carried Trinity downstairs to Pearl's.

"You're going to spend the night with Pearl," I said. "I bet you like that, huh?"

Trinity nodded.

I gave her a kiss on the cheek. "Of course you do." It was all playtime, candy and no such thing as bedtime down at Pearl's. I found her in the kitchen making a meat loaf. "Thank you for baby-sitting," I said as I let Trinity down. I went over and squeezed Pearl's shoulders. "I appreciate it. Getting some time with Oz to celebrate and, you know . . ."

"I don't wanna know," Pearl said, holding up her hands. She fixed me with a hard stare. "Is this how you plan on looking to-night?"

"Hush, Pearl. I just got to take the rollers out of my hair and change. And dinner's already cooking." Still, I gave Trinity a quick kiss and ran back upstairs. I took the rollers out and left my hair to fall around my shoulders, just the way Oz liked it. I put on a black strapless dress and my black *I'm not messing around* heels. I checked the smothered pork chops and vegetables on the stovetop. Every-thing was perfect.

"Oh! I almost forgot!" I ran over to the record player. I crouched down and went through my crates of records. Dinah Washington, I decided. I put the record on and looked around our tiny, neat apartment.

"All set," I said.

I meant to give Oz some time to relax when he got home, but I couldn't. I was so excited, I jumped on him like a cat the minute he came through the door.

"We're playing the Twenty Grand!" I said as I hugged him around the neck. He was dirty and smelled bad from work, but I didn't care. I watched his face as my words sank in. Everybody who was anybody had played the Twenty Grand. The Supremes. The Temptations.

He nodded. "Really?"

I let him go. "It's just another talent show, but still. It'll be big!"

"Yeah," Oz said as he got out of his jacket and kicked off his dirty, oily work boots. He'd graduated from college in the spring and was still stuck on the factory floor. He'd told me, "A monkey at the zoo has more chance of getting ahead around here than a Negro, seeing as monkeys are what they think we are anyway."

But he'd had another interview today for what he said was a job that would let him get his foot in the door good. I asked him about it as he walked over to the sink and put his lunchbox on the counter.

"Interview went like the other ones," he said, dumping stale coffee out of the Thermos. "Nice words and this and that, but . . ." He shook his head. "Who knows?"

I went over and rubbed his back as he rinsed out the Thermos. His muscles were knotted up under my hand. He shrank away from me. I stepped back, my feelings hurt.

Oz was so prickly now. The work stuff had him down. And then there was Tommy shipping out a few months ago. First Willa Mae gone, now Tommy. One time, when I was talking about going out on the road for an extra-long tour, he'd snapped, "Are you going to be the next one to leave?"

I went back to talking about the show, to remind him that it was right here in town. I hoped that would ease things a little bit. I'd turned down a few out-of-town gigs here and there to make him happy. But I'd spent those days cooped up in the apartment wishing I was someplace else.

He nodded along as I spoke, but I could tell he wasn't really listening.

Still, I pressed on: "You want to know when the show is?"

"Sure." He pulled wax paper from his lunchbox and folded it up to be used later.

"It's next month," I said. "That gives us a few weeks to tighten things up. And, you know, you and everybody can come and cheer us on." I paused. "Dinner and everything tonight was just kind of, I don't know, an early celebration. And to, I guess, try and make you feel better, too."

He leaned against the counter. "Thank you."

I reached out to touch his arm but drew my hand back, not wanting another rejection. I wasn't sure what to do. I wasn't sure how to make him happy.

"What can I do, Oz?" I asked.

He pushed off the counter and sighed. He looked at me for what felt like the first time since he walked through the door. "Nothing," he said. "You look beautiful. And dinner smells good. But I just need . . ." He gazed around the apartment. "I don't know what I need."

He kissed me, but it felt offhand. He glanced down at his watch and went over and switched off the record player. Then he turned on the TV, like he did every night around this time. He stood glued to it as Walter Cronkite flickered to life in black-and-white. The moment helicopters dipped into the frame, Oz crouched down and stared real close, trying to get all he could about the war. The only thing we had from Tommy were his letters, and, just like Tommy himself, they didn't say much.

On the night of the show, I was more nervous than usual. Backstage, everybody shimmered and sparkled, including me in a white dress that dripped sequins. Oz led me through the crowd of other performers. The place was alive with hope as everybody waited for their turn onstage. I could smell sweat mingled with perfume and powder. I could feel the vibration of jangled nerves—and they weren't just mine.

"Lots of competition," I murmured, holding tighter to Oz's hand.

"You're going to do fine," Oz said.

We came upon Mary and Celeste, standing off to the side of the stage. Celeste gave Oz a peck on the cheek. Mary did the same, then, as usual, called him Potato Boy and asked him how he was doing. He hated when she called him that. He was a long way from that boy—six years, in fact—and not as shy or as bad of a dresser.

Oz ignored Mary and turned to me. "I'm going out to watch from the audience." He kissed me and was gone.

Me and the girls circled up for our preshow lucky shot of bourbon. I did a second shot for double luck. I was nervous going out, like always, but the jitters fell away little by little with every note and with every step and turn me, Mary and Celeste did together. We sang a Supremes cover that everybody knew and everybody was with us, dancing and clapping and singing along, like we were the finale. I could've gone all night. When we left the stage, we were sweaty and high on that applause. We watched the last two acts from offstage—two quartets, back-to-back. They were okay, but they couldn't touch our trio. When it came time for the winner to be called, me, Mary and Celeste all grabbed onto one another.

"We got this locked," Celeste said, squeezing my hand. "No question."

"Shhh!" I said. "Don't jinx us!" But I was feeling pretty good about our chances.

Mary put her hands over her ears. "I just can't *take it*," she said. "Tell me when it's over!"

The MC was going on and on, dragging out the suspense. And then he said it. The winner. The crowd went into a fit of clapping and whooping it up. A young boy who'd performed earlier in the night pushed past us and went out to claim his trophy. He wasn't even that good. But he was cute, I guess.

I found myself clapping for him along with everybody else, even though I could feel something crumbling and caving in in me. I'd tried so hard. I'd been out on the road for years, away from my family singing my heart out. Trying and trying, but over and over it was always somebody else. When was it going to be *my* turn?

As I watched the MC lift the boy's arm in victory—almost yanking the boy off his feet—I thought about Oz. He'd never liked me out on the road, and these days he was liking it even less. Would he finally say enough is enough? That he'd been patient up till now? That I needed to face the fact that nobody wanted me and it was time to be the wife and mother *he* wanted?

I looked around, wondering where he was. And all of a sudden I felt frustrated and mad, like me and him had had a real argument about it and he'd said just those words to me. I told Mary and Celeste I was leaving and turned to go. I'd barely taken a step when I caught sight of Lloyd. He was walking fast in our direction, nudging people out of his way. He was smiling wide and all but shaking with excitement.

"Why you so happy?" Mary asked him. "Didn't you see? We just lost to a—" She looked at me. "How old is that boy?"

"Eight, I think they said."

"We just lost to an *eight*-year-old," she said.

Lloyd shook his head. "Ain't no losers here, little sister. We just won." He smiled as he rocked on his heels, with a glint of mystery in his eye.

I glanced out to the stage. The boy was doing an encore. I looked back at Lloyd, confused.

"We won where it *counts*, ladies," Lloyd said. Then he told us about some producers in the audience. A possible record deal. Our big break. Celeste and Mary jumped on him and almost knocked him off his feet. But I sank down and sat on the edge of an equipment box. I took a couple deep breaths because for a second there, Lloyd's words had sucked the air right out of my lungs. Right out of the room, even. But now, I could breathe again. Warm tears slid down my face, even as I smiled and laughed. I closed my eyes to take it all in.

This was it.

This was joy.

This was everything.

Oz

1968

"Are you happy for me?" Deborah asked.

Oz was lying beside her in bed. It had been a long night. The performance at the Twenty Grand. The celebration of their "big break."

"Of course I am," he said.

"I know you, Oz. Don't lie." Deborah pulled the covers up to her neck like a barrier between them.

Just a few hours earlier, she had run up to Oz overjoyed. He'd been surprised by how happy she was. After all, her group had just lost. But then she'd told him about the producers who'd been in the audience. Told him they were finally getting noticed. She threw her arms around his neck. He held her, feeling the fast thumping of her heart. His heart sped up, too, matching the excitement in hers. Then, as Deborah pulled back, Oz imagined her pulling away. Already off in some studio or on some stage far from home. Later, he'd smiled and laughed as they sat in the restaurant toasting and celebrating, but it hadn't all come easily. His mind kept toggling between happiness for her and, what? Loss for him. Now he didn't know what he felt. He just knew he couldn't get comfortable with it. He flipped over on his back and stared up at the ceiling. "It's just . . . it's all happening so fast," he said.

"Fast?" Deborah sat up. "I've been out there for years. *Years* chasing after this."

"All I'm saying is we need to talk about it."

Oz, after all, had news of his own. An interview he'd had weeks ago had finally ripened into a job offer. He'd learned it just that afternoon, before the show. The money wasn't the greatest and his office would be the size of a closet, but at least he'd be out of that factory and on his way. He was waiting until after the show to tell Deborah and to celebrate. He wasn't counting on any of what was happening now. It wasn't that he wanted her group to lose, but he didn't want a win like this either. What he wanted, if he was honest, was for her to have reason to be done with all of this and to live the life that he could give her now.

"What I think," Oz said, "is we need to see what we want to do and talk about whether this is the right time."

"The time is *now*, Oz," Deborah said. "Right now." She lowered herself to the bed again. "I can't talk about this anymore."

Oz turned on his side and looked at her in the dim light as she stared up at the ceiling, a tear sliding down the side of her face. He had the urge to trace her nose, in profile. She was so beautiful. Maybe even more so than on the day he'd met her.

Here, on the morning after, Oz stood in the kitchen down at Pearl's, leaning against the counter sipping a cup of coffee. He'd gotten up before Deborah and slipped downstairs. He could hear the floor creaking above his head, an indication that she was up.

"What you doing down here?" It was Pearl, coming into the kitchen.

"Just needed some quiet."

"Everything okay?" She went to the far corner of the counter and poured a cup of coffee. "How'd Deborah and them do last night? Did they take it?"

Oz shook his head. "Some little boy won."

Mr. Burton came in with the *Detroit Free Press* folded under his arm and said good morning. Pearl gave him his coffee and a kiss. He hugged her tight. Oz raised his mug and nodded hello, even though he felt a twinge of annoyance, watching Pearl and Mr. Burton smile and fawn all over each other like all was right with the world and they were the only two people in it. He was in this world, too, and, for him, it was off-kilter. He took a tongue-singeing gulp of his coffee, trying to rush it down so he could leave.

"Shit," he muttered as the pain subsided and his tongue went numb.

Mr. Burton glanced at him but said nothing as he went over and sat at the breakfast table in the corner. He snapped the paper open like he did every weekend morning. He read silently, then mentioned interesting tidbits to Pearl. He was telling her that it looked like Governor Romney was going to be serving in the Nixon administration. Then they started complaining about Nixon and what he was going to do about Vietnam when he took office.

Oz tossed back the last of his coffee, his charred tongue barely registering it.

"Whatever it is, I hope it means Tommy's coming home soon," Pearl said.

"Well, now," Mr. Burton said, "Tommy's just doing his duty. Being a man."

Oz was almost out the door, but he stopped cold at those words. His generalized sense of annoyance was crystallizing into something jagged and sharp, pointed squarely, if unfairly, at Mr. Burton.

"You don't know what makes my brother a man," Oz said, thinking about Tommy taking his father's punches. Worse still, recalling the making of the scars on his brother's legs and hands. And all that had come from it. He wheeled on his mother: "Mama, you want to stand up to your boyfriend for Tommy? You want to show up for your son, for once?"

Mr. Burton looked puzzled.

Tears rose in Pearl's eyes, but she said nothing.

Oz left the house picturing his brother as a man shivering and alone in some rice paddy halfway around the world. Then he saw Tommy as a boy, bloodied and maimed. He thought of Deborah and how when she was around, his mind was quieter. How this restless, remembering part of him would go still and settle down, like a soothed child. But Deborah was going to be a star now. Who would he have? And who would she have out there chasing after her on the road? He was thinking about what Robert had done.

He found himself pulling up in front of Lloyd's place. As he climbed the stairs of the rooming house two at a time, he took shallow breaths, trying not to inhale the smell of sweaty feet and rotten food. When Lloyd opened the door, he looked somewhere between surprised and wary.

"Can I come in?" Oz asked.

Lloyd hesitated for a second, then opened the door all the way. "Sure, man. Of course."

The twin bed against the wall was made, with its multipaneled quilt tucked neatly under the thin mattress. There was a small desk by the window with a perfectly aligned pile of papers, a pad with squiggly writing on it and a cup with pens and pencils in it. But what caught Oz's eye was the framed picture.

Oz whipped his head around and looked at Lloyd. "Where'd you get that?"

Lloyd didn't answer. He didn't have to.

It was Tommy, standing in a field of mud in his army uniform with his helmet sitting crooked on his head. He had his rifle over his shoulder and what looked like a puppy in a little sack at his side. He had that half smile of his that made one wonder if he was ever truly happy.

Oz snatched the picture up.

Lloyd reached for it, then drew back. He stood kneading his hands, his eyes on the picture until Oz put it back.

Lloyd motioned toward the folding chair at the desk.

Oz said he'd rather stand, so Lloyd sat. He nudged the picture back, away from Oz. He drummed out a nervous tune on the desk with his long, tapered fingers. Tommy had once told Deborah and Oz that Lloyd played piano, but he'd never thought himself good enough to accompany the girls.

Lloyd asked Oz, "What can I do for you?"

Oz glanced at the picture. It shouldn't be here. He looked back at Lloyd. "The thing with the girls. I want to talk about that."

Lloyd looked relieved. "Right. Yeah. Good things are happening there. It looks like we'll be getting a recording contract, no doubt. They're talking a pretty standard game."

Oz looked out the window and watched a few cars pass by. This was everything Deborah had ever wanted. "What are they expecting them to do? How long?"

Lloyd laughed and offered Oz a cigarette. Oz waved it away.

"They expect them to sing, man," Lloyd said, touching a lit match to the tip of his cigarette. He shook out the flame and dropped the smoking matchstick in the ashtray. "God willing, they'll have a good, long career. Traveling the whole world." Lloyd did a theatrical motion with his hands, as if he could see their names up in lights.

Oz looked out the window again and was quiet for a long time as he wondered how far and how long Deborah might be away. He felt himself toggling, just like last night after the show: happiness for her, loss for him. Oz shook his head, as if to clear it, then he heard himself say, "I don't think she should go." He couldn't believe he was saying it. But there it was, out of his mouth.

"What's that, now?" Lloyd's cigarette was hovering there at his lips as he leaned in toward Oz.

Oz turned from the window and looked at him. "I don't think she should go. See, I have a new job. And, well, we need a different kind of life than that. More settled."

Lloyd stubbed out his cigarette and laughed, like Oz was joking. Then the laugh faded. The smile fell away. He shook his head slowly. "Oz, this—"

"Being gone like that—"

"Now, wait a second. Yeah, she'll be gone sometimes. But not all the time, right?" Lloyd's voice was measured, as if trying to buck up a jittery performer. He got to his feet. "We can try and keep her home more. Would that help? Deborah would probably like that, what with Trinity being so little and everything."

"She can't sign, but she can perform around town," Oz said, offering his own alternative. "Or even, you know, Chicago or what have you. That's important to her. I know. So she can do that. I'd never stop her from doing what she loves."

Lloyd opened his arms in disbelief. "Does she know you're here?"

There was a long silence.

"I'm not trying—" Lloyd paused. "Look, they want a group, Oz, and Deborah's the lead singer in that group. They don't want the girls without her. Hell, they'd probably take her without them. You understand what I'm saying? She's not just good, Oz. A lot of singers are *good*. What she's got is that sparkle. That extra something that makes you think she was born to it."

"I'm sorry," Oz said. "But this is the right thing for my family. It's for the best. Everyone gets something they want. Deborah will keep performing. And the girls, you'll find something for them." He paused, holding Lloyd's gaze. "And I'd appreciate if you'd tell Deborah they pulled the deal or something."

Lloyd shook his head. "I'm not doing that. If you won't let her sign, fine. But you tell her."

Oz rubbed his temples, frustrated, his mind racing. He hadn't planned for any of this. But here he was. It was happening. "Lloyd, would you please do this?"

Lloyd shook his head.

Oz looked over Lloyd's shoulder, because he couldn't look at him right then. "I know what you are," he said quietly. "Deborah told me. About Chicago. The arrest at that homosexual place."

Lloyd took a step back, looking momentarily dazed, before recovering. "I don't know what you're talking about."

"I'll tell. I have a friend on the police force," Oz lied. "Everyone will know."

Lloyd's eyes darted over to the picture of Tommy, then back to Oz.

"Don't bring my brother into this. He's nothing like you."

"You don't scare me, Oz," Lloyd said.

"I'm not trying to scare you. I'm just trying to . . ." But what could he say? He *was* trying to scare him. Oz had to look away from him again. He glanced over at the picture of Tommy on the desk and thought, *You don't belong here.* He lunged forward and grabbed the picture. When Lloyd came at him, he shoved him back and ran to the door. Oz thundered down the stairs, with Lloyd's voice chasing behind him.

All Deborah talked about was the contract. At dinner, in bed at night or out on their evening walks, Oz would listen as she wondered aloud about what the contract would say and when it would be ready. They hadn't heard anything about the contract in days. About a week after Oz's visit with Lloyd, Pearl yelled up for Deborah to come downstairs to get the phone. She said it was Lloyd. Deborah jumped up from the couch and hugged Oz.

"Finally!" she said. On her way out the door, she stopped and turned to him. "I know you're not, you know, all behind this, Oz, but we'll make it work. You'll see. I promise. We both got something we want, right? You got that good job, and I got this. We're on our way!" She kissed him again and ran out the door.

Oz paced from one end of their tiny apartment to the other, wondering what Lloyd was telling her. Was he saying Oz had threatened him? Was he doing what Oz had told him to do? When Deborah came back through the door, the answer was drawn in tears on her face. She tumbled into his arms. He sank to the floor with her, rocking her as she told him there was no deal. They wanted something different. Oz told her it was okay. That she would keep performing.

He told himself: *This was the right thing.* For him. For her. For their family. He needed to keep it all together. And he could, now that he was making a better living. He would use it to make a good life.

Deborah

1970–1974

The bus finally came rumbling up to the stop.

"Come on, Trin," I said. "Ride's here."

When the door cranked open, I helped her up the steps. She had her coloring book and was being careful not to drop it. It was late morning on a workday, so there were just a handful of folks sitting scattershot here and there. I pointed Trinity to a seat midway down the aisle. She wanted the window, like always, so I let her have it. Wasn't much I wanted to see. But it was a pretty day, right there on the edge of spring.

Trinity was doing her best to color as the bus bucked along, jerking her crayon marks outside the lines. I kissed the top of her head, then watched out the window as we rolled down Woodward, grinding to regular stops to pick up riders. I stared out till we reached our stop.

"Careful, Trin," I said as she hopped down out of the bus right into a puddle of melted snow. "You did that on purpose, didn't you?"

She smiled up at me mischievously.

We both had on our red rubber boots, so I jumped down in the puddle after her, which surprised her and made her laugh. It wasn't enough to pull a laugh out of me. Not a real one. Hadn't had one of those in almost two years.

Me and Trinity quick-stepped it the rest of the way to the projects where my parents lived, passing a clothesline with white sheets waving in the breeze, like a silent surrender to crime and drugs and the deepest pits of despair. It wasn't the place I remembered from growing up. So much was going wrong. These days, the red brick apartments put me in the mind of a prison or asylum.

I held tighter to Trinity's hand and pulled her closer as we dodged a raggedy-looking girl dragging two little kids behind her. We hurried up the sidewalk with our coats unbuttoned and blowing in the breeze. Mama let us into the narrow entry of the apartment and wrapped me and Trinity in warm hugs. It smelled like disinfectant with an overlay of collard greens. A peek around the corner to the kitchen confirmed a pot simmering on the stove.

"How is he?" I asked Mama as I took off Trinity's coat, then my own, and hung them in the hall closet.

"Your daddy's stubborn as I don't know what, but what else is new?" She glanced in the direction of the living room, where the TV was going. "I'm gon' leave you and Asaline to your business." She smiled down at Trinity and grabbed her hand. "How 'bout some ice cream?"

"Mama, she hasn't even had lunch . . ." But she was already leading Trinity around to the kitchen. Asaline was in the living room with Daddy, waiting for me. I went over to his chair and kissed him on the cheek. "How you feeling, old man?"

"Not bad. Not too bad at all."

He didn't look good. He'd lost so much weight since the last time I'd seen him, maybe a month ago. He had a bad heart and Mama just about had to force-feed him, his appetite was so bad.

Asaline, never one to waste time, got right to the business of why he and Mama would be moving to Florida with her and her family. Asaline's husband had been looking for work for months, but there was none to be found for him around Detroit. Daddy had been putting up a fight about leaving for weeks. Asaline could win an argument by pure force of will. She declared victory now even as Daddy kept up resistance.

I patted him on the arm and said, "It's not safe around here anymore, Daddy, with these drugs and the way people are carrying on. It's for the best." I paused. "I wish I could go with you."

I half meant it. I thought I might be out touring an album at this point, or at least making one. But no. Here I was without a contract or even a group. I spent most of my time on the phone now, all but begging people to put in a word for me with this producer or that one. I went begging for gigs at clubs. And Oz was hardly home. He'd gotten his chance to come off the factory floor a while back and, a month ago, a promotion on top of that. Now he was at the office all the time. And when he was home, he only half listened to anything I had to say when it had to do with my plans to get myself some better gigs and another shot at a record deal. He'd fidget and take the conversation off in some other direction. One time, he'd even stopped and said: "I'm giving you the best life I can, Deborah. Can't that be enough?"

Now his thing was to call home from work every day, usually around lunchtime, wanting to know what I was doing or where I was going and giving suggestions on how I might make myself happier: *How about a movie with Pearl? How about going to lunch with a friend? How about taking Trinity to the park?*

Some days I wouldn't answer the phone, but he'd want a full accounting and have more happiness suggestions when he got home from work. I'd tell him at least some of what he wanted to hear—*I went shopping, I crocheted a new scarf,* whether it was true or not—just to shut him up. To stop him always checking up on me. But he never stopped.

I left Daddy and Asaline to the last of their arguing and went to the kitchen, where Mama and Trinity were finishing their ice cream. I leaned over and looked in Trinity's bowl. Chocolate. I thought about getting a bowl for myself but let that idea go good and fast. Hard as it was to get somebody to take notice of me, nobody'd want me waddling up onstage. Mama and Trinity were going on about Trinity starting kindergarten in the fall, which she was excited about.

"I think she's going to teach her teacher a thing or two," I said, picking her up out of her chair and putting her on my lap. "Isn't that right, Ms. Trin?"

She nodded and hopped down, independent as anything. She grabbed her coloring book and crayons. "I'm going to see Aunt Asaline," she declared.

We waved her off and Mama got up and poured two cups of coffee.

"Looks like y'all'll be going on to Florida," I told her. "Asaline's in there doing the last little bit of browbeating."

"Thank you, Jesus," she said, laughing, moving slow toward the table, carrying the two mugs. She hobbled something terrible now. Too much time bending, squatting and kneeling while cleaning other folks' houses in neighborhoods she never would've been allowed to live in, even if she had the money. I looked around the small, bright kitchen where I'd had so many meals and dreamed so many dreams about being somebody different from my mama and my sister.

"How you doin'?" Mama asked, side-eyeing me as she put my cup of coffee in front of me.

"Good," I said.

"Sure about that?"

I didn't answer.

She let out a weary breath. In the days after the abortion, she'd come to be careful about going too deep. About touching on something she sensed but didn't really want to know. She gave my arm a gentle squeeze, then spooned some sugar in her coffee. "Keep at it," she said. "You'll get another chance."

I took my turn with the sugar. It had been almost two years since Lloyd had called to tell me that Motown had decided to pull the contract.

"They're looking for a different sound, I think," he'd said.

I told him we'd keep at it. Then Lloyd left us. Gone, without a word. All I knew was that he ended up on the East Coast. Then Celeste got married. Moved to Indiana. And there went Mary, following Lloyd out to New York.

Mama patted my hand. "Just stick to your plans."

"Plans?" I laughed. Planning had only worked for Oz. That notebook of his was like a prediction book. Everything he wrote in it came to pass. I looked out the window. "Mama, half the kids who came up with me in these projects could sing and planned to be big-time. But you only get one Diana Ross."

Mama reached in her bra and pulled out a Kleenex. She gave it to me, then touched my face.

Asaline called from the other room. Bozo was on. Mama got up and hugged me around the shoulders, then put their ice cream bowls in the sink. "Come on, Deborah," she said. "Bozo's calling."

I hauled myself up to follow her but paused. "Let me warm up my coffee. Won't be a minute." I waited till she was gone and talking to Asaline in the other room. I went over to the sink and dumped some of the coffee out of my mug. Checked over my shoulder, then opened the cabinet where Daddy kept his bottle of Hennessy. I poured a couple glugs into my coffee cup and drank.

We moved to the suburbs in the summer of 1974. Oz was behind the wheel going slow on the tree-lined streets so Pearl could take it all in. She was in the backseat with her face turned to the window. Her jaw was set in a way that said she didn't care one bit for what she was seeing. I leaned forward and turned up the radio. It was the right kind of head-bopping song to lighten things up. *I'm not trying to be your hero . . .* floated out louder through the speakers.

Oz turned the corner onto our street. It looked just like the other streets. Pretty. Pleasant, I guess somebody might say. The yards were kept up nice with flowers and trimmed bushes. Oz glanced over his shoulder at Pearl and pointed to our house.

"That's it right up ahead," he said to his mama. "The tan brick with the big picture window." He sounded somewhere between proud and bragging. "She's going to love it," Oz said, glancing over at me.

He wasn't talking about Pearl, who was looking at the house like she didn't trust what it was up to. The *she* Oz was talking about was Trinity. She was about to have her own bedroom for the first time in her life. What nine-year-old wouldn't love that? Trinity was behind us, riding shotgun in the U-Haul with Tommy.

Tommy had been out of the service for around two years, but he still wasn't quite back. After Tommy survived his first tour in Vietnam, he'd volunteered for another round. I didn't understand why he'd do something like that, and in his say-nothing way, he never told us. The whole thing bothered Oz like nothing else.

When Tommy finally got home, on the night of his welcome-back party—a party specially planned by Oz—Tommy had eased away from the guests and left everybody to celebrate his homecoming without him. Him and Oz had argued after it. I'd only caught little scraps of their conversation and was struck dumb when Tommy said: "You should've let me die that night." There was heartbreak in his voice, but no stutter. Tommy had left the house looking wrecked.

These days, he spent most of his time out on the road. He'd pack up his camping gear in his pickup, Moody Judy, as he called his truck, because she broke down a lot. He'd be gone for months at a time, checking in every now and again on a pay phone from "the desert" or "the ocean" or "the mountains." He showed up when he was needed, like today, looking like a bearded mountain man. But mostly, he was out crisscrossing the country, leaving Oz with the kind of hurt that comes out as anger in a lot of men.

"I'm the one who's always been here for him," Oz had complained to me one time at dinner. "I'm the one who—" He cut himself off and stewed in it for a few days. When I asked him why he didn't just talk to his brother and see what was going on and let him know he missed him, Oz had mumbled: "I already know what's going on." And he hadn't said another word about it since.

I looked in the rearview mirror at Tommy in the U-Haul with Trinity. He was smiling over at her in the passenger seat and scratching the side of his face, his fingers digging into his beard. We pulled into the driveway with Tommy rolling the U-Haul up beside us in the double-car driveway. Trinity popped up and waved out the passenger seat window, excited. I waved back and blew her a kiss. Oz got out of the car, opened the door of the truck for her and caught her when she jumped down. The two of them raced each other to the front door.

As Pearl watched them, she said, "We cain't all run away from Detroit like this. We get a little money and cain't wait to run up behind white folk."

I put my arm through hers in sympathy and looked around at the well-kept-up ranches and two-stories. I'd wanted to stay in Detroit, too. One time, when me and Oz were out touring during our early looking, I'd told him it was important for Trinity to be close to family and it might be good for my career to stay in the city.

He'd shifted his eyes from the road to me and said, "You don't have a career. I wish you'd let that go and just . . . just see what we have now. Can you do that?"

The way he dismissed me and all I'd done—I was shocked. It broke my heart. How was this the same man who'd one time held me in my lowest moment and promised me that it would be all right? How was this the same man who'd hardly ever missed a show? How was this Oz? I went silent on him for the rest of the drive.

He apologized over and over again till he could get me to say I forgave him. I wasn't sure if I did. But I did let him drag me out to the northern suburbs. They were his promised land. It wasn't easy to enter, even with how good Oz was doing at work and how financially fit we were, having saved up plenty during our many years of living up in Pearl's attic. Detroit had its dangers, but the suburbs made me feel at risk in a different kind of way, because they didn't want us out there. Eventually, we found our house in a neighborhood where me and Oz didn't worry, as much, about finding a burning cross on the front lawn.

In that house now, I started the grand tour with where Trinity would sleep, because she was making such a big thing of it. I showed them me and Oz's bedroom. The guest room, where Pearl could stay, if she liked. She made it clear that she did not like. As she was turning this way and that to look around the empty room, I all of a sudden felt a nervous spell. It was a feeling that had started hitting me out of nowhere over the last year. It was like I couldn't catch my breath. Kind of like my stage-fright feeling. I excused myself and went to the bathroom.

"Pull it together, Deborah," I told myself, sounding like Mary used to before she'd push me out onstage. I wished like anything I had a drink. I took some deep breaths. I lowered the lid on the toilet and sat down. When we first went through the house, Oz kept saying, "Isn't it nice? Look at all the windows. It gets a lot of light, just like you wanted." I lit a cigarette and looked around at the nice counter. The nice sink. The nice tub. Nice black tile accents to go with the teal. Everything was so nice.

I tapped ash into the sink and rested my head on the heel of my hand. Tears fell like raindrops.

I jumped at the sound of a knock on the door.

"You all right in there?"

It was Oz.

"Yes. I'm fine. Out in a minute." I wiped my face. It took a second, because the tears wouldn't stop. I took some more deep breaths. It occurred to me that I should flush the toilet, like I'd used it, so I did. I took another couple drags on my cigarette, then stubbed it out and threw it in the toilet. I waited till I could flush again.

"We were about to send out a search party," Oz said as I came out of the bathroom.

"So, I can't go to the bathroom?"

"That's not—" He looked frustrated. "You were just gone for longer than the bathroom should take." He squinted at me through his glasses. He'd gotten rid of the round ones some years back. These were horn-rimmed, like he was all business. I adjusted them on his face. They were always going crooked. The lenses could usually stand to be washed, too, which was the case now. "I was just seeing if you were okay."

"I'm fine, Oz," I said, sliding past him, feeling the weight of him always wanting to know where I was and if I was happy. I found Pearl in the sunken living room. I made my voice sound light as I pointed to this corner or that one, talking about the couch we'd put here or there. I was shaking inside, though. Still with that stage-fright feeling. I couldn't wait to get home and get a drink. As I counted the minutes, I kept talking to Pearl while Tommy, Oz and Trinity went out to unload the U-Haul.

"So, this here's what you want, Deborah?" Pearl asked, interrupting me.

"What?"

"This." She opened her arms, like she was about to hug the whole room.

"Of course. It's—"

"Don't seem like you."

She turned to look out the big picture window. Oz and Tommy were pulling our short blue couch out of the U-Haul. We didn't have much. We'd brought the couch and our bed and a chest of drawers and Trinity's daybed. We had my crates of records, my record player and the flyers I'd kept from the many places I'd performed. We had dishes and pots and pans and a couple lamps. Other than that, there were clothes in suitcases and plastic garbage bags waiting to be carried in.

"Good to see them two together like that," Pearl said, still looking out the window at her sons. "They were so close as boys. I raised them to be that way. But now . . . I worry about them."

"Yeah. Tommy with the war and everything and being so . . . the way he is."

"It's not Thomas I worry about so much," Pearl said. "It's Ozro." I followed her gaze to where Trinity was talking to a little redheaded girl who had come over from across the street. The girl had something cupped in her hands. A mouse or something. Oz and Tommy were headed toward the house carrying the couch, sweating in the summer sun. "Ozro has a need for things to be a certain way," Pearl went on. "His idea of good. Like he's trying to keep a handle on a lot that ain't got nothing to do with the here and now."

"I don't understand," I said.

"That's probably best." She stepped up out of the living room. "I'mma go outside and see what this little girl's about, out here with Trinity." And then she was gone.

Oz

1975

Oz came home and found Deborah alone. She was sitting at the kitchen table having a glass of wine in the middle of the afternoon. She seemed surprised when she looked through the cutout to the kitchen and saw him coming through the garage door. She pushed the wine away, like it wasn't hers. Like a friend might show up and fill the empty chair next to her and drink it.

Deborah got to her feet and asked him, "Shouldn't you be at work?"

"Shouldn't you be doing something other than drinking in the middle of the day?"

"Shouldn't you be doing something other than checking up on me?"

"Well, if you would do what you should be doing, instead of that"—he glanced at the wineglass—"I wouldn't feel the need to check up on you."

He went over and snatched up the glass from the table. He smacked Deborah's hand away when she tried to take it back, a little harder than he intended, apparently, because she cradled her hand to her chest. He didn't apologize. He wasn't the one who should be apologizing for this. He stalked over to the sink. He dumped the glass, staring at her the whole time. He held her gaze until she looked away, ashamed.

"I wasn't checking up on you, by the way," he said, rinsing and drying the glass. After he put it away in the cabinet, he walked over to her and turned around to show her the back of his pants. "I'm here for this." He'd managed to split the seam of his pants getting out of his car at work. It had happened right before he was supposed to give a presentation to "the bosses." Somehow, he'd managed to hide the split by keeping his suit jacket in just the right place and keeping his behind out of view. "Can you fix it?"

That was a ridiculous question. Deborah could fix anything when it came to needles, thread, fabric and patterns. She made a lot of Trinity's clothes—smocks with matching pants were a specialty—and sewed in her own personalized labels.

Deborah smoothed her hair and opened her mouth to say something, then stopped.

"I'm sorry," Oz said, suddenly feeling bad about smacking her hand like that. It just happened. He didn't mean it.

Deborah nodded and said it was okay. That things had been hard. She went over and rummaged through her sewing cabinet next to the refrigerator, getting out her straight pins. The cabinet was a mess of threads and patterns and fabric remnants that Oz could never tolerate. He wasn't sure how she found anything in there. She waved him up on a stool.

"Hold still," she said as he wobbled a little.

"Careful, woman."

"Just let me see this . . ." she mumbled around the straight pins between her lips. "I've been wanting to get this waistband." The pants had never fit quite right in the waist. She got that pinned, then did the same with the split, without poking him. She waved him down. "Your pants, please."

He took them off and tossed them to her. As he stood there in his dress shirt, tie and underwear, he watched her lay the pants out on the counter. Her forehead was knotted up in concentration as she pressed the creases with her hand and carefully folded them.

She looked up at him and did a double take. "Why're you looking at me like that?"

"Like what?"

"You know like what." She looked down at his crotch. He clearly wanted her. She took off running. He chased her through the house. There was plenty of room to run because there was hardly any furniture to dodge. Over the whole year, Deborah had managed to buy only the kitchen table and chairs, even though there was plenty of money and she had a surplus of free time. It was as if she hadn't yet committed to the place.

Oz caught up with her and cornered her in the living room. She fought him off half-heartedly, swinging his pants at him. She let him push her to the floor and they made love on the carpet, with the sun streaming in warm and bright. Afterward, Oz lay there feeling nothing but good. They whispered and laughed about Oz's old sweater vests and what a dud he was at parties. He got quiet at that last memory. He didn't like being reminded of what Deborah used to do. It made him think too much about what he'd done. But he told himself he'd done the right thing because they had a good life now. She just needed to try to be happy in it. He rose up on his elbow and traced the freckles on her cheek.

"I know you don't like it," he said quietly. "But I think we can be happy here."

Deborah smoothed his mustache and touched the high bridge of his nose.

"We just need a clean slate," he said.

"Cleaned of what?"

He shrugged, thinking about all of the grime on his slate. "Anything you might have done to me or anything I might have done to you. Anything we might have done to anybody. Let's just let it be nothing."

"Anything we've done?" She sat up on her elbows.

Oz laughed, but it didn't sound right. "Look at you. Always so serious. I'm just saying . . . whatever." He glanced at his watch. "I should go."

"No." She pushed his arm down to hide his watch.

"You know I can't be late." Oz was keenly aware of being the only black man in the office for miles. He could make no mistakes. No missteps. Even a small one could ruin him. He got to his feet, even as Deborah reached for him again. He headed back to the bedroom to find a new suit. He glanced back to see Deborah hugging her knees to her chest and staring at their ugly, old blue couch. The only piece of furniture in the room.

Oz got dressed and went straight to the kitchen. He yelled out to ask Deborah if she wanted a sandwich. She said no. He made two ham sandwiches for himself and went to say goodbye. Deborah was pulling her blouse over her head when Oz stepped down into the living room with his ham sandwiches in hand, one half-gone already and the other wrapped in wax paper for later. He gave her a quick peck on the lips and she frowned.

"You taste like mayonnaise," she said.

He shrugged and said goodbye but paused at the step-up out of the living room. "I'll probably be late tonight," he said. "This stop home put me a little behind. You and Trin go ahead and eat without me." He stepped up, then paused again. "Any luck? With any of the women around here? Some of them might be okay to hang out with, don't you think?"

"What do you think?"

Deborah and the mother of Trinity's little friend from across the street would wave from the porch or driveway when they saw each other. They'd sometimes even meet in the middle of the road to say hi or something about the girls, if they were down by the road getting the mail at the same time, but Deborah generally did not feel comfortable with the other wives and Oz was wary, too. He'd found a letter in their mailbox a couple of weeks after moving in: *Don't give your nigger friends any ideas about joining you out here.* He and Deborah had no idea who'd sent it. Not a single neighbor was mean to them. Most of them waved or nodded when they saw them outside. The woman next door, Mrs. Neilson, had even brought over a vanilla pound cake after they'd moved in. But the letter had come from someone. So, they trusted no one.

"Well, don't just sit up in this house like this. Go visit with Pearl or—"

"Don't you have to get to work?"

"I'm just trying to . . . never mind."

He went out to the garage. But instead of leaving, he went around to the back of the house and watched Deborah through the window. She tossed his pants on the kitchen counter, then went to the cabinet and got down a glass. She poured herself some more wine. She sat down at the table again with a cigarette. Oz wondered how long she would sit there. Until Trinity got home from school? Was she like this every day?

He wanted to go in and shake some sense into her. Make her see that all she had to do was try. Why couldn't this life be enough? But he didn't go back in the house. He went around to his car and back to work.

Deborah

The Wiz was all Trinity could talk about, so when the show came around in the spring of 1978, we decided to make a night of it. After we got through the Fisher Theatre's golden doors and settled in our seats, Oz leaned over me and told Trinity, "One time, me and your mama saw the Supremes here."

"Uh-huh," Trinity said, with the *couldn't care less* tone of the preteen she was. She was huddled close together with her friend, Virginia, the little redheaded, green-eyed girl who'd come over from across the street the day we moved in. Virginia had a strange way of looking at adults without breaking eye contact—I don't think the girl blinked at all—and she'd introduced Trinity to hamsters and guinea pigs, which I didn't appreciate. But I was happy Trinity had her.

Still, friend or no friend, I worried. Trinity was alone in that neighborhood and that school. I was reminded of that every time she came home with questions like, "What's a porch monkey?" Oz said she'd grow a thick skin, but I didn't want my child to have to harden herself in order to go to school or just exist in the world.

Oz tapped my shoulder. "When were we here last? Sixty-eight? Sixty-nine?"

"Sixty-eight," I said, shifting in my seat and feeling the whole mood of the night shift with that question. That had been a full decade ago, back when I just knew I'd be a star. Had time gotten away from me that fast?

In the lobby at intermission, Oz gave a history lesson on the Fisher Building and its architecture, which put me in the mind of a real fancy cathedral with its arches and sophisticated paintings on the ceiling. "It was built in 1928 . . ." he read, straight from the brochure, while Trinity and Virginia sipped ginger ales, a special grown-up drink we'd let them have for the occasion. I took a swig of my tonic water. I was careful about drinking when I was out with Oz. He was noticing too much. I gazed around the crowded lobby, looking at nothing in particular, but my eyes caught on a familiar face. I stared for a second. I was pretty sure . . .

I tugged on Oz's sleeve. "I think that's Mary over there."

He glanced up from the brochure. "Who?"

"From my old group!"

I'd only seen Mary a couple times since she moved out East with Lloyd. She was leaning against a marble column, talking to another woman. When she saw me waving from across the room, there was half a tick of hesitation before she recognized me. I had a little pixie cut now, which was shorter than I'd ever worn my hair before, but I otherwise looked like myself. Me and Mary met in the middle of the lobby and threw ourselves into each other's arms, but careful not to spill our drinks. I found myself for a few seconds paying more attention to Mary's drink than to her. She was holding a glass of bourbon, neat. I thought of our good-luck shots and how I'd hold mine in my mouth for a few seconds before swallowing because I loved the sweet warmth of it.

"Well, look at you!" Mary said, holding me at arm's length so she could do just that.

"Look at me? Look at you!"

Mary had never been a beauty, but she was all right now, with her perfectly shaped afro and professionally tweezed eyebrows. She put me in the mind of Foxy Brown. She told me she was living in L.A. and was mainly into acting these days. She'd had a small part on *Days of Our Lives*, she said. She wanted to know if I watched the show and if I'd seen her.

I told her no on both counts.

But as she described her appearance as a nurse, I knew exactly the scene she was talking about. I'd been sitting on the couch watching *Days of Our Lives* like I did all the time when there popped up Mary on the screen, talking to Dr. Horton. I'd jumped to my feet, dancing around the living room, wanting to tell somebody, *Hey! That's Mary! We used to sing together!* But Oz was at work. Trinity was at school. I'd stood there through the rest of the show with every ounce of joy seeping out of me. What was wrong with me? I'd never wanted to be an actress. But still . . . I stopped watching *Days* for weeks, out of fear I might see Mary again. I'd roam the house looking for things to do, with the radio on for company. I'd sit at the kitchen table with a cup of iced tea, trying not to drink, till the quietness of the house made my ears hurt and I just had to pour myself a glass of wine or something stronger.

As Mary wrapped up her story about the show, she looked over to where Oz and Trinity were standing. Oz was eyeing us from across the room, his forehead scrunched up, like he was trying to figure something out. Trinity was pointing up at the arched ceiling, talking to Virginia.

"She's beautiful, Deborah," Mary said of Trinity. "She was just a little thing, last I saw her." She added, almost begrudgingly, "And how's Potato Boy?"

"Mary . . ." I cautioned.

"Sorry. And how've you been, Deborah?"

I told her life was just the way me and Oz had planned it. But every word I said echoed as I led her down the empty corridors of my life.

"Sounds wonderful," Mary said. Was that pity in her voice? She cleared her throat. "So, you still singing?"

"No. Too much going on."

She looked over at Oz. "Just as long as you're happy." She paused. "Losing that contract, that was, um, big. You ever talk about that with Oz?"

"Yes, well, I mean after it happened. Of course. He was a comfort, like always."

Her eyes went hard as she kept staring at Oz. She'd never really liked him, but the way she was looking at him was different than I'd ever known from her. "It was hard on Lloyd," Mary said in a real quiet voice.

"I'm sure it was." I didn't have sympathy for Lloyd, up and running off like he had, with no explanation, leaving us to fall apart. "It was a bad time for all of us."

I followed her hard stare over to Oz. Oz looked queasy. I tilted my head as I looked at him, like that might help me figure out what was going on with him and Mary.

Mary turned her eyes back to me. "It was good to see you, Deborah," she said. "I'll let you get back to your family." She reached out and hugged me, then pulled away, glancing at Oz again. She got ready to speak, then stopped. Finally, she said: "If ever you're not happy, you got reason. Call me."

Oz

During an interminable intermission, Oz watched Deborah and Mary across the lobby. He was too far away to hear anything, and he couldn't read lips, but he was good at translating Deborah's body language. She was smiling. She tilted her chin up and straightened herself until her posture was even more perfect than usual. Every few seconds or so, she'd smooth her paisley skirt along her hips, for no reason. She moved like that when she was uncomfortable. When Deborah's gaze met Oz's, she tilted her head, like she was trying to figure him out.

Deborah joined him, Trinity and Trinity's friend as they went back to their seats. But for the rest of the show, she was as silent as stone. For as long as they'd been together, from their very first date, she had interrupted every movie, TV show or play to give him running critiques. But not now. She didn't grab his arm and whisper: *This doesn't make sense* or *That song is silly* or *She/he can't act.*

When they got home, he said good night to his daughter and she gave him an awkward side hug. Hugs, conversations—they were all harder now that Trinity was growing up. She wasn't the giggly, curious little girl she used to be. She spent most of her time whispering secrets to her friend and, more and more, disagreeing with anything he had to say. He thought of her like a beloved book that was rewriting itself. Sometimes, in a language he did not understand.

As Trinity went off to bed, Deborah went to the cabinet and got down a glass.

"You can't lay off for just one night?" Oz asked. "Just one?"

As if in answer, she filled the glass to the brim with a white wine she'd pulled from the refrigerator. She drank deeply, looking at him over the lip of the glass the whole time.

This enraged Oz. He yanked the glass from her hand, sending wine splashing down the front of her dress and all over the floor. When she reached for the glass, he threw it in the sink, where it shattered. They stood staring at each other.

"What?" Oz yelled finally.

"Did you have an affair? Mary . . ." Her voice shrank and disappeared, even as her lips moved and her eyes filled with tears.

Oz blinked. It wasn't the question he'd expected. "Affair?" He shook his head. "Deborah—"

"Don't lie to me. Do you think I'm blind? Do you think I'm stupid? Do you think I couldn't see the way Mary kept looking over at you? It wasn't right. Something's not right . . ." She paced in front of the refrigerator, hugging herself. "She told me to call her." Deborah stopped and leveled her eyes on him. "I'll call her, Oz. I will. And she'll tell me."

He glanced out the window over the sink to the dark backyard, where the outlines of bushes and flower beds were visible in the dim light. He'd planted all of that with Trinity, not long after they'd moved into the house. He'd knelt beside her, just as his father had knelt beside him, explaining the importance of good, rich soil and the significance of every season.

More than that, Oz had cultivated and grown his family. This was all he had. This was what kept him steady. He turned back to his wife, with the words right there on his tongue. He would tell her about the contract. He would tell her about Lloyd. He would even tell her about his life before her and how the unspoken truth of it had led him—all of them—to this moment. But she would never forgive him. All of this—the very man he'd made himself into—everything he had, would be gone.

He opened his mouth and spoke: "I did it. I mean, yes. An affair. With . . ." He paused, considering a name. "It doesn't matter. It was nothing, Deborah. Nothing. I promise."

"Nothing?" Deborah collapsed like a rag doll suddenly left to stand on her own. Oz knelt beside her, trying to pick her up. But she kicked him as he grabbed at her flailing arms. She clawed him down the side of his face when he tried to restrain her. He managed to get her in a bear hug and hold her still, close to his body.

"Get out of my house!" She was trembling against him.

Oz let her go and she curled into a ball on the floor. He backed away, his hands in the air like he was giving himself up. "Deborah, just . . ." But what could he say? He went out to the garage and got in his car. He drove aimlessly for hours. *A woman can get over a cheating man,* Oz told himself. It was almost natural. He'd seen his mother do it. The wives and girlfriends of colleagues had done it. Deborah would, too. But she would never get over the truth.

The sun was up when he got home. Deborah was Frankenstein walking from the refrigerator to the counter, holding a package of ham. Her eyes were half-closed. She was hungover. Maybe still drunk. She stood over the paper sack she had open on the counter. Trinity's name was written on it, with a heart over the *i*. Next to the bag was a Twinkie. A lidless jar of mayonnaise. There were two slices of white bread, stacked one atop the other.

Deborah looked at Oz with bloodshot eyes. "Give her some

lunch money." Her voice was rough and splintered. She turned and shuffled out of the kitchen, holding on to the counter, reaching for the doorframe, then the wall, as she slowly, unsteadily made her way. At the sound of the bedroom door closing, Oz looked down at himself. His shirt and pants were a wrinkled mess. He went back to the bedroom. The curtains were closed against the morning light. Deborah was a small ball on her side of the bed. Oz had just intended to get his clothes out of the closet and go. But he was drawn to her. He started to crawl in bed beside her.

"Don't touch me," she said.

He knelt there for a moment on his undisturbed side of the bed, then got up. He grabbed a suit, a fresh shirt and a tie out of the closet and went to the living room to get dressed for work.

He was in the kitchen riffling through his wallet for lunch money when Trinity caught him. He'd hoped to leave the cash and be gone by the time she came searching for breakfast.

"God, Dad! What happened to your face?"

Oz put his hand to the scratches. They stung. "Nothing. I just . . ." What the hell was he going to say at work? They'd notice. They noticed everything about him.

Trinity was looking around the kitchen. "Where's Mom?"

"Sleeping."

Trinity's eyes narrowed on him. Deborah was as dependable as a new morning—no matter how bad the hangover.

He pulled a twenty out of his wallet. "Here's some lunch money. Your mama couldn't make lunch."

Trinity went over to the counter, as if looking for evidence. The lunch bag sat open and empty. The package of ham and two slices of bread were still sitting beside it. As was the mayonnaise with its lid off. And the Twinkie.

Oz held the money out to her again. "Here. Take this and go on to school now. Or, I don't know, make your own lunch. Everything's here."

"It's not time yet."

"Goddamn it, Trinity, then just . . . go somewhere!"

He slammed the twenty on the counter.

She flinched and backed away, covering her mouth, like she'd seen something unspeakable.

"Stop it!" Oz said.

She backed away again.

"I said stop it! You act like I'm going to hurt you or something!"

Tears were in her eyes. And it dawned on him that he'd never raised his voice with her. He'd scared her. She turned and went back to her room.

He stared off down the empty hall for a second. He looked around at the scattered lunch fixings and screwed the lid on the mayonnaise. Then he hurled the jar at the kitchen cabinet. He watched the white glob ooze down a cabinet door. He thought about talking to Tommy, someone who might understand him. But he let that idea go quickly.

The last time he'd talked to Tommy was three weeks ago. Tommy had called from Florida, where he was camping out in the Panhandle. Oz was sweaty from working in the yard and itching to get off the phone and take a shower. But Tommy was unusually chatty, so Oz had stood with the kitchen phone cradled against his shoulder, listening impatiently, shifting his weight from one foot to the other as Tommy went on about white beaches and orange sunsets. Then, Tommy said something that made Oz freeze where he stood. It was the exact thing Tommy had said after skipping out on the homecoming party Oz had thrown for him after Vietnam. "I'm trying to figure it out," Tommy said, "all the things w-w-w-we tried to run away from. In leaving Alabama." There was a pause. "I swear, sometimes I wish you'd let me die that night. W-w-w-we might both be better for it."

Oz had taken the phone from his ear and slowly placed the receiver in the cradle. He'd backed away from it, as if it were a bomb counting down to detonation. He'd taken a shower, dressed and gone down to his basement office to work, as if Tommy had said nothing at all. Over the following days, then weeks, Oz had studiously avoided answering the phone, fearing it might be Tommy calling from the road.

He leaned on the kitchen counter now and closed his eyes. It was all coming apart, this carefully cultivated life of his. The unspoken truth of it all, shared with his brother, was becoming an intolerable whisper in his head that he needed to quiet. He opened his eyes and set about cleaning the mayonnaise from the cabinet and the floor. He threw the jagged shards of the jar away. He put the ham back in the refrigerator and the bread back in the bag. He put the Twinkie in the box where it belonged. He flattened and folded Trinity's lunch bag so she could use it another time. He grabbed his briefcase and his keys and went to work. As if nothing at all had happened.

Deborah and Trinity became like a fortress against Oz, with their thick walls of silence. And when Deborah would speak, it was mostly to threaten to leave him. Everything Deborah did seemed calculated to punish him. She would leave the house and be gone for hours, with no explanation, which infuriated him. She stopped cooking dinner. She wouldn't sleep in the same bed with him. He and Deborah argued all the time. She made him so angry sometimes. Without thinking, once, he'd thrown a full dinner plate that had barely missed her head. He'd shocked Deborah—but not himself, necessarily.

Oz came to dread going home, so he stayed at work. He'd sit at his desk, doodling in one of his notebooks, remembering the lies he'd told and trying not to think about what Tommy had said. Once, he'd written *Just tell her*, but he'd only stared at the page, then closed the book and let the words disappear among his doodles of cars and faces without features.

He used to work hard while at the office late, but not anymore. Some time ago, he'd realized his work was going unnoticed. After a couple of promotions early on, he'd been in the same job for years, despite all the pats on the back. Despite swallowing remarks that ranged from clueless to racist. Despite the repeated declarations that "Oz is one of our rising stars!" He'd been passed over more times than he could count.

Work was as miserable as his marriage.

When Deborah's father died in the summer of 1981, they took his body home to Mississippi. Deborah asked Oz to go with her to the funeral. She had not asked anything important of him since his "confession." Over the past year, they had settled into a new normal. It was a routine of "trying," which meant self-conscious date nights. Fewer arguments. Spontaneous emotional outbursts from Deborah. Outbursts that would have Oz sheltering in his basement office, as if her tears were a tornado and he need only wait for the storm to pass.

Oz felt like Deborah's request for him to go with her to the funeral was a test. Was he truly sorry? He reminded her that he did not like churches. He reminded her where they'd gotten married, as if he needed to. He reminded her that he had not attended his own father's funeral. Not inside the church, anyway. She did not press him. But her grief was ambient. It filled every space in their home. When it met with Oz's guilt, he agreed to go.

The minute he and Deborah took their seats at the service, he knew he'd made a mistake. He could not get comfortable in the confines of the church pew. Deborah gave him sharp glances every time he moved. His Mahalia Jackson–adorned paper fan, identical to the ones fluttering in almost every other hand, proved useless at cutting through the heat that had inched over eighty degrees. He had not been down South since leaving Alabama in 1962, when he was seventeen. He tried to focus on the service to keep himself from thinking about just how close he suddenly felt to everything he, Pearl and Tommy thought they'd gotten away from. For them, it had been more than poverty and the humiliations of Jim Crow. For them, it had been life. It had been death. It had been the reason Tommy had said, "Sometimes, I wish you'd let me die that night."

Oz tried to quiet his thoughts. He focused on the hat on the head of the woman in front of him, trying to name each flower. The hat was black with black daisies and a sizable black mum. What were the other flowers, all done in black? Even as he tried to keep himself grounded with his guessing game, his mind jumped the state line and landed in Alabama, on the day of his own father's funeral.

On that day, Oz had stood across the street as everyone filed into the church. He'd watched through one of the windows as mourners walked past a casket that had to be closed because of the condition of the body. There was not much of a body left. They all gave their condolences to Pearl. She didn't deserve it, Oz thought. She was to blame for so much, including the fact that Oz could not bring himself to enter that church. He went back across the street to watch and wait in the swelter of that June day. Two hours later,

Pearl emerged from the service dry-eyed and unreadable. Tommy's face was a pained grimace as he struggled to carry the casket with the other pallbearers. His hands were still bandaged from what he and Oz had endured a week before. Oz's forehead and cheek were flecked with painful cuts from shattered glass. Oz caught his brother's eye from across the street. He knew what Tommy was thinking and shook his head. He could not join. It was all he could do to stand there and bear witness. Tommy nodded. He understood. Oz did not stay to watch them load the casket into the hearse. He could not bear that. He knew his father would be carried away and buried soon enough. He was doing his best to put everything to rest.

But he was restless now, as he sat uncomfortably beside Deborah in the church pew. Everything in him felt unsettled as her voice rose to join the congregation in singing, *I see a band of angels . . . and they're coming after me . . . Ain't no grave . . . can hold my body down . . .* A chill went through Oz even as everyone around him fanned hard against the heat. It was the cold realization that, yes, he'd tried to hide himself behind a Midwestern accent, new ways and the love of his family. And, yes, he'd tried to bury the truth of who he was along with his father. But he was suddenly seeing a kind of resurrection, as he stared in despair at the open casket at the foot of the altar.

When Oz got home from Mississippi, he immediately went back to the bedroom he shared with Deborah, dropped his suitcase and opened the top drawer of the chest of drawers. He reached to the back to grab the cigar box he kept in there. He opened the brass closure to reveal a smaller box inside. That smaller box held a ring. He hadn't opened the boxes since leaving Alabama, though the ring had called to him many times, perhaps loudest on that night in

1967 when Detroit erupted into a fiery Armageddon. He took the ring out and held it in the palm of his hand. He saw the hand that had once worn it reaching up through a cloud of smoke. His father appeared to him, short and bespectacled, like he was in life. Oz heard his voice and his familiar words: *Every evil you do, son, it'll catch up to you. In time.*

He dropped the ring back in its box and slammed the drawer shut.

Deborah was there, her eyes full of suspicion. She did not trust him now. His anger, his silences, his late nights at work—they were all signs of betrayal to her.

"What is that, Oz?" she asked, looking at the chest of drawers.

"Nothing."

"Oz—"

"Nothing!"

As she came near, he shoved her back. Hard. She stumbled and slammed into the doorframe. Oz hadn't meant to push her that hard. He hadn't meant to push her at all. "I'm sorry," he said, reaching to help her.

She waved his hand away as she gazed up at him from the floor. Was that shock and terror in her eyes?

Oz stumbled back, unnerved. *Look what you've done . . . Again.* "I didn't—"

"What's wrong with you, Oz? Have you lost your mind?" She rubbed her back and grimaced.

He backed away. Had he lost it? He looked at his hands, as if they had a mind and a will of their own. He crossed his arms and trapped his hands under them. He'd meant to keep her safe. And yet, there she was, pulling herself off the floor, rubbing her back from where he'd hurt her.

"I'm sorry," he said.

Oz drove home from a late night at work. Traffic was light on I-75. The black Pontiac in front of him was barely going above the speed limit. Still, he stayed behind it at some distance in the right lane. Then, he closed his eyes and kept them that way. He pressed the accelerator. His pulse quickened. His grip tightened on the steering wheel. The engine hummed and his Cadillac vibrated. He gave it more gas and imagined the crash before it happened. He yelled. His eyes flew open. He saw that he was just short of tapping the Pontiac's bumper. He slammed on the brakes and pitched forward. He loosened his tie as he fought to catch his breath. He pulled off the highway onto a road he did not know. He turned into the parking lot of a large Presbyterian church and took the ring out of his pocket—he had started carrying it now. Oz held it up, as if he could see through it to another dimension.

"Why are you here now?" He was speaking to his father. But in thinking about that funeral and about how he'd pushed Deborah and about the lies—all of the lies—Oz knew the answer to that question. "Please . . . just let me be," he said. "Like before."

There was an eviscerating silence in response, and he got back on the road.

At home, he sat in the garage until he felt like he could go inside and be who Deborah and Trinity expected. He heard the television going in the family room as he opened the door to the kitchen. When he walked by, he peeked in and said hello. His wife and daughter were sitting together on the couch watching *The Facts of Life*. They looked surprised to see him. He went on. He did not have it in him to feign interest in whatever Trinity had done at school or whatever was upsetting Deborah.

In the bathroom, he stripped down to take a shower. While he waited for the water to get hot, he stood in front of the mirror and did something he hadn't done in a long time. He practiced his vowel sounds—*A, E, I, O, U*—and said his words—*I can't. Good afternoon. How are you all?* Everything came out sounding desperate and choked. Not like him at all. He'd worked so hard to lose every vestige of who he used to be. But to become who?

He stared at his reflection as a mist settled on the mirror. Oz had always looked a lot like his father. Through the gathering steam, it was as if the face staring back at him *was* his father's. Oz blinked and wiped the condensation away, but nothing changed. He put his hand to the mirror, as if he could feel the high cheekbones, the straight nose, the dark stubble on his chin.

"You weren't so old, were you?" Oz whispered, half expecting his father's soft voice to come to him and remind him that he was only thirty-seven when he died. *Parents seem so old when you are young,* Oz thought. But here was Oz, his thirty-seventh birthday just weeks away. It was as if they were meeting here—a generation apart, but at the same stage in life. Oz squeezed his eyes shut again, then opened them. It was the same face staring back at him, but there was shock and terror in his father's eyes now. The last thing Oz had seen when he'd looked upon his father's face for the last time.

Though he barely had an appetite, Oz got dressed and went back in the kitchen to find his dinner. He was pulling his foil-wrapped plate out of the oven when he heard Deborah.

"How was work?"

He glanced over at her through the cutout in the wall. She had one hand on the kitchen table as if to brace herself. Her eyes were glassy in that dim light. She was wearing her nightgown with the daisies on it.

"Fine," he said. "The usual. You know."

"No. I don't know."

He pulled back the foil on the plate. Steak with onions and mushrooms. Mashed potatoes and green beans. "Don't be crazy," he said. He went over and tossed the foil in the garbage.

"I'm a lot of things," Deborah said, "but I'm not crazy." She lowered herself into the chair, as if coming to rest after a long journey. "We hardly see you. And when you're here, you're not here. I've tried, Oz." Tears slid down her cheeks. "What am I doing wrong? Just tell me." She held her hands out. Not reaching for him, but more to show the emptiness, Oz thought.

He stared down at his plate. Then he pushed back from the kitchen counter and went through the doorway to where she was. He stooped down and grabbed her hands. They were warm and soft. She smelled of wine and toothpaste. A reflexive flash of rage went through him about the drinking, but then it was gone. And he felt nothing at all. Just numb.

He looked at Deborah's wet cheeks. At her mouth, which was a perfect Cupid's bow. He remembered her smiling that first smile at him. Deborah dancing with him. Deborah singing. She did not sing anymore, not even around the house. He squeezed her hands.

"You don't have to do anything. It's just . . . I've got a lot on my mind. That's all."

"I'm sorry about that. We can talk, you know?"

"I'm fine," Oz said. "Just not feeling like myself." He went back to his dinner.

Tommy called Oz out of the blue. It was to meet for lunch to celebrate Oz's thirty-seventh birthday. Oz thought maybe Deborah had asked him to do it. Tommy wasn't traveling so much these days, but there was still distance between the brothers. It had grown out of Tommy having said he wished Oz would have let him die and Oz hanging up without a word. They hadn't spoken about it since, though they did see each other from time to time at family get-togethers. It was so uncomfortable that Oz had considered saying no when Tommy called, but then he thought again. He missed his brother. And Oz finally wanted to talk about it all. Needed to. It was eating him alive.

Oz looked out his office window. People were down on the sidewalks in light jackets or no coats at all. The first of October, and it was a beautiful Indian summer day. He grabbed the spreadsheets he'd been looking at and put them in his briefcase so he wouldn't forget to take them home tonight. He closed up the case and set it beside his desk. He left his suit jacket draped over the back of the chair and walked the few blocks to the restaurant in the sunshine.

The little mom-and-pop place where Oz was meeting Tommy was a blue and silver shrine to the Lions with a few tables and plastic chairs that didn't encourage lingering. But it was clean enough and the ribs were good. Tommy was already there when Oz arrived. Tommy waved him over as if the place was huge and a flag-down was necessary.

Tommy stood and hugged Oz like a long-lost friend. Or brother.

Oz was barely settled into his uncomfortable chair before Tommy asked him, "So, h-h-h-how you been?"

"Good. And you?"

"Can't complain."

Oz nodded, not quite knowing what to say.

Rosco, the counter guy, tall and bouncer big, came over and dropped their plates in front of them.

"Thought I'd go ahead and order," Tommy said. "I know you don't usually have a lot of time."

Oz thanked him and looked at the spread. A half slab of ribs with slaw and macaroni and cheese for each of them. Rosco hovered at the table, talking to Tommy and Oz about the Lions and how he thought they were going to do against the Bears. Rosco had concerns and needed to hear that everything was going to be all right. When he left, the two brothers laughed about it, then looked at each other like they both had something to say but didn't quite know how to say it. They smiled awkwardly, then concentrated on their plates. Tommy looked up occasionally to share a story from the barbershop where he worked. Tommy had good stories about the men who sat in his chair and the absurdity, the monotony, the poignancy of their lives. When Tommy's plate was nearly clean and his stories fully told, he leaned back and asked Oz, "So, how you been? Really?"

Oz felt the weight of the ring in his pocket. He reached in and closed his hand around it. The ring was as warm as it had been on the night it slipped from their father's sweaty hand. He took the gold band out of his pocket and put it on the table between them.

"W-w-w-what's that?"

"His wedding ring."

Horror rippled across Tommy's face and he recoiled, sitting as far back in his chair as he could. "W-w-w-where'd you get that?"

Oz held his brother's gaze in silence.

Tommy looked away.

Oz sat back and rubbed his eyes. They were tired. He hadn't been sleeping. "Lately I've been . . . I've been remembering him. A lot, Tommy. Since, you know, Deborah's daddy's funeral . . . and our conversation. Since you said what you said."

"Don't do that."

Oz rubbed his eyes again. He rubbed his whole face, as if scrubbing it clean. "I keep remembering this time when I was walking home with him. We were on that dirt road between the house and the church. I was, I don't know, eight or nine. Remember when I stole that boy's marbles?"

Tommy nodded.

"Daddy was asking me what kind of punishment I thought I deserved—"

"Of course he l-l-l-let you pick your punishment," Tommy cut in.

Oz looked down at the table, feeling gutted. When it came to Tommy, there had never been a question about punishments— rhetorical or otherwise. Tommy's punishments had always come swiftly. Frequently. With uniform brutality.

One of those punishments appeared right before Oz's eyes:

He and Tommy are boys. Oz is ten. Tommy is eight and small for his age. Pearl has Tommy on her hip, moving toward the back door of their house in Alabama. There are angry welts and open wounds on Tommy's legs from where a leather strap has split the skin from ankle to thigh.

"Hurry, Mama," Oz says. He's several steps ahead of Pearl and his eyes are flicking nervously around their dirt patch of a backyard. Oz is worried that she won't go. But she is in arm's reach of the door, as close as she's ever come to leaving. Oz runs ahead of her, cutting through the peanut field, which is an eruption of yellow blooms. He hears Pearl breathing hard behind him. Then, as if out of nowhere, there is his father on the edge of the field with his shotgun slung over his shoulder, striding in their direction. He is not a big man or at all physically imposing. In his soft-spoken way, he asks Pearl where they're going.

"Nowhere," she says. "Just . . . nowhere."

Oz's father looks at him, his eyes sad and confused. "You gon' leave me, too?" Oz immediately feels guilty. But he is doing this for Tommy. He'd imagined himself coming back home to check that his father was okay and helping out on the farm.

Pearl lets Tommy down and his sweat-drenched face contorts into the very image of agony. Tommy collapses to the ground. Oz puts his arm around his little brother's waist to hoist him up.

"Y'all stick together," Pearl says as she walks ahead with their father.

They all go back to the house in silence. Inside the house, Pearl asks if she can clean Tommy up. Get some salve to put on his legs, which are now caked with blood and dirt from the field.

Oz Senior shakes his head. "He need to learn, Pearl. How many times I done told you?" He pauses and lets out an exasperated sigh. "That's the boy's problem. You always coddling him."

As Tommy settles uncomfortably, painfully, on the couch, Oz Senior dares him to sit with his legs crossed again in the sissified way that had gotten him in trouble in the first place.

"Be a man," Oz Senior says. Then he leans forward to hold Tommy in a stare. "And talk like one, too. Not like some damn stuttering fool. In fact—" He gets up from his chair and grabs Tommy's bony arm, pulling him from the couch. He nudges him in the direction of the kitchen, with Tommy grimacing and falling, then shuffling along stiff-legged.

Pearl is on her feet. "Please. He ain't done nothing. It's me. I'm—"

"Quiet, please, Pearl," he says.

Pearl eases down in her seat with her hand to her mouth, rocking back and forth. Oz Senior points Tommy to a chair at the kitchen table. He disappears, then reappears with a bowl and slides it in front of Tommy. He reaches in and pulls out a hot pepper.

"This here's for the Father," he says, holding it up. He plucks another pepper from the bowl. "This one for the Son." He reaches in again. "And this one for the Holy Ghost." While Oz Senior cannot read the Bible, he has much of it memorized. And when he can't remember, he improvises. He drops all three peppers back in the bowl and says, "You eat every one of 'em and it'll fix that stuttering. And even burn that sissy outta you. See, a faggot cain't stand fiery judgment. You understand?"

Tommy nods.

Their father pats his cheek and says, "Good boy."

He walks back to the main room where Pearl and Oz are. He sits in his chair, looking exhausted. Oz is sitting on the floor, stealing glances at his brother. Tommy is at the table with his bloody, dirt-caked legs dangling like raw meat. Some of the wounds are weeping blood through the dirt. Tommy starts in on one of the peppers, and his nose begins to run. Tears and snot stream down his face. It is the first time he has cried through all of it, and Oz suspects it is the heat from the pepper, because Tommy, as little as he is, as many bare-legged beatings as he's taken for crossing his legs like a girl, as many times as he's been called a sissy and a stuttering faggot—he has never been a crier.

Oz tries to signal him. To tell him he will figure out a way to come through the kitchen and eat the peppers. But Tommy does not look up from the bowl.

"Now, Ozro," his father says, "I know what you thinking, 'cause you a good boy. But you gotta let him handle his own, all right? We all gotta handle our own." Oz Senior gets up and comes over to where Oz is sitting. He kneels down. "He need to be a man." He touches Oz's chest. "Like you." He touches his own chest. "Like me. I didn't have no daddy to show me the way. Just your grandmama. You know that. But y'all got me. And I'mma show y'all right from wrong. That's my job, son."

Oz doesn't know what to think. He looks to Pearl on the couch, but she has slipped away. He can hear her crying in her bedroom behind a closed door. His father pats him affectionately on the cheek, just as he did with Tommy, then stands and walks back to the bedroom. "Let me go check on your mama."

Oz hears their murmuring from behind the closed door. He catches his father saying, *It's all gon' be all right . . . Tommy understand.* He hears Tommy sniffling and choking in the kitchen. He puts his hands over his ears and runs outside. He runs through the field, his feet getting tangled up in peanut plants and tearing away a spray of yellow flowers. He doesn't know what to do, so he keeps running until his feet find the road. And the road dead-ends.

Oz blinked and it was as if the years had flown by and here he was sitting across the table from his brother again, both of them fully grown. Though, Oz was realizing, neither of them were ever that far removed from the boys they'd once been. Oz asked Tommy: "Did you mean it? What you said. That you wish I'd let you die that night?"

Tommy shook his head. "N-n-n-no. I just . . . I wish it was different. I w-w-w-wish . . ."

Oz looked down at the table. "What I was saying earlier, about walking home with Daddy and him asking what kind of punishment he thought I deserved, I was trying to get to what he told me. He told me, 'Every evil you do, son, it'll catch up to you. In time.'" He paused. "He was right. I see it with Deborah—"

"H-h-h-he wasn't right," Tommy said, lurching forward. "He was n-n-n-n—" Tommy stopped, his mouth working, fighting for the words. "N-n-n-never right."

Oz looked at the poster of a roaring lion on the wall behind his brother's head. "He was just thirty-seven, Tommy. Just like me. Today."

"That don't m-m-m-mean nothing," Tommy said quietly.

Oz looked at the ring at the center of the table. He slid it back and put it in his pocket.

"W-w-w-what're you gonna do with that thing, Oz? It n-n-n—"
Tommy stopped again. Struggling. He closed his eyes, then spoke
in a rush: "Needs to be buried. All that." Tommy went quiet for a
second, then pleaded: "M-m-m-make peace, Oz. W-w-w-what do
you think I was doing? Out there on my own?"

Oz realized his brother didn't understand. Their stories were
vastly different. Peace would not come as easily to Oz. Oz carried
a kind of guilt and regret and fear of himself that Tommy didn't
have. And for good reason. He stood and told Tommy he needed
to get back to work.

Tommy blinked. "Y-y-y-you sure? Maybe—"

"I'm sure."

Tommy followed behind him, just as Oz remembered him doing when they were boys.

"Hey," Tommy said, "w-w-w-why don't I walk back with you?"

"I'm okay, Tommy. I know how to get back to work."

Tommy nodded, then looked around like people might be
eavesdropping. "Look, I'm n-n-n-not supposed to say, but Deborah's having a surprise birthday party for you tonight. Even with
the trouble, she loves you."

She shouldn't, Oz thought. Then he said, "She made me promise
a thousand times that I'd leave work on time. And bring home
some ice. The ice was a dead giveaway."

Tommy smiled.

Oz patted his brother's bearded face. "When are you going to
shave this thing, Grizzly Adams?"

Tommy stroked his beard and shrugged.

Oz went his way, waving goodbye. Then he stopped and said,
"Tommy, at your physical, for the army, what did you tell them? About
your legs?" Oz looked at Tommy's melted-wax palms—the very last
punishment his brother had ever received. "And your hands?"

Tommy eyed Oz with suspicion. "W-w-w-what I thought best."

Oz nodded. "Not the truth, then?"

"No. N-n-n-not the truth."

Oz went back and pulled Tommy into a hug. "I'm sorry I made it so bad for us," he said. He pushed away from his brother and turned so Tommy couldn't see his face. Oz wasn't crying but he thought he might if he met his brother's eyes.

Tommy called out to him, asking again if he could walk back to work with him, but Oz shook his head and waved goodbye without turning around. He took the corner and went toward his office. Then he stopped, as if running up against a brick wall. He fingered the ring in his pocket. He took it out and peered through the hole at the cloudless sky.

After

What are your future plans?

Trinity

1988

I had a few minutes to spare before my radio news update. I was religious about recording it. The last time I'd tried to do a live news report, it had been an unmitigated disaster. Now, all I had to do was play my track at the top and bottom of the hour when I got the cue. I bopped my head along with the final notes of "Won't Get Fooled Again," then listened as the DJ growled, "That was the Who, baby, right here at New York's favorite place for classic rock!"

That was a vast overstatement. Our station was no one's favorite for classic rock. Or for news. But that line was my cue. With the push of a button, there was my voice delivering an update on the Tawana Brawley case. Perfect. I looked across the hall to the DJ in the other booth. We gave each other a thumbs-up. He was a short, middle-aged white guy, balding but defiant about it. The hairs that grew beyond his half-moon bald spot were collected and pulled into a thin ponytail that hung down to the middle of his back. He insisted on being called "the Sensei" and, as the name might imply, was obsessed with all things karate. No one knew his real name, except for maybe the station manager who'd hired him. I took note of the fact that he was wearing the Bruce Lee T-shirt that only appeared on days he was praying for luck.

I yawned and stretched. It was six in the morning and the first news break of the day. I wandered down to the break room, which was essentially a closet with a coffee maker and a vending machine crammed in the corner. I brewed a pot of coffee. There was usually a pot waiting, courtesy of the Sensei. But he'd come in a little late and frazzled, which probably explained the Bruce Lee prayer T-shirt. I stood around, arms crossed, breathing in anticipated caffeination bliss, waiting for the coffee maker to drip its last precious drop into the pot. I rinsed out two mugs, filled them up and took them back down the hall. It was musty and overly warm in the hallway. There was the scent of mildew, too, from the carpet. I waited outside the DJ booth until I got the signal to go in.

"Thought you might want some coffee," I said, shouldering the door open.

He accepted with gratitude and gestured for me to sit on the stool across from him. "So, how's it going? Things are sounding good in there. Like you've definitely got your sea legs."

"Definitely." I'd landed in New York and gotten my radio job in November of 1987, not long after graduating from college. My unmitigated disaster had occurred during my first month at the station. I was in the booth doing a live news hit when I dropped the printout with all of the stories on it. It happened midread. I couldn't readily retrieve the page from where it had slid under a cabinet. I tried to remember what I'd printed out. Something at the harbor. Yes, okay. I blurted out a couple of disjointed lines until the sound of my voice saying the most idiotic things—*Fire at the harbor . . . no, it wasn't a fire . . . I mean . . .* —sent me into a hyperventilating meltdown, live on air. Unknown to me at the time, the Sensei had cut back to music after my first few sputtered words. He'd come running into my booth, waving his arms like he was flagging down a ride.

"Whoa, whoa, it's okay, kid." He'd been nothing short of my

savior that day. He'd sat with me, counseling deep breaths and offering a "sweetener" for my coffee. Said sweetener turned out to be Wild Turkey. I declined. I was not a drinker.

The Sensei had talked me down mostly by cataloging, in some degree of detail, his own personal failings and embarrassments in an effort to show me that it wasn't so bad. "Nobody's gonna remember nothing like that," he'd said, waving his hand dismissively. "Now, you wanna know what people remember? How's about getting completely shit-faced and calling your boss a dumb cocksucker—which, by the way, he was—live on air and being tossed out on your ass like yours truly? That's something that'll follow you around. Careerwise."

The day after that pep talk, of sorts, he'd worn his Bruce Lee shirt to work, hoping it would cast its lucky charms on me and I'd have a good day of news updates. Whether it was down to me just pulling it together and putting it all on tape, or the grace of Bruce Lee, who knew, but I did do okay that day and every day after and was now feeling like a pro here in my third month on the job.

Looking at him in that T-shirt now, I asked what the occasion was. Why'd he need luck today?

"Ah, yes, young lady, I got myself what you'd call a date with Destiny." He paused and grinned. "Literally. That's her name."

"Let's see if it's prescient."

He looked like he wasn't quite following.

"Nothing," I murmured. "Carry on."

"Anyways. I met her down at the bowling alley the other night." He winked.

The Sensei lived in Hoboken. The earth may as well have been flat in this regard. The world ended for me at the edges of the Hudson and the East River. When I imagined him in New Jersey, I really just pictured Bon Jovi music videos featuring him.

"I'm hoping to get lucky indeed, if you get my drift," he said, smiling wide.

"Another good one," I said, rolling my eyes.

He sipped his coffee and shrugged. "Don't knock it till you try it." He eyed his mug, as if trying to figure out what was in it. "That's a mighty strong cup you're pushing, kid!"

"I needed it. It's that kind of morning. Didn't get much sleep."

He raised an eyebrow. "You telling me you actually had a late night out doing something fun?"

"No."

He pointed his mug at me. "See, what you need is to go out there and get yourself a life."

"Thanks," I said, sliding off my stool. "But I'm all set."

"See there. Look at you."

"Look at what?" I was headed for the door.

"So defensive about your boring old spinster lifestyle."

"Well, when you describe it in those terms, of course I am." I went through the door. "But good luck with Destiny." I paused with the door open. "And you do realize that no one's real name is Destiny, right?"

He nodded. "Yeah. Started out as a 'stage' name"—he did air quotes—"but she likes it and it works in the real world, if you ask me."

"Welp, let me know how it goes." I paused again. "Wait. No. On second thought, no details. Maybe just a simple devil horns to indicate you had a good evening. And perhaps just quiet, private despair if things don't go your way. I can pick up on that, no problem. Deal?"

He raised his coffee cup in a goodbye salute.

In my own booth, I checked the wire to see if there was anything I could use to freshen up my next couple of news hits. There was an interesting murder. A car accident. But I was tired. I decided to stick with reruns. I sat on my stool and swiveled around like a kid, even though I hated when the Sensei called me that. Kid. Twenty-two may have been young to him, but I hadn't been a kid in a long time.

And the Sensei was, all things considered, wrong about me being a spinster, too. I got out and about plenty, usually with Jonathan. We'd met at my second job, which was an evening shift at a Pizzeria Uno down on Third Avenue, just around the corner from my apartment. Jonathan was a fellow waiter and would-be playwright. And then there was my roommate. I'd rented a room in an apartment with two guys—a Dominican and a Korean—when I'd first arrived in New York. After about a month, I'd found myself spending many of my nights in the Dominican's—Manny's—room. He was the complete opposite of Jonathan: Manny was tall, Jonathan was short; Manny was analytical, Jonathan was all emotion and drama; Manny enjoyed any and all sports, Jonathan played only darts. Badly. They were both very nice and generally available when I wanted company, which were minimal requirements, I knew, but enough for me. There were no strings or expectations. Relationships were cleaner that way. Easier to make a break when the time came. And it always came.

I rubbed my eyes and took a big sip of my coffee, willing the caffeine to do its job. To wake me up. To stop my brain from drifting off into its dreamy voice-from-beyond place. It had indeed been one of those mornings after a troubling night. Last night, I'd abandoned Jonathan at a terrible play staged in his classmate's loft and gone home, where my mother called to talk about declaring my father dead. It was the first time she'd ever brought up something like that. I was stunned. When I asked her why she wanted to do that, her answer was:

"Because."

"Because? Seriously? Because?"

"I don't need your permission, Trinity. I just— Look, I'm ready to do this."

Her words sounded a little elongated. I wondered if she was drinking again. She'd been sober for years. I didn't want to ask her because I was afraid to know the answer. "What if I'm not ready?" I asked instead.

She was quiet for a moment. "I want to do this. I've talked to somebody—"

"Who?"

"Somebody I used to know. Lloyd. You probably don't remember him. You were little. But he helped me understand some things."

"That makes no sense."

"It does to me."

"It just seems very sudden, Mom." Once the words were out of my mouth, I heard how ridiculous they sounded. It would be seven years this coming October. "Where is this coming from? What's changed all of a sudden?"

"Me. It's time to be done with the heartbreak." There was a long pause. "Trinity, I wish I could explain myself to you, but . . . I'm doing this. Okay? I'll talk to you later."

And she'd hung up.

It's strangely calming watching towels being tossed around in a dryer. I said this aloud to Jonathan as we sat in the laundromat waiting for my last load to go through its final turns.

"Uh-huh," he said, clearly not paying attention. He was hunched over a folding table, obsessing over the play he'd written. As he looked down, he nervously ran his hands through his hair, which was as shaggy as a sheepdog's. The dark scruff on his chin was edging toward unkempt. It was his look, along with the shredded jeans and white T-shirt.

"Why don't you give it a breather," I said.

He glanced at me with tired, red-rimmed eyes, then gathered up his papers and worked them into a neat stack. He tucked the stack under his arm and came over to where I was sitting by the window. He slid into the hard plastic chair next to me with a deep sigh. It was late. We were exhausted after working our shift. We were the only two left in the laundromat.

"Tell me honestly, Trin. What did you think? When you read it?" He nodded toward the stack.

I had successfully avoided this conversation for a week, largely by avoiding quiet, alone time with him. But here we were. I prided myself on being honest, but I also understood the need to some-times shade the truth. This went back to a Christmas when I was a kid. Tommy had gotten a paper doll for me, complete with paper outfits. But it wasn't what I wanted, and I told him so. It hurt his feelings. My father took me aside later and said, "Sometimes, it's more important to say what someone needs to hear—in this case it would be *thank you*—rather than whatever's true to you."

Looking at Jonathan with his tired eyes and knowing his sensi-tivity about his writing, I offered, "Well, it wasn't bad." It was, in fact, *astoundingly* bad. It was about a clown having an existential crisis, complete with every sad-clown cliché imaginable.

He leaned back in the chair and hugged his stack of papers to his chest. "'Wasn't bad.' That's not a compliment."

"Well . . . sorry," I said, realizing I could have done a better job at shading. Mercifully, the dryer buzzed, and I got up to grab my towels.

He tossed his neat stack of papers into the chair I'd just vacated. They separated and splayed, with some threatening to fall to the floor. "This is trash." He came over to help me fold towels. "If I had your story," he said, "*that's* what I'd write."

"My story is not very interesting."

"Are you kidding me? Everything with your dad and your mom? All the drama and—"

I stopped with a towel in midfold. "That's not a story, Jonathan. It's not a drama. It's my reality."

"Exactly! And it's incredible. You want to talk about not interesting? *I'm* not interesting."

Indeed. He was a textbook "good kid" from a loving, intact family with no skeletons to speak of. But that wasn't the point. "You know," I said, "for a generally thoughtful guy, you can be anything but, when it comes to your 'work,' or whatever you call that." I nodded toward the disheveled stack of papers in the chair.

He stopped folding and watched me for a second. In response, I picked up the speed of my folding, ready to be on my way.

"You're right," he said. "It can appear that way when it comes to my craft."

I rolled my eyes. "Your craft? Please."

He took up another towel and started folding again. "Say what you want, Trinity. But this is what making art is all about. Life."

"No," I said. "It's *my* life. *My* reality. There's no making anything from it."

I am not crazy. But there were times when I thought I saw my father. The most recent time was on the seventh anniversary of his disappearance. October 1, 1988. I was at the A&P shopping with Manny. He was over in produce while I was in canned foods trying to decide between two different brands of pinto beans. That was when I saw what looked like the back of my father's head, bobbing near the end of the crowded aisle. It was his shiny scalp under the thin veneer of hair that got my attention. I stood watching for a second and recognized the way he tilted his head to consider a can of green beans. And the way he moved—quickly, decisively—as his hand darted out for the Green Giant brand. Then he pushed his cart to the end of the aisle and turned the corner.

My heart was pounding. I reminded myself: *This has happened before* . . .

What would he be doing in Union Square of all places? On a Saturday afternoon? I felt compelled to follow him. I shoved my little red cart down the aisle, zigging then zagging between shoppers, wincing and apologizing whenever I rammed someone with my cart. I hung a right, just like the man in front of me. Then I saw him in profile in frozen foods. Not full profile. His head was turned in such a way that all I could see was his ear. He grabbed a couple of Swanson's TV dinners. I suddenly had this image of my father alone, eating in front of a television in some bleak Alphabet City apartment with a bathtub in the kitchen.

I inched my cart forward as the man moved away from the TV dinners. I stopped when he turned back abruptly and grabbed two more boxes. I wondered: *What would he do if I walked up to him? If I grabbed him by the arm and demanded to know, "Where have you been? Mom is declaring you dead!"* I inched up a little closer. "Dad," I said, watching him turn away from the frozen dinners and me and move toward the ice cream.

Two men in the aisle looked back at me, then went on with their shopping. I didn't belong to them. The man I'd called Dad kept walking, after tossing a pint of vanilla ice cream into his basket. Breyers. Was that the brand he liked? Was that the flavor? I couldn't remember. I was seized by panic at my inability to remember. What else had I forgotten about him?

"Hey!"

I whipped my head around toward that call. It was Manny holding up a bunch of bananas with a bottle of sparkling apple juice under his arm. I turned again to find that man. He was nearly at the end of the aisle.

"It may be him," I said, abandoning the cart.

"What—?"

I hurried down to the end of the aisle.

I felt strong arms grab me from behind. I looked back. "What are you doing? I'm trying to catch—"

But the look on Manny's face was so sad for me that I stopped.

"It's not him, Trin. Come on."

"How do you know?" I strained away from him, trying to look around the corner of the aisle.

"Because it wasn't him those other times."

I kept pulling away, even though the man was well out of view now.

"Please, Trinity." Manny nudged me to the cart. He looked off in the direction I was looking, but he was still holding on to me. "We should pay for this and go. This is getting out of hand."

I blinked at that, as if coming out of a trance. There was nothing to see now, apart from an aisle crowded with strangers. After going through the line and paying, Manny put his hand at the small of my back and tried to guide me in the direction he'd have me go. I jerked away and got behind the cart, pushing it forward out the door.

"I have it," I said.

As we walked home down Third Avenue, Manny said, "I think you need to support your mother in doing what she's doing. I think that's why this is happening."

"So, you're a psychiatrist now?" I shoved the red shopping cart along as fast as I could, so determined was I to put some distance between the two of us. But I couldn't gather any speed. The cart had a bad wheel that wobbled and spun around and occasionally locked up. Manny smiled down at me, his white teeth practically sparkling in the radiance of his face, which would typically be my undoing. But at the moment, it infuriated me.

"I'm your friend, Trinity," he said quietly. Friend. Roommate. Sex partner. We were a slippery mix of all those things. "And I'm telling you, you have to, I would say, let go. These 'sightings,' they aren't good. Your father needs to find rest." He made the sign of the cross.

I shoved the cart along, the many cracks in the sidewalk making the wheel issue that much more pronounced and frustrating. I elbowed his hand away when he reached to help. He shrugged and tipped his Yankee cap to me, then clasped his hands behind his back, in the way he did when he was about to make a point.

"On the way up to see my buddy in the Bronx, you made us get off *a million stops* early when you thought you saw your father, remember? It wasn't him. And at Cozy Soup 'n' Burger that time, remember? You followed that man for blocks up Broadway before—"

"I *know*. Shut up. *Please*."

He was quiet for a moment, but I knew he wasn't finished. He could not leave a point unmade or a thought unexpressed. "I just worry," he said. He put his hand on the cart to stop me. He looked at me, his head tilted to the side. "Do you truly believe that's him? In your heart?" He touched his chest with his fist. "And that he's wandering the streets of New York City?"

The door to the Chinese restaurant Jonathan and I liked swung open behind me, and I got out of the way. I took a moment to really consider Manny's question. I was sane enough to understand that my father was not likely walking around New York. But then again, he could be anywhere, couldn't he? Assuming he was alive. And I assumed as much.

"I don't know," I said, grief swelling in my chest.

"You're being pulled along by a ghost," he said. "I'm afraid of where he'll lead you. That's all. I don't mean to disrespect his memory."

Manny could not be disrespectful even if he wanted to be. He'd told me that when he was a boy, he'd wanted to be either a priest or a professional baseball player. His asthma sidelined him and nagging spiritual doubts kept him out of seminary. Still, he went to Mass every Sunday. He worshipped the Yankees. He was now in law school, driven by a desire to do some kind of public service, after taking a physician-like vow to "do no harm."

"I feel like it's just one terrible thing after another," I said, surrendering the cart to him. He managed it with one hand as we walked on.

"Al dedo malo, todo se le pega," he said quietly.

"What does that mean?"

"All bad things happen to the injured finger. That's the general translation."

"Um, and what does *that* mean?"

He laughed. "Well . . ." He laughed again and looked skyward with some degree of concentration. "Okay. I've ruined the feel of it. It's supposed to be profound, if you hadn't noticed. But basically, it's like saying bad things attract bad things. So, you hurt your finger, you're bound to keep hitting that hurt spot." He grabbed my hand and kissed my finger. "And I'm sorry."

I leaned into him as we reached the corner of Twelfth Street. Our street. "I'm sorry, too," I whispered, too low for him to hear over the traffic. I could feel the pain, but it wasn't in my finger. It was a kind of radiant ache that was everywhere.

Deborah

1989

I stood in the middle of the living room greeting everybody who'd come to pay their respects to Oz. I was nodding along with Oz's old secretary, Mrs. Jackson, sipping my tonic water and sick in my heart.

The after-funeral get-together wasn't my idea. Lloyd, of all people, had thought it up.

"I still miss Mr. Armstead," said Mrs. Jackson. "But at least you're getting some closure now." She reached out and squeezed my arm. "This must be so hard on you. And your daughter." She motioned across the room to Trinity.

"It is," I said, glancing over to where Trinity was standing on the edge of the crowd, looking like she'd rather be anyplace other than where she was. I felt the same way.

Mrs. Jackson excused herself, saying she didn't want to take up any more of my time, as I had other people waiting. A tall, dark-haired man who used to work with Oz came up next. I'd seen him before at a couple work functions but didn't know him. He was a handsome enough man, but he looked like he'd had a broken nose that didn't heal right. The work friend was telling me how sorry he was for my loss and what a nice guy Oz had been. Then he was standing too close to me, smiling in a lazy, flirty way, asking, "What are your future plans?"

I excused myself without answering and walked to the back of the house and my bedroom. Future plans? I near about choked as I took out a cigarette and lit up. What I really wanted was a drink. But I was clawing my way back from my crash off the wagon after learning about what Oz had done to me. After humiliating myself onstage. After going on to drink like a woman with a death wish for some weeks after. Poor, guilty-feeling Two Cents had all but made himself a one-man, twenty-four-hour AA hotline. And I thanked God for him.

I closed the door of my bedroom behind me and put my sweaty glass of tonic water on the bedside table. I sat down and exhaled two streams of smoke through my nose, like an angry bull, then rubbed my tired eyes. I looked around the room. I hadn't changed a thing since the day Oz disappeared. I'd wanted everything the same. But now I couldn't stand to look at the sameness.

Laughter rippled through the living room, and all I could think was: *They're all out there saying goodbye to a stranger.* How could I have been with Oz for so long and not seen what he could take from me? I put what Lloyd had told me about Oz up against what I remembered of Oz comforting me over losing that contract. It was all a lie. The man had slowly put me in a cage in the suburbs and was sitting there holding the key, all the while making me think I was free.

I'd thought about telling Trinity when we were together this morning in my bathroom, while I was getting ready. But I'd looked at her sitting up on the counter with her coffee, her makeup a mess from sleeping in it after driving home. She looked miserable as anything, and I thought: *What purpose would it serve?*

There was a knock at the door. I thought I'd slipped away without being noticed. I looked at the last bit of my cigarette—I wouldn't even get to enjoy it in peace. "Damn it," I muttered under my breath. I was too tired to get up and open the door. "Yes? Come in."

Tommy peeked his head around the door. "W-w-w-wanted to let you know Willa Mae's on the line." He looked at the phone by the side of the bed. "You didn't hear it ring?"

I glanced at the phone. "No—well, yeah. I just didn't get it."

As I picked up, Tommy slipped out of the room, saying he was going back to hang up the other phone.

It was good to hear Willa Mae's voice. We'd been such good friends when we were young, working together in the hospital kitchen. But we'd lost touch after she'd moved back down South. I'd called her to tell her about Oz's funeral, but she couldn't make it. I told her now how much we missed having her with us. She gave her condolences but was mostly quiet, though she apologized over and over for "Oz being gone."

"None of this is your fault," I told her.

She said she kind of felt like it was. I imagined it was because she'd put us together. I tried to make her feel better. Couldn't tell if it worked. She didn't sound good. She said her goodbyes and hung up.

I took a last drag from my cigarette as Tommy came back in the room and sat down beside me on the bed. Lloyd had told him about Oz, not long after he'd told me. Tommy had apologized on his brother's behalf. He said he'd known Oz to do harm out of love.

"That wasn't love," I'd said. "If it was, he would've known he wasn't just taking some contract from me. It was like he stole my soul and left the rest of me to wilt and die." I thought now about "future plans" and shook my head.

"What?" Tommy asked.

"One of Oz's work people asked me about 'future plans.' And I

realized"—tears rose in my throat—"I don't have any future plans.
All I've got is this house Oz left me and the job where he used to
work. *His* leavings. Not a damn thing of my own."

Tommy leaned forward with his elbows on his knees, his broad
shoulders slumped. How could I pour out my grief on a man who
was full up with his own? It had been less than a week since Tommy
had called and said: "Lloyd's gone. What am I supposed to do now?"

I'd been right to suspect that Lloyd was sicker than he'd said. It
had been more than pneumonia. He had AIDS. Him and Tommy
kept it from me for a good while. When they finally told me, I was
as bad as Lloyd's family in being scared to come back around him.
But it was that picture of Tommy that Oz had stolen from Lloyd
that broke my heart and tugged me back. It had been there on the
side table in the living room for years, silent witness to Oz's deceit.
Tommy had told me about it and asked for its return. Lloyd cried
when I showed up at the apartment and gave it back to him. He
touched the picture like he was reading braille. He'd gone blind by
then, so he couldn't see Tommy standing there, with that half smile
of his and a puppy peeking out of his knapsack, but he knew what
was there. He told me: "Tommy found that puppy in that bombed-
out village. He tried to save it, but it got away from him not long
after that picture."

Lloyd's passing wasn't the out-of-nowhere shock of having
somebody here then all of a sudden gone, like with Oz. But it was
still a trauma. With Lloyd, Death had crept up real slow, slouching
in the corners of the apartment and lounging in the halls of the
hospital, drawing out every second of suffering.

"How're you doing?" I asked Tommy, realizing as I said it that
I'd asked the same stupid question people were asking me tonight:
How are you doing?

How do you think I'm doing?

The state of Tommy told me all I needed to know. His beard wasn't trimmed. Whiskers were working their way down his neck. His white dress shirt was wrinkled. And his eyes were bloodshot, staring off at nothing. "Forget it," I said. "I know how you're doing."

"I think it's gonna be a little graveside service," he said, looking down at his hands. "Maybe with y-y-y-you and me and Mary. And Trinity and Mama."

Lloyd's family didn't even want him back to bury him. "Whatever you think's best."

Tommy shrugged. "It's not what he would've w-w-w-wanted." He lowered his head. "Couldn't ever give him that. Till it was too late. And even then . . ."

I touched his arm. "You gave him what you could."

"No, I didn't."

"You had your reasons."

He snapped his head around and held me with those bloodshot eyes. "I had *somebody else's* reasons. The reasons of a little boy who was made to hate himself." His face broke with grief. "Lloyd, um, he w-w-w-wanted me to come out there. To New York with him w-w-w-when I finished up my first tour in Vietnam, all them years ago. You know what I did?"

He didn't wait for my answer.

"I reupped." He put his head in his hands. "Trying to run away from him and from what I was." He looked up at me, tears in his eyes. "I w-w-w-went out there and risked dying instead of loving him back like I should've. Like I *do*. H-h-h-he had the good sense to give up on me. Then I got him back, and he had this plague."

I reached out to rub his back and comfort him, but he stood up and wiped his eyes dry in one quick move. "We better get back out there." He nodded toward the living room. "Especially you. They're probably looking for you." He moved toward the door, then stopped. "And thanks for doing this. The big party. I know it was for Lloyd."

I waved him toward the door. "You go ahead. I'll be out in a minute. Maybe put on a little music. Lloyd'd like that."

The corner of Tommy's mouth lifted into a half smile, with his eyes just brimming. Then he left.

I remembered Lloyd sitting up in bed playing the keyboard. It was just weeks ago. He was blind. Frail as a baby bird. His voice, feeble as anything. But he played and we sang "Try a Little Tenderness." Then he stopped and asked, "Are you going to say a proper goodbye to Oz?"

"What do you mean?"

"A preacher. A funeral. The whole thing. And a big party."

I looked at him like he'd lost his mind, then realized he couldn't see me and said, "Have you lost your mind?"

He shrugged. "Maybe. Things aren't clicking upstairs like they used to." He put a long, bony finger to his temple. He smiled. Lloyd's beautiful teeth were yellowed, but clean. Tommy saw to just about every toothbrushing, every sponge bath, every gentle washing of what was left of Lloyd's beautiful hair. "Nobody's going to mourn me, Deborah."

"People love you."

"They used to love me. Before they knew me." He turned his face away, toward the window. If he'd still had his sight, he would've seen it was a clear spring day, with the sun high in the sky. "Maybe that's what Oz was scared of," he said, with the surprise of somebody who'd just tripped over a good thought. Then he shook his head. "I don't know. I'm so tangled up in dying . . . I like to think that somewhere, somebody's having a good time over somebody's homegoing. It won't be mine and Oz's is the one we've got . . . And it'll be good for you, too. Because—" He paused and crinkled his forehead, like he was straining to get his thoughts together. "See . . . if you could forgive me, you'll forgive him, too. Damn sure not now. I get that. But one day, you'll want to feel like you did right by him, even if he didn't do it by you. But don't take this as some noble words from a man with one foot in the grave. I just know that the goodbyes are important. As much for him as for you. And Trinity. And—" He'd stopped, tears sliding down his hollow cheeks. "And my Tommy."

I came back to myself, all by myself in my bedroom. Glasses were clinking outside the door. I got up and went back out to join everybody. I didn't see Trinity anywhere around. Mr. Adler told me she was out on the porch with Pearl. I went over to the record player and dropped the needle on some Otis Redding. I closed my eyes as I listened: *You won't regret it, no, no, young girls they don't forget it . . .*

Life goes on. Seems like it moves faster just when you get the understanding that it's been passing you by. After Oz's funeral, I was thinking about "future plans" when I got a call. It was to see if I could do a jingles session in Chicago.

"We heard a couple of the Chevy spots you did," the voice on the other end of the line said. "We thought you might be a good fit."

I told him I'd think about it, but I didn't trust out-of-the-blue calls like that from men making music promises. Then a couple weeks later, I got a call from one of the arrangers I'd worked with on the Chevy spots. He told me that the call I'd gotten was on the up and up and that I should give it a shot. I did, and before I knew it, I was singing little ditties for everything from McDonald's hamburgers to United Airlines. A couple months after I got going good, I was making nice money at it. And I was finally making my plan for the future.

I squinted into the summer sun as I walked down the driveway to the mailbox, thinking about how I was going to lay out my plan for Pearl. She was on her way over. I glanced down the street. There was no sign of her white LeBaron just yet. At the mailbox, I flipped through the flyers and bills. As I turned to go back up the driveway, I noticed Virginia's mother at her mailbox. We met in the middle of the street, like we did sometimes. We traded hellos and updates on the girls, probably things we both already knew from our own daughters: Virginia was working in finance in London now. I acted like it was news to me. I told her Trinity had just become a newspaper reporter in New York. I suspected she was acting like it was news to her. I asked how she was doing, after the divorce. She asked how I was coming along but never mentioned Oz. And then we said our goodbyes and went on our way. We were good neighbors, but not friends. We hadn't found a way to bridge the things that still made us a little foreign to one another—my blackness and her whiteness and the different ways we understood the world. But even so, we'd somehow raised two girls who were close as anything.

As I walked up the driveway, I caught sight of Pearl driving toward the house. I waved to her as she pulled in, and my mind went back to that question of how best to lay out my plan for her. Pearl was cautious, just like Tommy. And just like me. But what I wanted was to dare to do something different. To have a life not as somebody's wife or widow or mother. And I felt like this was my time. I just wanted to make sure I wouldn't let Pearl talk me out of it, because I'd already talked myself out of it a time or two.

I dropped my mail on the table by the door and hugged Pearl as I let her in. "How're you holding up, old girl? How's Mr. Burton."

She swatted my arms away. "Who you calling *old*?"

Quiet as it's kept, at fifty-nine to my forty-five, she had more zip than I did. Pearl fanned herself with her hand as I followed her to the kitchen.

"Good God," she said. "It's hot." She opened the fridge and got out a pitcher of iced tea. I got down two tall glasses. She dropped a few ice cubes in each one. "How you keeping yourself, Ms. Deborah?"

"Oh, you know. Just doing a little bit of this and that."

"Are you, now?" She poured the tea. "Do tell."

I bit my lip, not quite ready. Thing was, my plan was sounding silly and reckless as I kept thinking about it, and I was talking myself out of it again. I swiped the two full glasses away from Pearl and carried them to the living room.

"You need to leave your haven of the suburbs and come do some work with me," she said, settling on the couch. I put her drink on a coaster on the coffee table in front of her. "We working on our Devil's Night strategy right through here. You need to come on and do some patrols with me and my block club, come fall."

I pictured Pearl, Mr. Burton and a pack of old ladies walking around their neighborhood with baseball bats and crowbars, looking for the arsonists and thugs who made Detroit a living hell on Devil's Night, the night before Halloween. They'd set fire to just about anything, unleashing terror on a city that was already, in so many places, a bombed-out, boarded-up ruin. Pearl and Mr. Burton had had a scare a couple years back on Devil's Night with a shooting not far from their house. An old man they used to look in on was shot dead in the street. They'd become almost radicalized about saving, if not the city, then at least the few blocks around their neighborhood.

For folks out here in the suburbs, Virginia's mama included, on Devil's Night or any other, Detroit was more like another planet than a bunch of neighborhoods with good people like Pearl. The way they talked about it, you were as good as dead if you so much as breathed in the city's atmosphere, which was thick with drug deals, crack house fumes and stray bullets. That was if the alien life-forms didn't get you first. I didn't necessarily feel that way, but it was hard to ignore what was happening in Detroit. It was so bad in the projects where I'd grown up that I was grateful as anything that my family had gotten out back in the seventies. Now I sat here watching it all from a safe distance, which was just fine with me.

"I'll think about the neighborhood watch, Pearl," I said. "We'll see."

She got up and went over to the big picture window. "It's beautiful out here, I'll grant you that much. Lawn's still looking as good as when Ozro was here making sure he was outdoing everybody else."

I went over and stood next to her at the window.

"You know," she said, "sometimes I feel like I ain't rightly grieved him. Even with the funeral and all that. It just don't seem real without knowing what happened, you know? I cain't hardly believe the streets just swallowed him up."

To my mind, that was one of the things that had Pearl out in the street trying to fight crime. Maybe saving somebody else's son.

"All right," Pearl said. "This moping, this ain't what we about today." She went over and grabbed her purse from the chair. "Before I forget . . ." She rummaged around. "Here!" She pulled a business card from her wallet and walked it over to me. "This here's a lounge one of my friends just opened. It's nice but in need of a good singer." She passed the card to me.

I looked down at it. While I'd gotten myself comfortable singing in the studio, I didn't have the nerve to go back on a stage. Whenever I thought about it, all I could see was the stumbling, slurring mess I'd been, crawling around on my hands and knees like a dog. "I don't think the stage is for me anymore," I said, passing the card back. "But thank you."

She took it back, even as she said: "This is what you love, Deborah. I think you need to get back on that horse."

It was time to let her know I was on a little bit of a different horse. "Look here, Pearl. I want to tell you about something I've been thinking about doing." I took a deep breath and spit it out: "I'm quitting my job. I'm going to do jingles. Full-time now."

She cut her eyes at me.

"I know, I know. That job and Oz's boss saved me when I needed it. But I hate it. You know that. I can't stand it. With this, though . . . I know it's not, you know, all I want it to be, but it's—"

"Deborah, you'd be walking out on a sure thing, leaving that secretary job."

I felt a little glimmer of agreeing, but I kept pushing. "Look, I've been thinking about it a lot. It's good union work. And I got a little nest egg saved up for lean times. The way I figure it is, I'll spend a few days in Chicago every week, record what they need me to record, pocket a good chunk of change, then I'm back here. It'll be, I don't know . . ."

Pearl eyed me close for a second, then smiled. "Something to get you outta this house, for one." She looked around the room. "It might be good for you. I don't know. Crazy, but good."

It was like I could feel my whole body and my mind relax. I didn't understand how much I needed this till that very moment. Somebody to say, *You're right, Deborah. Do your thing, girl.*

The phone rang and I jumped. Then I remembered. "Oh! That's Trin! She was waiting for you to come over. Said she had some news."

"I don't know if I can take any more news today," Pearl said.

"I'm sure it's good," I said, reaching for the phone. That was my hope, anyway. When I heard Trinity's voice, I waved Pearl off to the kitchen. "Just a minute, Trin. Pearl's getting the kitchen phone."

Pearl picked up. "What's the big news?"

"I'm doing great, Pearl," Trinity said, laughing. "So glad you asked. And, yes, the new job at the paper is going along well, too. Your interest in these things is so welcome."

We laughed and talked about the job. She'd wanted to be a reporter since she was a little girl, learning to type on Pearl's typewriter. She'd told me: "I like telling stories. I like trying to figure out what makes us who we are."

Pearl told her my news about me quitting my job and striking out on my own. Then the conversation slipped into silence and Trinity cleared her throat.

"Well, I guess I've procrastinated long enough," she said quietly.

My stomach knotted up. "What's going on, Trin? What's wrong?"

"Well," she said, "I don't know if *wrong* is what I would call it. But it is"—she paused—"really, really unexpected. I can't stress the unexpected nature of this enough."

"Stop it with that, Trinity," Pearl said. Worry always sounded like anger with her. "What is it?"

"Please don't be mad, okay? But, Mom, you're going to be a grandmother. And, Pearl, you've been a great grandmother. But now, well, think of it genetically."

I didn't feel like a woman about to be a grandmother. With every month that went by, I felt younger than I had in years. I was commuting back and forth to Chicago for work, and I liked my little "jingle life." I didn't too much know, from session to session, what product I'd be singing about before I got there. I'd just show up at the music house, get in the studio, pop my headphones on to listen to what they wanted me to do, then do it. And the music, it wasn't bad. The musicians and arrangers were good and serious about what they were doing. Everybody wanted a hit. Everybody wanted to do one of those little jingles that stuck in your head like the *Plop plop, fizz fizz* Alka-Seltzer song or *If you've got the time, we've got the beer.*

It meant residuals, which was what you were after, but it was also something to be able to say, "Hey, I'm singing on that."

I paid more attention to commercials now than I ever had before. I was watching one with some of my music friends at a sports bar in Chicago after a session. The three of us were all staring up at the TV listening to an ad for Tropicana orange juice.

"It's kinda catchy," William, one of the guitarists, said.

Cindy, a singer, nodded. "Not a hit, I don't think, but not bad."

My fellow music folks had made it their business to keep me company on a lot of the nights I stayed over for work. At least a couple of them would take me to dinner or to a game or have me over. We'd become good friends. After Cindy and William dropped me off back at my hotel, William jumped out of the car and caught me at the automatic glass doors. We stood close together, hunched over against a coat-cutting wind, with him finishing up his cigarette.

"So, maybe on your next trip," William said, "we can, I don't know, grab some dinner someplace nice. Not some sports joint. What do you say? Maybe just us two?" William was round in the middle and losing his hair up top, but he was nice and good company. He was divorced with two kids and maybe could've stood not to eat so many hamburgers, which was what he had almost every time we all went out somewhere. "Or maybe you could come and see me play some night," he added real fast. I think he noticed I was holding back.

"I'd love to see you play," I told him. He played in what I heard was a pretty good blues band. "Especially if y'all ever make it up to Detroit."

"Good," he said, smiling. "Good." He flicked his cigarette butt to the ground and crushed it under his shoe. "Well, I won't keep you out here in this cold. Have a good night and . . . okay . . . have a good night."

I watched him jog back to his car and waved to him and Cindy as they sped off, kicking up gray slush behind them. There was a tiny flutter in my heart as I realized he'd just asked me for a date. I smiled to myself all the way up to my hotel room, even though I didn't like William that way. He was nice and all but not my type. Still, to feel wanted . . . How long had it been? And what was my type anyway?

Up in my room, I took a long shower, thinking about what it might be like to be with somebody. I'd only ever been with Oz. The other time, which was not of my choosing, obviously didn't count. What might it be like to fall in love and have everything, *everything* be true? And then I thought, *Some things were true with Oz, weren't they?* I did love him. Had he loved me, too?

I got out of the shower and dried down. As I lotioned up and put my night cream on, I thought, *My skin's still in good shape.* I touched my face. *It's still got some spring to it.* I looked at myself from different angles in the mirror. I was about to be a grandmother. A *grandmother*. I didn't feel old, despite the crow's feet and the occasional fine line.

"There's still life in me," I said out loud as I rubbed excess night cream on my elbows. I pulled my nightgown over my head. "Well, see, that's the problem right there," I said to my reflection in the mirror. I had on a blue flannel nightgown with little pink flowers on it. It was comfy, but it wasn't what anybody in their right mind would call sexy. I looked like a grandmother in it.

"Who do you want to be, Deborah?" I asked myself.

I wasn't sure. But I was excited—and maybe a little scared, too—to be asking myself something like that at this stage in life. But I was about ready to find the answer.

Trinity

1990

He was the babysitter of last resort. Manny was working. His mother was, too. All of my friends had jobs. There was no other choice. The Sensei was the eldest of eight and a favorite uncle, so he was no stranger to kids. Still, when he came through the door rubbing his hands together saying, "Okay, take me to the little dude," I had second thoughts. But the sight of his girlfriend coming in directly behind him made me feel infinitely better.

"I brought reinforcements," the Sensei said. He motioned toward Destiny, the woman I'd immediately disliked, based only on her name. I'd had a chance to meet her during my last days at the radio station, and I'd come to love her. She was incandescently blond with a pleasant round face that had seen too much of the tanning bed. She was funny and kind and a strangely perfect match for the Sensei, who I warned not to blow it. She was also good with kids, having raised two really sweet ones of her own. Still, I had to reassure myself about the safety of my kid: *It will only be a couple of hours, and he'll be asleep for most if not all of it.*

Destiny gave me a big hug. "I know you're nervous leaving him with us. Don't worry. We've got it covered."

"Thank you for coming." I squeezed her back.

I introduced them to my son. He was seven months old, and I was still getting used to saying *my son*. I was not someone who ever expected to be a mother. It wasn't part of my plan at all. *My son* was a complete birth-control-failure accident. But keeping him was the best decision I'd ever made. *My son*, with his toothless smile and sweet smell, was the joy of my life. I gave Destiny and the Sensei his routine, which wasn't much, and told them that Manny would be there to relieve them in a couple of hours. And I stressed that we called him O, instead of Ozro, which was his name. We'd started off calling him Oz, but maybe two weeks in, it didn't feel like it fit.

Back when we were trying to get the fit right, I would shake Manny awake in the middle of the night, wanting to discuss it.

"How about O?" Manny had suggested one night, groggy and squinting like a mole in the glare of my reading light. "We can call him that. Or his middle name—Manuel, yes?"

"Why would you want to do that?"

"Jesus, Trin." He pushed my reading light away. "It's a nice name. I'm offering a suggestion. You woke me up to talk about alternatives. Here I give you some, and look." He mumbled something about hormones, which upset me. He got up from the bed. I could hear him in the kitchen running water. The floor moaned as he paced. Then he came back in the room and leaned over O's crib. From the light coming in through the window, I could see Manny was patting him and checking that he was still breathing. Manny did that all the time, thinking he was being subtle. He'd had a baby sister who'd slipped away in the night.

"I'm sorry," I said as he finished his baby check.

He climbed back in bed and suggested again that we call him O. I agreed.

"Why can't you be sane like that on the regular? Why do we

always have to argue on the way to the inevitable agreement? Why are you like this?"

"I wish I knew."

Here, a few months after that discussion, our little boy's name, O, seemed right.

I watched the Sensei and Destiny hunch over his crib, oohing and aahing.

"He's gonna be a real lady-killer, this one," Destiny whispered. "And look at all that hair!"

I smiled. O had a mass of thick black hair that stood up against any effort to smooth it. It made him look like he was perpetually frazzled.

"And how are things with my buddy Manny?" the Sensei said, looking over his shoulder at me. "You gonna make an honest man outta him?"

Destiny elbowed him in the side. He looked at her like, *What? What did I say?*

"Your buddy?" I raised an eyebrow. "Didn't realize you two were close."

"Close enough for me to be worried about whether you're still busting his balls every chance you get."

"I don't—" I held up my hands. Why would I even get into this discussion with him? I herded them out of the bedroom and hugged them both goodbye. I went back to O's crib and kissed him on top of his bushy head and breathed him in deep.

"I love you, and I'll see you soon," I whispered. I never left him without telling him that.

I pulled away and made sure again that they had my number at work and Manny's mother's work number, just in case. I repeated that Manny would be home in a couple of hours. I said it that time mostly to make myself feel better about leaving. Sometimes I

thought Manny was better with O than I was—singing Spanish
lullabies to him, settling him down quicker than I could, telling
him stories about the Yankees—which made me feel terrible and
competitive. I didn't know Spanish. I didn't know or care anything
about the Yankees. But just then, the thought of Manny coming
home to pick him up and carry him around the apartment gave me
comfort, because it would comfort my son.

Manny and I had talked about "making it official." I'd brushed
it off like it was something we might want to think about, but what
was the rush? In the meantime, we'd decided to be "exclusive,"
which had meant saying goodbye to Jonathan—a process that was
incredibly fraught. Jonathan and I had carried on a casual relationship up until I learned I was pregnant. It actually took a minute to
be sure O was Manny's. For Jonathan's part, he'd gotten a lot of use
out of the "drama" and had written a well-reviewed play on paternity and patriarchy that was running off-Broadway.

"You see what I mean now?" he'd said to me. "Life. Art. It's
everything. And I didn't even have to steal your mom and dad's
story, although, I admit, I tried. Couldn't pull it off."

As for Manny, he was understandably furious about it all, and it
was almost the end of us. But we were good now. I'd never been
exclusive with anyone for any amount of time, but I wanted to try
with Manny. To what end, though, I wasn't sure. I didn't see the
point of marriage. My mother asked me about it all the time. Even
Pearl, who had an allergy to marriage for herself, kept asking me,
"So, are y'all gon' do this? You got that baby now, you know."

Yes. I knew.

I suspected Manny had gotten to Pearl. I was sure he'd enlisted
my mother and Tommy, too. They loved him. Everyone loved
Manny. I loved Manny, but maybe not enough. Sometimes I wondered if there was something wrong with me. This was one of those

times I missed Virginia. She would know just what to say in this moment about what was wrong and what was right about me. She lived in London. We didn't talk or see each other nearly enough. The last time we were together, I was at her flat and still dealing with my Jonathan/Manny situation. We were sitting on the floor of her nearly empty main room, hunched over takeout of the spiciest chicken curry I'd ever had in my life. Between tongue-incinerating bites, I was sharing my angst over two-timing. She'd told me, "It's like you're waiting for something, Trin. You've always been that way. I don't think you even know what it is."

The minute I got to my desk, I called home to check on O. He was still asleep, the adults were watching *Enter the Dragon* and all was well. That was followed by a meeting with my editor, who sent me out to Staten Island to cover the case of a girl who was killed in a robbery at a drug stash house.

"A bullet to the head for a girl dealer?" my editor said. "With all the shit that happens around here, that shit right there doesn't happen all that much. Looks like they've finally collared some guy for it, too. Go out there. Get the story."

My trip to Staten Island took me to a housing project in New Brighton. Even on a bright summer's day, the red brick midrise was bleak, surrounded by black wrought iron fencing that looked more like caging. Still, there were bands of children going about the business of being children, playing chase on a small patch of grass. I had a vague memory of going to the projects in Detroit to visit my mother's parents. The pictures of those moments were fuzzy in my mind, but they popped with color and sound and smell. I recalled the warmth of my grandparents' apartment and the aroma of coffee, no matter what time of day it was.

It was stale food and mildew I smelled now as I entered the apartment building in New Brighton. I went up to the third floor and down the dimly lit hallway—*Why is there always so little light in these places?*—to the apartment that belonged to a friend of the dead girl. It was overly warm inside and thick with the overhang of cigarette smoke. There was a baby—a little girl, maybe a year old—holding on to the coffee table, turning up a bottle that had fruit punch or some other red liquid in it. I resisted the urge to issue a warning about sugar and the little girl's teeth. I waved and smiled at the baby. She paused in her bottle-draining and smiled at me, then got back to business.

The friend indicated I should have a seat on the couch then immediately said she didn't know anything about the shooting. This was to be expected.

"Okay," I said, showing her my little tape recorder and pressing record. It was my dad's mini–tape recorder that I now used. It was in the briefcase my mother gave me when I went off to college. "Can you just tell me about her, then? You're her best friend. What was she like?"

At this, out came the girl's story. People want to tell you about the people they love, especially if they've lost them. And, in the telling, I was good at hearing how it all fit together. Having grown up an outsider—"the only one of your kind," a kid had once said to me in school, like I was an exotic zoo animal—I was a good onlooker. Inclined to examine people, the *lives* of people, with the overly observant eye of a girl always trying to find where she might fit in.

When the young woman finally finished telling me how wonderful her dead friend had been—including, to my surprise, as mother to the little girl toddling around the room—I thanked her for her time and gave her my card, just in case she thought of something more she wanted me to know. Sometimes it was in that follow-up call, after they'd had some time, that real revelations came: *I didn't feel comfortable saying this before, but . . .*

I waved goodbye to the little girl, wondering how much more unkind life would be to her. By the time I got back to my office it was late. A friend, Josh, at the desk across from mine asked what I was working on.

"Dead girl on Staten Island," I said, plopping down in my chair, exhausted. I tossed my notebook on my desk.

"Drugs? Prostitution?" Josh sat forward. "No. Wait." He threw his hands open theatrically. "Housewife in a love triangle? Killed by husband? No. *Lover!*"

"I like that last one," I said. "And your enthusiasm. But drugs— that's the answer I'm looking for. Thanks for playing."

Josh stood and tossed the remains of his lunch or dinner—who knew, maybe it was breakfast—in the garbage. "Want to come with me and grab a soda while I have a drink or three?"

It was tempting. I was tired. And I could use a lift after slogging through the details of a girl's brutal, all-too-short life, but I had work to do.

"Come on. You know you want to," he said, waggling his eyebrows up and down.

"I do," I said. Then I pointed to my notebook and tape recorder. "But I need to see what all I have so far."

"You and your work ethic," he said. "You will die alone." He saluted, then made his way to the elevator bank.

I picked up my notebook and flipped through, mentally reconstructing a life. What were the days, months and years like for her? What might she have become, if she'd lived in a different world? Fatigue set in as I thought through her story. I got up to get some water and clear my head, but my phone rang, and I sat back down at my desk. It was my mother.

"Just checking in on you," she said.

I sat up. "I'm fine. Is everything okay?"

"No. I mean yes. Everything's fine. Good. Just wanted to call and see how the baby's doing."

My mother had been great helping with O after he was born. She'd slept on our lumpy couch for a week and dispensed all manner of motherly advice. It was like we were coming to know each other in a new way. Now, as I listened to my mother talk about her latest trip to Chicago and the friends she hung out with and the fun she was having, I thought about what Virginia had said: *It's like you're waiting for something.*

My mother seemed to have found her something. She was as happy as I'd ever known her to be.

What about me?

When I got off the phone with her, I didn't have the mental capacity to do any more work. I couldn't help wondering how my mother, *my mother,* suddenly had a more exciting life than I did. I packed up my briefcase—my father's briefcase—and went to join Josh at the bar across the street. A couple of our other colleagues were there with him. He ordered me my customary Shirley Temple, a drink I genuinely liked, and we all talked about the stories we were covering. A fellow crime reporter ran down details on jury deliberations in the Central Park Jogger trial. A political reporter talked Dinkins and crime and we all ruminated on that for a bit. They wanted to know about O. I happily pulled out my wallet to show everyone pictures. I was the first to get up to leave. I wanted to get home to my kid. Besides, it was never fun being the only sober person at a party. But then the whole table broke up.

I walked with Josh to the subway. It was late summer and unpleasant in the way only August in New York can be, with the sharp smell of urine floating on the thick air. We were talking about work and life and marriage and Josh asked me what I was waiting for with Manny.

I told him I didn't know.

Then I was at his apartment.

Then I was in his bed.

I got home just after midnight. Manny was up. He was sitting in a chair in the main room, with O resting on his chest.

"You just got him back to sleep?" I asked.

"Where've you been?"

"Been?"

"I tried you at work. Several times."

"We went for drinks. After."

"Who?"

"Just a bunch of us from work."

"And that's all?" He stared at me without blinking. "Just drinks?"

I blinked, then couldn't meet his eyes.

"What did you do, Trin?"

"I'm sorry. It just . . . happened."

"'It'?"

I didn't say anything. I didn't have to.

"*It* doesn't just *happen*, Trinity. Jesus!" He shook his head and closed his eyes. "What's the matter with me? This is you. You're not serious. You don't want this."

I set my briefcase on the floor. I drew in a deep breath. "Just let me—"

"Yeah. No."

He got up and took O to our bedroom and closed the door.

Deborah

1991

I drove back from Chicago in an early March snowstorm that near about struck me blind. It was a long, slip-sliding trip, with curtains of snow closing up around the car. I was scared as anything as I crept along, hunched over the steering wheel trying to see my way clear. There was at least one jackknifed semi on the other side of the highway. I passed so many cars that had spun out or slid down in ditches, I just knew I'd be next. By the time I got home, I was so grateful to be pulling into the garage that I wanted to kiss the ground.

Inside the house, I flipped on the kitchen light and dragged my suitcase through the door. I checked the answering machine on the counter. There was Trinity, asking if I could call her back, but saying she didn't want anything in particular. Just to say hi. There were a couple hang-ups, then Tommy. He was stuttering and backtracking to resay things so much that he got cut off in the middle of saying, "Me and Pearl are—"

"I'll call you back later, Mr. Tommy," I said.

I got myself out of my boots and draped my coat over a kitchen chair. I poured a tall glass of Pepsi and took a minute to relax, because that drive had worn me out. While I sipped, I thought about making myself a sandwich for a late dinner, then figured I'd do that later. I lugged my bag back to my bedroom, thinking about what Trinity had asked me, last time we spoke: "Don't you get tired of going back and forth like that? Especially in that weather? Why don't you just move to Chicago?"

I propped my suitcase by the bedroom door. "I'll get to you later," I said to it. "I'm too tired for that right now." I put my Pepsi on the nightstand and fell back on the bed, staring up at the ceiling. *Why don't I move?* I wondered. *Just go all the way?* I sat up and looked around. Everything was like I'd left it. Like I liked it. My perfumes lined up over on the dresser. My bed made nice and neat. I ran my hand over the floral quilted bedspread, thinking about home and what made it so. This wasn't how I'd expected to live in this house—all by myself—and yet, here I was. Doing just fine. On my own, but not feeling so lonely anymore.

I turned the clock radio on and got undressed. The DJ was introducing another "oldie." Another "dusty."

I laughed. "That wasn't that long ago, Mr. DJ," I said as . . . *Whoa, ah, mercy, mercy me* . . . vibrated out through the speakers. I recalled seeing Marvin one time, years before that song and that earthquake of an album came out. It was back when I used to go to Motown. He'd waved at me as I sat out there on that hard bench, hoping to see a star. I smiled at that memory, and others that were coming back to me. It had been a long time since I'd looked back at that time in my life without thinking about what could've been and regretting a lot of what was. It had been a while since I'd looked back and smiled. But I felt, just then, a little flicker of my old joy. It was a shadow of what it'd been, but it was there.

I harmonized with Marvin, then glided back to the bathroom, moving to the rhythm of the music, still smiling. I took a shower, and as I lotioned up after, I heard the doorbell. Then keys in the lock. It was Tommy, using his key after a warning ring, like he did sometimes. Still, when I heard the door open and close, I called out, "Tommy? That you?"

He hollered back that it was.

"I'll be out in a minute!"

"It's m-m-m-me and Pearl," he called back.

That was strange. The both of them coming, especially at that hour. Pearl usually liked to be home with Mr. Burton at night. I hurried and got my pajamas and a robe on and went out to meet them. As I approached from the hallway, I hollered out, asking if I could get them something to eat or if they wanted something to drink. I found them at the kitchen table. The light over their heads was dimmed.

"What did I do to deserve both of y'all here tonight?" I turned the dimmer knob to bright and stopped dead at the sight of them. "What's going on?"

They looked all business.

"W-w-w-we need to talk," Tommy said, trading a glance with Pearl.

All of a sudden, little prickles of worry rolled up my arms.

I eyed Pearl. She was staring out the sliding glass door to the snow mounds on the patio. I slid into a chair across from them. "What is it?"

Tommy put his hands out, like he didn't know where to start.

I glanced at Pearl. "Are you okay?" She finally looked me in the eye, but before she could answer, I turned back to Tommy: "Is it Trinity? Oh, no. The baby!"

Then the phone rang. They both looked at it. Then at each other.

"You need to get that," Pearl said to me, glancing down at her watch.

"I don't under—"

Tommy scrambled over and grabbed the receiver off the kitchen wall and answered. He held it out to me with his hand over the mouthpiece. "Here!"

Still confused, I got up and went over to him. I put the receiver to my ear. Then I dropped to my knees.

Before
and After

Ain't too much space

between the worlds of the living

and the worlds of the dead.

Oz

1981–1991

Oz leaned his head against the cool window of the Greyhound bus and closed his eyes. Night had fallen, so there wasn't much to be seen out the window. What mattered was that he could feel the miles rolling by as they rumbled along. And as he got further and further away from Detroit, he felt more and more like he could breathe. True, the heavy air in the bus smelled of sweat and dirty socks, but his chest felt less constricted than it had in some time.

He was headed south.

The bus jolted and rattled. His eyes flew open. He looked outside. He couldn't make out much more than shadow and light passing by the window, but he imagined the scenery probably wasn't much different from what he'd seen when he made this journey in the opposite direction, some nineteen years before: long stretches of forest and highway. On that first trip, he was with Pearl, Tommy and Willa Mae.

Pearl had told him and Tommy: "We going to Detroit to be with my people. We cain't stay down here. We won't survive the haunting."

Back then, Oz had carried with him the same kind of expectation he had now: *There will be freedom, there will be a chance at redemption when I get where I'm going.* But that trip north had been a journey of forgetting. Going back down South was a passage into memory.

He closed his eyes again as the bus moved through cities and towns and crossed state lines.

In Birmingham, a coffee-dark young man wearing a white T-shirt boarded and sat across from Oz. As Oz watched him dig through a camouflage duffel bag, he wondered if the young man was in the military, headed home for a visit. It made him think of Tommy getting back from Vietnam, proud and angry, like he'd passed some test he'd been forced to take.

Oz had been guessing about his fellow passengers since Louisville, trying to figure out the different stories of the people who got on or off the bus. He considered basic clues: what they had on, how well or badly groomed they were, how old they looked, what color they were.

What would that young man guess about him, Daniel Ozro Armstead Junior, sitting there in his white work shirt that had given up its starched crispness many miles ago? Oz's striped tie was in a neat coil in the seat next to him. He was wearing dark blue, pleated dress pants. He'd left his suit jacket back at the office and hadn't even considered going back to get it or anything else. His Stacy Adams shoes had once been spit shined. What else? A wedding ring. A thick, but simple, gold band. Not unlike the one he was carrying with him in his pocket. He didn't have any bags, which should have made him look suspicious to anyone paying any attention. The only thing he carried with him, in addition to the ring, was a pen and a little wire-bound notepad, about the size of his palm. He kept those things in his breast pocket, like he was still at work.

"Where you headed?" Oz heard someone say. He dropped his

guessing game about himself and looked up at the young man who was asking.

"Home," Oz said. "Just down the road."

The young man smiled. "Me, too. A little ways out past Eufaula."

Oz nodded, but never said exactly where his home was.

"Got a wedding," the young man went on.

"Congratulations."

"Oh, no!" The man spit out a laugh and shook his head. "My *friend's* wedding. I still got some time out here on the market."

"Well, enjoy the market," Oz said. "Time's a creeper. It's up before you know it."

"You ain't never lied." The young man chuckled like he'd seen this firsthand. But Oz guessed he was too young to have a real understanding of what time can do to a man—especially when it catches up to him. When Oz had been around his age—early twenties, Oz guessed—he'd thought he could outrun time. And tragedy. Build a life fortified against it all. He was wrong. He reclined his seat as far back as it would go, signaling that the conversation was over. He closed his eyes, but he wasn't sleepy, which made him think of his father.

"I'm just resting my eyes," his father would say whenever Oz caught him asleep in his chair or dozing in the grass. He'd jump right up and get back to doing whatever it was he was meant to be doing. It was as if the need for sleep was a sign of weakness for him, and he needed to show he was strong. Strength was important to his father.

Oz changed positions in his seat as he tried to redirect his thoughts. He angled his knees toward the window, rested his elbow on the armrest and propped up his head on his hand. Not the best, but comfortable enough. He looked at his watch. It was past midnight. His birthday was over. Only hours ago, he'd been with his brother. Only hours ago, he was supposed to be at home, celebrating with his wife and daughter. Only hours ago, he'd wandered around Detroit with his father's words running over and over in his head: *Every evil you do, son, it'll catch up to you.* He'd passed the bus station. He'd doubled back and gone inside, as if pulled by an invisible tether. He'd stood in the vestibule thinking of Alabama, the ring in his pocket and the haunting he was trying to survive. He'd gone to the counter and bought a round-trip ticket, determined to lay it all to rest. For good this time.

The bus bumped and shuddered. Oz popped his chair upright and clicked on the light above his head. He couldn't sleep. They'd be rolling into Eufaula soon and dropping off his neighbor across the aisle. Then onward home. He looked around the bus at his fellow passengers. He'd guessed all he could about them. He went back to trying to guess more things about himself, the man who'd boarded without so much as a change of clothes. Without a word of his leaving to anyone. To look at Oz in his white shirt, dark blue pants and black shoes that had lost their shine, the people on the bus would not guess that he'd just turned thirty-seven years old. He looked considerably younger. There was something boyish about him. Probably the slightly bucktoothed smile he'd gotten from sucking his thumb too long. He looked like the kind of lean, strong young man who would live forever.

Oz got off the bus and stood in the parking lot, breathing in exhaust fumes. He was back in Alabama, but not quite home yet. Their bus had limped into the station before dawn and was not able to go on. It would take some time for another bus to arrive. Standing on the edge of the parking lot, which was almost empty, he asked himself, "What the hell are you doing here?"

It was as if he'd just awakened in some stranger's bed, confused, not able to remember how he'd gotten there, but knowing enough to worry about what might come of it. He glanced back at the bus station, which was lit up but dead inside. *I can just go back home*, he said to himself. He patted his pockets. He had his round-trip ticket and plenty of money. He had a roll of cash in addition to what he kept in his wallet. His father had carried his money in just the same way.

"Insurance," he remembered his father saying. "You always gotta have insurance in life, Ozro." Oz touched the roll that bulged just slightly in his pocket, thinking about how he could go back and it would be like none of this had happened. "I'll just have to make up a story about where I've been," he said aloud, eyeing the bus station again. "I'll just go back home." But then he thought, *Home*. He was almost there. He looked around. He spotted the young man across the lot, loading his camouflage duffel into a waiting car—a Lincoln Continental. Under the lights in the parking lot, Oz could make out that it was a model from the seventies with a white top and whitewall tires. It looked well cared for. He took it as a good sign. He waved, crossing and uncrossing his arms above his head as if flagging down a rescuer in the distance.

"Hey!" he called out.

The young man looked up at him. Oz hurried over but stopped well short of the car.

"Well, if it ain't my bus-mate," the young man said.

Oz gave him his warmest smile. "Look, you said you were headed someplace outside Eufaula." It was a question, but Oz didn't speak it that way.

The young man nodded. "A few miles south. Why?"

"Good, good. Look, they said they don't know how long it's going to take to get another bus in service. I'm wondering, can I get a ride? Out to Dothan? It's not that far out of the way, and I'll pay you for it."

The young man looked at Oz for a second, assessing him. He leaned around the car and conferred with the young woman behind the wheel, then straightened up and looked at Oz again, like he was still sizing him up. "You ain't got no bags?"

Oz shook his head. "I'm just—" He laughed nervously, just short of a cackle. He hoped he didn't sound like the crazy man he felt like now, with his thoughts whipsawing this way and that. He opened his arms, as if to say, *I'm harmless.* "See, it was kind of an impromptu trip, and I didn't line up things like I should have." He pulled his wallet out—not his money roll, his insurance—and riffled through it. He took out a twenty and handed it over.

The young man stuffed the bill in his pocket and jerked his head toward the car. "Come on. I'm Isaiah."

"I'm Daniel," Oz said. He wasn't sure why he'd introduced himself by that name—his first name—but there it was. Out of his mouth. "It's Dan for short," Oz added, to convey an air of authenticity. He thanked Isaiah and hopped in the back behind the girl in the driver's seat.

"You got people here?" Isaiah asked, looking at Oz in the rear-view mirror.

"Uh, no. I don't."

"Yeah? So, you here on business or something, then?" Isaiah turned and looked at Oz full-on, examining him.

"You could say that." Sweat was pooling under his arms and pinging out on his forehead. Oz smiled, mainly because he didn't know what else to do to signal again that he meant no harm. He rolled down his window to cool down some. "Thank you both again," he said.

"You welcome," Isaiah said. "We don't mind helping a brother out when we can."

Oz was good with people, a skill he'd worked on because he was naturally shy. Everyone at work generally liked him. He liked to think that was even true of himself as Daniel. Dan. He rested his head on the back of the seat. He closed his eyes as the sweat dried on his face. The air was mild and felt clean. It was just like he remembered early Octobers in Alabama. When Oz was younger, he never thought he'd know Octobers anywhere else. After their home was lost to the fire, he, Tommy and Pearl had moved in with his grandmother—his father's mother—just down the road. The place was a mess of stained furniture, broken chairs that Oz didn't know why they kept and a kitchen sink and counter that seemed to sprout dirty dishes. Pearl slept on the stained couch and Oz and Tommy shared a blanket on the dirt-caked floor, ever on the lookout for invading rats and snakes.

One night, Oz looked up at Pearl on the couch. He could tell by the rhythm of her breathing that she was crying. Oz was too numb to cry. Too bottled up with all the things that Pearl had told him and Tommy they could never say about what they'd just been through. But he did ask: "What are we going to do now?"

That was when Pearl had said: "We going to Detroit." She spoke without hesitation, like she'd been thinking about this for some time. "To be with my people. We cain't stay down here. We won't survive the haunting." She said it in a firm whisper because Willa Mae—who lived there, too—was just on the other side of the room, sleeping on her own patch of floor. "Thomas, is that all right with you?" Pearl asked him.

Tommy didn't answer. He had gone mute in the days after attending their father's funeral, where he'd insisted on helping to carry the casket with his injured hands. He blamed himself for everything that had happened.

Oz nudged him. "Did you hear Mama?"

Tommy shifted under the afghan their grandmother had crocheted but said nothing.

"He said yes," Oz whispered to their mother. "Tommy wants to go." Tommy *needed* to go. They all did if they were truly to start again. Pearl was right about survival. Oz thought he might die or do something to himself if he stayed.

Within two weeks, they were on a bus bound for Detroit, with an overworked, beaten-down Willa Mae smuggled out like a runaway slave.

After they left, Pearl rarely spoke of Oz Senior or any member of that family again. But Oz was like Lot's wife, Pearl had told him. He couldn't help but look back. That was because he knew that what he was leaving would never leave him.

Dozing in the backseat of the Lincoln now, it was as if Oz could suddenly smell the acrid smoke of a burning house. The stink of burning flesh and hair. It was as if the air blowing through the window was turning the skin on his face to ash. Blowing up his nose, in his mouth, choking him. He grabbed at his throat, as if that might open his airway.

"Hey!" Isaiah said. "You all right, man?"

Oz opened his eyes but kept clutching at his throat. He couldn't breathe. He saw the outline of a man so outsized that he took up his entire field of vision. Hands were grabbing at Oz, and he jerked away violently, sliding down in the seat even as he swung wildly.

"Hey! Hey!"

Oz's eyes focused. It was Isaiah, leaning over the front seat, reaching for him.

Oz choked out, "I'm fine, man. Just"—he reached out and

rolled up the window—"I think I fell asleep. Had a bad dream." He laughed unsteadily. "A nightmare. Just that fast."

They rolled into the stillness of dawn, with the sky blinking awake in shades of pink and blue.

"Up here," Oz said, pointing. "This is it." They were getting close to where his old house used to be. "You can drop me off right here." He could see that no one had rebuilt that broken-down shack. From a distance, it looked like the remains of the house had been swallowed up by a field of green.

The woman pulled to the side of the road. Oz looked around, as if to gather up his things. Then he recalled that he was both passenger and cargo. He thanked them both again as he got out of the car. Isaiah got out, too, so Oz walked around to shake his hand. When Oz went to pull back, Isaiah held on.

"Look here," Isaiah said. "We could use some extra bills. You know. For the ride."

Oz yanked his hand back. "I just paid you twenty dollars." He nodded toward the road. "That was more than fair. You can get on your way now."

Isaiah shrugged. "Yeah, but see, we gon' need them extra bills."

There was no mistaking what was happening, still Oz's mind whispered in surprise: *I think this man is trying to rob me* . . . He thought for a second about what to do. He'd been a decent boxer back when he was a boy sparring, but he was not a fighter. The best he'd ever been able to do was outrun whoever was after him.

"Come on, Dan. I seen what you got in that wallet." Isaiah glanced back at the driver, who Oz now saw was pointing a gun at him. "We ain't got all day." He motioned toward Oz's wallet in his back pocket.

Oz looked over his shoulder at where his old home had been, then back at Isaiah and the woman. "I paid you fair and square. I'm not giving you another dime."

Isaiah looked at the car, then back at Oz. "You realize she will shoot yo' ass, right? That ain't no toy she holding."

Oz shrugged, like a man who had nothing to lose. "Tell her to go ahead."

Isaiah glanced back at the car. "Damn it, man, why you trying to be a hero? Just gimme the money."

Isaiah leapt forward. Oz swung at him and missed. But his second punch landed on Isaiah's chin. Isaiah shouldered Oz to the ground and rained down blow after blow. Oz was flat on his back. He tasted blood in his mouth as he swung, his fists catching mostly air. Isaiah rolled with Oz in the dirt and ripped his wallet from his back pocket. He scrambled to his feet with Oz grabbing at him as he struggled to get up. Isaiah kicked him back down. He pulled the cash from the wallet and threw the wallet back at Oz, then ran to the car.

"Stay down!" the woman yelled, firing off a shot in the air as Isaiah hopped in the passenger seat. The Lincoln sped off. Oz spit blood into the red clay at his feet and brushed off some of the dirt that clung to his white shirt and suit pants. He limped up the road to where his old house had been. He waded into the field and stood there, looking at the verdant rows of bushes all around him. Peanut plants, with their deep roots, ready for harvest.

"It's what you cain't see," his father had told him the first time Oz had joined him in the field. "All that going on under your feet. You pull it up, and you got yourself something." And his father had tugged the green, bushy crown up from the ground. He shook off the dirt so Oz could see the peanut pods that had grown. His father had smiled and said, "That's something, ain't it?"

Tears came to Oz's eyes. He wandered further into the field.

Their house had been set off the road on its own small plot. They'd never owned that land.

"Never owned a thing," Pearl used to say.

Oz felt a new wave of fury at Pearl. If she'd just come home that night, when he and Tommy had needed her, their lives would have been different. His father might not have had to die in the prime of his life. And Oz might not have found himself back here, in the prime of his. A father dead, a son uncomfortably alive—both in their thirty-seventh year.

Oz stumbled away from where their house had been, hurrying toward the road. His jaw was aching from where he'd been punched in the face by the man who'd robbed him. The funk that clung to him from the long bus trip was rising up and threatening to make him sicker than he already felt. When he reached the road, he kept going. He was in the middle of nowhere. He walked toward where he remembered the town to be. The leather from his nice dress shoes chafed and cut into his feet. He came upon a Gulf station that had a pay phone. He still had his money roll, but he didn't have any change. He didn't want to go in there. He was filthy and bloody. But he had no choice.

He went in and grabbed a Coke out of the cooler, as casual as could be, and took it up to the counter.

"You all right there?" the counter man asked him. Oz heard everything but genuine concern in the man's voice.

He nodded. "Just the Coke, please." He tossed a ten on the counter. The man held the bill up to the light. He tossed it in the cash drawer and slid Oz's change back to him, sizing him up the whole time. Oz nodded thank you and limped out on his aching, blistering feet. He went over to the pay phone. He'd lied when he said he didn't have any family around. He wasn't all that eager to make the call, though. But he did.

"Why're you here?" Willa Mae asked Oz.

Oz took a long pull from his can of Pabst in response.

He and Willa Mae were sitting on her porch in lawn chairs with McDonald's bags balanced on their laps. She'd driven him from Alabama back to her little ranch house across the border in Georgia. As they rode along, Oz, with his battered face and blood-streaked white shirt, had told her that he looked way worse than he felt but he wasn't up for much talking right then. So Willa Mae had driven on in shocked silence for miles, past signs advertising boiled peanuts, past crosses marking church after church and past fluff-laden cotton fields. She would occasionally glance at Oz, no doubt storing up her questions until just the right time, which appeared to be now, as they sat together on the porch at the onset of evening. Her queries came out pointed and impatient: "You and Deborah having problems? Something happen?"

"It's, um . . . I guess you could say that." That lie was laughable. The problems he was having with Deborah were manageable and of his own making. She wasn't the one he couldn't live with. The best he could manage was, "I'm just trying to get some space. That's all."

"And I'm the only one that know you here?"

"That's about right, yes."

He took another swig of beer as he looked at his cousin. He worried that the years reflected on her acne-scarred face were etched by trouble, not time. He recalled her leaving Detroit over a decade ago when the city was burning and tanks were rolling through the streets. She was chasing after what she thought was a prophetic dream. Oz had mostly been out of touch with her, which was something because they'd been so close. A bond that had formed when they were kids. Back when Willa Mae was in the care of a mercurial aunt who would toss out random scraps of affection between long stretches of neglect and occasional acts of cruelty. Oz remembered once coming upon Willa Mae crying after Aunt Bee had said she had a hard time looking at Willa Mae's face, with her acne bubbling up like it was. Oz had sat quietly with his cousin until the tears passed.

But there were plenty of other times when Willa cried for reasons unknown to Oz. It was usually when he and Tommy were on their blanket on the floor at their grandmother's house trying to sleep while Willa Mae was on her side of the room. She would sometimes whimper without ceasing, until Oz fell off to sleep. During the day, Oz would sometimes catch her at the front door, broom in hand for her endless cleaning jobs, assigned by Aunt Bee. She'd be looking past the dirt patch of the front yard out to the horizon. Once, while Oz was tinkering with the broken-down truck parked beside the house, she had come running outside, her face radiating a rare smile. She'd wanted to know if he'd fixed the truck and if maybe they could go for a ride. He hadn't, but he promised her he would.

That skinny, smiling, quick-moving girl was only vaguely recognizable in the woman sitting across from him on the porch. She was heavier now. She walked with a cane, too. She'd mumbled something about a car accident when Oz had asked about it.

He leaned in and asked her, "So, how've you been, Old Willa?"

"Don't change the subject on me, Oz. This ain't no buddy-

buddy catch-up. Look at you, showing up here in your work clothes and dress shoes, day after your birthday. And you trying to tell me it's you needing some space from Deborah?" She paused, apparently giving him a chance to answer. When he didn't, she said, "Boy, if you think I believe that, then I guess you think I'm a new kinda fool, don't you?"

Oz shifted uncomfortably in the lawn chair—and in the clothes he was wearing. He had taken a shower and changed and was now outfitted in another man's baggy jeans and Incredible Hulk T-shirt. "I have some unfinished business, Willa. Same reason you came back this way." Oz dug his Big Mac carton and fries out of the bag and started eating. The burger was like tasteless, damp cardboard, but he hoped a full mouth would shut down the conversation, and it did for a time. They sipped their beers and ate their burgers and fries to the evening calls of crickets.

When Willa Mae finished, she closed her empty burger carton and picked up where she'd left off: "And what's this 'unfinished business' you got, Oz?"

He closed his carton slowly and turned his beer can up to get the last swallow, giving himself a beat to contemplate what he might say. "It's me," he mumbled. "It's my daddy."

"All right. Now we getting somewhere."

He swallowed and inched closer to the truth. "You remember how he was?"

She closed her eyes, as if tracking it all in her mind, and nodded.

When they were young, Oz had indeed managed to fix that old truck and the two of them would go out on drives together. Short ones, because the truck was still prone to breaking down, but long enough for him to listen to every sadness Willa Mae needed to share and to tell her about life with his father. The good, the bad, the unbearable. But he hadn't told her everything.

She leaned forward. "You can talk to me, you know that, right?"

He crushed the Big Mac box against his knee and searched the tree line, thinking he'd heard an owl hooting out there in the twilight. Finally, he said, "When it all happened with him, the fire, I mean, I . . . well, Tommy . . . I didn't—"

Oz shook his head, unable to speak.

"You didn't what, Oz?"

Oz shook his head again, his eyes burning with tears.

Willa Mae looked like she had more to ask, because clearly there was a lot more for him to say. But when she did speak, she said simply, "He gone, Oz."

Oz got up from his chair. He paced from one end of the porch to the other, then stopped and looked around as if men in white coats might show up to drag him off the moment he said what he was thinking. "No," he said quietly, fingering the ring in his pocket, "he's not."

"It's all right, cousin," she said. "Come on. Sit back down."

He looked around. He should not have called Willa Mae. He should not even be here. He should have walked on until his feet bled and the road ran out beneath them. He realized he was sweating, even in the mild evening air. He wiped his brow with the hem of the Hulk T-shirt and sat down.

"You in a bad place, Oz." She leaned back in her chair. "And ain't nothing wrong with that. What I think is . . . see, we got this veil between us and the dead—"

"I don't want to hear any of that Voodoo witchcraft stuff, Willa," Oz said.

She ignored him and went on: "When Aunt Bee was lonely and wanting some company, she could be real nice. She'd sit with me and we'd talk, and she told me one time that ain't too much space between the worlds of the living and the worlds of the dead. We can get to them, through the right channels. But more important, they can get to us." She looked out to the gathering darkness, as if on guard. "I'll tell you this much. If your daddy mean you harm, he ain't getting to you here."

Oz needed look no further than above his head to see a manifestation of what Willa Mae meant. The ceiling of the porch was painted blue. Willa Mae would tell anyone who'd listen that blue was meant to trick haints into thinking they'd come upon water. And everyone knew that a spirit could not cross water. Everyone knew that water, even if it was an illusion, could keep you safe from whatever was haunting you.

But Oz knew better. And he was coming to believe that maybe this was a haunting he was not meant to survive.

Oz called home after he'd been at Willa Mae's for about a week. He sat on the butt-dimpled couch next to the end table with the telephone. He paused with the receiver in his hand and his finger in the numbered hole ready to dial. He took a deep breath, then dialed the numbers. The phone rang on the other end of the line. The pickup was fast. It was Pearl. Oz held the phone to his ear while she said, "Hello? *Hello?*"

He hung up.

Later that night, he sat on the couch and dialed home again. He got Deborah. Her voice was sharp and anxious. "Hello? Is somebody there?" she asked.

He hung up.

The days tumbled one over the other. Most days, Oz would sit for hours in Willa Mae's back bedroom, where he'd been sleeping. He would look at the items he had spread out on the dresser: his return ticket to Detroit, his cash roll, his small notebook, his father's wedding ring. He would get up and touch every item, then go back and sit down and stare at them some more.

He did at least sometimes leave to get some air. He would take Willa Mae's car up the road to the convenience store, passing desolate, decaying houses along the way. If not for the fact that there were sometimes people sitting on the porches in their plastic chairs, he'd swear the homes were abandoned.

The convenience store was just a little bit more than a hut that sold candy, cold drinks, cigarettes and the like. Customers could also get a good catfish sandwich or catfish with two sides and corn bread from a window in the back. He saw the same people in there doing the same things all the time, and he blended right in. After all of his work to lose his accent, it had found him again. His vowels softened. Relaxed, as if at ease. He sounded just like everyone else when he asked or answered a question as he stood in line, holding his fish plate or Coke. Or sometimes both.

Once, he was in line behind a tight knot of three girls. Teenagers. All three looked fast in their too-tight jeans and breast-cupping tank tops. They sounded older than they looked, too, given the amount of cussing they were doing.

"Hey," Oz said. "Watch your language, girls."

They laughed at him and rolled their eyes. The girl at the front of the group shoved M&M's and Hershey bars and money toward the man behind the bulletproof glass. Oz watched them leave with their bag of candy. He was thinking of Trinity. He thought of Trinity whenever he saw a girl of any age. He was thinking he should have said something to her about boys and being careful. But she wasn't of that age yet. Then he thought again: She was sixteen. She was *sixteen*. He'd been right there and hadn't even noticed she was at the age and probably needed to hear that. How useless he'd been.

The cashier broke him out of his trance, asking him to pay for his plate. The paper plate was sagging in his hand now, the grease having soaked through. Oz paid the man, then went outside and stood watching those girls disappear down the road.

Back at Willa Mae's, after he'd eaten his lunch, he called home again. He got Trinity. But she hung up on him so fast at the sound of nothing on the other end of the line that Oz was left stunned by the dial tone and her lack of curiosity about who might be calling. There was no desperate-sounding *Hello, hello? Is somebody there?* like Deborah or Pearl. There was only the briefest chance to announce himself. When he didn't, she was gone. He felt a strange mix of pride and heartbreak in that.

Willa Mae caught him staring at the receiver in his hand. "How'd it go this time?"

He hung up and eyed the receiver in the cradle. "You know, right there at the end, I was barely there when I was there . . . What's worse is, when I was there, I wasn't myself. I put my hands on Deborah. Did you know that?"

Willa Mae's eyes widened, and she shook her head. "How would I know something like that, Oz?"

"I pushed her," Oz said. "Hard. It was like I was gone for a second. Then I came to, and there she was on the floor."

"I don't believe that. That ain't you."

"It's not me. It's him, Willa."

Willa Mae grunted as she sat down on the couch next to him. She looked like she didn't want to speak the words, but still she said: "What happened with your daddy, Oz?"

Oz pictured the dresser in the back room and that ring gleaming on it next to the bus ticket he meant to use to get back home to Detroit. All this time, he thought it was a matter of going back to where he'd grown up to put those demons to rest. But it wasn't as simple as that. There was no big moment of resolution when he was standing in that field. He was coming to believe his demons had a price.

He recalled what he knew of demons. There was a Bible lesson he'd learned as a child. It had come back to him on a night he went to church in search of Pearl. It was the night Tommy was talking about when he told Oz: "Sometimes, I wish you'd let me die that night." That night, their father had come upon Tommy up in the loft of the barn. Tommy was with a boy from down the road. They were just playing cards, Tommy kept saying to their father. But he was so scared, and his stutter was so thick, it was hard to make out much more than "C-c-c-cards."

"That's all, Daddy," Oz said, trying to help. "Just cards." But Oz had no idea. He'd been in the kitchen eating leftover grits, hunched over the radio, trying to keep time with Little Eva.

They were all standing out in the yard now. Night was falling.

Their father adjusted his glasses in his slow, deliberate way. "Thomas," he said. "I think you doubt the kinda man I am. I think you doubt the kinda man you can be. Come on in the house, son. It's time to become a believer."

Tommy looked at Oz, his eyes wide and pleading. He went down on his knees.

"Daddy, please," Oz said. "Nothing's going on with Tommy and that boy."

Their father looked off toward the house and slid his hands in the pockets of his overalls. He rocked back and forth on his heels. Then he turned back to a kneeling Tommy. "Thomas," he said quietly, his eyes welling up, "what kinda father would I be? You know I ain't had one, so I gotta be a *good* one to you boys." He nodded, as if making up his mind. "This for the best. One day y'all'll look back. Y'all'll understand when you got families of your own." He held his hand out to Tommy. "Come on, Thomas."

Tommy was still on his knees, tears streaming down his face, keening like he already had a loss to grieve. Oz tried to imagine what the punishment might be this time. Probably another bad beating. Maybe with the whip. But hadn't Tommy been beaten enough? Oz took off running down the road. He was looking for Pearl. He found her at church, alone in a pew. The sun was all but down, so the sanctuary was dim and shadowy.

Oz knew Pearl had to hear him gasping, trying to catch his

breath, but she didn't turn. As he crept toward her pew, close to the altar, he recalled that Bible lesson he'd learned as a child. The preacher had told him and the other children: "Don't come up around the altar when we're casting out demons up here. They can jump out of that person and straight into you." As proof, the preacher had told a story about Jesus casting out demons and sending them into a herd of pigs. The pigs, so afflicted, so tormented, had thrown themselves off a cliff and perished in the sea.

As Oz approached Pearl's pew, he wondered if there were any demons left floating around waiting for him. He was so unnerved, he stopped halfway up the aisle and called out to his mother: "It's Tommy. Daddy's got him again. Are you coming home?"

"In a little bit," Pearl said, still not looking back at him.

Standing behind her pew, Oz couldn't see Pearl's face, but he knew she was in tears because of the choked sound of her voice. "I need to commune with God," she said. "I need to . . . I need to know what to do."

"But—"

Pearl put her hands over her ears and curled forward as she said, "Thomas is fine. Thomas is fine. Go home, Ozro. I'll be there in a minute." She straightened, then looked over her shoulder at Oz and said, "Y'all stick together." She was wild-eyed, like Oz imagined a demon-possessed person would look.

He ran back in the direction of home, tripping over rocks that seemed to rise up in the darkness to hinder him. From down the road, he saw flames illuminating the sky. He prayed, "Please, please, please . . ." as he sprinted toward what awaited him at home.

He looked up at Willa Mae now and said, "I was so . . . I didn't want to understand Tommy when he went his own way to deal with his demons. Traveling all over the place like that."

Willa Mae's brow knotted up in confusion.

He let her know about his brother's wanderings and calls home, though he did not tell her everything. "But Tommy was right," Oz conceded, picturing those tormented pigs running off, trying to get free. "He was right, going off on his own—"

"That's some nonsense, Oz," Willa Mae cut in. "And you just said you always knew where he was. The boy checked in." She paused. "Look here, let me call. Just to let everybody know you with me. That everything's okay."

Oz shook his head. He asked her not to do that. "It's not okay, Willa. I'm not okay." He got up and went back to the back room, ignoring Willa Mae, who was calling out to him. He felt a shadow in the shape of his father rise on the wall beside him. He let the shadow lead. In the room, he grabbed the bus ticket from the dresser and took it to the bathroom. He stood over the toilet, ripping it up. He flushed it.

"Is that what you want?" he asked the shadow. "The end of my family, too? Is that the price? Is that your punishment for me?"

The next day, Oz went to the convenience store and asked for a job. The man behind the counter recognized him. Even seemed to like him because Oz was always friendly when he came in. He told Oz that he owned the place and that he couldn't pay much, but if Oz was willing to open the store in the mornings, he could use him.

Oz accepted, needing to be of use.

What he liked most about the job was that it paid cash and no one asked who he was, beyond his name. He was Dan to them. As the months passed, he established a kind of rhythm. He always got to the store just a little earlier than Catfish Kenny, the tall, rangy, fish-eyed man who worked the catfish counter. Oz would unlock the door to the store, which was heavy and fortified by security bars. He liked the quiet during his time alone there. He would walk down the aisles, checking that everything was in its place: There was all of the candy in the right boxes; potato chips, jerky and cracklin's were fully stocked; the sodas and beer and water and milk were all cold. And so it went until Catfish Kenny came in and leaned on the counter to share one of his "eye-openers." The latest centered around the president.

"Ronald. Wilson. Reagan," Catfish Kenny would say, widening his fish eyes for emphasis. "Six letters in every one of them names. Six. Six. Six. The mark of the beast. You see what I'm talkin' 'bout?"

Oz would express mild skepticism, then go up behind the bulletproof glass that divided the cash register from everyone else. He'd sit on his stool and read magazines about health and fitness. He avoided anything that made him think of that other life.

Sometimes, though, while on his stool, Oz would look up the wall next to him at row after row of cigarettes. His eyes always came to rest on the green and white pack of Kools. Deborah's brand. Once, it was as if he could see Deborah reaching for one. He knew his mind was playing tricks on him, so he closed his eyes. But there she was, behind his closed lids.

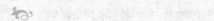

As the seasons turned and the years went by, Oz kept calling the house. He staggered it out to avoid creating a pattern. After a while, it was only Deborah who picked up, and Oz imagined Trinity off in college. That was his hope. He called Tommy and Pearl, too. He never spoke, but he tried to gauge everyone's *hello*s. How flat they sounded. How rushed. How happy. How sad. How quickly they hung up on him.

Tommy would always stay on the phone the longest, as if waiting for him.

He wasn't sure what to make of Deborah's *hello*s, but a couple of times, he was sure she was drunk. Once when she'd either dropped the receiver or not put it down properly in its cradle, he'd heard her humming in the background. He wondered if she was singing again. She had stopped even singing around the house when he was there. Then he heard her heavy night breathing—not a snore, but close. As he sat listening to her sleep, he missed her. He longed for her. He allowed himself to think about the sound of her voice, the curve of her hips, the smell of her hair. But he would not let himself speak to her.

He hung up, like he always did, telling himself that everyone was okay. Better, even, for him being gone from a life he'd built but had never fully inhabited, no matter how he'd tried. Every year, it was as if he was shedding the vestiges of that life like another skin. Peeling back to someone he barely recognized.

Oz hovered outside the boxing ring, giving instructions. He could do this all day, but, as it stood, it was what he did at night and on weekends. He had set up a boxing gym in a barn. The barn belonged to a customer at the store. The customer had told Oz the space was his if he cleaned it out and made good use of it. So Oz had gotten a couple of guys to help him haul out a rickety old tractor and rusted tools. They'd swept up God knew what all from the floor. They'd built a serviceable boxing ring and hung heavy bags and speed bags. Oz had put up posters of the greats: Joe Louis, Muhammad Ali and, of course, Sonny Liston.

So, you Sonny Liston now?

"Left foot forward," Oz said, climbing into the ring. He was talking to a young boy who had the slight build of a bully magnet. "How does that feel?" Oz asked as he put his hands on the boy's shoulders to square him up.

The boy—Dre—made a noise around his mouthguard and nodded.

"All right," Oz said. He went through the same thing with the boy's sparring partner, Antonio, another knobby-kneed and -elbowed foal of a boy. He stepped back into a corner of the ring and watched as the boys danced around each other. Dre was little but wily, lunging in first with wild, windmilling punches. Antonio hunched down and covered his head, trying to block the onslaught.

Oz had not intended for the gym to be a place for kids. He'd meant it to be a place men could come and blow off some steam. Find some escape, however briefly, from the troubles of life. Then, Antonio and Dre had appeared with three other boys. Oz had made them all leave. He never saw the other three boys again, but Antonio and Dre kept coming back, racing their bikes around outside and tearing up the yard, which wasn't much more than a patchwork of dirt and weeds, but still. Oz shooed them away like stray dogs. Then one night, Oz looked up and they were inside the gym. Willa Mae had let them in because she had a soft spot for discarded children. She'd given them brooms and rags and told them to earn their keep with a little work. They were sweeping and wiping down anything in their path. They were conspicuously averting their gaze from Oz, as if hiding their eyes might keep their whole person entirely concealed.

But Oz saw them, all right. And he noticed how Antonio moved quickly and carelessly with the broom, humming and bopping to whatever was playing on his Walkman. And how tight-lipped serious Dre was, his untamed mass of curls bobbing with every overly aggressive wipe-down. Oz had told himself that he'd let them finish, pay them, then tell them this wasn't a place for them. But then, he'd felt sorry, because, of course, what he also saw was something of himself and his brother in them, just as he saw Trinity in most every girl. How could he not?

As Oz watched them now, dancing around the boxing ring, their jabs grew sluggish and ever more graceless. He told them to call it a night.

They both said in unison, "Thanks, Mr. Dan."

As Oz hopped out of the ring behind the boys, he asked, "Hey, how come your buddies didn't come back with you? Those other three boys?"

They glanced at each other. "Dre told them you real hard on kids," Antonio said.

Dre smiled, his teeth straight and white, but unusually small, much like himself. "You got you a real bad reputation with kids out there. *Real* bad."

"And they never ask why you keep coming back for that?"

"The money," Dre said. "But I told them you ain't hiring no more."

Oz didn't even pay the boys anymore. He looked at Antonio. "Come on, man. Why would you let him be out there telling tales like that?"

Antonio shrugged. "'Cause this is our place." The two of them bounced off to get some water.

Oz walked through the gym, exchanging hellos with some of the regulars, a handful of guys who sparred and worked the bags with the zeal of fighters training to go twelve rounds. But all the men who came in that gym, even the ones in excellent shape, were swinging at impossible dreams. When they left the gym, it was back to their problem homes and piecemeal jobs and the street corners and clubs where they drank and joked and smoked and used their boxing skills on anyone who made them feel like lesser men.

Oz went over to the door where Willa Mae held court every night. "How's it looking, Old Willa?"

She glanced down at where she kept the cookie tin, which was now a money tin. "How you think it's looking?"

There were a few dollar bills along with a scattering of quarters and dimes and pennies.

"You need to make these boys start paying some real money, Oz or Dan or whatever the hell I'm supposed to be calling you."

Oz waved a dismissive hand. "I'm not going to bother them. They give what they can," he said.

"Yeah, well, I think they can give more than they claim they can." She pointed to one of the young men going at a speed bag. "Look at the gold chain on that one."

"That's not everything," Oz said. He glanced over at the water jug, where Antonio and Dre were shoving each other and laughing. He felt something in him lighten. He felt like maybe he was making good use of this place, like he'd promised to do. He had a need to do something right. Something redemptive. Something good.

Oz moved into the RV Willa Mae kept parked in her side yard, next to the carport. It had a tiny bathroom and kitchenette and a bed. He lived mostly in blue jeans and white oxfords, though both items of clothing had sharp creases where he'd ironed them. Those clothes, that small RV, the convenience store, evenings and weekends in the gym, the ever-present company of his demons—that was the extent of Oz's life. And he wrote it all down in his notebooks, not unlike he used to do when keeping track of his life's goals. He kept the notebooks stacked in cubbies and on shelves in the RV. The notebooks were held together by rubber bands and organized by year. And the years did pass quickly.

In the spring of 1989, Willa Mae told Oz he'd been declared dead. "Deborah called and invited me to your funeral."

Oz was sitting at a picnic table in the backyard, going over the books from the convenience store. He'd taken over that job from the store's owner the year prior. He was waiting for himself to feel something about the news of his passing. But it was like rain pinging against a window. It hit but washed over him without soaking in.

"Well?" Willa Mae said, sitting down across from him and propping her cane against the table. "That don't mean nothing to you?"

Oz put his pencil down and squinted at her. The sun was shining behind her, making her seem to glow. He cupped his hand over his eyes to see her better, then glanced at the house. "I wonder if I'll be able to go up on your blue porch now." He meant it as a joke, but it came out as dark as he felt.

"Seem to me you been a ghost for a long time, Oz," Willa Mae said. She had long ago stopped badgering him about calling home or even going back. He was the only family she had around here. The only friend, too, as far as he could tell. About a year after he'd moved in, she'd told him about her losses. After leaving Detroit, Willa Mae had followed those dreams of hers to Alabama. She'd found Aunt Bee right where she'd left her.

"I guess I was looking for some kinda . . . I don't know," Willa Mae said. "But all them dreams I had? Wasn't the sign I thought. She was like she always was—mean one minute, then the next minute trying to be nice, like she ain't never said or done nothing wrong to me. She never said sorry. But she didn't have long to live, and she was by herself. I couldn't leave her like that, even though she done me bad a lot. So I stayed and took care of her till she passed. I hoped it made her happy because, when you think about it good, she ain't never had much in her life to be happy about."

Willa Mae had left Alabama after that, "following behind a no-count," and settled across the state line in Georgia.

"That was why y'all hardly heard from me," she'd told Oz. "I was too wrapped up with that fool."

She'd married him. Put up with him, until he almost killed her. He'd slammed their car, with her in it, into a tree after yet another night of too much drinking and arguing. Willa Mae could never say why she'd gotten in the car with him that night. She'd known better. She'd even known better than to marry him, and yet . . . "It was love. Loneliness. I dunno."

The husband had walked away from the accident with barely a scratch, as had happened with most every half-witted, blackhearted thing he'd ever done. But the firemen had to pry Willa Mae out of that car. The doctors had done the best they could with her shattered leg, but she'd been left to limp through the rest of her life on a cane. Willa Mae attributed the good fortune of her husband leaving to Aunt Bee. "One thing that woman did do was pass on what she knew about curses. I put a root on that fool. Drove him clean outta his mind. Ain't got no idea where he ran off to. But I ended up with this house, so it wasn't all bad. I guess Aunt Bee did leave me with something good, in her way."

Willa Mae had been alone in the little ranch house ever since. Until Oz.

She reached out and touched her cane, which was propped against the table. She held Oz's gaze. "You telling me you really don't care that you dead to them now?"

"I imagine that's how it feels for them," he said quietly. Then he asked, "Are you going? To my funeral?"

She made a dismissive noise. "I cain't be up there fronting when I know what's what." She gripped her cane and hoisted herself up to standing. "I feel guilty enough as it is. I'll call with my condolences when they bury you."

Oz started having nightmares after learning about his death. Some-times it was him being put into a coffin, unable to speak or move but very much alive. Someone would close the lid—he could never make out a face—and lower him into the ground. He couldn't yell for help. He couldn't move. He'd wake up screaming and clawing at the covers. On other nights, his nightmares were about fire.

In those dreams, Oz has just left Pearl at church. He is walking toward their house and an inferno. The heat is like a wall, but he punches through. His father is inside the house with his hand on the windowpane, like he is saying hi. But he is looking at Oz in shock and terror. And then it is Tommy's face, still-water smooth, that Oz sees, even as the color of that moment drains away before Oz's eyes. Tommy's calm face, the rhinestone-studded velvet that is the night sky, the red glow of the flames—they are all the color of ash. There is only the yellow of the curtains at the window, un-dulating around Tommy like a frame. Oz would always wake up in a sweat, never having reached his brother. And that dream—the grief and regret he'd felt in it—would haunt him all day.

Oz awoke from that dream one winter morning and got dressed in his creased jeans and starched white shirt. He threw on his jacket and braced himself against a brisk wind. He drove to work in the black Dodge he'd bought off a neighbor some years back. When he got to the store, he did his checks. Everything was as it should be. He listened to Catfish Kenny's "eye-opener" about the United Nations and a one-world government and being tracked by our Social Security numbers, which were, in fact, the mark of the beast and a sign of the end of the world. Oz expressed his usual skepticism, then went up behind the bulletproof glass and made some change. He went across the street to the phone booth outside of Pig Meat Barbecue. He dropped in some coins and dialed. He checked his watch. Maybe he'd catch Tommy before he left for work. If he was still working as a barber, like before. Oz would try to see what he could hear in his brother's voice, like he did whenever he called.

"H-h-h-hello?"

Oz felt an immediate sense of relief at the sound of Tommy's stutter and was about to hang up, but he didn't this time. He kept thinking, *Tommy's alive*, as if this was a surprise.

Tommy said hello again.

Oz moved to hang up; then, in an uncertain whisper, Tommy said his name. "Oz?"

Oz hung up, like the phone was electrified. He walked quickly back across the street and back to the store for a full day of ringing up customers, restocking and half listening to Catfish Kenny. At the gym, he talked with the few guys who'd come in. It was cold, and there was no heat or air-conditioning in the gym. But Antonio and Dre were there, flailing at each other in the ring. Rain, shine, whatever the season, they showed up. They were older now, with Antonio hitting a growth spurt and teenhood. Dre was on the edge of adolescence, but his height had barely budged, which made Oz wonder if that was why he wore that cloud of curls on his head so high.

Oz signaled to them that it was time to go. "Let's call it a night, guys," he said.

Both boys bounded over and pitched themselves through the ropes, tumbling out like acrobats.

All that energy, Oz thought. *Must be nice.*

He was tired from his restless sleeping and endless bad dreaming. He told the boys to leave the cleaning until tomorrow and corralled them to the car. He dropped Antonio at a tiny duplex, where he lived with his grandmother. He watched the porch light come on and Antonio disappear safely inside. He pulled up outside of Dre's house, one of the many desolate, decaying homes Oz passed every morning on his way to the convenience store. Dre lived with his mother, a known addict, who spent more time "away," as Dre described it, than there. As usual, no lights were on, but Dre jumped out like it was nothing and ran to the front door. He let himself in. Oz sat waiting for a light and for Dre to flash it three times. That was the signal that everything was okay inside. But there was no light. After a couple of nerve-racking seconds ticked by, Oz got out of the car and ran to the front door. Just then, a light came on, the door swung open and there was Dre.

"Is something wrong in there?"

Movement over Dre's shoulder caught Oz's eye. He could see through the open door into the front room. It was empty, save for a beanbag chair up against the dingy back wall. A bony wraith of a woman was sitting on it, hunched over, staring in Oz's direction but somehow straight through him. She was scratching furiously, like a rodent, at something on her arm. Oz was sure that woman was Dre's mother—he could see something of the boy around her wide-set eyes.

"Is everything okay?" Oz asked.

Dre looked confused, then glanced over his shoulder. He stepped out and closed the door behind him, appearing embarrassed. "She got troubles. That's all."

"Can I help?"

Dre shook his head, then cleared his throat. "Um, I forgot something. I was in the house, and I remembered I forgot."

"What is it? Is it in the car?"

"Oh, I didn't leave nothing. What I forgot, or what I meant to do, was ask if I can, you know, have my birthday party at the gym." He paused, apparently sensing Oz's aversion even before Oz spoke. Then, he pressed on: "All the guys, my friends at the gym, they think it'll be fun. I never had a birthday before," Dre said, his voice cracking, as if to remind Oz that this was a boy on the brink of manhood. "I mean. I had *birthdays*—lots of them—but it's, you know . . . Thirteen's a big one, and seem like I should have a party for it. That's all."

Oz glanced at the closed door behind Dre, thinking of the woman on the other side of it. Given the state of the boy's homelife, he wanted to say an immediate yes to the party, but birthdays were so hard for Oz . . . "I don't know, Dre. Birthdays are . . . A party? At the gym? I'll have to think about that."

Dre smiled, his tiny Chiclet-like teeth glowing white against the darkness of him. "I know you will, 'cause you nice, Mr. Dan."

Oz watched Dre go inside to whatever awaited him. He got in his car and drove off, thinking about birthdays. He did not celebrate them, his or anyone else's. Every passing birthday marked another passing year. Everyone—Deborah, Trinity, Tommy, Pearl—they'd all grown older. But his father, not so. He was another year gone, with Oz trying to make up for it.

Back in his RV, he was cold. He was lonely. He felt unlike himself.

Like who, then? he wondered.

He fell asleep, balled up on his bunk with his clothes on. But he jolted awake in a sweat, looking around wildly. He'd been dreaming about his own birthday party. The one he'd missed. He'd been dreaming about Antonio and Dre fighting in the backyard with his father. About his father, looking at him in shock and terror.

Oz got up and stumbled out of the chilly RV into an even colder night. He went in the house for some water and warmth. Standing at the sink filling up a second glass, he waited for his mind to clear. He waited to feel more like himself, or the self he'd gotten used to being. He wondered if this was how Deborah felt with one of her hangovers—like there was a film separating her from the world. His tired eyes caught on the kitchen phone. Thickheaded, in a groggy stupor, he went over to it. He just wanted to hear everyone's voices again. He dialed Tommy's number first. After a few rings, his brother picked up. His voice was deep, but he'd been asleep, so it cracked. Almost like Dre's: *You nice, Mr. Dan.*

"No, I'm not," Oz mumbled.

"*Oz?* Th-th-that you?"

Oz jumped and yanked the phone away from his ear. He put his hand to his mouth, as if to stop more words from slipping out.

"Oz?"

Oz heard his brother's voice hanging in the distance between the phone and his ear. He looked at the receiver, caught between the habit of hanging up and a sudden urge to answer to his name.

Oz waited at the gate. He got up and paced in front of the long row of seats, stretching his legs. His knees were bothering him. He'd been jumping rope too much at the gym.

"Not as young as you used to be," he mumbled to himself as he kicked his legs out to loosen up his knees. Tommy's plane had landed. He could see it out the window. After a few minutes, Tommy emerged from the jetway. It had been the better part of a decade since he'd seen him, and Oz thought Tommy wore the years well. He'd filled out a little. His face was rounder. His waist thicker.

Oz raised his hand as if to say, *Here I am*. Tommy nodded in Oz's direction from his place in the line of deplaning travelers. The two brothers approached each other slowly. Oz had missed him, without question, but he didn't move to hug Tommy. And Tommy didn't reach out either. They stood awkwardly in front of each other. Tommy was holding a small gift-wrapped box with a red bow, like it was Christmas.

"How you doing, Tommy?" Oz asked.

"Fine. You?"

"Okay."

They stood together for another uncomfortable second, with Tommy looking at him like a rare find. Something to be studied.

"You want to, um, maybe grab a bite to eat?" Oz asked, pointing off vaguely. "There are places around here . . ."

"Yeah," Tommy said.

Oz led the way out of the airport to the parking lot, with no need to stop at baggage claim. Tommy had his overnight bag slung over his shoulder. This was going to be a short trip. That was one of the many things they'd discussed, when Oz decided to answer the third time his brother called his name.

As they came upon the car in the lot, Oz told Tommy how good he looked and how good it was to see him. Tommy accepted the compliments but offered none to Oz. When they'd spoken on the phone, Tommy's surprise at hearing Oz's voice had quickly turned to anger and a rat-a-tat of questions: Where are you? Why would you do this? *How* could you do this?

Oz had agreed to meet Tommy in Birmingham after Tommy promised that he'd keep everything between the two of them. Like they'd always done.

Y'all stick together.

They pulled into a Waffle House and Oz followed Tommy in, both of them hunched over against spitting rain. Within seconds of sliding into the booth, Tommy leaned forward and said: "Don't y-y-y-you think it's time to come home?"

Oz looked down at the table. "Can we not talk about that right now?"

"Can we n-n-n-not—what?" Tommy's elbows were on the table and his fists were clenched.

"You want to hit me, Tommy?"

Tommy's jaw tightened, but he pulled his hands back and put them under the table. "I told you not to let Daddy get in y-y-y-your head, Oz."

Oz didn't respond.

It was quiet until Tommy said he wanted to go to their old house.

"It's all farmland now," Oz said, remembering how unhelpful his visit had been. "There's nothing left."

"I don't care. I w-w-w-wanna see it."

Oz shook his head. "I've seen enough."

The waitress walked up. They both turned their attention to her. Both of them ordered pancakes and coffee. As boys, when their father was away, Pearl would sometimes make them breakfast for dinner. It was a special treat. Both of them, when they grew up, would always order breakfast whenever they could. It was lunchtime now, but close enough to dinner, in Oz's mind. He noticed that Tommy had almost smiled when he was giving his order.

When the waitress left, Tommy said, "Look, Oz, y-y-y-you can't keep this up. You gotta, I don't know . . . What about Deborah? Trinity? Mama?"

"They deserve better," Oz said.

They ate the rest of their meal in silence. As they left the restaurant and walked back to Oz's car in the rain, Tommy said, "I n-n-n-need to go back."

"It won't make it any better," Oz said, unlocking the door, in a rush to get out of the weather. "Trust me on that. It may make it worse."

Oz got in the car, but Tommy stood immobile by the passenger door.

"I thought you'd made your peace," Oz said.

Tommy just stood there, his face gleaming with droplets of rain.

Oz let out a heavy breath and put his head back on the headrest. "Tommy . . ."

"I'll go back on m-m-m-my own, then."

Oz closed his eyes in frustration, then motioned for his brother to get in the car. It was more than a three-hour drive. They did most of it in silence. By the time they got to Dothan, they had outrun the rain and were rumbling into the day's dying light. Oz pulled off the road near where he believed the house used to be. "Over there." He pointed.

The two of them got out of the car and walked through what looked like a barren field, with the harvest having long passed and planting not yet done.

"I think the house was right here," Oz said. He motioned around himself, as if he were standing in the middle of one of its rooms. And suddenly, Oz could not move. He looked at his brother, the one person in the world who had witnessed what Oz had done.

"It's all right," Tommy said quietly.

Oz had told himself that for years. It was how he was able to leave Alabama. It was how he'd been able to build a life with Deborah and Trinity. But it had all been false. "Tommy," he said, grabbing his brother's arm.

"Look, Oz—"

Oz was looking, but he wasn't seeing what Tommy was seeing.

Oz is seventeen, running toward the conflagration in front of him. The church and Pearl are behind him now, and he is still praying, "Please, please, please . . ." He looks over his shoulder to see if, by some miracle, his mother has followed him home.

Thomas is fine. Thomas is fine. Go home. I'll be there in a minute.

But there is no one else on the road with him. Tommy and his father aren't in the yard where he left them. He runs to the barn, yelling their names. They don't answer.

Flames are shooting through the roof near the back of the house. Oz sprints up to the front porch. He opens the door, and it is as if he has unlatched the gates to hell. He is overtaken by a rolling column of smoke. He pulls his T-shirt up to shield his mouth and nose and squints as he feels his way through the front room. He sees Tommy crab-crawling toward him. Oz crouches and grabs his brother under the arms.

"Where's Daddy?" Oz asks over the roaring of the flames and the groaning of the house.

Tommy points toward the back of the house, where the walls are aglow.

Oz drags his brother out the door and down the stairs to the yard. He brings him to rest in the vegetable garden. Tommy is coughing and hawking up phlegm. Still, he's trying to speak.

"He w-w-w-wouldn't let me go," Tommy says, holding out his hands to Oz. His palms are so red, it's as if blood has boiled to the surface. Oz is sure the skin is breaking.

Oz runs back in the house, his T-shirt pulled up over his nose and mouth again. He finds his father on the floor of the front room.

"Come on," Oz says. "Hang on to me."

His father pulls himself up, grabbing Oz's pants and shirt and shoulders. But he doesn't move toward the door. He is asking for Tommy. In a choked voice, he tells Oz Tommy has to go through the fire. They'll be like Shadrach, Meshach and Abednego. Oz pulls his father closer as flames, like fingers, reach for them. Oz drags him toward the door. His father is coughing so much he can barely speak, but Oz hears him croak out, "It's his punishment . . ."

Glass shatters. Oz ducks, but shards slice through his forehead and the side of his face. Tommy is trying to climb through the broken window, but he can't pull himself up. Even if he could, a line of flame is blocking his way. Oz pauses. He looks at his father in his arms. His father is weak, but he mumbles, "You bleeding, son. Come on." His father appears to muster whatever strength is left in him and grabs at Oz's shirt, trying to yank him toward the front door and the outside and air they both can breathe. But seeing his brother's anguished face at the window and feeling his father's desperate effort to get him to the door and to safety, Oz is a tangle of emotions.

"Why can't you leave him alone?" Oz cries, anger unspooling itself. "Why do you make me choose?"

Through a cloud of smoke and rage, he pulls his father back from the front door. "Stop hurting him!" Oz shoves him toward the back of the house. Then time slows and the rage quiets. The roar of the flames goes silent, and Oz sees what he has done. He leaps forward and catches his father's hand, but it is sweaty. It slips from his grip. His father's wedding ring slides off and that is all Oz is holding. His father's eyes, full of shock and terror, are locked on his as he stumbles and falls backward.

Oz lunges and grabs at him. To save him. But the flames roar again and the ceiling creaks and beams crash down, crushing a chair and the table. Oz covers his head and ducks. The room swims before him, even as he searches frantically for his father. He can't see him anymore—but he hears him. Wailing. Calling his name. Oz can't breathe. He falls to the ground and drags himself to the door, the house falling apart around him. Tommy is there. He pulls Oz down the stairs to the vegetable garden. Oz is coughing and convulsing and through tears he sees Pearl running through the yard. He is like an anguished child, relieved at the sight of her.

"Y-y-y-you're bleeding," Tommy says to Oz. "Y-y-y-your face."

"Where's your daddy?" Pearl asks, falling to the ground beside Oz. She asks that question again and again, until her voice disappears into sobs, and she says, "Oh, God."

Oz's lungs are burning. He is still fighting for every breath as he lies prone on the ground, but he turns his head to look at their house. It is a shell with orange light still undulating toward the sky.

He tenses and throws up. Pearl rubs his back and sobs. He loves her. He hates her.

"Why weren't you here?" he says in a rasp. Then he closes his eyes.

It was late. Tommy and Oz stopped off and got a motel room between Dothan and Birmingham.

They sat down beside each other on the edge of one of the beds, neither one of them saying a word. The truth was right there, laid bare between them—always known. But unspoken since that night.

On that night, Oz had listened from his hospital bed as Tommy, with his hands bandaged and as big as mittens, spoke in the quietest of voices. He told him and Pearl that Oz Senior had held his hands over the flames of two candles, trying to purify him. But when the burns on his palms became unbearable, Tommy knocked over the candles. They'd rolled away and set the house on fire. Tommy had tried to get their father out of the house, but their father had said the two of them would be like Shadrach, Meshach and Abednego in the fiery furnace, from the book of Daniel. Not so much as a hair would be singed on either one of them, and Tommy would emerge cleansed. At last. And so, he'd grabbed Tommy and held him down.

When Tommy finished, Oz said, "I killed him. I killed Daddy."

Tommy, who was sitting on the edge of the hospital bed beside Oz, said he'd seen it through the window.

Oz told Pearl to call the police, so they could come and arrest him.

"No," she said. She sat in the chair rocking back and forth, back and forth, shaking her head. She was crying. Then finally she dried her eyes and said, "I ain't turning you and Tommy over to some

Alabama police. I cain't have that for y'all . . ." She stopped rocking and looked from Tommy to Oz. "We gon' put this away, okay?"

Tears slipped down Oz's face. "How? He was my daddy. He was trying to *save* me, and look what I did to him." Oz buried his face in his hands, thinking of the father he'd loved and wanted to please, despite everything. *That's my boy . . .*

Pearl nodded, tears in her eyes. "I know."

"You should have been here," was all Oz could say.

"I'll carry the blame, okay?" she told him and Tommy. "I'll carry it from here."

And Oz had tried to let her.

Tommy got up now from the motel room bed next to Oz and went over to the desk. He picked up the present he'd brought and gave it to him.

"I forgot all about that," Oz said quietly.

"A very l-l-l-late Christmas present," Tommy said, working hard at a smile.

Very late, indeed. It was the end of February. Oz turned the gift over in his hands. How could they be thinking about Christmastime or any other time when there was *that* time? Still, he apologized for not having thought to bring anything for Tommy. Tommy joked that Oz had always been thoughtless, and then, suddenly, Tommy's eyes were shining with tears. They both knew that Oz had been thinking of his brother when Oz had done the worst thing a son could do.

Oz pulled the bow loose and removed the wrapping paper. It was a picture frame. He turned it over.

"That's Trinity," Tommy said, as if that was necessary. Oz would have recognized her anywhere. She hadn't changed much since the last time he'd seen her at sixteen. But she was clearly all grown up. And she was beautiful.

He cradled the picture in his hands, gazing down at it. "I don't deserve her. Never deserved any of it." He looked down at his hands, thinking of how he'd been in those last days with them. Angry, consumed by guilt, afraid of himself. Always remembering what he'd done in a split second. All of the guilt and regret in the world couldn't change a thing. That was what he was thinking, after that time he'd shoved Deborah. It was the same thing. What could he destroy in a moment? If he lost himself again? "I never wanted to hurt them," he said.

"Y-y-y-you're not some outta-control monster, Oz."

"That was my daddy. Look what I did to him. When even you tried to save him."

Tommy went over and sat down again on the bed next to his brother. "Oz, even the w-w-w-worst criminals get visitation—and you ain't the worst. Y-y-y-you need to come back with me."

Oz shook his head. "He's not finished with me yet, Tommy. I tried to let Pearl carry it. All those years. But that was wrong. This is my punishment. I would be locked up right now if we'd done the right thing. I'm trying to make up for it all, but . . ." His words fell away.

Tommy got up and paced the room. He told Oz that it had taken him a long time to see that none of this was his fault. He told Oz that he would come through it, too. Then he begged his brother to at least call home.

Oz said no. This was his life now. He didn't deserve that other life.

But Tommy wouldn't hear it.

On a clear evening in early March, Oz sat on the couch in Willa Mae's house with the phone in his hand. Tommy had told him that Deborah would be coming in from Chicago that night. That he and Pearl would be there at the house with her. And for Oz to call.

He sucked in a deep breath and dialed the numbers. It was Tommy who picked up. He heard his brother's muffled voice telling Deborah to come to the phone. Oz was tempted to hang up, like he'd done all those times before, but he stayed on.

"It's me," he said, when he heard Deborah. "Oz."

There was commotion on the other end of the line. Like she'd dropped something. Then he heard her voice again. "Oz?"

"Yes," he said. "It's me."

He heard rustling and more commotion on the other end of the line. "I can't believe this," she whispered. "I don't understand. How're you . . . ? I buried you . . ." Then she said, "No. I don't guess I did." Suddenly her voice was muffled. He heard her say, "Did you know about him? All this time?"

She wasn't talking to him. He heard jumbled replies from Pearl and Tommy.

After a beat of silence, he said, "I know all of this is . . . it's a shock is what it is." Oz looked down at the Lemon Pledge–shined wood of the end table. "It was a shock to me the day I walked off. I can't even believe—"

"You left us?" she cut in.

He hesitated. "You could say that."

"I *could say* that? You just said you walked off."

"It's not as simple as that. It wasn't so much a leaving as a being led away." He paused. "I don't know where to start."

"You could start by coming back here."

"That's not an easy thing, Deborah."

"What in God's name is it, Oz? Is it the affair? The stuff with Lloyd? I don't understand."

And so, Oz told her about himself.

Trinity

1991

Manny arrived at my place on time. On my way to the door, I popped in the bathroom to do a quick check of my hair and makeup. I turned to see my profile in the mirror. Not my best. I was covered in a fine sheen of sweat. It was overly warm in the apartment. I kept the heat higher than someone else probably would because I was always worried about O getting cold. I took a wad of toilet paper and dabbed at my forehead and chin—the shiniest places.

I tried to look good every time Manny brought O home from spending time at his place, in the hope that Manny might notice. But he could still barely look at me and it had been over six months since I'd cheated and moved out.

I gave myself another visual once-over, then went from the bathroom to the door, which was a mere four steps. Everything was a mere minuscule number of steps from everything in my tiny studio apartment.

I opened the door to find Manny with O limp in his arms.

"He's out like a light," I whispered.

"Yup." Manny stepped past me and went over to lay him in his crib. He put the duffel bag with O's things on the floor. "We had a busy day with the family. You know, church, dinner, the usual." He gently extracted O from his puffy winter coat, careful not to wake him. He glanced over his shoulder at me. "He had his bath already, and you can see I put his pajamas on, so ole boy's good and powered down for the night." Manny bent over and kissed him on the forehead. "See you next weekend, little man," he whispered.

O flinched and stirred but didn't wake up.

Manny brought O's coat to me over by the door.

"I'm glad you guys had a good time," I said as I held on to the coat. "And how have you been?"

"Oh, you know. Keeping busy."

"Any interesting cases?" Manny was a lawyer now. He'd gone to a white-shoe firm, which had surprised me, given his legal aid leanings. But he'd weighed his law school debt against the future and had gone in the direction of paying the bills and a college fund for O.

He shrugged. "No cases you'd be interested in on your beat."

"Try me. I can get into white-collar crime as easy as any other." Actually, I was trying to get out of the crime coverage business altogether. Murders, rapes, robberies—they were weighing on me. I needed different stories to tell.

"Nah." He moved past me toward the door. "Look, I'll be by next Friday as usual, unless you want to have the Sensei—"

"Salvatore," I corrected.

"Right, right. Sorry."

The Sensei had asked us to call him by his real name, Salvatore, some time ago. He said he saw us as family now, so it was important. And shock of shocks to me, I saw him as family, too. He was one of O's favorite people and a dependable babysitter who sometimes shuttled O between Manny and me.

"Anyway, just let me know about picking him up." He smiled. "I'm going to take him shopping for his first Easter suit. And my mother already got him a bunny outfit," he said, chuckling.

Easter was still a few weeks away. I reminded Manny of the schedule: "I have him on Easter."

"You sure?"

"Of course I'm sure." I'd planned the month very carefully because of it.

He clenched his jaw. "But you don't even go to church. You know Easter's important in my family. I'd like to have him then. At least on Sunday."

"I know, but . . . I'll think about it, Manny. All right?"

He reached for the doorknob. "Let me know when you know on the drop-off."

Our exchanges were often so cold. So businesslike. "Manny," I said, trying. "Please. I told you I'd think about it." I paused. "And I hate that it's like this between us. You know that, right?"

"Well, it didn't have to be, did it?"

"No," I said quietly. "And for the millionth time, I'm sorry. Okay?"

"Right."

"Don't do that."

His fingers played at the doorknob. "Look," he said. "I've gotten serious with someone. I thought you should know."

"Oh." I suddenly felt weak, like I might need to sit down. "Oh," I said again, like an idiot.

"Yeah. She's nice." He nodded toward O's crib. "And he likes her, so seal of approval."

"He's barely a year old. He's too little to be relied on for a 'seal of approval,'" I snapped. Then it hit me. "Wait, you've had him around her? Without telling me?"

"I don't need your permission for my son to meet my friends. Like I said, it's serious. And you know I'm not going to just have him around some random booty call." He looked at me hard, as if to say, *But you would.*

"You know I would never do that."

"Really? History—"

"Fuck you, Manny. I messed up one time—"

"Just the one time? Really? You sure about that?"

"We weren't *together* together back then." It was the ever-lurking specter of that paternity scare. Manny had never fully gotten over it.

"Sure. Whatever you say." He opened the door and stepped out into the hallway. "I'm not doing this with you, Trinity."

"I didn't ask you to do anything with me."

He pulled the door almost closed, then pushed it open again. "I loved you. Do you hear me? I *loved* you. I wanted a life with you. And you fucking stuck a knife in and gutted me." He jabbed his finger at me. "You know why?"

"Shut up. Go. Okay? Leave."

"Because, Trinity, you don't know what you want. The girl who couldn't quite commit? I used to think it was a challenge. Here, let me fix the poor, broken girl with all of my love." His tone was mocking. "I was an idiot, right? If only I'd known."

"Yes. I know how fucked I am. You've told me. Daddy issues. Abandonment issues. The whole gamut. I'm aware." I tried to push the door closed, but he was holding it open with his foot. "Move, Manny. I mean it!"

"You don't know how to be with anyone, Trinity. There's nothing anyone can do to make you happy. And I don't want that tainting my kid." He pointed toward O's crib. "You hear me? I don't want that hurting my son."

"What are you going to do, Manny? Marry your perfect girl—who's had a perfect life, I imagine—and take my kid away from me? Is that what—"

There was a cry from the direction of O's crib. We both froze and looked. He was up on his knees, gripping the bars with his chubby little hands. Fat tears were sliding down his cheeks. He looked like he'd seen a monster. Two of them.

I ran over and picked up my little boy. "Hey," I said. "It's okay. Everything's just fine, okay?" I *shh*ed him and danced across the floor with him to calm him, glaring over his head at Manny. Wanting to hate him. But Manny looked as close to crying as I'd ever seen him. He was standing in the doorway twisting his baseball cap in his hands. I imagined he wished he could disappear through the floor. He came over and kissed O on the mess of curls atop his head.

"Sorry, dude. Daddy's sorry. Okay? Daddy's sorry."

Then he looked at me like he wanted to speak. He didn't. Neither did I. Still, in that instant, we made an unspoken truce. He put his cap on and left.

I went home for Easter. It was not one of my usual holidays for going home, but my mother had begged me to come. Something was up. She didn't want to talk about it over the phone, but she assured me it was something that could wait until I got there. I had O with me on the trip. Manny and I had come to an easy, civil agreement about Easter, for which I was grateful.

"Your family doesn't get to see him as much as mine," he'd said. "My mother can wait until he gets back to humiliate him with the bunny outfit."

When I walked in my mother's house, the vibe was subdued, with my mother and Pearl in the kitchen going about their work quietly. But there were the usual hugs. Shock at how big O was getting and delight at how busy he was. Mr. Burton took my bag to my old bedroom. I felt like I should have done that myself, given that he was getting up there, past seventy. But he insisted. I helped my mother and Pearl in the kitchen, pitching in where I could with the side dishes, while O toddled around at our feet. I wasn't much of a cook. When I thought about how much takeout and thrown-together macaroni or bean-based meals O and I ate, I always wanted to do better.

Pearl and my mother wanted to know the usual things, even as there was the undercurrent of the unspoken: *Something's odd here* . . .

Pearl asked about work. I told her it was fine, but that I was getting a little restless. My mother wanted to know how things were with Manny. Things were serious indeed with the "perfect girl" he'd told me about. Turned out, he'd asked her to marry him. It felt fast and unsettling, but I told my mother: "She's nice. O likes her. They invited me to the wedding. It's, um, in a couple months. June."

"Is this girl pregnant or something?" my mother asked, incredulous. "Why so fast?"

I shrugged. "He told me 'when you know you know' . . . What *I* know is that he's rushing to get on with his life." And out of mine.

"And you going?" Pearl said.

"Yes." Manny and I had our truce, after all.

"I'm sorry," my mother said.

"What? It's fine. As long as Manny's happy and O's happy—"

"Are *you* happy?" Pearl asked.

"I, well, I'm fine."

Fine. Everything is fine.

I put my coat back on and escaped to the backyard, where Tommy was at the grill. They'd decided to forgo the traditional Easter ham in favor of steak.

"What's going on, Tommy?" I said, cozying up beside him at the grill for a little warmth. "Things are . . . weird."

"Huh?" He poked at a rib eye with his giant two-pronged fork. It sizzled and flames flared up.

I knew he'd heard me. I knew he knew what I was talking about, which made me more concerned. "Why am I here?"

He closed the lid to the grill. "Your mama's got some news for you."

"What is it? Is she sick or something? Has she been drinking again? Is this an intervention?" Then it occurred to me that people don't arrange their own interventions.

"N-n-n-no. Nothing like that."

I let out a relieved breath.

"Shhh-she'll tell you," Tommy said. "No bad n-n-n-news."

I nodded, feeling even more relieved. It was probably something with her singing. She wanted to surprise me. I'd let her do it. Tommy asked what I was doing with myself out in New York. If I was doing anything other than working.

"I'm dating a little. Nothing serious." In truth, I'd gone out with Josh once after cheating with him on Manny, but that had been a grievous error. I'd talked about Manny the whole time, to Josh's understandable displeasure. Things became uncomfortable at work. I was greatly pleased when Josh took a job at the *New York Post* and left. I hadn't dated, flirted with, slept with or been otherwise interested in anyone in months.

"It can be h-h-h-hard," Tommy said, "finding the right one."

I took this as an opportunity to cautiously approach *his* love life. Word was, he had one now. "And how are things with you? How are things with, you know . . . ?"

He tilted his head, like he was thinking about it. "Not bad."

"And any reason why you didn't bring him?"

He looked embarrassed. "Just w-w-w-wanted to keep the circle small, with everything. That's all." He smiled and reached around to pull his wallet out of his back pocket. "I don't know if you w-w-w-wanna see him, but . . ." He plucked out a folded-up snapshot and gave it to me. "That's him. That's Dom."

It was a picture of Tommy standing next to a tall, slightly round, bearded man with white-gray hair. "Very handsome," I said. "Something of a silver fox, isn't he?"

If Tommy could have blushed, he would have been beet red. He had rarely ever talked about his personal life, apart from the occasional mention of a "friend" here or there. Even when Lloyd was alive, he'd referred to him as his friend and kept any details about their relationship to an absolute minimum. It was terrible, watching him be so careful, even when Lloyd was dying. He never wanted to give anything away. Never wanted to make anyone uncomfortable. But over the past few months, Tommy had been dating Dom, a man he'd met at a "mixer," as he described it. The term "boyfriend" was a bridge too far for Tommy, but he was as happy as a teenager falling in love. And it struck me that falling in love when he *was* a teenager was something he never could have talked about.

"Can't wait to meet him," I said, sliding the picture back. I hugged him and kissed him on the cheek. "I'm glad you're happy, Tommy."

He patted my hand. "Not quite as h-h-h-happy as I'd like to be . . ." He shrugged and his smile dissolved. He opened the grill and started moving the steaks to a waiting platter. "Why don't you go help Mama and your mama." I wanted to give him another hug because of that sudden sadness in him, but I went inside. I helped my mother and Pearl put the green beans, potatoes and other sides on the table. Tommy delivered the steaks, and we all settled in. We made small talk, but there was no getting out from under the weird vibe. Finally, I said, "Okay. What's your big news, Mom?"

Mr. Burton cleared his throat conspicuously and looked uneasy.

My mother put down her fork and glanced at Pearl, who was sitting next to her. Then she looked across the table to Tommy. She wiped her mouth with some deliberation. "It's your father, Trin."

"Okay . . ."

"He's . . . he's alive." She paused, then rushed out: "And okay. He's, um . . . he called a couple weeks ago."

It was like trying to make sense of a riddle. "I'm sorry. What?"

"Your father is alive, Trinity," she said slowly, as if talking to a dense child. "He called me—"

"Wait. I don't—"

"I know. I know." My mother put her napkin on the table slowly. "He's a little . . . he's a little fragile, right now. Everything's fragile right now."

I was at a loss. O was squirming in my lap and tugging at my sleeve. I reflexively fed him some mashed potatoes.

"He's got a lot of guilt," Pearl said. "Trying to find a way to unwind it . . . that's hard."

Mr. Burton excused himself to go in the other room. Within moments, the sound of the television disrupted the stunned silence around the table. I felt like I was floating above it all, too distant to fully take in anything. "I don't understand this."

My mother told me all that my father had told her. I didn't know what to think or believe or how to look at Pearl or Tommy. Tommy wouldn't meet my eyes, in any case. O started twisting away from me in my lap, and I realized I was holding him tighter than before. "I'm sorry," I whispered, kissing the top of his head.

"Trin, are you okay?" my mother asked.

"No."

"Your daddy'll be in touch with you soon," Pearl said. "That'll go a long way." Then she looked at my mother. "If he came back, Deborah, would you have him?"

My mother bit her lip and looked thoughtful. "I don't know," she said. "I talked to him again this morning. I need to see him. Look him in the eye when we talk. That's when I'll know what comes next."

Oz

1991

Oz stood in the cashier's booth looking at the picture of Trinity he kept on the counter next to the cash register. It was the one Tommy had given him. He said aloud: "What now, Trin?" He had not yet spoken to her, though he talked to the picture regularly, as if in preparation for a real conversation, even as he worried that she would not want a real conversation with him.

He'd made a mess of everyone's life, not just his own.

He thought of Deborah. They'd spoken on Easter morning, and she'd told him: "I need to see you. But I don't want you here. Not yet, anyway. What are we going to do about that?"

When she'd suggested coming to him, Oz had hesitated. *How will she see me now?* He'd considered the shabbiness of his small, penitent life. The RV. The unheated, un-air-conditioned gym. His failure to make amends, as he had intended. His failure to find anything close to peace. He was confronted with the reality of her in this place seeing him differently. *Feeling* something different for him. Something other than a love that was, for Oz, somehow fossilized in amber. Frozen in time.

When Oz did finally answer Deborah's question, he'd said, "Can I think about it?"

Here, weeks later, he was still turning it over in his mind.

He glanced at his watch. It was still early in the evening, but it was time to close up. He needed to get to the gym for something else he'd been putting off. He grabbed his notebook from the counter where he'd been jotting down his thoughts, like he did most days. He dropped the notebook in his bag along with his pen. He did his regular inventory check, then locked up. He drove slowly to the gym. When he arrived, he sat in his car procrastinating some more. Oz had decided to let Dre have his birthday party at the gym, just like Dre had asked. But Oz was having a difficult time going inside, for all the reasons he didn't want the party in the first place. He checked his watch. He was quite late. He reached over to the passenger seat and grabbed the vanilla cupcakes he'd picked up at the Piggly Wiggly on the way.

Inside the gym, there were balloons tied to the four corners of the boxing ring. There was a long food table, also festooned with balloons. Oz saw the hand of Willa Mae in all of it. There was a smattering of regulars milling around. Some of the gym's nicest guys. But there were no kids, apart from Dre and Antonio, who were over at the food table stuffing back hot dogs. For once, Dre's riotous curls were tamed. Marshaled into neat lines of cornrows, all marching toward the back of his head.

Willa Mae approached Oz. "You couldn't get here on time? That boy's been waiting *hours* for you."

"It's, um . . . you know . . . I'm sorry."

She made a noise in her throat, then pointed to a far corner. "If that one over there could make it, anybody could."

Over in the corner stood the wraith of a woman Oz had seen in the front room of Dre's house on the night Dre had asked for the party. Dre's mother, Oz had guessed. She was squinty-eyed and strung-out looking, but there she was, standing against the wall. Oz took his cupcakes over to the table and told Dre happy birthday. Dre mumbled, "Thank you." He otherwise ate his hot dog in hostile silence. When he was finished, he walked away.

"You late," Antonio said. "It's almost over." He shook his head in disappointment and plucked a cupcake from the box and left Oz at the table.

Oz walked around the gym, saying hello to everyone, feeling terrible. When the party was over, he helped with cleanup. He said good night to Antonio, who was rushing out the door with Willa Mae, headed home to help his grandmother with something. Oz spotted Dre beside a far wall, sitting on a crate. He pulled up another crate and took a seat. That hostile silence from before settled in and sat between them for a long while. Oz broke in, telling Dre he liked his hair. Dre touched his cornrows, glared at Oz, but said nothing. Oz stared off straight ahead toward the open barn doors, where the evening light was ebbing away.

Finally, Dre said, "Where were you?"

Excuse after excuse readied itself for deployment—worked late, couldn't get away—but Oz opted for a truth. "You know," he said, "I have troubles sometimes, Dre. And my troubles got the best of me tonight. And I let you down. I'm sorry about that."

Dre glanced at him, tears welling in his eyes. He said quietly, "My mama's got troubles, too."

Oz looked around the gym for her. But it was empty.

"She ain't here no more," Dre said. "Was only here for a minute, if that."

Oz nodded, struck by the everyday, normal way Dre spoke. This was his life. Then Dre said he'd had fun tonight, with his friends. With the men who showed up for him. Then he and Oz talked about Dre's mother again. And troubles. And how sorry Oz was. For everything.

When Dre nodded and said, "It's okay," tears rose in Oz's throat. He was surprised by how much the forgiveness of this boy meant to him. As the two talked some more and Oz listened to the innocent, sometimes outlandish hopes of a thirteen-year-old boy, he felt a stirring in his chest. It was a feeling he hadn't had—hadn't *allowed* himself to have—in a long time, but he held on to it as he and Dre left the gym and as he got the boy safely home. He stopped at Willa Mae's house, which was quiet and dark. And after the briefest moment of doubt, Oz grabbed the phone in the kitchen because that feeling he had, it was still stirring in his chest, warm and awakening. It felt good. It felt terrifying. It felt something like being a father.

Trinity did not hang up on him. She did not yell at him. She said only, "Dad? Is this really you?"

It was not the sixteen-year-old girl he'd last known. Which, of course, he understood, but to hear it . . . a voice that was new, yet known. "I'm sorry," he whispered. He tried to explain himself in a stuttering, almost Tommy-like rush.

She listened with the quiet air of a rational adult. She did not absolve him, but she did not condemn him either.

He wondered, *Why doesn't she get mad? Why doesn't she just go off on me?*

She told him she had a son.

Tommy had shared this with Oz, but Oz still could not imagine it.

"His name is Ozro," she said. "We call him O."

"That name. It has so much weight on it . . ."

"He'll make it his own," she said.

"When I first held you," Oz said, looking down at his empty

hand, "you were so tiny. It scared me. I promised you I would do my best to be a good father. When I was not even a good son. And look at us now. I'm so sorry." What Oz would not give for her forgiveness. For a way forward.

He could hear her sniffles on the other end of the line. He could never stand it when she cried. He heard himself promise that he would see her soon. He told her Deborah wanted to come down. To see him.

"Well, then, why won't you let her?" Trinity said. "Stop punishing yourself. Stop hurting her. Stop hurting me . . . Try thinking of someone else's pain, Dad."

Trinity

1991

There was a flash of red hair at the airport gate. It was Virginia, just arrived in New York. We practically knocked each other over as we hugged. It had been more than a year since we'd seen each other. We talked on the phone as much as we could, but that was expensive, and it also wasn't the same. Virginia was fully settled in London now and had no plans to ever live in the States again.

"I missed you so much, Trin!" she said, lifting me off the ground.

"Same," I said, hanging on and immediately bursting into tears.

"Hey, hey, don't do that," she said, looking at me with the same intense, unblinking gaze she had as a kid. She pulled me in for another big hug.

"Thank you so much for coming," I said. "You didn't have to do this. With the long flight, the jet lag . . ."

She waved my words away. "With everything you have going on? There's no way I'm letting you do this on your own. I'm your lifelong plus-one, no matter where in the world we are." She held me out at arm's length. "You look great. We'll deal with your"—she motioned toward my face and frowned—"makeup situation in the car."

I wiped my eyes, no doubt smearing mascara even as the tears kept coming. "How am I going to keep it together through Manny's wedding?"

She hugged me again. "It's okay. It's going to be all right."

Virginia's arrival time was so tight that I drove the rental directly from the airport to the church, with her saying she would "just slip into a nice tea dress in the backseat." It wasn't as easy as that. There was a fair amount of struggle in that backseat, with the blue silk of her dress occasionally floating up and her feet touching the roof of the car. When she was dressed, out the corner of my eye, I could see she was holding something red and yellow over the seat. "How do you think O will like this?"

I glanced at it. "It's a truck. He'll love it."

"Great." She tucked it in her purse.

"He's with Manny and his family."

"Mm-hm. And how are you feeling about that? And the rest?"

"Fine."

"Right." She hoisted herself up and climbed into the passenger seat. "I know it's hard to see him marrying someone else."

"I never said I wanted to marry Manny."

"Right. Anyway, I can't put lipstick on that pig, but"—she rummaged around in her purse and pulled out a tube of bloodred lipstick—"we can put lipstick on *you* and you will at least look great tonight, even if you don't feel that way."

"I told you, I'm *fine*."

"Sure you are."

Manny's wedding was beautiful. An explosion of white hydrangeas and gold ribbons. He was as handsome as I'd ever seen him in his tuxedo and bow tie. At the reception, I watched Virginia do the electric slide with O in her arms. A Whitney Houston song was on and they were following along with Salvatore, Destiny and a clutch of O's cousins.

I danced for as long as I could manage it, then said an early goodbye to Manny and his bride. I told Manny I had a headache, which Virginia said was a terrible and transparent excuse. While I yelled it over the thumping beats from the DJ, she stood by with a stiff smile. Manny interrupted and yelled back, "Can I talk to you outside?" He turned to his bride, who was radiant in white and framed in a cascade of curls. "I'll just be a minute."

I congratulated her again and hugged her goodbye. We were official co-parents now.

Manny pointed outside to the patio that looked out on Long Island Sound. I followed him out the door into the night air and immediately felt better. Though being at his wedding was abject misery, being with him had generally always been easy.

It was a pleasant night. A handful of guests were out for a smoke or just enjoying the view. Manny exchanged hugs with some and got pats on the back from others as we passed. He stopped and leaned on the railing.

I stood beside him, looking out to the lights floating on the surface of the water. "So, what's up, Manny? You want me to take O home with me so you—"

He laughed. "Did you see him in there? Dude's having a blast. No. Plan A is still good. He'll go home with my sister and her kids. You can get him from there in the morning. Go out and have a girls' night with Virginia." He looked over his shoulder. A dancing scrum was visible through the tall windows of the reception hall. "Look. Your mom called last week." He glanced at me. "She told me about your dad."

"She shouldn't have done that."

"She's worried about you. She's just looking out. Told me to keep an eye on you. That's all."

"You don't have to keep an eye on me, for Christ's sake. I'm fine."

He looked at me with raised-eyebrow skepticism. "Really? I'm just saying, in your shoes, I might not be so fine." He shrugged.

"Okay. I'm not fine," I allowed. "I'm just so . . . angry . . . sad. Everything. When I talked to him, it was almost like talking to a stranger. While, at the same time, I feel like I didn't say enough . . . My mother is there now. With him. I thought she should go on her own. Said she needed to look him in the eye, to know what comes next. I wonder what she'll see in him. What *I'll* see, when we get together again."

He nodded. "How could you not wonder?"

"And worry."

"Yeah. And worry." Manny backed away from the railing. He looked at me with the softest eyes and said, "I'm here. If you need anything. Okay, Trin?"

I nodded. I couldn't speak.

He looked at the reception hall behind him. "I'd better get back before she misses me." He squatted down and did a runner's lunge, then a little bit of body-twisting limbering up. "I've been practicing my Hammer dance. I'm telling you, you don't know what you're missing by leaving."

I laughed. "No. I know what I'm missing." Then my laughter caught in my throat, and I said, "She's a lucky girl."

Deborah

I'd been waiting for the storm to come. I'd been waiting for the urge to reach for a drink and crash headfirst off the wagon. But I wasn't feeling that. I felt calm—hurt and mad, but calm. A storm might break in me later. And maybe it might be so big that it'll take me down to a new bottom, but there was just that calm as I pulled up outside Willa Mae's. There in the side yard next to a carport was the RV, looking a lot like I'd pictured. But I couldn't see Oz living in that thing. I got out and walked up to the front door, my eyes catching for a second on the porch ceiling. It was as blue and lovely as the sky above.

Willa Mae let me in. I didn't know whether to hug her or hurt her. She stood back, like she didn't know what to do with me either.

"How you been?" I asked, nodding in the direction of her cane. She'd been young, skinny and able-bodied, last I'd seen her.

"Not bad," she said, glancing down at the cane. "This ain't nothing but a little something to keep me standing."

"Good," I said, worried about her a little. I walked over to the window and stared out at the RV, which, on closer look, I could see was grayish and dirt streaked. I said what I was thinking when I first drove up: "He's been here all this time? Living in that thing?"

"That's his prison, Deborah." Her tone said, *Anybody can see that.*

The living room of our house was almost bigger than that RV. I tried to picture Oz locked up in it, staring at me out one of those little windows. "Willa, what's he like now? Truly?"

"Same," Willa Mae said. "Different. Tortured. All that." She came up and stood beside me at the window.

"You should've told us, Willa. We mourned him. Had that funeral and everything. You knew that. You called me that very day and didn't say word one about it."

"I know, but more important, *he* knew, and he wanted to stay where he was at. And I couldn't tell what he didn't want told . . . How do I say this?" She paused. "When I was a girl, Oz was kind to me when I needed every kindness. Even when he was hurting. Me and him, we was kin that way." She pointed out to the RV. "But let me ask you this. Say I'd told you when he showed up here. Or when I called you on his funeral day. What then?"

"I would've come down here. Like I'm here now."

"And what you think's gon' happen? With you here now?"

I looked out at the RV. "I don't know."

"Right," she said. "Come on. I'mma get gone and stay that way for a little bit. Give y'all some time."

I followed her out through the kitchen and the back door. She stopped at the steps leading up to the door of the RV to let me go ahead. "It's a lot," she said. "I know." She leaned forward and hugged me kind of stiff, then let go and left.

Before I could knock on the door, it opened and there was Oz in ironed blue jeans and a white oxford. "Come in," he said.

I did and looked around because I couldn't look at him. Not head-on. Not yet. I took in the short length of the RV, the small counter, the pull-down table, the driver's and passenger seats up front. My eyes came to rest on the little windows that looked out on the carpet of green grass in the side yard. I imagined Oz had planted and cared for it.

He cleared his throat, then said, "It can get hot and stuffy in here this time of year. You want to go back in Willa's?"

It was definitely hard to breathe, but I didn't know if it was the stuffiness or the nervousness or our nearness. "No," I said. "Out here's fine."

He lowered the windows I was looking out of and let in a soft breeze and birdsong. He motioned for me to sit at the pull-down table. There were two worn upholstered seats across from each other. In the back of the RV, I could see a narrow bed with a blanket pulled tight and tucked in under the mattress. Oz was across from me at the mini sink, so close I could touch him, even without stretching my arm out all the way. And I did reach out but stopped with a hair's breadth between my fingers and his shirt. He was pouring coffee into two mismatched mugs. One was green and chipped at the lip. The other was white and coffee stained. I pulled my hand back and put it in my lap as he made to turn. He put the mugs on the table and nudged the white one in my direction as he slid into the seat across from me.

"It's good you're not a big guy," I said. Then the smallness of what had come out of my mouth hit me. Me and Oz had spent years together, talking about any- and everything. But here I was struck dumb like we'd just met, not knowing what to say.

"It's tight quarters," Oz said.

I asked if he minded if I smoked. "I'm trying to quit, but, well, it's not going so good."

He nodded. "Go ahead."

I lit up, then looked at him. Truly looked at him. For the first time. And he was looking back at me. He still had a boyishness about him, but I could see where age had touched him, right there along the temples, leaving streaks of gray hair. Those soft brown eyes of his . . . they were still the same. But they did look weary as they searched my face . . . For what? Understanding? Forgiveness? Something more . . . ?

"Look at us," I said quietly.

"You look good, Deborah. Time's been kind to you."

"Has it?"

He looked down at the table.

I gazed out the window and took a long draw on my cigarette.

He got up and grabbed another mug to catch my ashes. As he settled back in again, he said, "I'm going up to New York next month. Around the Fourth of July. To see Trinity. I . . . um . . . I think it'll be good to spend some time."

"It would be more than good, Oz. It's necessary." My eyes drifted to the shelves going up the narrow wall behind his head. There were stacks and stacks of what I recognized as his notebooks. I wondered what kind of plans he wrote down these days. "Willa Mae said this is your prison."

He blew on his coffee but didn't say anything.

"What do you mean to do, Oz? Just rot out here?"

"I don't know. I just let it lead me."

"Let what lead you?"

He was quiet for a moment. "This feeling."

"Guilt?"

He shrugged and glanced to his left, like there was somebody there. Then his eyes came back to me. "What did I look like trying to be happy in the life I had? After what I'd done? What do I look like trying to be happy in the life I have now?"

"Were you ever happy, Oz?"

"I was."

"People don't usually have affairs when they're happy."

He made a noise, like something was caught in his throat. "I never had an affair."

"You said—"

"I know what I said, but it wasn't true." He stared at me for a long moment. "What would you have done, Deborah, if I'd told you the truth? About all of that with Lloyd and your contract?"

"I would've left you."

"That's what I thought." He looked down at his hands. "I did terrible things to hold on to you because you made me happy, or"—he paused—"you made it less bad. You made all this stuff in my mind quieter. Loving you let me live, for a little while . . . But I made a mess of it."

"Yeah. You did." I tapped the ash from my cigarette and took another drag.

"Do you want a divorce?"

I stubbed out my cigarette. Divorce had not crossed my mind. I hadn't thought that far ahead. And then it occurred to me. "Oz, you're dead. I don't even . . ."

He sat back and blinked, like he was surprised to hear me say it.

"I mean, in the eyes of the law," I said.

"I am, I am. I just—" He shook his head. "How do you come back from the dead, Deborah? It's like I'm somebody else here. That's how I live, see? Like there was no you. There was no Trinity. There was no Oz, outside the one who murdered his daddy and has to pay for that. But now here you are . . ."

"Oz, I—"

"Never, for not one day, did I not love you."

"I love you, too, Oz." Behind the worry lines and signs of age on him, I saw through to the boy I used to know. "I think, sometimes, about those innocent days—"

"I was never innocent."

"With me you were." I remembered him in his sweater vest and the potato and with his notebook and all of his plans.

"Was I?"

"Yes." My voice caught in my throat.

He leaned forward, like he was about to share a secret. "I feel like he's always here now," Oz said. "Right there out the corner of my eye. I feel like I don't know what bad might be in me to make me do more bad to you and everybody I meet. How do you get free of something like that?"

"I don't know, Oz, but locking yourself up here . . . What good has it done?"

"None."

Looking at Oz, alive but not well, I felt a heaviness. Grief, I think, because it was finally, *finally* real to me. I was mourning the loss of him and everything.

I held my hands out to him on the table. He took them. His hands were dry but warm and strong, as he held on.

Back at home, I caught myself looking for Oz's black Cadillac to come up the drive. When I was over visiting with Pearl, I'd sometimes find myself watching the door, like he might come walking through. He didn't. We talked, though. Saturday morning, two Saturdays after I saw him, he called and said he wanted to thank me again for coming.

And I thought about that call all day. The way he sounded—shy, like the boy I used to know—and what he'd said about me bringing light and how he'd felt. I thought about it even up till Tommy and Dom came to pick me up hours later. When I told them about the call and that it was a good one, Tommy said he considered that a good start to a night out.

Him and Dom took me to Two Cents' club, of all places. Which, for me, was a bad start. I hadn't been back there since my downfall. If I'd known where we were going ahead of time, I might not've gone. The place felt the same but different when I walked in. It was more than the after-hours club it used to be. It had an updated dining room that was packed tight. The stage up front was nicer than I remembered, with professional-looking lights and a good pianist playing on it. I tried to concentrate on the food, which was good, and the company, which was better. Me and the boys were just getting to dessert—a chocolate lava cake—when Two Cents stopped by the table. I hadn't seen him in a long time. I'd stopped using his "hotline" for help, not long after that night in his club. No matter how much he told me not to be embarrassed around him, I still was. But he seemed just like normal. Still as skinny as a junkie and as talkative as anything.

"It's good to see you, sis!" he said, folding me in a big hug. "Where you been keeping yourself?"

I told him about my work and all the time I spent in Chicago.

He seemed surprised I was still singing, and jingles at that.

"It's not what I'd ever planned for myself, but it's been a good surprise and not a bad living."

He nodded and looked around, then said in a low voice, "Look, would you be interested in maybe gracing us with your talent tonight?"

"I don't do that anymore," I said.

"What? You just told me you sing jingles."

"That's different. I don't do live, public stuff anymore." I eyed that stage. While it was updated, it was the same place I'd known one of the worst moments of my life.

Tommy and Dom piped up with encouragements.

"It's just like getting back on a bike," Tommy said.

"And how would you know?" I asked him.

He shrugged and exchanged a glance with Two Cents.

"Wait," I said. "Did y'all plan this?"

Tommy shrugged again and said he thought it might do me good.

I shook my head. "Y'all don't understand. It would be . . ." Every time I looked in the direction of that stage, I saw myself falling and crawling on my hands and knees. And, what's more, I was scared that if I went anywhere near that stage, the storm would break.

"It's all right," Two Cents said. "I understand. More than most." He hugged me, then turned to Tommy and Dom. "It was a good try." He went off to work the room some more. I went back to my chocolate lava cake and conversation with Dom and Tommy, nervous and not trusting myself. I wanted to go home, but I didn't want to mess up their evening. We sat back and listened to the piano player give it his all. I could feel Two Cents' eyes on me from across the room.

"What would I even sing?" I said out loud.

Dom and Tommy looked at each other, then at me, like they were surprised I was still thinking about it.

"Just some standards, Deborah," Dom said.

"The s-s-s-stuff you love and haven't done in w-w-w-way too long," Tommy said. He smiled. I kissed him on the cheek and thought about it some more, then got up and went over to Two Cents.

"Are you going to try and make me feel bad all night?" I asked him. "With all your staring?"

"Naw. I'm just trying to remind you who you are, sis. With my eyes." He made his eyes wide and smiled at me.

"I'm scared."

"You should be. You alive."

I followed Two Cents back to the kitchen, which was where the piano player was taking a break. The whole time I told myself I hadn't agreed to do anything yet. I was just going to ask some questions and meet the piano player. He was a young one. Maybe late twenties. He was trying to break into R&B, he told me. He showed me what was left of the set list. It was all songs I knew and would do okay with.

"Classic tunes for a classic songstress," Two Cents said.

"Probably more of a relic than a classic." I went over the list again. "But we'll see how we do."

He squeezed my shoulders. "It's all you, champ. Go on out there and knock 'em out."

I followed the pianist out onstage, nervous as anything. I asked a waiter to bring me a glass of water so I could deal with my dry mouth. When he delivered it, I put it down on the little table next to the mic and told everybody who I was. I nodded to the pianist, and we slid into the first song. My voice felt froggy, but I think the comfort of those old songs helped me loosen up. The lyrics were more memory than words to me. Every party. Every turn on the stage. Every dream. They didn't break my heart as bad as I thought they might. But they did nick it good. I found myself looking around the audience and realized I was searching for Oz. Like maybe this gig was like so many others before it, with him out there sipping on a drink and watching. But no. Not this time.

I went out and waded in among the tables. I danced with a handful of husbands. Winked at wives. It felt right. It felt good. As the clock slipped past ten, I asked the pianist if he knew "Happy Feelings." Sure enough, he looked at me like, *Is that a serious question?* Everybody loves a Maze groove, even without a full band. And we did groove. He played, I sang and the audience came in on the chorus. At the end of my mini set, the love that came back to me, it was like nourishment I didn't know I was missing.

When it was all wrapped up and everybody was heading home, I sat on the bench next to the pianist and took off my heels while I waited for Tommy and Dom to bring the car around.

"You wanna give me some of what you got?" the pianist asked.

I smiled as I rubbed my aching feet. "I think I just went out there and had a good time. That's all I did." I wasn't thinking so much about what it ought to be. Or what I felt like I was missing. Or all the ways I could humiliate myself again. I just played the room I was in. And I played it good.

Oz

1991

It was just after ten on Saturday night, and Oz was closing up. But things were in full swing at the barbecue joint across the street, with people talking and laughing out in the parking lot, and bass bumping out of a glimmery Mustang parked under the streetlight.

Catfish Kenny was wiping down the counter and putting paper plates away. "What you got up for tonight, Dan?" Catfish asked. "Got my group coming by to plot strategy. You know you welcome to come." Catfish and his group, three other like-minded men, were always "strategizing" and looking for signs of the end times. Oz had heard more than enough of their "eye-openers" about Ronald Reagan, JFK, MLK and various portents of the apocalypse.

"I'll leave the strategizing to you," Oz said. "But I won't be long behind you leaving."

"Suit yourself," Catfish said.

It had been a busy night. Oz had moved plenty of beer and wine and chips and such. He didn't feel bad about knocking off before eleven, his usual quitting time. He planned to call Trinity when he got home, to give her his arrival information. His Fourth of July trip was only days away. Whenever he and Trinity spoke, he mostly listened. Drinking in everything she said, like a man too long in the desert. She was a good mother. She worked hard but didn't much care for her job anymore.

"I think I'm looking for purpose, Dad," she'd told him.

He understood that search. He was still looking, too.

He glanced at the clock and thought about Deborah. He imagined she was still out with Tommy and Dom, based on what she'd told him that morning when he'd called to thank her again for coming down. To thank her for bringing him a little light and some moments free from his searching. There had been such a stillness in him that day and such a strength in her as they held hands across the narrow table. Upon leaving, Deborah had paused for a moment, framed in the doorway of the RV. She'd told him, "Don't think too hard on all of this, Oz. Just try and do the next right thing. Then go from there." And she'd smiled and hugged him and said goodbye.

Oz could still hear her voice as he went up behind the bullet-proof glass and counted out the cash register. He put the cash in an envelope and handed it to Catfish. "Think the boss will be happy with this," he said.

Catfish nodded as he stuffed the envelope in his breast pocket. He patted it and headed out. Oz turned the Open sign around to Closed on the barred door. But just as Oz was turning the lock, Antonio and Dre came loping up.

"It's kind of late for you two to be out roaming the streets, don't you think?" Oz said, opening the door for them.

Dre rubbed the feathery beginnings of a mustache above his lip and smiled. "It's Saturday night, Mr. Dan. What else you expect us to do?"

"Be home studying?"

Antonio laughed. "We just getting some snacks for our movie."

"We rented *Total Recall!*" Dre put in. "You wanna come watch, old man?"

"Maybe next time," Oz said. "I have plans."

They exchanged an amused glance. "Well, look at Mr. Dan," Antonio said. "Plans."

Oz laughed and waved them off. He told them they could grab a thing or two they wanted and that it would be on him since the store was closed and he couldn't make change for them. They ran to the candy aisle like it was Christmas.

"Don't bankrupt me, now," Oz said.

He went back to the booth to get his things together, so he'd be ready to follow the boys out. Make sure they got to Antonio's house safely for their movie night. He was stuffing his lunch bag into his duffel, imagining all the trouble boys like them could get into, when he heard the bell jangle on the door. He glanced up, thinking maybe the boys had left, but they were still there in the aisle, negotiating over Reese's Cups versus M&M's.

He came out of the booth and saw a young man in a bomber jacket heading back to the beer section.

"Hey, man," Oz said. "We're closed. Not selling anything more tonight. I was just about to lock up."

The man ignored him and disappeared behind a potato chip display and opened the door to the cooler at the back of the store.

Oz muttered under his breath as he returned to the booth. He didn't feel like dealing with this. He decided he'd avoid the hassle and arguing by letting him get what he wanted. Free stuff always made things easier.

Antonio stood pondering the chip display and plucked out two bags of Lay's.

"All right, boys," Oz said. "Let's hurry up."

They said okay, even as Dre darted off to the soda cooler.

The man in the bomber jacket emerged with two forty-ounce bottles of Colt 45. Looking at him full-on, Oz was sure he'd never seen him before, which was unusual. Most people who came in were regulars. There was something about the way the man kept looking around the store, as if tracking the movement of the boys and monitoring the door. Oz didn't like it.

"I can't make change for you," Oz said. "But it's your lucky night. Go on and take those."

The man put his beers on the counter, like he hadn't heard Oz.

"Take them and go," Oz said. "Have a good night."

"I will," the man said. "But I want what's in the register first."

He pulled a gun from the back of his pants and aimed it at Oz. He held it sideways, like a gang shooter on television. Oz looked into the young man's eyes. The look that came back to him was serious, but unsteady. Oz wondered if the gunman was new to this and posing. He couldn't be more than nineteen or twenty. Not even old enough to buy that beer on the counter. Oz glanced at the nose of the gun that was pointed at him. The gunman's hand was shaking. Oz was in the booth, behind bulletproof glass, but he raised his hands reflexively. He'd been robbed at the store before. A couple of times. The first time, he'd hit the floor and taken shelter under the desk in a corner of the booth. He'd yanked down the phone and loudly called the police. It was enough to scare them off, thankfully, because help was always slow to come, if it came at all. The other time, Oz had pulled out the gun he kept in the booth with him. In that instance, Oz was the one who had the shaking hands as he stared down the robber, wondering if he had it in him to take a life again. The robber had run off, and Oz had taken the gun home and kept it there.

As he stood with his hands raised, considering what to do, he caught sight of Antonio and Dre, crouched down and creeping slowly up the aisle. He didn't want them trying to be heroes. There was the glass between him and the gunman. The boys had no protection.

"I'm not playing," the gunman said. "Gimme what you got in the register."

"I told you, there's nothing in there. It's already cashed out."

The gunman whipped his head around, just as the boys went into a running crouch on his left. "Stop!" He aimed toward them. "Get y'all's asses over here."

Antonio and Dre came over, saucer-eyed, with their hands raised, but still holding on to their potato chips, Reese's Cups and bottles of grape soda.

"Man, if you want to check, be my guest," Oz said, opening the register. He opened the door to the booth and moved out of the way as the gunman pushed past him. The man eyed the empty slots, then looked around wildly. "Where's the safe?"

"Safe? We don't have a safe, man," Oz said, easing out of the booth and over to stand with the boys.

The gunman looked confused. Then he held Oz's gaze. "I don't believe you." With that shaky hand of his, he raised his gun and held it on Antonio. "Open the *god*damn safe or I'll shoot him."

"Man," Oz said, "I'm telling you, we do not have a safe." He looked around. "This is it. You got us at closing time. I'm sorry. All I have is what's in my wallet, and I'm happy to give it to you." Oz paused. "And I have a money roll in my pocket. You can have that, too." The boys were huddled up close to Oz. He could feel them trembling on either side of him. Antonio, who was staring down the barrel of the gun, was crying and, in the quietest whisper, calling for his grandmother.

Oz's heart was thumping loudly in his chest, but the rest of his body was oddly calm. He shoved the boys back, so they were wedged between his back and the candy aisle. Then, there was an ear-popping *bang*. A fiery flash. Oz's chest exploded. He fell back. His hand fluttered up to his chest.

The man with the gun looked surprised. He bolted for the door and Oz raised up to follow him. But it was as if Oz's body wasn't his own. He couldn't get up. He heard one of the boys whimpering and breathing hard behind him asking what he should do. He couldn't tell which one it was.

"Call nine-one-one," Oz said. There was a gurgle when he spoke.

Antonio ran up to the cashier's booth. Oz could hear him fumbling with the phone and punching in the number. Antonio's voice shook as he tried to explain what had happened: "In a store . . . man with a gun . . ." he stammered out.

Dre was staring down at him. "You gon' be okay," he said. "You'll see . . ." His voice broke and he looked terrified.

Suddenly, Oz was seeing Tommy's face. Tommy used to be scared all the time. Oz wondered what his brother had discovered when he'd gone off to find himself. His eyelids suddenly felt impossibly heavy. There was a gentle smack on his face. He opened his eyes and there was Deborah, framed in the doorway of the RV, smiling at him.

He smiled back and tried to speak.

"What?" Dre said, his ear close to Oz's face.

"I'm supposed to call my daughter," he said. *We had plans.* Hadn't she grown up well? Her boy, *her* Oz, what was he like?

He saw that shadow in the shape of his father—another Oz— moving around the store with Pearl. He raised a hand and pointed: "There he is. See? He's fine."

"Shh, shh. They're coming. They told me they're coming."

That was Antonio. He was back. He'd gotten so good in the boxing ring.

Oz was reminded of Tommy, dancing around their makeshift boxing ring in the backyard, with rust-colored dust rising around his skin-stripped legs.

"They're coming, okay?" Dre said, his voice shaking. "Okay, Mr. Dan?"

"Oz," Oz whispered. The gurgling in his chest was so bad he could barely talk, so maybe he didn't say it at all. But he was thinking, *My name is Ozro. Not Dan.* His eyes moved from one boy to the other. Tears were glistening on both boys' cheeks. Oz grabbed at Dre's T-shirt. He wanted to tell him not to cry. "Look out for each other," Oz said, his voice suddenly stronger and echoing in his ears.

The boys nodded.

"Promise?"

They promised him.

And suddenly, there was that stillness Oz had felt before. *This is the right thing*, he thought, as his head came to rest on the arm of one of the boys.

Now

Everything at rest.

Deborah

We got the news early in the morning on Sunday. Me, Pearl and Tommy met Trinity down South that next day. It was a long, quiet ride from the airport to the country, and Willa Mae was waiting for us at the door to her house. She had on a black dress. The full skirt was caught in a gentle wind that did nothing to ease the summer heat. She led us from her house to the trailer in her side yard where Oz had lived. She opened the door and waited on the outside steps because it was so tight inside that trailer with the four of us.

"I ain't changed nothing," Willa Mae said.

His prison, Willa Mae had called it. When I was there before, I'd stayed in the place where Oz had asked me to sit, looking but not moving around the RV at all. I made my way toward the back now to where he had his bed made nice and neat. There was a bottle of Old Spice and some Speed Stick deodorant—the very smell of him—sitting on the lip of his tiny sink in a broom closet of a bathroom. There was his striped tie coiled in a drawer. He'd had it on the day he left. In a little cubby, he had a handful of white, starched shirts hung at just the right distance apart so as not to squish together and wrinkle. And there was the one pair of dark blue suit pants. He had them hanging in front of his blue jeans. They were the pants that matched the suit jacket I'd given to Trinity when she'd headed off to college. Why'd he keep those artifacts from a life he'd left?

Trinity saw those pants right when I did, and the look on her face was a mix of surprise and sorrow. I hugged her close but stayed quiet. We all stayed quiet. That little RV was silent as the grave. I eased into a seat at the fold-down table that wasn't much bigger than a TV tray, remembering that time I'd sat across from Oz.

Pearl stood with her head bowed, touching the bed where Oz had slept, shaking her head. Finally she said, "Me and Ozro, we talked about forgiveness. And him blaming me for not—"

"Ma . . ." Tommy cut in. "It's n-n-n-not the time." He was standing by the door.

"No, Thomas, I'll grant Ozro that. Maybe I should've left your daddy. I surely should've been there when y'all needed me. That's the biggest regret of my life."

Tommy looked away.

Pearl went on talking to him: "Your daddy was the only thing I'd known since I was a girl. I didn't know how to leave. I didn't know how to stay. I told Ozro I was sorry. I told myself I was sorry. I tell your daddy I'm sorry every day, even though he's gone. And I do hate he's gone, especially that way." Tears rose, and she wiped her eyes. "I had to forgive myself. Whether Ozro forgave me or not, I don't know, but I hope he forgave himself."

Tommy moved his hands around, like he didn't know what to do with them. He turned around and went back outside, where the sun was shining and the sky was blue and the world was still turning, like nothing at all was wrong. Pearl excused herself and followed him out. We heard quiet voices and crying, then Pearl saying, "I hope you forgive me, too."

Willa Mae cleared her throat and stepped inside the RV. She

pointed us to a shelf over one of the upholstered seats. The one I'd noticed when I visited. She nodded toward the stacks and stacks of notebooks on it. Bunches of them were held together by rubber bands.

"Them's for you, Trinity," Willa Mae said as she fanned herself. "He always said that. So, there they go."

Trinity thanked her, then went over and took down a stack. She pulled off the rubber band holding them all together and opened a few. She looked over at me. "They're arranged by date," she said. She flipped through, reading quick. She looked up again at all of us, confused. "He called himself Dan."

"I never liked it," Willa Mae said. "He was always Oz. My good cousin."

"Where can we claim his body?" I asked. It was one of the few things I'd said since the ride to the airport, the flight to Georgia and the drive out to Willa Mae's. I was holding the white mug that Oz had filled for me when I was here. I remembered looking across the short space to the counter where the coffee maker sat, with him just a hair's breadth from my fingers.

And, just then, tears fell.

Trinity was home with me for a week after we got back from Georgia. She spent most of her time at the kitchen table going through her daddy's notebooks, with her own notebook right there next to her, stopping from time to time to write something down.

One night, just before bed, as I was on my way to the kitchen for some water, there she sat at that table. I touched her shoulder. "How you doing?"

She glanced up from her page with the look of somebody still half in another world. "I didn't know. What he did to you."

I slid into a chair next to her. "That wasn't for you to know."

"I'm sorry, Mom."

"It's all right, Trinity. I'm not that woman anymore. And he wasn't that man anymore, last I saw him." I looked at the stacks and stacks of notebooks on the table. "Sometimes I can't believe this is all we've got left of him."

"I know. But in some ways, it's a lot, isn't it? It's like he left me one last thing. A chance to know him. Maybe not in the way I would have liked, but still . . ." Trinity reached out and grabbed one of the notebooks in front of her. "He wrote down everything. His boyhood, his upbringing, what he did to his father . . . his whole life."

I nodded. "I think he was looking for himself in all that."

"Do you think he was at peace. In the end?"

I thought for a second. "I hope so."

Trinity nodded. "I'm glad I got a chance to talk to him. I'm glad of that. I was so angry at him sometimes. But he let me be angry, and I think that helped ease it." She stopped for a moment, her eyes shining. "I think he was looking forward to coming out to New York. I really do."

I squeezed her hand. "He was." I smiled as she wiped her eyes. I glanced at the notebook she was writing in. "That's a lot of notes you're taking. What're you doing there?"

She leaned back in her chair. "I don't know, but I think I'm going to write about it. About him. A big article, I'm hoping. Or maybe even a book. I think it will help me understand him. The lives he lived. What do you think?"

"Well, just make sure you give me a say, too." I got up and touched her face. "Don't stay up too late, okay? And don't get lost in all this."

She promised she wouldn't, then she rubbed her eyes and said, "I need to call Manny anyway, before it gets too late."

"Everything all right? With O?"

Trinity closed her notebook and moved to stack her father's notebooks one on top of the other. "Yes, no issue there. Manny's just, I don't know. In crisis. He's thinking about leaving the firm. It was never a good fit for him in the first place. He never wanted to be that kind of lawyer. He was, understandably, chasing the money." Trinity looked at her watch. "I'm just going to be a sounding board."

I raised an eyebrow. "Isn't that something his wife should be? A sounding board?"

Trinity leaned back in her chair and crossed her arms. "We're just talking, Mom. Like we do all the time. We have a good friendship. Stop looking at me like that."

"I'm not looking at you like anything. I'm just wondering what his wife thinks about you being a sounding board."

Trinity got busy moving the notebooks around again. "I don't know," she said.

"I'm just—"

"I'm not the other woman, Mom, I can assure you. I would never do anything like that. Yes, I've been the Thoughtless Woman, the Noncommittal Woman, the Serial Dating Woman, but never— knowingly—the Other Woman. That's not what's happening here. Manny and I are just . . . we're good friends. That's all."

"If you say so." I patted her on the shoulder and went on to get my water. "Just be careful there."

"There's nothing to be careful of," Trinity said as she put her notebook under her arm and headed off to the other room to make her call. "We're what we've always been to each other. That's it."

Trinity

1993

In the backyard of my mother's house on the last day of spring, two years after my father was killed—four years after his big funeral—we had a wedding. There was a pergola drenched in white daisies in a particularly bright corner of the yard. A handful of chairs were lined up in front of it, awaiting guests. My mother stood beside me and told me that she and my father had gotten married in a small apartment with even fewer guests and barely any flowers to speak of. She said it was better than she'd imagined it could be. She looked wistful as she picked one of the daisies and smelled it.

"I do miss him," she said. "And for what we had, when we were young, before everything . . . I'd do it again." She gave me a watery smile, then excused herself to go get dressed.

I went and found Manny in the kitchen. He was adjusting O's black suit and fuchsia bow tie.

"I think you're the most handsome ring bearer I've ever seen," I said to O, bending to kiss him on the cheek.

He tugged at his tie, looking uncomfortable. "Thanks, Mommy."

He was three and tall for his age. He'd gotten his height from his father. He ran off through the sliding glass doors in search of what, I wasn't sure. People were starting to gather in the backyard and take their seats. As Manny and I watched, I pointed off to a quiet corner of the yard. "We buried his ashes there. Just Mom, Tommy, Pearl and me. No big hoopla like the first funeral with the burial at the cemetery then the big party here at the house." I thought about it for a second. "He's a man with two gravesites."

Manny made the sign of the cross, then slid his hands in his pockets. He looked around the backyard. "It's good," he said. "Getting to see where you grew up and hear your stories. Even the hard ones. *Finally.*"

"Well, what with all you've had going on, it's been hard to get a trip to the Midwest on your calendar."

He gave me a look.

"Sorry." I put my arm through his.

Manny was separated and now moving toward divorce. An amicable one. He and his wife had been happy. At first. But, as they approached two years together, they found it wasn't working. Manny said he'd rushed things. He left their perfect house in the Hudson Valley and moved back to the city. He left his white-shoe law firm and went to work for the Legal Aid Society. He said he needed a new start.

"Thank you," I said, "for being my plus-one for this, seeing as how Virginia couldn't come." Virginia was at home in London, waiting for O and me to fly out there next week. It would be a welcome-to-the-family visit. Virginia had just had a baby girl that she was happily raising on her own.

"I don't mind being the backup plan," Manny said.

"You've never been the backup plan."

He looked at me, like he had no words. He touched my hand at his arm. "We should probably get out there. It's about time for the main event."

We went out through the sliding doors and found a seat near

Pearl, Mr. Burton and Willa Mae. Willa Mae had come back to Detroit, but it would be a short trip, she'd said. She had a boxing gym and a bunch of boys and young men to get back to, including the two boys my father had saved.

"They miss him," she'd told me. "And they're good boys. I'm thinking Oz saved them twice. At that store and with that gym. I'm gon' try and keep them saved."

I missed my father, too. But it gave me a measure of peace to know that he'd died for something good. I settled back in my seat and listened to a cellist play a song I didn't recognize. And soon enough, there they were, the men of the hour. Tommy and Dom, in matching black tuxedos with fuchsia cummerbunds and bow ties. Tommy caught my eye and winked on his way up the aisle. He'd been reluctant to do it, at first.

"It's not legal," he'd said. "And never will be." But with every day of wedding prep that passed, and I think with all the excitement he saw in Dom, something shifted in him. This morning, he'd told me that it was the happiest day of his life. A day he thought would never come. A day he had, that morning, shared with Lloyd at the cemetery.

Watching him make his way up the aisle, it was one of the happiest days of my life, too. Manny nudged me and pressed a wad of Kleenex in my hand, whispering, "You never prepare for emotion."

After the ceremony, Tommy and I danced on the patio under twinkling white lights. He looked down at me and said, "I w-w-w-wish Oz was here. I miss him. I w-w-w-wish he'd survived it."

I wished it, too.

"I always thought, out of the two of us, he w-w-w-would."

"You're both strong, Tommy. In your ways."

Tears came to his eyes. "That old ring of Daddy's? I took it out to the cemetery this morning, while I was out leaving flowers for

Lloyd. I buried it in a little shhh-shallow hole. I think Oz w-w-w-would've wanted that."

I hugged him and said, "Everything at rest." Then I put my head on his shoulder and we swayed through the last strains of "I Say a Little Prayer."

Later, I stood on the edge of the patio watching Pearl and Mr. Burton dance to an Anita Baker number, as performed by my mother. My mother was out in front of her band, which was made up of some of her Chicago friends and Two Cents. They were on a small stage we'd built in the corner of the yard. Pillars at the four corners of the stage were strung with lights and it looked kind of magical.

Manny approached at my shoulder and remarked on how lovely it all was.

"It came together so nice," he said, tapping my arm. "Here. I thought you could use one of these." I looked over my shoulder and saw he had two Shirley Temples. He plucked out the maraschino cherry from his drink and added it to mine. I loved the cherries. He hated them. We both rocked a little to the music as we sipped our drinks.

"You know," he said, "life is short, Trin. I've come to understand that, with everything I have going on."

I followed his gaze. He was looking across the patio at O, who was rolling down a slope in the lawn, his jacket, cummerbund and tie long ago discarded.

"But it can be good," he added.

"It's getting better, I think." I bumped my shoulder against his. "What was that you said about my injured finger?"

He threw his head back and laughed. "Oh, one of my most profound sayings?"

"Yes." I laughed. "That one." But then my laughter tapered off to nothing, and I felt like I might cry as I said, "Things don't hurt so much anymore, Manny."

He looked down at me and grabbed my hand. He kissed my finger. "Good," he said. "That's what we're going for." Then he looked startled as he glanced at the finger he'd just kissed. "Oh, I'm sorry. That's not very platonic co-parent of me, is it?"

"No. It's not." But I smiled at him. Honestly, Manny and I had no idea what we were to each other or what we would become. I thought about life, the varied lengths of it and the many ways we could spend it. I watched Pearl and Mr. Burton, swaying together on the dance floor. They had no intention of tying the knot, but they were happy. I looked at Tommy and Dom. It wasn't legal, but they were as married as anyone I knew. My eyes fell on my mother, jamming with her friends, and I thought about all she'd been through and what she probably regretted. But she hadn't regretted it all.

"Less pain," I said. "That's definitely what I'm going for. And a lot more from life, if I can get it."

I looked at Manny and raised a questioning eyebrow. He smiled and let me pull him out to the patio. We fell in step together. And we danced.

ACKNOWLEDGMENTS

I am most grateful to my editor at Berkley, Amanda Bergeron, who journeyed with me over many rough patches in the writing of this novel. Her smart suggestions and endless encouragement helped see this story through to a strong finish.

I would also like to thank the entire team at Berkley for their support and care in publishing both this novel and the one before it. I am humbled by their belief in my writing and their enthusiasm about putting it out into the world.

And many, many thanks to my agent, Michelle Brower, for being a steady hand and a trusted guide. I do not know where I would be without her.

Significant portions of this novel take us through fraught moments in our nation's racial history, including the 1967 riots in Detroit. The *Detroit Free Press*, with its exhaustive reporting on the unrest of the era, was an essential source for research. The Detroit Historical Society's Detroit 67 project also provided oral and written histories that proved invaluable. The voices of those who shared their personal stories about life in a city coming undone informed my writing about that period.

I would like to say a special thank-you to Mark Leepson, who has written movingly about his time in Vietnam. I first found his story in the pages of *The New York Times*. I appreciate all he later shared with me about the draft and his service. It helped shape

Tommy's experience. A special thank-you also goes to Karen Taylor Good, who taught me everything I needed to know about the jingle business in the eighties and nineties in Chicago, which is part of Deborah's narrative.

Additionally, I am deeply appreciative of friends and fellow writers who read earlier drafts of this novel and provided valuable notes. They helped make the book better.

Finally, the writing of *Life and Other Love Songs* took place over some difficult years that included the sudden death of my father, Nathaniel Wells Jr. The loss brought into focus the fragility and the beauty of this life. And the importance of family. There is no greater gift.

Life

AND OTHER

Love Songs

———

ANISSA GRAY

———

DISCUSSION QUESTIONS

1. In tracking the course of Deborah and Oz's relationship, what are the key turning points, for better or worse?

2. Even though Deborah objects, Oz refuses to enter a church, even to get married. Why does he shun religion?

3. Oz commits an unthinkable transgression against Deborah. Can his reasons for depriving her of her dream ever be justified?

4. Deborah pursues stardom from the time she is a young girl. Though her career does not go as planned, is she still a success in the end?

5. In Detroit, the 1967 riots send shock waves through the city and the nation. How does the unrest trigger reminders of a tragic past for Oz and Tommy?

6. Family secrets and generational trauma are at the heart of *Life and Other Love Songs*. How do those issues fray Oz's relationships with everyone he loves?

7. Oz and his family migrate from south to north and from inner city to suburbs. What is the significance of regional and economic mobility for Oz?

8. What in Trinity's family life steers her toward becoming an observer of others as well as a reporter?

9. What is the role of guilt in the lives of the characters, particularly Oz? Does Oz make amends for his transgressions?

10. Oz's relationship with Willa Mae is among the most significant in the novel. Why does she keep his secret?

11. Tommy spends years trying to outrun a troubled personal history. Does he truly make peace with his past and himself?

12. Who bears ultimate responsibility for the death of Oz's father? Did Pearl play a role?

13. What is the significance of the title, *Life and Other Love Songs*?

A CONVERSATION WITH ANISSA GRAY

In *Life and Other Love Songs*, a husband and father disappears without a trace, and his family must figure out how to keep living while coming to terms with his absence. What inspired this idea?

A few years ago, I heard a story about a husband and father who simply vanished. The disappearance—and the questions it raised—reverberated through that family in profound ways for generations. And I wondered: What would happen if the fate of a long-lost loved one was eventually revealed? What would happen if that revelation called into question everything the family thought they knew about that person? And so emerged the story of the Armstead family.

In both your debut novel and *Life and Other Love Songs*, you do an amazing job of portraying complex family dynamics. Why is it so important to you to center your stories around complicated family relationships?

Whether it's family of origin or chosen family, these are the people who have perhaps the most profound influence on our lives. I am one of five children, raised by a stay-at-home mom and a father who worked a lot of long hours outside of the home. Growing up in such a large family, there was a fair amount of conflict but also love and joy. All of these things—conflict, love and joy—are central to life. They're also the building blocks of great storytelling. This is what pulls me back, time and again, to examine the complexity of relationships in all varieties of families.

A major theme in this novel is generational trauma. Tell us about your decision to explore this.

Exploring the complexity of family relationships means excavating family history. Our family histories can hide traumas that impact us, generation after generation, in both subtle and profound ways. Reckoning with those issues, particularly those that cause shame and silence, such as abuse, is of course best done in therapy. But for me as a novelist, those issues and the mechanics around dealing with them make for emotionally rich stories. I find a lot of satisfaction in developing characters who not only delve into the genesis of their family's struggles, but who also find ways to cope. For the family in *Life and Other Love Songs*, that is the ultimate goal. Understanding the past but not being bound to it. And bequeathing something better and healthier to the next generation.

The book also explores how buried secrets can unravel a family. Do you think the Armstead family would have been better off never having their family's hidden truths come to light?

There's a famous AA saying: "We're only as sick as our secrets." In that sense, secrets are seen as an impediment to recovery. That is true in a broader sense as well. It takes a lot of mental energy to keep a secret safely tucked away. And then there's the added stress of worrying about being found out. In *Life and Other Love Songs*, the chief secret-keeper in the family is Oz Armstead, a husband and father. We see the emotional toll it takes on him and his family. We experience how far he's willing to go to keep things hidden. It is only after the secret is revealed that the family finds a way to knit itself back together. So, for this family, bringing those hidden truths to light is a form of salvation.

Let's talk about Oz and Deborah's relationship. Why did Oz stand out to Deborah at the rent party, when she could have had anyone?

Deborah is accustomed to being center stage and the center of everyone's attention, most especially the attention of young men. While she enjoys that, Deborah is also not entirely comfortable in the spotlight. She suffers from a great deal of stage fright. When she spots Oz at the party standing by himself and looking very uncool, I think she sees something familiar. And when she finally speaks to him, what strikes her most is how he listens to her and seems to care about what she has to say in ways that other boys do not. It makes her feel special. It makes Oz special to her.

Pearl is such an interesting character, having been married and given birth to Oz at the tender age of fourteen. Oz describes her as "somewhere between mother and sister." Who inspired her character?

My late maternal grandmother, Florence Gennette Johnson, is the inspiration for Pearl. By the time my grandmother was fourteen, she was married to my grandfather and had had my mother. During the time I was writing *Life and Other Love Songs*, she was in the last years of what had been a long and eventful life. While my grandmother differs from Pearl in significant ways, what I wanted to capture was her resilience through often difficult circumstances. Pearl is a reflection of that.

How do Oz's past traumas affect his relationships with every-one he loves?

One of Oz's chief goals, when his family arrives up North, is to lose his southern accent and make himself over. He wants to bury past traumas and be someone else in this new place. Because Oz is hiding his truest self, it makes it difficult for his wife and daughter to know him. It's something of a different matter with Oz's brother and mother. They know the truth of who he is. And the secret he is trying to outrun. This creates a unique strain on those relationships, which leaves Oz, in many ways, very much isolated and at an emotional distance from much of his family.

In Detroit, the 1967 riots send shock waves through the city and the nation. Why is this especially significant in the novel?

In 1967, the family is living near the epicenter of the uprising, looking on as the city erupts into a conflagration of anger, destruction and fear. It is an important historical linchpin, as the novel shows a family trying to navigate the racial tensions of the times. The moment also offers an important glimpse into Oz's *personal* history. He and his brother witness part of the riots from a street corner in disbelief. As Oz watches a city's racial reckoning, he is also reckoning with very personal internal divisions. In the fiery destruction around him, he sees a significant reminder of his past.

You've worked in journalism throughout your career. Tell us about Trinity's decision to become a reporter.

For Trinity, the journalism seed was planted when she was a young girl, learning to type by retyping stories from newsmagazines and newspapers. Additionally, growing up as the only black girl in her neighborhood, she was somewhat isolated. Always on the outside looking in. This made her a keen observer of others. At one point in the novel, while covering a story, she says that she was inclined to examine the lives of others with the "overly observant eye of a girl always trying to find where she might fit in." While Trinity searches for her place in the world, she finds satisfaction in writing about what she sees around her.

There are so many emotional and pivotal scenes in this novel. Which was one of the hardest scenes to write?

I don't know that it was necessarily the hardest scene but writing about the 1967 uprising in Detroit turned into an incredibly surreal and emotional experience. It was 2020, and I'd written the scene and moved on to another part of the novel. Then suddenly, there was the murder of George Floyd and protests in the streets and renewed conversations about race. In the midst of this experience of history repeating in real time, I went back to those pages I'd written. I found them to be flat. More research-driven than personal. I threw them out. I rewrote that historical scene of the 1967 riots with a sense of shock, anger and fist-in-the-air revolution that I was suddenly feeling in my own time. It's not that I'd never personally experienced racism. Certainly, I have. It's that it was the first time I'd ever seen a larger movement of that kind to address it.

In the days, months and years to follow Oz's disappearance, Deborah and Trinity come to realize they may have never truly known him. Do you think you can ever fully know a person?

No, I don't believe we can ever truly know someone. Even those we know quite well. Oz shows us a somewhat extreme version of this. But what is also significant is that building intimate relationships can open the door to getting to know *ourselves* better. Our close connections with others, particularly when there are moments of disagreement, can force us to become more introspective and see things about ourselves that may surprise us. As Oz's family tries to come to terms with all they discover about him, Deborah and Trinity are also forced to turn inward and gain a better understanding of themselves.

Which character do you think changes the most over the course of the book?

All of the characters undergo a kind of metamorphosis in some way, but it is perhaps Oz who changes the most over time, in my view. Oz starts out as a young man overburdened by secrets, wanting to be someone other than who he is. He builds a life that is designed to block out the past. But by the end of the book, we see not only who he used to be but who he is. And we watch him make the ultimate sacrifice as he tries to become someone better.

Do you relate to any of the characters in the book? If so, who and why?

For me, I think it's more a matter of what I admire in many of the characters, and that is a sense of resilience. Virtually all of them experience some form of loss: There is Oz's disappearance, Deborah's lost dreams of stardom, Trinity's lost stability when her father disappears. But even with the losses, there is this journey toward something better—even if that journey takes them to some incredibly dark places, which is particularly true for Deborah and Oz. In the end, I believe they all manage to find some measure of light.

What do you hope readers take away from reading *Life and Other Love Songs*?

At the heart of *Life and Other Love Songs* is a family's very intimate, personal history and all of the ways in which it comes back to haunt a husband and father and everyone he loves. What I hope readers come to see as that story unfolds is how life and love can endure through it all.

What books are on your nightstand?
The Heaven & Earth Grocery Store by James McBride. I'm a huge fan of James McBride, from *The Good Lord Bird* to *The Color of Water* and beyond. I always look forward to anything from McBride, and I can't wait to dive into this one.

Stone Blind by Natalie Haynes. This novel is a retelling of the story of Medusa and Perseus from Medusa's perspective. I have a general interest in Greek mythology. Add a heavy dose of feminism, and I'm in.

The Sullivanians: Sex, Psychotherapy, and the Wild Life of an American Commune by Alexander Stille. I'm spending a lot of time reading about cults right now as I research my next novel. This book recounts the disturbing history of a commune hidden in plain sight on New York's Upper West Side. An incredibly compelling read.

Photo by Bonnie J. Heath

Anissa Gray is the author of the novel *The Care and Feeding of Ravenously Hungry Girls*. She is also an award-winning journalist whose work has been featured in *The Washington Post*, CNN, and The Cut. She lives in Atlanta, Georgia, with her wife.

CONNECT WITH THE AUTHOR ONLINE

AnissaGray.com

AnissaGrayAuthor

AnissaGrayAuthor